The Gamecocks

Stephanie M Sellers

Copyright © 2013 Stephanie M Sellers

Spread Eagle Publishing

All rights reserved.

ISBN: **1482681188**

ISBN-13: **978-1482681185**

Publisher's Note

Scanning, uploading and distribution of this book via the Internet or other means without permission of publisher is illegal and punishable by law. Do not commit piracy.

This is a work of fiction. Names, characters, places, and incidents are the product of the author's imagination or are used fictiously, and any resemblance to actual persons, living or dead, business establishments, events, or locales is entirely coincidental.

DEDICATION

For the lost boys.

CONTENTS

Acknowledgements
Guide to Lumbee Vernacular

1 Tenacity and Providence Hook Up at Forks in the Road...p.1

2 Tons a Reckoning for a Pardon on da Preacher...p.15

3 Thicker 'n Thieves...p.33

4 I'm Not Supposed to Tell. I'm Not Supposed to Tell...p.56

5 Totens and Little People...p.79

6 Momma Always Said...p.83

7 Irony Under the Twinkling Weeping Willow...p.115

8 Turquoise, Hot Pink and Orange Make the Colors of Fire...p.137

9 Slick, Slide and Alibi...p.161

10 Straight Back Chairs and Copper Stills...p.178

11 Say that Again, Boy...p.203

12 You Were Always There for Me...p.213

Cover Image Credit and Content Credits...p.237

In Reflection...p.242

Author Bio...p.245

ACKNOWLEDGMENTS

In **The Gamecocks** Jake Wilkes risks all for a friend whose death made headlines. Imagine Larry the Cable Guy, on a mission, and you will fully appreciate **The Gamecocks**. Satirical Literary Fiction unfolds historical mysteries while carrying friendship to a dangerous level. Set in rural North Carolina where moonshine, conjuring, church and fifty five thousand Lumbee Indians truly are as much a part of the beloved culture as America's largest ongoing mystery, The Lost Colony.

Origin theories, based on research, human behavior, psychohistory, and sociolinguistics, focusing on the Lumbees' endangered vernacular, are fully explored. So their colorful language is in full bloom adding provocative awareness to their unique culture. And while a primary goal of this work is to provoke the reader to question the self existential crisis, ethnicity's value, and present day culture's stress on social status, as it relates to a happy life, it also strives to unlock the notion that American History as taught in our classrooms is concrete. Like Einstein said, "The important thing is not to stop questioning." This work is ideal for Social Studies, Sociolinguistics, Culture and Historical Theory curriculum.

Simply put, **The Gamecocks** braids Southeastern North Carolina's past and present culture, focusing on Lumbee Indians, with messages on being happy with who you bes, fate and second chances.

Therefore, I am deeply grateful for Christian Soldiers and Providence. Our present day rural South is a love affair of cultures and faces, the differences that keep us curious and aspiring self existential quests. For the professors who delve into sociolinguistics on Lumbee English phonology and for the tribe for keeping it on the swamp. Preserving the Lumbee endangered language and culture is chief. I appreciate all who create technological information systems. And I am thankful for all who took time and effort to record history as it was occurring, on stones, scrolls and in caves.

American history was written by the conquerors. It is biased and limited. And while storytelling within family and community groups is crucial for preserving history, sadly it is fleeting as value systems separate us. So I want to thank a dear Lumbee Indian friend for the precious insight. And I must thank my dear codger cowboys, living and not, who told so many lies on our horseback trail rides I thought they were airing out storylines.

Guide to Lumbee Vernacular

A-prefixing is not common. Example: He was a-looking for the cooter. A-prefixing is more common with older Lumbees. So is the pronunciation of 'i' to 'oy' such as, high sounding hoy, which is a Portuguese language tradition.

Dropping 'g's from plurals is a Portuguese tradition.

Mon means man and is used at beginning of greetings and is from Elizabethan era.

Juvember means sling shot or forked stick and is from Portugal. Is Elizabethan era.

Mommuck means wild mess or treat something badly and is from the Elizabethan era.

Toten means omen and is sign of death. Can be smelled or heard and is from Elizabethan era when token was interchanged with toten.

Meddlin' means interfering.

Crone means push down.

Ellick means a cup of coffee with sugar.

Lum means belonging to the Lumbee community.

Crotched up means caught up.

Dib means a baby chicken.

Nary means not any.

No'rs means nowheres.

Malahack means mess up.

Thou or Thoust means you and is from Elizabethan era.

Kin means family or treated as such.

Index means to stop.

Hope m' die means hope m' clare.

Gut of snuff refers to quantity of snuff contained in animal intestine. Whether or not the snuff is in plastic or tin the term is still common.

Gyp means a female dog.

Haint means a ghost.

On the swamp means being with other Lums or in the neighborhood.

Baccar means tobacco.

I'm means I have and is from Elizabethan era.

Weren't means wasn't.

Jubious means strange.

Yurker means mischievous child.

Gyarb means a mess.

Across the river means on the other side of the tracks.

Headiness means very bad.

Pleasure it means enjoy it.

Listen at means listen to.

Bes means is and is from the Scotts.

Breath it means to tell.

Cam means calm.

Colic means illness and is from early English.

Catawampus means not square.

Swanny means swear.

Brickhouse means upper status.

Liketa means nearly.

Buddyrow means friend.

Bate means lot.

Kiver means cover and is from Elizabethan era.

Liable to means likely to.

Kyarn is something nasty or rotten.

Sorry in the world means sad.

Chicken bog means chicken and rice.

Chunk means to throw.

Conjure means to invoke spirits like a magic charm.

Put a root on means to cast a spell on someone.

Cracklins is a crisply fried slice of hog skin like fatback.

Fetched up means raised up.

Fine in the world means doing well.

Gambrel is a carcass stretcher.

Gaum is a mess and is from Elizabethan era.

Goanna is fertilizer.

Chauld means embarrassed or disgraced.

Cooter means large swamp turtle.

Cuz is greeting for fellow Lumbee.

Damn Skippy means right! Is an affirmative to a speaker.

Gallanipper means a large mosquito-like insect and mosquitoes.

In the pines means snobby or uppity.

Orta notta means should not have.

Pappy sack is male child endearment.

Pearly means a small dainty piece.

Pocosin means big swamp.

Pone means a loaf of bread.

Pow wow means a Native American Indian celebration.

Pure means certainly.

Purty means ridiculous-looking.

Pumpkin seed refers to a bream family fish.

Pyert means lively.

Slam means very.

Smash means to press.

Sow cat means endearment toward a child.

Sweetnins means cakes and pastries.

Mension means measurement and is from Elizabethan era.

Hit means it.

Hosen means hose.

Housen means house.

You see me means you just ask me about it.

Wit means knowledge.

The Gamecocks

Prologue

The juvember had been tossed to the wayside and Jake Wilkes was sent hurling-

Chapter 1

Tenacity and Providence Hook Up at Forks in the Road

Jake's long arms sprung down and gave the podium a couple of knocks. The grumbles hushed and he executed his best dimpled grin. "This is brand new for some, but for others like our genealogical researchers you're familiar, but haven't made the connection. Think about it. History was written by the conquerors. If we'd been properly educated by the Portuguese and all the other early explorers ya'll wouldn't be so burdened by it." One dimple dug deep as his elbow slid across the podium and his shiny whites beamed down the center aisle. "Ya'll sound like cloggers down there." Smiles spread, so Jake sucked in a fresh drawl of brave and went straight on to his next note card as his blue banner hanging overhead, 'North Carolina's Lumbee Indians and America's First Christians,' replicated a guillotine as it popped and rippled and a small plastic lid rolled off his head.

"Humph. Now it's believed by some that the Templars had a fleet of ships at La Rochelle France, even though there's no proof." As chins cocked Jake slapped the podium. "The Templars didn't want ta leave proof. They had too much ta risk. They hit the trail runnin' off to the New World on old Viking routes on a pre-Columbian voyage. And like we were just talkin', on Portugal, the Knights Templar did not disband."

Jake backed into the screen and the knight moved as if declaring the caption, "Protect Christian Pilgrims," precisely as he proclaimed the creed and some guests awed. The bearded Knight Templar wore a white mantel waisted with a wide red tie embossed with golden threads. It bled from his grasp in one hand and his other held a silver cup as he toasted an ominous hand hewn cross.

"Christian crusaders?" The dark little lady in the blue pantsuit snapped, "I know I'm in the right room." Two rows back a Lum sniveled, "Bes a-gaumed up talk. Haint hittin' on Indians er nuttin' like," while others mocked the screen's bright image adding sir and knight to their names. "Sir Knight Whopicoddle White Hide," was followed real quick by "Idiotgidhisself kilt don'tshuddup," and the growl fumed straight on, but that hard bent Jake stretched even taller.

"They simply changed their name to Knights of Christ. And the temple they built was renamed to the Order of Christ. In 1492, this group from Portugal provided navigators for Christopher Columbus and the Order's cross was sewn on the sails of his ships. But there's no evidence you can get yer hands on. Is there?" His jaw aimed across the back rows. "Course not. Too much at risk. Anyone have a guess what they're called today?" Jake leaned across the podium. He smiled real cheesy-like from one side of the room to the other like some fool was really gonna raise his hand. "Anyone know what links our Lumbee Indians to the Holy Grail?" His boot vibrated against the podium's trim and the sniveler snarled, again. "Hope m' die."

"Now, I detect some of you here still don't get the connection. Sounds like a couple are touched even. Anyone know what pidgin the Lumbee's speak? Where the languages connect?" Jake squinted and pursed his lips like he had an osmosis lead line to tug up an arm.

After he'd planted his seedy greens across every single row and didn't get a sprig of reckonin' he doggedly continued, flipping over note cards as he proceeded. And the prim lady seated nearby hurriedly marked her notepad. But both whoahed real sharp like when an aged Lumbee in overhauls, from deep within the Lum group in the back rows, raised his weathered hand. His huge shiny palm glimmered as his scarred blackened leather knuckles spread. "Hope m' die, n'er had no White man a-meddlin' on the swamp like dis," his riled voice deepened his atypical tenor into a bon a fide bass, "and right in my face, too. Orta notta munk up our chances a-gettin' federal funds, boy. Look at me. I'm Cherokee." His chin lowered and squint glared as he rattled, "Tell me I haint."

"Put a root on 'at boy," a young Lum yelped through his baccar filled mouth. A nasty black line drooled down his chin as he spit into a well used bandana. Shook off what didn't make the cloth onto the carpet and rubbed it in with his work boot.

"Uhm- uhm," the aged Lum's grunt vibrated like it was rattlin' sticky phlegm. His whiskers danced like corn silks on fancy colored Indian corn and his blue eyes sparked like prize kernels heatin' up to 'xplode.

Jake zealously tapped the slide projector's screen and its retraction bar dinged the backside of his head. He politely winced as he worked to still the waving screen. But his hands still shook like he was sifting beans. And all the while, the heated Lumbee guest was showing off his hawkbill as the screen lit up with an image of the holy tablet. The Lum flicked the shiny silver blade and scraped out a crusty black line from under his thumb. Perked the blade up in his overhauls' front pocket and with mesmerizing Mediterranean blue eyes glared up at Jake from under a canopy of wily gray curls. "The

Lumbee Council'll hear 'bout you a'fore mornin', you see me."

Finally, the cop on duty as umpire shifted from the rear corner halfway up into the room so all the Lums could view him straight on.

Jake's slim muscular build and farmer's tan complimented his hayseed hair and green eyes. They sparkled like North Carolina's emeralds dug up fresh from a shiny clay bed. "Okay. On to another psychohistorical fact: In 1656, historian William Dugdale wrote that explorer Sir Walter Raleigh visited the area where the section of holy tablet was discovered and was told a story about the Templars hiding treasure there." Jake aimed at the screen's image where an aged map with a yellow cross marked the spot. "Raleigh obsessed over the treasure seeking and even persuaded his wealthy wife, Elizabeth Throckmorton, Maid of Honor to Queen Elizabeth I, to buy land there and hired a crew to dig the ruins of the Templar preceptor. It was rumored nothing was found.

In fact, Raleigh has a whole string of raw deals where he claims to have found nothing. Nothing. Yet he was desired and commissioned. Sent out time after time." Jake spun in a circle. Landed square on his boot heels and cocked a half grin. "No one with any logic would keep spendin' money on a lost cause. Raleigh was a con man, the kind who would sell out to the highest bidder. And there were plenty more like him waiting in line for a chance to find treasures. Treasures like the Knights Templars' collection of Christian relics. The stolen relics." Jake licked his lips and scanned the room.

"Privateer pioneers like Raleigh are why the philosophers of the Christian crusades, the Knights Templar, created a system of trust. Some say there're groups today using that same system." Jake thrust his palms together, threw them up into the air like he was setting a bird free and lit up their eyes. "It was so simple." His wide smile faded as he leaned across the podium. "You tell and you die."

The audience gulped, near about in perfect unison, sat back and stared straight on.

"Tracing the movement that led to the quest for peace," Jake's water glass slid, but he quickly recovered it, "as well as the quest for the Holy Grail and other Christian relics, leads to," he took a sip of water and languished over it, "leads to the Lumbee people." When the screen beheld a beautiful woman with long dark wavy hair framing her bare brown bosom the men grinned. "Their language is rich with Portuguese."

Quick as a kid on a wild hare Jake planted a paper wad against the side wall. "Lumbees call the slingshot a juvember or juvemba. The Portuguese use the same word to describe a young kid." He flipped the juvember around and the band flopped. "It's a kid's toy. Juvember is also the name of a Portuguese village." He smiled and nodded and some guests responded kindly. "Pocosin, say that around here and first thing that comes to mind is swamp. Pocosin is the name of swamps all around the southeast. In Spanish Portuguese it means little without dry land or swamp. And common Lumbee names like Chavis, Chaves, Cheeves and Cumbo are Spanish Portuguese and African. Though the Lumbee deny any African heritage. But Lumbee DNA says the same thing as their language does." Jake hoisted the juvember up like a flag. "So it ain't a surprise to anyone that in 1754 the governor counted not a single Indian in Bladen County."

Jake backed up to the screen and framed it with his outstretched arms. One draped over her head and the other cupped the rest of her. "Our Lumbee Indians' physical appearance and language, along with documented logistical sightings prove they are, without doubt, America's first Christians." While guests were still lock jawed and flabbergasted into complete silence Jake took full advantage. "Lumbees," he yelled, "are North Carolina's Pilgrims. They are the true Native American and must be justly recognized." He took two long forceful strides to the podium for a sip of water. When he nervously slammed the water glass it splashed onto the prim lady's lap and soaked her notepad. Jake stood aghast, but she excused the mishap with a surprising smile that lifted her eyebrows till it took off ten years.

"Pilgrims?" one Lum shouted.

"Holy nothing, we're Indians, you fool."

A young freckled Lum dressed in a worn thin flannel shirt and similar jeans bolted up and aimed his judging finger. "What kind of gungi dis guy got?" His soprano rose as he reddened. "Bes sense a no man I got ta hear. Malahacked kyarn from wheretell I'm don't cyare." And he plopped back down into the metal chair. "Called it Grail 'er something." Another young Lum screeched. The umpire grasped his holster as his belly flapped up and down over his belt and laughter rolled over the room. "Gungi went out with 'nam." But when the blue pantsuiter scowled he leapt back into cop mode like a basset sniffing the air.

"Youse got a truck to haul my bate a' loot or youse gonna be a cheat and just dole off a pearly piece?" The overhauls man stomped his thick soled boots on the carpet and chunks of smelly stuff popped off. Other Lums remarked that they'd pen out their addresses and to send theirs express mail, too. Others wanted to know where to find Grail Gungi and who had seeds. "Holy, Holy Grail!" the baccar spitter hit his top leg like he was winning a bet. "We's rich! Got da load of relics. Whad e'er dat bes. Mail my piece to da swamp, overnight 'xpress, cuz." And a curly orange topknot jerked the back of the baccar spitter's tee shirt so hard it choked him. With clenched jaws she commanded, "Down."

Jake wrenched his hands then politely grinned. "This isn't about treasure. It's about the origination of a people. This is about Lumbees claiming their heritage as America's first Christians and their position as Native Americans. Can there be a mightier pride for any group to claim? They are traced back to the first explorers, the Portuguese. Naturally, they blended with native Indians and their other neighbors, the Africans, and of course with the English pilgrims." As clogging and fuming forced forward from the back rows Jake forced a thick notebook from the podium's shelf. "This explains everything. We have to work together on this."

The back rows shuffled. Lums bolted straight up and Jake was asked exactly how many people he'd told his cockamamie ideas to. "Youse a sharp 'un, but we's already Christian." Fireworks fumed from the curly orange topknot. "We want our rights as Native American Indians. We have Lumbee pride!"

Other guests shrunk into their chairs. The ump called for order. And the prim lady up on display next to Jake grew thinner and paler until she faded into the beige wall as nothing except a little pink hole where her thin pink lips sucked in streams of air. But as Jake spun away from the audience and wildly grinned like an unashamed unconscionable thief the prim lady resumed breathing normally, if not heavily.

Metal chairs bounced against the royal blue carpet. They rattled. Clanked. Scraped and slid down the beige walls as the Lums in the back rows hauled ass. "Leave peaceably now," the officer ordered as he motioned others to the front of the room. Still, a few Lumbees hurried straight on through the genealogical aristocrats who parted like sliced white bread as the Lums crammed the front desk for copies of Jake's articles and his business cards. Several threats were overhead. Some outright yelled. "Ain't worth killin'!" But the gracious genealogical aristocrats tried to calm them, including the dark skinned blue pantsuiter. "Bless your darlin' heart, I know this isn't what you wanted to hear, chile."

The officer quickly braced open the outside double door. "Make sure you have everything. Building's gonna be secured here shortly." They peeled tires. Popped over wheel bumps. And as metal scraped against metal orange yellow sparks sparked and their call for attention was declared by an officer's siren when circling blue lights rounded off the evening's presentation.

"Certainly, they're not what Queen Elizabeth had in mind," the prim lady turned up her nose and fanned her damp notepad as she and Jake waited behind the bolted double glass doors. "That is, if you are correct."

"I wasn't done." They exchanged shrugs as Jake moaned at the strewn mess of note cards then suddenly grasped her shoulder. "You got it. You did. Didn't you? You may be the only one."

After a bat of her eyes he loosened his grip and she braced as tall as her thin five foot frame allowed. "You didn't get through all your notes. That's a shame. All that work." Her skinny finger traced her matte pink grin. "And the paintings and maps, your presentation was so clever and organized." When the screen's bright reflection caught her glasses she squinted and then raised her eyebrows and took the time to read the information the riled guests had upstaged.

Excerpt from the 1871 North Carolina Joint Senate and House Committee as they interviewed Robeson County Judge Giles Leitch about 'free persons of color' living within his county:
Senate: Half of the colored population?
Leitch: Yes Sir; half of the colored population of Robeson County were never slaves at all...
Senate: What are they; are they Negroes?
Leitch: Well sir, I desire to tell you the truth as near as I can; but I really do not know what they are; I think they are a mixture of Spanish, Portuguese and Indian...
Senate: You think they are mixed Negroes and Indians?
Leitch: I do not think that in that class of population there is much Negro blood at all; of that half of the colored population that I have attempted to describe all have always been free...They are called 'mulattoes' that is the name they are known by, as contradistinguished from Negroes...I think they are of Indian origin.
Senate: I understand you to say that these seven or eight hundred persons that you designate as mulattoes are not Negroes but are a mixture of Portuguese and Spanish, white blood and Indian blood, you think they are not generally Negroes?
Leitch: I do not think the Negro blood predominates.
Senate: the word 'mulatto' means a cross between the white and the Negro?
Leitch: Yes sir.
Senate: You do not mean the word to be understood in that sense when applied to these people?
Leitch: I really do not know how to describe those people.

"They'll come around, eventually." She curiously clutched at her neck. "You realize though, you won't take this podium again."

"Can't say I'd blame 'em. But this is just the first. I still have the surrounding counties." He set his jaw like he was bracing for a punch. "Don't know exactly what I'll do next. Got a professor up at Chapel Hill willing to listen, but I don't have time to be tracking up there and back. Don't know if he'd be any real help anyway." He palmed the glass then cocked an eyebrow. "Gotta put my boot down on what'll put the word out best."

"You could always just tell me."

"You have ties with the Lumbee?" His Adam's apple bounced as the prim lady marched to the podium. First she held up his thick notebook, 'Black Purse Papers and Beyond: A Study on the Lumbee Subculture by Jake Wilkes.' "This took some grit young man." Then she pulled out one of Jake's note cards, marched it over and flipped it up in his face. Underlined in thick reverberating lead was, 'You tell. You die.'

"Yea, they're the ones who cut my brake lines."

Her thin lips curled down into wrinkled pockets. "This is Providence." Her itty bitty blues stung. "You must tell."

His passion boiled into a heated roar. "If I had any sense I'd walk away before I went missing." He bit his lip and flatly waved at the remaining guests staring from the other side of the room while the blue pantsuiter and her gentleman friend stepped up to the podium. When the gentleman took a business card and gestured good-bye Jake eased a nod. Then gave his attention back to the prim lady as he traced the deep scar on his cheek to the corner of his mouth with his pointer finger.

"You couldn't be dragged away." Her bony features boldly stabbed. "And I'm the only one here willing to help."

The prim lady's living room was elegant and uncluttered with pastels and layers on layers of sheers over the tall windows. From the first meeting Jake heated up her house like a red hot coal under winter quilts. The prim lady didn't miss a move as Jake sunk into the divan and propped up his socked feet on her free retirement center's monthly magazine spread open on the maple coffee table.

She resigned to her desk, positioned where her angular profile turned from sharp to mellow as their meetings lingered into the late hours. Stacks of shorthand surrounded the backside of her desk in manila files. Each labeled and dated. Jake bled the story in thirty minute swells. With a pink highlighter she slashed at her typed shorthand notes and asked for details, editing his dictation until her pages were mazes. Then Jake resumed. The prim lady's chest heaved as she typed the fight scene, biting her bottom lip until she didn't have a lip at all. "Are you sure you want to be compared to a dog?"

"Yes, that's how it was." Jake sunk further. His arms were so long and her sofa so dainty that his muscular forearms hung off each arm rest. She momentarily admired him then instructed him to close his eyes. "Go back there. Smell the summer grasses and the pits of your arms. Can you hear the mosquitoes?" Her voice hypnotized Jake every time. "Here we go into the thicket where Bruce destroyed your innocence." She typed as he spoke letting her shorthand typos fly by. "Tell me everything you see. The types of trees. The vegetation. All your secrets in the dark woods. Why are these people so important to you, Jake?"

His eyelids quivered and jerked open. "Allies are allies, Miss Lucy."

"Mmm." Then she presented a title and he balked. After thirty minutes the collaboration intensified. They debated verbiage, content and structure. After a fair amount of haggling they decided. Introduce the story when the boys were thirteen, because, as they fully agreed, that pubescent period when the brain's neurotransmitters aren't completely formed made for a fair amount of undisciplined and uncensored drama.

Two weeks later Jake picked up their efforts. She even included a cover page with her suggested title. "Trying to get us killed?" Jake skimmed the first chapter's pages. "I'll take it to the office. Read it there." When she inquired about security he informed her that only he and the manager had a key. "Don't worry. Plagiarism is the last thing on her mind these days."

"Actually, it's leaks to the council that concern me." When the prim lady's pointy nose stabbed at the air like an ill tempered finger Jake's tender touch melted her and she returned his pat along with a gentle push toward the door. "Jake, when I agreed to co write I didn't imagine my reputation being at risk. This little town, you know people are talking."

"Then you must a' heard by now. Everyone in town knows."

Her eyebrows awaited like a cast fifty pound test line suspended over white water as her gap caught a feisty trout.

"You're helping me write a business plan to expand the winery."

And with that, her gauzily white cheeks perked up like she was still sixty. "I have a lot to learn about you. How many more secrets are you keeping from me, Mr. Wilkes?"

Jake winked good bye and drove to his inherited career with a thousand stories on the tip of his tongue.

Tuesday mornings at Lucretia Winery inventory was verified for the afternoon's data entry. Phone messages were checked. And coffee was poured. The distillery practically ran itself. Trained and experienced employees entered monitor readings. The manager oversaw it all and presented any issues to Jake. The biggest problem at Lucretia's was goat escapees.

After the manager butchered the last escapee the task of goat fetching was delegated to the folks at the cheese store. So that morning's goat chase was enjoyed through the gallery's giant front window by both Jake and the manager. They grimaced as the goat popped across employees' car hoods into a truck bed. Then it hopped out and sped like a rabbit between vehicles. Once cleverly cornered by a maintenance worker on a three wheeler and two squealing ladies between its fence and a tractor trailer the frisky goat was scooped up and dropped into the pasture.

"Liketa snub off a front leg so it'd end that mess." Cassie finished the last of her coffee and shook her curly orange topknot like it was a fire cracker set off as a signal to work. And she did. With a fisted hip and seriousness about her like a judge with a gavel she told Jake that if he couldn't see to snubbing he'd better come off the hip with some more funds. Jake agreed to allocate funds, once again, on goat fencing and retreated to his office with the manuscript.

He placed the cover page face down on his desk. Flipped it over and tapped his chin as he fret over the suggested book title. Flipped it back. Flipped it over again. Spied Cassie's orange head bobbing as she read out another amended list of morning duties to her store personnel, and flipped it back down, just in case she wanted to confer or hand out another pink slip. When she was out of sight Jake began reading Chapter 1, Tenacity and Providence Hook Up at Forks in the Road, as he sipped the tepid remains from his favorite cup.

The thicket's stomped clearing held Bruce and Jake in their own trap. The young teens barely moved as the swarm surrounded them. It hummed above in a polite tone as if waiting on an invite and then in a whoosh, droned down welting up their tender flesh as if the mosquitoes truly were sin eaters suspicious old timers threatened instigators with. The teens popped their bare arms and swatted their faces. "Keep your mouth shut, cuz." Bruce's warning slapped like sharp cymbals against the mosquitoes' hypnotic hum front row of the fiddling katydids' background chorus in the late summer night. The boys' sour adrenaline fumigated the air as they breathed like bulls sucking in scents of hot cow heat until the air between them became as thick and nasty as death's awaiting dinner bugs.

Bruce eased up a bit from his crouch and carefully looked around. His crown of dirty blonde ringlets caught the moonlight and glimmered like a willowy dandelion's seed head momentarily marking him as just another sweet young boy. His hair tussled about while he fought the stinging mosquitoes. And his ringlets danced like willowy seeds while the night wind sang for its seeds to parachute free.

Tree frogs chirped like little baby birds as his old malahacked silver cup tapped. The fluted form hung off a long twisted wire from a Loblolly branch above his humble still, crafted from his old man's cast out pieces. The cup sang its tings and pings against the looped wire like it was being strummed to rally Bruce's turning and burning. The cup would ting and the baby birds would sing. It was all so pleasant. No one would have ever known from just listening to the sweet chorus the boys had all that ol' kyarn on their hands. The enchantment was so absolutely intoxicating, that for one second, Bruce looked like one of those spirits Lumbees tell to show up and help out strangers in need.

But then as he fully stood his ringlets left the light for the moon's shadow. He was not little at all. Bruce Black's thirteen year old chest puffed up under his threadbare tee shirt like an ancient bare-chested Croatan's out on the edge of the Carolina Coast doing his time on night watch. The cup's chorus twirled into a tight mesh as the wind suddenly blasted up from over the pond's dam and the baby birds smashed down. Stunned into silence. Bruce checked for the neighbors with panoramic vision then scornfully glared down to his side as tender young Jake petrified. Their eyes locked. Caught in a trance; Jake just let those mosquitoes feast as Bruce's cold Lumbee Indian grays threatened.

And don't think for one second them totens didn't pay it no mind, 'cause at the same time the boys were 'bout ta go around the choir director's baton poked straight up and jerked down the entire band from the late summer night's stage. The background music whoahed like a rough riding plow mule; with a screech from all the bullfrogs, just like they'd been stomped. The katydids did it, too. Then a whippoorwill's alarmed whip followed by several lame tree frog chirps. The baby birds squalled and the silver cup scraped around the Loblolly's trunk like a guillotine crunch.

And then it all stopped and got real still and quiet for one solid second, so the last critter's position in the band was amplified; a lone mockingbird's mock of an alpha arf. That very instant it became so still and dark, even the mosquitoes left. Like no spirit wanted ta be around for what was gonna happen next, not even a dark toten.

Jake's heartbeat pounded, but he didn't dare open his mouth to speak because there was a squealing, reeling voice in his head, absolutely screaming, "Mommy!" Even if he were blind drunk from their homemade hooch he knew not to tell, or let it slip, ever, as his quivering finger pointed to the dripping blade. It all happened so fast.

Bruce's top lip rose like a wolf's does before he eats his prey. He held the blade out from his side and shook it. "Bes just like a dog shakes, ha?" Bruce mimicked a dog shaking off its wet coat. His blonde ringlets whipped around his stoic grin. Then he bent straight over and used the German Shepherd's cream colored undercoat right at her butt to wipe off the blade, and smirked. Miss Scarlet wouldn't bark at Bruce again.

The dog was so beautiful. The moonlight covered her body as if the Little People had kivered her up with a holy blanket as her dark blood seeped into the bright sandy soil. Jake clamped his eyes shut, afraid he'd cry if he kept gawking. He caressed her outstretched body like his love alone really could've saved her. And instantly, tears formed, so he opened them. Too weak to move, Miss Scarlet whined as the whites of her eyes flared up at Jake. "Oh, my God," he panted. Her chest heaved for one last drawl of breath and that is when her hushed hollow howl totally consumed the boy.

Miss Scarlet died with her mouth hung open. Her pink tongue that had soothed and welcomed him so many years hung lifeless and still. Jake quickly grew hot as the moment marked him. His blonde bangs shivered as he trembled, filling up with a passion so powerful right there and then he became a man.

Bruce still scowled directly over him.

Jake cracked his knuckles as his hot glaring greens aimed like poison tipped arrows. Sweat oozed down his back as endorphins rushed down his spine. The sultry summer heat combined with his red hot fury made his armpits so sticky he had to pull at his pits to loosen the stuck fabric. Then Jake's thin legs tightened till his bones felt like steel. And his skinny frame actually thickened so much he had to roll his shoulders to keep from ripping his shirt. Then as Miss Scarlet's ears flopped lifeless like rags on a clothesline Jake became so empowered he unconsciously grit his teeth and bared his cusps as he fought the urge to choke his best friend.

Face to face with the threat, Bruce's thick lips parted. "Swanny, I'm had to do it." Hushed, but feminine, like most Lumbee males; it did nothing to distill his ferocity. "You gonna stick around and bury that? Don't count on me. I'm berries to pick. Shine to cook. Time's money, cuz."

"I hate you! Just shut up, you stupid Lum."

Bruce's gapped lips closed then slowly and wickedly curled up at the sides as he held the blade out in front of him like a fencing sword.

Jake blew as a snarl twisted his hot face. "She wasn't gonna do anything. She was just warning you." Consumed with the urge to kill, his fists were so tight they pulsed. The hair on the back of his head rose like a dog's sharp hackles and from deep in his chest he heaved a gruesome growl. "You make me sick." He panted. "Why didn't you just shoot her some more hot dogs? You got a pocket of 'em! You just suddenly forget how to shoot that damn juvember? You just get that stupid all of a sudden? Huh? Huh? Did cha?" His nostrils flared as a drizzle of snot rimmed his snarled lips.

Bruce leaned back. "Bes tired of it. Dog was a-gonna mommuck up my source and then I bes, I mean we, bes climbing that hill over at the creek to get my Muscadines. Now Buddyrow, can you see us a-toting buckets up and down that hill? Gotta be four miles a' nothin' but ass 'n elbows. Damn, Skippy." Bruce rolled his bottom lip down till it doubled. "It's just a dawg."

Bruce rested his hand on Jake's expanding back and the bullfrogs began to croon again just like a haunt had told 'em to. The katydids fiddled and the Muscadine grapes sparkled like they were just flicked with fairy dust. The damp night air settled down and covered them with heavy swamp scents and the freshness of Long Leaf Pines. "You ain't gotta deal with no crap from nobody. I don't care if some fool's got money or not, or a fool showing you a piece of paper saying her dog's better than my momma's mutt. Nobody's gonna run over me, or you. You always been there for me."

"I can't do this anymore." Jake balanced himself clenching a thick vine and took calculated breaths like he was birthing some big awesome thing he'd just as soon kill when a sweet cool breeze filled his senses and suddenly the nightsongs come screeching back into his ears while Bruce swatted at the stinging mosquitoes. "Gallanippers gonna gaum me up wid colic. Mess of 'em in these woodses tonight."

"You sure do get on the swamp when we're out like this." Jake's angst amplified between his gritted teeth as he glared up at Bruce. "You sound like your old man."

"Bes what the bate of 'em do, Buddyrow; keep the tribe." Mosquito blood was smeared over Bruce's cheek like a battle star, like he did that day when they were only five when their backyard opened up to all the sorry in the world.

"Gawd, just talk plain with me," Jake's burning eyes filled. "It's not like you're gonna turn me into a Lum." Bullfrogs croaked rib-dat as Bruce bellowed, "Gotdat, Jack!" and he leaned against Jake's shoulder. "You better not breath it, not to one or I'm put a root on you. And be all the sorry in the world having to do that to you, Jake."

"Yea, nothing comes between good ol' boys and their precious damn shine." Jake cleared his hot face from the grape pickin' gyarb as he held down one nostril and blew out a stream of snot. Then the other. And the diversion served well as it rinsed off Bruce's hand. As their standoff over the dead dog subsided a car turned up the hill toward the neighbor's back yard. When they hunkered down deep behind the grape vines they disturbed the plump Muscadines bobbing near their heads and the air surrounded them with sweetness. Bruce popped one into his mouth and used his chin to direct Jake to do the same. Bruce spat out one seed, then another. Jake bit down. The grape burst wet and cool inside his hot dry mouth, but the connection with Miss Scarlet's blood pulsing from Bruce's faster-than-light gaping hole sent Jake hurling. Jake gagged and grape spewed along with leftover taco salad.

"Baby," Bruce spat as he popped Jake on top of the head. With the car long gone Bruce directed, "Get home. When your mama smells you munked up wid the colic, and bes all chauld over, tell her you fell out the tree house. Gotdat, Jack!" In the thick of the vines with the moonlight behind him Bruce mirrored his sinister old man. "I'm not your cuz. Talk normal ta me. Got that?" Jake spat out the lingering stomach acids as he held his knees.

"You bes right, my friend. You taint got no Lum blood. No warrior in you a'tall, blanko baby." He hovered like a snake aiming to strike. "I'm said it. Tho says a word I'm ta put a root on you. Made dat son a' Dodger's bust his head on a rock right there at school. Fell off that teeter totter and bes sense of a jack rabbit. Say he's gonna be like that straight on." Bruce's arrogance spat off his shoulders like a heavy poison, so real it stank. "I know all 'bout conjuring. 'Member that when youse telling what's up to yer perty white Mommy."

"Shut up." Jake stripped leaves from a nearby maple and to wipe a spew of vomit from his shirt. "She'll want to check me out. I can't tell her I fell. She'll never believe it." As Jake bolted Bruce grabbed his arm, flung him to the ground, and kicked his shin so hard it sounded like it cracked. But it was only Bruce's worn boot separating from the sole, again. As soon as Jake was sure his leg wasn't broken he stopped rubbing and rocking and glared up at Bruce like he could kill.

Bruce rolled. "Haw! She'll believe it now when ya' take them britches off." Up like a shot Jake kicked back and snarled, "Tell your dad you fell out trying to catch me." And right then the bullfrogs up and croaked all together like a big fat clap. "The Prince got a boo boo?"

Bruce's eyes doubled before he doubled over and in one deep guffaw coughed out the pain. "Swanny, you done mommucked up now. Youse fixin' ta gyet crotched up now. Don't cho ever call me that." Bruce's nostrils flared wrongsididas with his thick lips poked out like he was fixin' ta bite. But Jake just shook his burning foot. "I'm done, Bruce. I'm not cookin' any more. I'm done. I mean it. Do what you want with my share." Bruce blinked so many times, like he was shifting gears in a runaway truck. "Fine by me. Gets better with age, like women."

"What? You have a girl now?" Jake licked his dried lips as Bruce's throaty whisper heated Jake's ear. "We were yurkers then. Kids experiment. Bes all." His head rolled side to side as the shiny blade rolled over and over in his palm. "We were drunk."

"Not every time, Bruce." Jake's tender voice cracked. "In the pick up last summer, we weren't in the back just waiting on falling stars. You know it." Bruce held the blade at Jake's cheek. "I was just gettin' off. Understand?" A lone mockingbird cried out a drawn out version of his neighbor's call, "Whip-poor-er-will!"

Bruce didn't tote buckets heaped with grapes that night. Jake didn't either. They toted shovels from the still site to bury Miss Scarlet. A pent up angered passion fueled a fast humongous hole out by the baccar field off the road a ways. And Miss Scarlet's body sunk into the summer warmed soil as Jake tossed a handful of stones across her sandy topped grave. He prayed aloud that he was sorry and wished he could take it back and could've done something to have stopped everything as Bruce kept watch.

Chapter 2

Tons a Reckoning for a Pardon on da Preacher

Exhausted from a full day at the winery and God's honest truth, the mental exhaustion from heaping out all the memories, Jake takes a break from dictating his story and stretches his legs in long three foot spanned steps on out to the fall evening's cool front porch. Her quaint old house sits back off the road, lined with pecan trees, only four miles from the winery. When a rush of cool wind sharpens his senses and rustles the fallen leaves Mr. Fisk's sweet sour mash tweaks his senses and a smile.

Jake casually leans against a column and stares off into the bare limbed sky. The black limbs thin out into a deep purple sky with a three quarter silvery blue moon cresting over a thin maroon waft. Refreshed, he returns to the living room to discover she is in the kitchen preparing her usual, tea for two and pimento cheese sandwiches. He lingers over her desk, reading her latest revision as she brings their evening treat and suggests he read reclined on the divan.

When the cover page still has her suggested title, <u>Lumbees Undone</u>, his tongue curls up over his top lip like a clamp. He props up his socked feet and reads Chapter 2.

Everything changed that summer. Bruce was busy working with his dad at the Lumber mill. And at night, Bruce's lone flashlight trailed off into the timberline as he lumbered off to turn Muscadines. His dad had turned too, Evangelical.

His dad sweat out distilled Saturday night sugar on Sunday mornings while he swore down from his pulpit at his wide eyed followers. His followers were mostly Lum winos, some aged street people and a few totally ignorant Lums who thought they'd discovered a gifted prophesying preacher who talked just like them. His dad was crafty enough to surmise in sermons that withheld donations meant the Lord's gifts withheld, like not enough work or food or shine to wash down the desperation. And it worked. After all, his dad operated the most popular shoe and shine outlet in town. Lots of 'em got work time to time. And God's honest truth, they all got shine. All in all, crafty Black made it work for him: Despite institutionalized English education Lumbees kept their hundred year old vernacular. They called it 'Keeping the Tribe' and they called Bruce's old man Preacher Black.

Jake's mom, Mrs. Wilkes, said Preacher Black was eccentric and dressing all in black was just another one of his oddities. "He'd a never made as a preacher if he'd taken up cockfightin' like the others do. Deep down he must've had a good soul. Lots of men get caught up in alcohol." She also said people who'd been real bad and got saved became holy rollers. While Bruce told that his dad just had a bad losing streak and wanted to earn his money back and that his dad would be back at the card table as soon as he got his funds together. From the way it looked, if Bruce was right, his dad would be playing soon. They got a new roof on the house. It needed it. A two k bribe got the drive paved from the mailbox up to the house and graveled the dirt road one hundred feet on each side. They got a new truck, a camper and a jet ski. All black. Told his dad can write it all off on his Jesus work.

And to top it all off, Bruce's dad also got a hair transplant. He looked like a sun burnt yellow onion with long wispy roots flying over his prickly forehead. He couldn't wear a hat till the swelling went down. Stuffed in his Sunday best, Bruce's dad paraded inside the gas station, paid for the fuel and then entered the bathroom on the outside of the cinder block store.

Jake went behind the store and leaned against the free air's sign post with his cowboy hat over his eyes and a bottle of water in his hand. The summer heat rose up scalding until he was forced to fan himself with the brim while Bruce sat lurking in the new truck, the new dirty black truck. Even with the graveled section dust clung like sin.

Bruce continued stealing peeks so Jake waved and satisfied, Bruce leaned deep into his seat and draped his arm out the open window down the length of the door to show her off. Her long black hair and loud obnoxious laugh were hard to ignore.

Bruce stabbed his chin up in the air like he always did when he was figuring out what to do next as Jake approached. Then Old Man Black flung open the bathroom door. "Gaummed dat up! Worse 'n stink bugs on soft taters!" At the precise moment Jake popped the top of the hood of Old Man Black's new truck. "Whoa, mon!" Old Man Black sounded like a stobbed screaming woman as his alligator boot steps quickened. "Geyt! Bes waxing my truck, yurker!" He looked like a cartoon character marching across the steamy hot parking lot stuffed in his black suit with sweat dripping down his red hot temples like a wrestler on a pay off, but nobody with a lick a sense would've dared laugh, out loud.

Jake nervously waved him off while Bruce begged, "You don't want this slacker kiverin' our truck with paste wax. He'd munk it up." As Old Man Black got closer he slowed down. Jake wasn't hard to recognize. It's just that every skinny thirteen year old boy in Cameron wore boots and cowboy hats. They all pulled time putting up hay for the Thomas's. Wore the same soiled jeans day in and day out so they wouldn't wear out their school jeans and hung out at the store to ask for more paying chores. What else was there to do in the middle of nowhere, North Carolina? That was, other than working shine or plain mischief that wouldn't fetch a dollar.

Old Man Black walked around his truck checking for yurker marks. He said so out loud and then went on to grumble under his breath about suing and having plenty of church people who'd stand up in a court of law and testify against Jake if there was so much as a new pit or wad of gum on the undercarriage knowing full well there wasn't a single soul around from his church. "Swanny, thought I had me a wood toter. You bes lucky today. Don' see no yurker marks no'rs." He pumped the fuel while inspecting his image in the side mirror and adjusted the small Testament in his suit coat's front pocket. He pulled out the hanky, wadded it up and poked it back down to the bottom of the pocket and sat the Testament on top so it would stand out and anyone could easily identify him as a solid man of The Word.

Robin leaned over Bruce's lap and her long neck stretched till her head was clear out of the window. "Hey, Jake, how's your summer vacation?"

"Hot, but I'm making a little money." Jake threw cool water down his hot throat.

Bruce winked. "Me too."

Robin politely smiled. "What time is it, anyway? I told Mom I'd be back by four. We just got back from the nursing home. We sing for the residents. Preacher Black visited our church and we teamed up. Our congregations are both so little." Robin hadn't taken a breath when she fully leaned over Bruce and asked, "What church do you go to, Jake?"

"It's three-forty-five. We're Presbyterian." After he answered Robin, Jake smirked at Bruce. "You sing hymns? How's that going for ya?" His dimples dug into his sun kissed cheeks and his green eyes shone like a happy cat's when Robin responded, showing off her glistening whites framed with her full red lips. She grew more beautiful each summer. Mesmerized, Jake leaned against the truck. Perspiration dotted his top lip and as Robin shared his wanton moment, whether consciously or not, she licked her lips when Jake waved his cowboy hat over his broadening chest and purposely flexed his pecs.

And Bruce braced his hard arm in the window frame like a hot engine rod fixin' ta 'xplode. "Like singing anything else." Bruce's smug answer ended with rolling eyes. Then he turned to Robin. "I'm good at it. Huh?" As Robin nodded her long black hair bounced against her chest's padded buds.

Jake smiled as he fanned his heated face. "Hey, I know where you can get some good peaches next year."

Bruce scowled at Jake's implication and Robin eagerly leaned up for a better view out the window. "Next year?" she chirped. "We'd like 'em now. Right, Bruce?" Jake's big white teeth were as white as his sun bleached blonde crew cut.

"Dad's congregation keeps us up in peaches," Bruce cleverly replied.

"I see that." Jake's head rolled like a ball in a poured cement ditch.

Teased to the hilt Bruce licked his front teeth as he glared up at Jake with his steely grays. "Dad's really into church now. Got religious friends all over town." That's when Jake's head stopped still.

"It's three-forty-five," Robin whined. "I better not be late, Bruce. You know Gili. I mean Mom." Her forehead wrinkled with worry. Everyone knew Gili. She'd made the restaurant notorious. Gili's; don't complain or it'll come back burnt, cussed brown.

Jake daringly leaned into the truck. "Do you work at the restaurant?" His full head fit inside forcing Bruce to press back against the seat to keep from being cheek to cheek. "Dad takes us there a couple of times a year. Never seen you working there."

"Well you don't come often enough. I grew up working at Gili's. But I have a lot of demands on my time. I have flute, dance and compete over at the team penning off Highway 42. My horse is double registered. Anyway, I'm not there every night." Robin turned to Bruce and then to his dad who sat snugly behind the wheel. "Are we ready now?"

"We're always ready to carry out the Lord's work, Robin." As Preacher Black tucked his chin and smirked over at Jake his eyes squinted from the sun. "Wanna come, Jake? Bet you know the words to a few of our hymns." The magnifying sun made his pale eyes look like hollow yellow holes. "Presbyterians got lots of the same songs as us chosen folks."

Robin's wrinkled forehead relaxed as she sighed up at the truck's ceiling and rolled her eyes. "Preacher Black, are we headed somewhere else to sing? I mean, I thought we were just singing at the nursing home? If we're gonna be any later I'll have to ask Gili." Robin pulled out her cell phone and flipped it open. When the recording requested the caller try again or leave a message Robin flipped it closed. "Can't get through this time a day. They're all ordering take out."

"Thought we'd do atonement at Gili's. She'll set us up wid a mou'ful me bringin' her sow cat in." Preacher Black's deep guffaw eased into a sly smile. "I'm smashin' the gas for a bate a' Gili's. Hold on, yunguns."

As Bruce shook his bangs free from his sweaty brow the blonde ringlets parted to make way for the shame. His eyebrows united and his chin darted about, but there was nowhere for him to hide. Bruce's nose pointed up in the air all around the big blue sky like a bird dog trying to lock sights. "Orta notta eat free thyere again this week."

"Shush, boy. She's got in for me, now." Preacher Black patted the Testament held up in his suit coat's pocket.

A car pulled up behind their truck, impatiently honked for a turn at the gas pump and his dad turned the key. Jake threw back the last of his water. But his dry throat wasn't eased. "Later, dude." Bruce mouthed bye as Robin stared dead ahead. And Sinister Minister wrapped his big open hand across Robin's bare knee and rested it there as he steered away from the gas pump.

Two weeks later, Mrs. Wilkes explained to her son, "Imagine that. An overhead limb breaks the man's neck. Just imagine that." Jake welcomed the little fairies that lowered him into the recliner to sew his gapped lips shut while his mother handed him the newspaper clipping. "Working in that dangerous environment all his life and struck down by a limb on the path to his truck. It's so odd. The man just turned his life around and the Lord calls him up. It's the craziest thing. Look, Preacher Black made front page. That must be inside his little church. It's just the craziest thing ever."

Jake sat listlessly scanning it, over and over. Black's obituary didn't say anything about Preacher Black being a former gambler, or one of the meanest, orneriest, most foul Lumbee fools no one with a lick a sense would e'er stow up in a corner without a loaded gun or sharp blade or simply no will to live on any longer. And the newspaper clipping didn't mention a single one of his numerous overnight stays at the county jail. Why Black had been there so many times they kept his favorite breakfast on hand, pig brains. His obituary could have simply stated that Black was a well known moonshine operating possible wife killer and confirmed child abuser. That would have at least given it a redeemable amount of honesty. Jake crushed it and sat seething as his leg vibrated like a muffler on a runner's worn shock until his mother told him to sweep off the steps where, safely outdoors, he promptly cussed, under his breath.

Straightaway, the funeral was held. And just as straightaway, one thing was very obvious. Old Man Black stirred up quite a following and that's probably why all the facts weren't included in his obituary. There'd a been a riot. Every single parking place around front was taken. Mr. Wilkes drove around the block searching for an open parking spot. Twice. It was astounding. In less than two months Preacher Black had conned nearly three hundred folks into joining his church operating out of the old shoe store right there on Main Street.

The same shoe store that served as a front for his moonshine. One of his Lum friends owned the store. Black just utilized it, for a fair fee. Anyone in Cameron knew. The shine was received in boot boxes and shipped out in boot boxes, an easy farce for any law outside of Black's payoffs. Work boots are even close to the same weight. There were times so many boots were going in and out a few outsiders got curious. So the old fart set up a resole booth. Really though, it was plain fact that Old Man Black weren't never worried 'bout nobody doggin' on his biz, cause hardly no Lum was ever born meaner than Black.

(There's an old rumor. Been around forever and kept anyone from ever crossing Black. When Black was fourteen he was forced to leave the tribe and wasn't allowed back. He was that mean. As a child, Black cut his teeth on a blade and then as a yurker, cut his cousin. On account Black wanted his new leather jacket. His cousin nearly died, but totens carried that bleeding child's scent to his momma and she found him just in time. She used her blouse to make a tourniquet and then threw her own blade down at the Black's front door and warned that their boy'd be dead before sunset and that she wouldn't need no blade for gettin' it done. Black was on his own since. Stole what he couldn't earn out of his loggin' wages and likker funds. And no Lum would touch him on account he threatened his toten to chase 'em for eternity if they did. But that's just rumor.)

"Don't touch anything in here." Mrs. Wilkes instructed as they stood at the entrance of the stale old shoe store turned church. Her jaw literally vibrated as she hissed. "This place is going to be full of thugs and scallys. I just know it. We better just sign our name and leave."

Mr. Wilkes winked at Jake and cleared his throat as he steered his wife inside like she was a little pinto pony. "Now there's a thought. You know the Lumbee are suspected to be descendants of The Lost Colony." Mrs. Wilkes looked right through him as he continued. "It's legend that Sir Walter Raleigh wanted to form a new society here, a secret one, like the banned Templar Knights. And the Grand Master of the Templar Order, de Molay, who was burned at the stake in thirteen fourteen by King Philip of France, the same King who pressured the Pope to disband the Order, issued a curse."

Mrs. Wilkes was on the purple side of rage by this point and shook like she had her own little earthquake going on under her meager heels. "Don't fill his head with that mess," she hissed. "Those boys'll beat him if he repeats that and you know it."

But Mr. Wilkes held his son's full attention. "The King and the Pope both died within the year. Eyewitnesses say de Molay wasn't even screaming and didn't show any fear. I can see Chavis Black being that way." Mr. Wilkes penned the family name into the registry in the foyer 'cause Mrs. Wilkes' couldn't. Her fists were still clenched. He hummed in reflection and added, "He was always talking about puttin' a root on someone." He smiled down at Jake. "Good thing you made friends with the family."

The registry book was cream colored with blue lettering and blue lines. Jake asked for the pen to write best friend beside his name and that was the beginning of the best funeral the little town of Cameron, North Carolina ever had. Or at least the most talked about. As Mr. Wilkes was about to hand over the pen he noticed the alternating nude to bikini clad busty blonde stretched down its side. It was from the strip joint down in Fayetteville. He slyly grinned as he held it out and shook it like the ink might be low. The nude lady flashed and flashed as his smile grew and grew. But when Mr. Wilkes was about to put the pen in his Sunday suit coat Mrs. Wilkes elbowed her mister and he dropped it. "I said, don't touch anything in here."

As Jake unconsciously quipped, "Good-gooboly-goo," way too loudly, like he and Bruce always did when something incredible happened, Mr. Wilkes popped the top of his head. And they all gawked as the humongous shiny white hertz out front, slid in to triple park. They were surrounded with church goers' cars and jar runners' trucks and drunks' clunkers and there wasn't a single solitary police car around, marked or not. Must've figured everyone safe with Black out of the game. Jake pinched his palms to hurt so he wouldn't laugh out loud. And as he fought his growing grin, his dimples dug in till he became absolutely adorable. His mother didn't notice, but his dad did and that time thumped his bony shoulder, real hard, and instantly, Jake's smile flipped.

The store church was full of greeters and weepers. From the yellowish brown skinned and curly headed folks it looked to be mostly Lums up where Bruce stood next to his aunt, two old uncles, and loads of kin in every degree. He looked like a man in his ironed black pants, white shirt and an oversized tie. His work boots were either new or stained with black shoe polish to match his pants. Bruce saved his money, hoarded it. Wouldn't buy anything new and the absolute last thing he'd ever buy is a pair of boots to wear only once. From Jake's position, it looked like Bruce was holding together. When Jake had gone over two days prior, Bruce was hot, fast to cuss and told him to get out. Mrs. Wilkes said he was hurting. Mr. Wilkes said he would turn out just like his dad and for Jake to leave him alone.

Bruce spread his arms open for his dad's store church followers and his dad's old drinkin' pals along with regular family folks and his co workers from the Lumber mill. Then Bruce longingly smiled as his favorites appeared. The jar runners openly weeped and with good reason. They didn't know if they'd be making payments on their wide screen televisions and vibratin' beds the next month. The bate of 'em had goods on pawn and Buy Here Pay Here Cars that'd be repossessed without a minimum payment.

Cassie and her seven youngins were lined up red faced and snotted like they'd cried all the way there. They were a sight with their spankin' red faces, curly orange heads and blue eyes. Poor things, looked like they were out of washing powders again. Cassie was a number one runner. Never cheated Black, ever, and had been a regular part of the household. She even helped build the bathroom addition. Regular handy woman; had a butchering outfit on the farm where she worked for rent and acted as a nurse, too. She'd patched up and doctored up pert ner everyone in the store church that had a connection to running, and concerning the Blacks, she knew every scar and how it got there.

Cassie sought out the only Black left and Bruce took to her hug like a calf to a bottle, holding her so tightly her back ribs showed through her thin pink blouse. "My little pappy sack, youse got a long row now. But youse pure got a bate a' friends who'll be there. Ya know our numbers, Shug." Then Bruce hugged Pig Pen, Cassie's oldest boy and the rest of her youngins. Then Old Rodger Dodger who pitifully shook as he explained that his brain damaged son only got out with the group home's nurses. Bruce patted Dodger's back with a genuine look of remorse for puttin' that root on his boy. Even his nose turned red. Then Bruce bear hugged Snap, a tall lean Lum with grave overbearing. Next, Bruce tenderly hugged Edge, Snaps' adopted daughter who fetched up alongside the stills like Bruce.

Bruce shook hands with young Thomas Magee and his older brother who mourned in reserved fashion like their parents beside them. The Magee family did not look into Black's black coffin. And neither his jar runners nor their families lingered over Black, but took fast checks making sure he was pure dead and then took seats. They pulled out napkins from take-out places and threadbare bandanas and wiped their noses and youngins' noses and waited for commencement.

When Jake spied a teacher he tried to guide his parents to take a seat. "Mrs. Albers, it's so good to see you. You never age." Mrs. Wilkes politely hugged her, the kind women do so boobies don't touch.

Mrs. Albers was due to retire, past due from the look of her long ear lobes. They wiggled. "Oh, thank you." They slowly released their hug, but kept hold of one another's forearms. "Mrs. Wilkes, you are so blessed. Jake is such a good student." She glanced at Bruce. "I wish they could all be so well behaved." She waited for Mrs. Wilkes to say something derogatory about Bruce's behavior on her invitation to bite, but when she only received a polite smile she looked around for another target.

Mr. Wilkes grasped Jake's shoulder, held it firm, and said, "Jake is one of a kind. I have big plans for him."

Jake peered up at him, which wasn't that far, about five inches and he'd be just as tall. Jake noticed it three months ago, when his dad had needed reassurance. He had crept into Jake's bedroom and slipped his hands under the sheets. "I have big plans for myself." Jake informed his old teacher. "Dad just has to fund them."

Mr. Wilkes turned pallor as Bruce squinted over at Jake and he responded with a raised eyebrow and just like that it was understood. Secrets kept the youngsters' friendship bound like slaves to silent echoes. And the silent echoes crashed into their youthful faces aging them like life's mean hand.

When Mrs. Albers smiled her tiny yellow brittle looking tea stained teeth gritted together in Jake's face. The sight, along with her liniment and tuna scent, forced Jake to wince. She pursed her lips in deep thought. "That's right. You want to be a veterinarian." When the skin on her neck wiggled along with her earlobes, like a gobbling turkey, Jake grinned like he had just stolen a cherry pie.

"He's wanted to be a vet since his first pet chicken." Mrs. Wilkes explained. "He named it Fluffy."

"Oh, that's just precious." Mrs. Albers' limp hand swatted the air. "I just love coming to these things. I always learn so much. People are so interesting, so unique." Her shoulders rose up and down like her blades were clapping for more. And pure arnt if she didn't get it.

Dan the Man's oversized square frame blocked the light at the front door entrance. Bruce defensively stood up taller, but it didn't help him appear intimidating. Dan the Man could've easily snapped Bruce's head off with one hand. He was the biggest human being ever seen and so ugly strangers to town were known to plow into cars while staring. His nose so bulbous and pits so deep roly-polies hibernated in 'em. Their antenna stuck out like whiskers. He had no neck, shoulders wide as the front of a town car's bumper with his head up in the middle like some kind of evil voodoo doll hood ornament made by an unskilled witch. His ears looked like they'd been stretched out, but thick and had so many rises a toy car could run around in there for an hour and never hit the same rise twice. And his lips were too big, even for him. His lips hung all red and drooled shiny like the backside of a mare after foaling.

In the doorway, holding all eyes and the light hostage, he was so extra cross, so extra riled, so extra rabid; his forehead was waded like a blanket over his beady black angry eyes. He was so fearsome that folks sitting clear on the other side of the room shrunk down into their chairs so as not to bring any attention to themselves. But his anger was null and void if he was lookin' to collect on any a Black's bad bets. As soon as Black got it he spent it: The sense of a honey badger eating everything in sight just 'cause he could with no idea when or even if he'd come across another meal. And Dan the Man was like a honey badger on account he'd eat anything and looked like a mean ass honey badger and sounded like one as he breathed his nasty breaths like a dying man grasping for air. He plum growled.

For one full gawl dern minute all Bruce or Jake could concentrate on was Dan the Man's brand new work boots. He boldly smiled at Bruce straight on and then over to Jake. He sported a new tooth, too. Gold enamel framed a perfectly white porcelain crown. His giant broken horse-tooth was fixed. The upper one he had broken just a few months before when he got dared to open a tin can of beans down at Old Man Black's likker works. He'd done it for years successfully, but his giant horse tooth had been weakened from years of acidic gastric juices. Dan the Man had always out drank the others, forcing himself to vomit to make room for more.

Oh, man, and if Dan the Man's new boots and shiny tooth didn't make a donkey out a' that entire shoe store church funeral neither did knowing the place still had four nights of hard work in the back all wrapped up on pallets marked as a defective boot shipment to be returned to the manufacturer. Every single jar runner in the store church knew and was hoping on that last run. But to get that run they'd have to deal with Dan the Man.

The quiet was broke when Dan the Man stomped down the aisle and stopped cold when Bruce locked on him like a hawk on an old farty possum. Dan the Man took off his hat and then with all the gall of an indolent yurker, and with his beady eyes still locked with Bruce's, he eased a nod directly at him to show off his new hair transplant. The long wisps flew over his big old head like fishing line teasing a fat cat down in its bank hole.

His hair transplant was just like Preacher Black's. He sported a puffed up noggin all discolored like flesh does when it fights decomposing in yellow and brown and pink to red with purple dots. Oh, man, did he have guts, big buffalo guts. Bruce signaled to Jake with his arrogant half a smile, chin up, but not too high, and nose flared. Either Bruce had just fueled osmosis and put a root on Dan the Man or was settin' a dare, a dare so big, so stinkin' crazy, Jake thought he smelled it and his leg quivered in anticipation of the first cue. He rubbed it down hard a couple of times to keep from running up to Bruce right then to plan something extra rotten for nasty old Dan.

Still, the Wilkes family managed the procession line, hugging each of Sinister Minister's relatives as Jake kept a check on Dan the Man. Jake casually adjusted his suit and peered over his shoulder just like in the old timey detective shows. Mrs. Wilkes said polite things about being sorry and it being sudden. While Mr. Wilkes said things about how good it was to see everyone coming to support Bruce. Mrs. Wilkes said, "Bruce will have it hard now that he's all alone." And one of Bruce's cousins said that Bruce will not be alone. Bruce's cousin, his mom's sister's son, Mark, explained that they agreed to move in with Bruce and help out. Bruce rolled his eyes, making it look not nearly as agreeable.

While slyly, Dan the Man slowly slinked in, almost like he was afraid to walk the procession line. His boots scraped across the tile like a cooter's toenails tapping and scraping, and spreading grossed out chill bumps up and down the line. Dan the Man eased his hat back on and retracted from the line. Even his neck sunk in deeper like a nasty ol' cooter when he turned around and headed to the far wall where he pilfered with an orange and yellow funeral wreath.

His big fat clumsy fingers fiddled with the wreath's envelope until he got the card out and he stared at it a long while before a young lady approached and he held it out to her. "For my only real friend all my life," she read aloud. "See you on the other side. Love, The Man," and handed it back to him. His thick pimple pitted chin twitched as she patted the middle of his back and told him, "That's lovely, so touching. It has to be the sweetest thing I've ever read on a funeral card." And with that he hung his big fat head so lowly his hat tumbled off. Another lady bent straight over to retrieve his hat, so far over in fact that her lacy black slip showed, but Dan the Man didn't even stare. Didn't gawk. Didn't say a thing out a line, only took the hat as it was handed back and covered his face with it as he hurriedly broke off into the back room where the pallets waited.

Mark said they'd move in the first of the month, when rent came due at the trailer park. Mark looked about six, wiry, curly headed and had those mesmerizing Lumbee blue eyes. Bruce's aunt stood closely to Bruce. "I'm Bruce's Aunt Thelma. Lizzie'll finally rest in Heaven now. She won't have to worry about her youngin' with me. I'm strict and all about higher education. We don't even speak their vernacular. Know what I mean?" Thelma wrapped her arm around Bruce's shoulder and they all nodded and smiled. His Aunt Thelma looked like all the other Locklears; light yellow brown skin and light brown curly hair with cheekbones high and nose broad with a wide bus. And she wore a fine low cut dress, not too low, but just low enough to make Jake blink when he did he best not to keep looking down the valley.

Both Mr. and Mrs. Wilkes solemnly empathized as Thelma held on to Bruce's rigid frame. Mrs. Wilkes sniffled. "Lizzie must have been her nickname. We went to church together for fifteen years and I never heard her called anything other than Gladys."

Thelma licked her bottom lip, made a quick scan of who was in line and then stepped closer to Mrs. Wilkes. "Gladys Elizabeth White," she nearly whispered, "an old English name. It was too stuffy for us on the swamp and Lizzie fit her. She never met a stranger and treated everyone like they were special. We sure miss her." Thelma's eyes welled up.

"I know she's happy to have you watching over him now. We're just through the woods, the yellow house. The boys have a path cleared. You let us know if you need anything. I mean it, Thelma. A ride to town, church, stay with the children, it's going to be an adjustment for all of you."

"Thank you," she softened as Mr. Wilkes offered his hand to Bruce. They shook, but Bruce didn't make eye contact with him. Instead, all chauld up, Bruce sought Jake.

Like a toy soldier Bruce held out his hand for Jake. But Jake jerked him up to his chest and used his chin like a clamp over Bruce's shoulder. After Bruce trembled, just the slightest, Jake let go. Bruce's dry lips opened and a white sticky string from his top to bottom lip stretched. Jake considered wiping it off, but was afraid people would talk. So instead, he handed him a tissue from his Sunday suit as he licked his own lips. Bruce read the cues and used the tissue to wipe his mouth.

Bruce swallowed, "We're taking his body to the cemetery off Old Plank Road, the Black's plot. It's private, right after this. Comin'?" His eyes begged. As Jake affirmatively sighed Bruce squeezed his shoulder.

The Wilkes stood over Old Man Black's body. His once saggy fat jaws were folded like sheets down to the satiny white pillow and his black suit finally fit his deflated frame. His lips were painted pink and the same pink was circled around on his cheeks like the coroner had tried to make him seem happy. The heavy furrows across his fire damaged forehead and around his eyes, which came from leaning over likker kettles and stoking fires, defined his true temperament: cross. When Jake tried to see how his eyes stayed closed he was surprised as threads were exposed when the left eyelids separated. He quickly pointed it out to his dad. "The temperature difference, son. Come on, let's find a seat." The jubious eye deal spooked Jake so he just had to look again. An eighth of an inch open and all he could see was a dirty white cloud.

The uncomfortable metal folding chairs clanked, rattled and squeaked against the old tile consuming the building the same way the stink loomed. The big room with its ten foot ceilings and old plaster walls trapped all the scents from old shoes and new, armpits and cardboard boxes, old dust, pine logger's dust, to the orgy of cologne, all sprinkled with the aroma of an open jar of rotgut. It was freshest on the breath of folks sniffling behind the Wilkes. Jake bent over and pulled up his socks to sneak a look over his shoulder.

Dan the Man took up two chairs and his sidekicks, Wart, and Mr. Fisk were there and if it weren't a miracle enough to see those dudes in a church, Scarecrow was there, right behind Jake. He'd met 'em all through the years and avoided 'em like lipstick lips on Sunday mornings.

With stinging dry eyes Jake studied the lady front and center with short brown hair, big brown eyes and a tight navy suit. She shifted her hips seducing the white podium marked with black scuff marks around its base with one finger, outlining its edges, over and over. Her pale skin was over powdered. Her lip gloss didn't have any color, just wet. But she must have been wearing fake eyelashes. It was as if she had tried to make herself appear homely or plain. But it didn't matter. She had boobs the size of cantaloupes.

Mr. and Mrs. Wilkes studied one another while Jake grinned straight on at the fruit offering. The lady scanned the room, from one side to the other, gradually taking order. She scanned persons as they entered from the foyer, from the side door and then the ones lingering at the racks of soliciting material on missionary work where boots and shoes were still displayed for sale, and she even scanned the ceiling. So Jake looked, too. There were only aged beige ceiling tiles, tube lighting along the walls and the one new chandelier. And then, when he followed her view, turned around like an owl and a camera was visible. Jake made his eyebrows dance up and down for the camera and Wart gave him the evil eye so he jolted back around and when he did that sexy lady winked right at him. So Jake sat back perfectly still.

Preacher Black's black coffin was right in front of her. The white podium was the only thing between her and the black coffin. The stand held The Holy Bible. Its golden edges sparkled like a butterfly's wings on a spring day. "Fellow friends, members of the Congregation, and relatives of the dear departed, I am Preacher Lilly." Her voice was silky smooth, like a Southern Belle's from one of those old black and white films where moss hangs from shady trees and everything looks sprawled out and welcoming. Jake swallowed the extra drool pooling in his mouth while Preacher Lilly's cantaloupes shifted as she took a deep breath. "Our dear brother, Preacher Black, or simply, Mr. Chavis Black, has left us to live in Heaven. As any one of us can testify, this man was a saint!"

The Wilkes family checked this news with the other wearing the most perplexed pusses imaginable while other funeral attendees gave Preacher Lilly, Amen's. Then all of a sudden, a sly smile radiated from Jake's bashful batting eyes. Bruce had Preacher Lilly's picture pinned on the inside of his closet behind the hanging flannels and pullovers right in the middle. Fayetteville's infamous 'Starlight Club' was lettered in flaming yellow across her spread eagle legs with the pole acting as the 'l'.

Right after he had acquired the hot 'Glossy Flossy' Bruce told Jake that she had offered to teach him everything he'd ever need to know in life and Jake's eyes had 'bout fell out of his head like they were right then as Preacher Lilly swung her head around and moaned. "Dear brothers, we're gonna miss this man. This man brought so many of us to the Light. He even turned stone to life. This building was nothing but an old shoe store." She winked, plain as day, at the group of scallys behind Jake. "Now it's a beacon of Light, a holy vessel, a watering hole for the down-troddin' and poor." Poor was so drawled out it had two syllables as her lips pursed up like a hooker's in the movies. "Preacher Black turned all us 'round from the dark to the Light." She swung her head and moaned again as funeral folks shouted, "Amen."

A man testified that Black gave him money for food. Another squealed, "He lifted me up." One of the scallys behind the Wilkes whispered, "He gave him a bottle."

"Sisters and Brothers, our Bible teaches us that a man in the Lord is a new man! A reborn spirit! Of the flesh of the Lord. Preacher Black gave me new flesh." With her flexed palms Lilly traced her body from way down at her firm hams and back up to her bouncy lopes, attaining an unconscious rise from Jake's member and most likely every other man. "From his flesh, the Spirit moved him in me, to be new, alive, to feel His power."

"Amens," swelled up through the room as young Jake was slowly hypnotized. Her head swung around. Her brown locks slapped her cheeks and full mouth hung open and then suddenly, she stopped. Preacher Lilly sashayed to the front of the coffin and looked down at Black's corpse and began to shamelessly shake her head as the two blue hams wiggled a quick jig. "Look at him." She spun around with her arms spread back like an abandoned baby doll. "Look at this man of God. Surely there's not one of you who hasn't been touched by his testimony." Folks responded with raised arms, shouts and moans.

Then a loud squeak demanded all eyes as a metal chair strained against the tile. A woman abruptly stood in front of the Wilkes with both arms thrust to the ceiling. "Preacher Black gave me love, pure love." She cried, "He showed me the way. He led me from Hell, Sister." A lady in front of her stood and slapped a tambourine. One poor lady who was moaning pitifully was handed a tambourine from another grieving lady until they were everywhere. And they were all pretty, tightly dressed and had great fruit plates, every single serving.

Mr. and Mrs. Wilkes darted at one another as the shiny tambourines mesmerized and excited everyone surrounding them when suddenly, Jake jumped. The row of scallys directly behind the Wilkes had clapped their hands. Preacher Lilly thus begged all to stand and sing. Some stood, ready to sing. Others were clearly hypnotized and too enthralled to leave their seats.

Preacher Lilly stretched to the ceiling, "Come together, now. Let's praise God for sharing this man with us. Even though it wasn't long enough, it was just enough. Oh, Preacher Black, what are we going ta do now? Who we going to call? Who is going to guide us, comfort us, lift us up and give us the power to go on? I tell all ya'll, it'll be Preacher Black's spirit alone. God didn't allow that man to be so low down mean for so long, to change and walk in the Light for no reason at all. No. Our Lord has plans for all of us. His plan for Preacher Black was to live on in us. We carry his spirit in us." She thrust her head around so hard that her short brown hair flew off her head right onto a man in the front row, but she didn't get upset.

And neither did he. But his fast wife did. She hastily pawed the man's new little brown pet from his caressing hands and slammed it up against the wall where it slid down to the tile and landed like a balled up kitten with its tail on end.

That Preacher Lilly loosened the bobby pins from her long brown hair and cried, "It's all right, Brothers and Sisters. It's a sign. It's a sign from Preacher Black." Her hips thrust back and forth in a quick snap. "He wants us to be ourselves, be free, move in the spirit that moves you." Quick as a pig on a cob she crone down the lid of the coffin and jumped up on top of it. With a gasp, Mrs. Wilkes bit her bottom lip just as many of the funeral folks who were standing, all ready to sing, sat.

Preacher Lilly stretched her arms up over her head until her little blouse untucked from her skirt and the buttons holding in her cantaloupes poked up like little pearl onions, threatening to come a-loose. In one long swoop her long brown hair seduced other women into motion. Tambourine ladies gyrated like long liquid lines from the ceiling to the floor as men clapped their hands. Still fully hypnotized, Jake fit in four claps before his mother slammed down his hands.

Jake enjoyed his dad's beet red face while his mother breathed out a freight train into his ear. And Preacher Lilly kicked out in anguish. "Is there anyone out there who wants to testify? Get up here and tell it. Tell what our dearly parted Preacher Black did for you. Don't let this moment pass you by." She swung her long brown hair and when she stopped it fell in wild directions all over as the cantaloupes peeked out. "We are only dust in the wind, ya'll. Be free. Loosen yourselves from this world. Feel His love. Only God's love'll set you free." Then she formed big circles with her outstretched arms.

Slipped in her high heels on the slick black coffin and one of the pearl onion buttons popped off. And Jake quietly mouthed, "Only God's love will set me free."

She used her toes to peel off her heels and each landed with a clunk and many a man's wagging tongue. Then stood spread on Black's coffin like she was daring someone, anyone to come get her off.

Jake licked his lips at the sight of her lacy bra. He leaned forward from his chair as if he'd go up to testify and test one of those cantaloupes. But Lilly moaned as she twisted on top of the coffin causing Jake's lap to get so hot and tight he had to glance down and check for a wet spot only to notice his dad's similar predicament.

Directly behind them, as if a megaphone was growling out grief's despair, Dan the Man stood and cast a dark shadow all the way down to the front row like a hurricane creeping in from dark water. Jake covered his lap as Dan's deep testosterone driven voice broke, "I gotta testify." From a deep crater, a volcanic abyss, threatening the building and all inside he testified. "I feel him. I feel his presence, Lilly." Jagged and torn, deep and scary, Dan the Man cried. So big. So surreal that others joined in wails.

"Get up here." Preacher Lilly eased off the coffin. Raised the lid back up and peered in as she directed Dan the Man to also look at the corpse. Her waving outstretched arm drew him nearer and nearer while his quivering bottom lip dripped drool. She kept coaxing, waving and wiping her tears until Dan the Man broke. He took one look and fell to his knees as his head ducked in and out of the silky death bed in sequence with his fitful cries.

Dan the Man jerked and wailed in fits over his mean old poker playing friend's corpse for what seemed like half an hour. And instead of inviting him to take a seat up front so the funeral could proceed Preacher Lilly rubbed his back. "Mon, my ol' buddyrow you da only real friend I ever knowed. Only one I took kin to. You never laughed at me or put da jokes on me. You took my momma soup." Dan wiped snot with his sleeve. "I'm a-sorry." He shook like a quake with vibes so strong the attendees shook. "Black, you jus made me so mad. Almos' don't believe hit." He inhaled a train of sighs. "Till I see you here. Thoust took a lot a' licks in your days, Black. Your head bes a rock. Even a steel-toe boot couldn't kill ya. Member dat? Black!" His wails pierced the bones of every single witness in the store church on out to the passersbys on the sidewalk who blocked much of the light as they spied through the entrance glass.

Then Dan the Man picked up the corpse by both shoulders and Black's heavy head fell backward flush to his back. While funeral folks gasped, Mrs. Alders screamed, when he cradled the corpse's loose head. "Tain't never had no real money before. You orta notta took hit. Lordy, help me take this back. I didn't mean hit. I'm just awful mad." Dan the Man kissed the corpse on the cheek and gently placed him back down. Then rose like the mighty giant being he was as he held them all hostage.

With eyes so wide open they looked like they'd pop out a' the sockets and a clamped jaw like a vise, his giant fist punched a hole straight up in the ceiling right next to the new gold plated chandelier and he fished for the electrical wires dangling near the overhead light. When he couldn't reach them he cried out like a squealing baby. Remorse hung his thick oversized lips into an exaggerated frown. He spread his fingers out like he was in shock and his big spider palms threatened them all. "Bring him back!" His booming demand thumped in their chests. "You girls come put yer hands on him! Conjure up his life breaths!"

That Preacher Lilly, right up behind him, continued to disdainfully glare with her hands on her hips when Dan the Man commanded her, "Come here!"

Mrs. Wilkes whispered that it was time to leave, but Mr. Wilkes shook his head as poor Bruce approached Dan the Man. Even with a stiff back and his muscular build the closer Bruce got to that giant nasty the more he looked like an elf. The chairs behind the Wilkes squeaked as the scallys; Mr. Fisk, Wart and Scarecrow leaned in to quietly talk to one another. While up front, that Preacher Lilly positioned herself smack dab between the giant angry ugly and young Bruce.

With her back to the frightened attendees Preacher Lilly whispered to the angry ugly as he bent down into her face. Then he looked away from her and out into the crowd as Bruce stoically approached the coffin and looked in. He growled like bear, pushed Preacher Lilly aside, and tore into Dan the Man like a raving maniac. Bruce swung and kicked at Dan. But Dan held Bruce's face in his palm, keeping his punching fists and kicking feet from reaching. Preacher Lilly said something else, something stern, but the words weren't clear over Bruce's growl.

It made Dan shout out, "Tyake me, Lord! I's jus a low down drunk. Tyake me! Tyake me!" He cried in mighty jerks as the room echoed his giant wails and Bruce crazily climbed up Dan's outstretched arm. And folks cheered, "Go, Bruce! Get him," and "Pull his eyes out!" and one even screamed, "Climb up there and bite off his nose!"

The chairs behind the Wilkes screeched and squalled and crashed against the hard tile floor as the scallys rushed up front. Mr. Fisk and Wart fumbled with their baggy pants' pockets and pulled out what looked to be wooden clubs as long limbed Scarecrow lurched to Dan. "I'm a-gonna whopicoddle his ass!"

Mrs. Wilkes then shouted for mister to call the police, but he insistently pointed out a man in a worn out corduroy blazer with an empty holster. Their heads snapped back to Dan and Bruce as Mr. Fisk and Scarecrow peeled Bruce, now frenzied mad like a raccoon took fresh from the wild, from Dan the Man's arm. Bruce punched at the bate of them and got in a couple of good whacks before he calmed to a slow foaming mad.

Jake leapt around his dad's legs and ran to his best friend. Scarecrow hovered over Bruce and held his jean jacket around Bruce's face, like a shield. But when Jake called out, "Let's get out of here. Come on," Bruce pushed Scarecrow aside. Scarecrow quickly shined his silver badge at the boys and jutted his chin at the man with the corduroy blazer who had a sweet forty-five pointed directly at Dan the Man.

With Bruce still under his arm, the boys hurried on numb legs down the cracked tile aisle when Lilly's pearl onion button shone up from the rank floor like a cornucopia symbol of pure raw lust. Jake scooped it up without missing a step. Then the chandelier bulbs popped; crack crackle pop, one after the other and the boys looked back toward the black coffin's happenstance as if the Little People purposely busted those bulbs over Dan the Man's suffering head. Glass penetrated his weakened flesh and blood spilled in streaks down his face like black reflected prison bars in the dim light.

Dan the Man was on his knees. Scarecrow dangled handcuffs over Dan's head. Wart and Mr. Fisk stood to the side or rather wobbled at Dan's side, flabbergasted with seemingly sober eyes, as they nervously worked to lift the giant man's hands up into the handcuffs for Detective Scarecrow.

And low and behold, that Preacher Lilly also had handcuffs and hers were humongous. She held them down in Dan the Man's face as he sulked like a cow sucking in a deep breath before a long drawn out bellow; the forlorn cry of the beast's suffering. Then those two perky navy blue hams wiggled up in the air as Lilly bent straight over to clamp the humongous restraints around Dan the Man's thick ankles. Simultaneously, both Jake and Bruce hollered, "Good-googoboly-goo," as Mrs. Wilkes hissed and pulled her son's shoulder and became real pissed when he resisted. She even stomped.

But everyone else in the shoe store turned church shine distributing building looked on catatonic like, too. Too flabbergasted not to look, still too scared to move, and real excited they didn't have to pay a dime for the best show in that little town for at least two generations. Dan the Man was ne'r 'bout hogtied belly down perpendicular to Black's black coffin with the tall law and all the church people saying, "Amen."

Chapter 3

Thicker 'n Thieves

As Jake eases the prim lady's divan back onto its cherry lion claw feet and declares the spring is repaired she blushes and suggests he purchase a belt. "Aiming to, Miss Lucy." Then headlights illuminate the layered sheers and he rushes to the window. "For a secluded place in the country you get a good deal a' traffic."

"Some of the farmers' wives take jobs in town. Insurance." She takes her seat at her desk. "I made your revisions last weekend." As she holds out a clip bound chapter he can't help but notice the original on her desktop. "Back up copy." She rests her hand on it. "Had any calls?"

"Is it all over my face?" He flashes a shiny white. "I almost drove over here to tell you, but it was a Wednesday. Thought you'd be at church." She poses like a gopher on look out, so Jake divulges. "There's a Lum out there thinks I'll hand over a reward for information. Wanted to know what it's worth." When Jake picks up the stack like he's set on reading she taps her hard soled slipper on the desk leg and like a hawk sets sites and aims her bright blues. "What?" he asks. "You could be in with him for all I know."

She smacks her lips. "As a history major with a minor in religion my concern is in the honor of recording history as it occurs. As the co author of your novel I subsequently intend to document the outcome."

"You're doing a fine job, too. Like how you put it together. So what do you predict'll happen?"

"The Lumbees will have to face facts that they are like all other Americans and blend in. They will abandon their vernacular. The Lumbee Council will most likely face charges and disband and welfare will fill the gaps as a socialistic government does to prevent their entire community from becoming a burden and a nuisance."

"You're so invested."

"Well of course I am. My lineage affords me honor as second nature."

"Oh." Jake marches to the window as headlights mark the sheers again. "Tell me one thing."

"You're in a mood, Jake." She motions for him to sit.

"Why do you think the council will take the fall?" When an engine backfires Jake jumps from the window's view and he flattens against the wall. His contagious panic sends her to her knees holding the back of her chair like the spindles will block bullets. He smiles first and they shrug off the paranoia as the vehicle's vibrations fade.

Jake plops down on the divan. "Have you told anyone about, uh, my story?"

"Not a soul." She lightly pants.

"Me either. My girlfriend thinks I'm helping one of my employees. She knows I'm not expanding the winery. Had to tell her something."

She jabs him with her little blue eyes like they're prickly pin tips. Then with a thin pointer gives him a heaping dose. "One of your employees? One of the Lumbees I suppose? Did you give her a name?"

"Yea, I told her it was Dodger." His top lip curls. "So what?"

"No woman is going to let that go unchecked. Uh-huh. She's mentioned this at some point, Jake. You disappearing on Friday nights. Half the time you end up here on Sunday afternoons. I don't care if she is working. A woman keeps tabs on her man."

Jake grins. "You're right." His long arm swings at the sheers across the room. "That was probably one of her bus boys. They don't make nothing at Gili's, minimum wage. She gives 'em a twenty just to go check on her horse."

"There you go. Stop worrying, pony boy."

"Pony boy?" He reads over the first page and she straightens her desktop. "Really, do you think the council knows about us?"

She leans against her chair. Slides her crossed legs out in front of her and admires an old English countryside oil painting. The fox hunters behind the old pitted glass proudly announce a kill as a child pours refreshment into silver cups lined up on a linen covered table under an outcrop of leafy trees. "Would it make a difference? Would you quit?" Her itty bitty blues bite. "Just walk away?"

"No. Like I said before, there's too much at risk."

Her pale heart shaped face tilts. "For history's sake or your friend's?"

Jake's hips shift down into the worn divan as he props his socked feet onto the magazine she keeps on the coffee table and he reads over their progress as she dives into translating shorthand into prose.

This time Henrietta has shortened her name to H. Prickenrath on the cover page. "Like your new writing name, Miss Lucy. Elusive." Her nose jabbed up at the air and took her top lip with it.

Chapter 3

Thicker 'n Thieves

Jake's new sports car gleamed showroom shiny inside the garage and Jake hid behind a post as Bruce drove by for the third time looking for it or the old family clunker, Crash. A lot's changed since that summer when they were thirteen. But from the hide and seek game going on it was plain to tell that the boys were still boys.

From his hidey hole, Jake admired the hot pin stripe on Bruce's ride. His rims were all right too, shined it up good. When Bruce slowed down on the fourth attempt, Jake stepped off the front porch where it was easy to hide between the post and his mom's clematis vine. Bruce pulled up into the drive and turned down onto the sandy area where Jake usually parked. Bruce leaned against what once was Old Man Black's Jesus truck, waiting for Jake with a wide grin, waving his ball cap. "Come here, you." The truck shone like new. Bruce was all cleaned up, even wearing jeans without holes.

"Whew!" Jake whistled. "Buddyrow must have a date."

The scent of aftershave and mint gum tumbled from Bruce's shaking head. "Where's Crash?" Bruce strained to get a view into the back yard. "Why'd you hide up there anyway? You stink-bomb, you were laughing when I came by. Huh?" When he bit the tip of his tongue and smiled his teeth shone too.

"You betcha. Laughing good. Not often I get one over on you."

"That's right. Take it in, boy."

"Got my car inside. Knew when you came by the first time you were looking for me. You never drive that slow."

"You finally sell Crash?"

"We're restoring it."

"Crash? It's junk. Your dad bought that thing when you were born."

"Makes it a classic."

"Do what you want." Bruce threw up his hand. "I think you've lost your mind."

Jake rounded out his right cheek with his tongue.

"Liar, you had me." Bruce squints. "Really, where is it?"

"It's in the shop, nothing big, just hoses and lube, stuff to keep it going."

"You really think it'll be worth something one day?"

"I don't know. Dad holds on to it just in case. He worries I won't be able to make the payments on my new car. Least I'd have something to get around in."

"He ought'a be making the payments." Bruce's resentment deepened his tenor Lumbee voice.

"Dad's business is slow. Advertising is one of the first things to get cut. My vet's only keeping me on because I'm the one people ask for. He's let two others go. One of those was part time, after school, like me."

"It's tough everywhere. Thelma's lucky to be with the State. Says she missed being laid off based on seniority by one year. She says it's fate, the move here, the new job. She's engaged to him now."

"The round guy who pulls out his ear hairs and looks at 'em? Oh, man, and you're gonna have to live with him." Jake slapped his thigh and Bruce swelled up and stood tall as if he was about to make an official announcement for a political campaign. "No. I haven't told her yet, but she's gotta move. I got a buyer for the home place. I'm going to college, Jake, and buying a new spread."

Jake worked down the hairs on the back of his neck with one hand and patted Bruce's shoulder with the other. "Gawd, that's great. That's the best thing I ever heard. What are you taking?"

"Business, two year degree at the community college. Going to have a legal operation."

Jake peered into the back of his truck and quickly guesstimated the number of empty sugar bags in the nearly clear trash bags. "Legal likker?"

Bruce popped Jake's shoulder. "Yep. No more smugglin' hog corn. Cassie's boys'll be in uniform. Drivin' big rigs and their teedum drunk days'll long gone. You see me. I'm going to have a winery, a fine place, with wood floors, cheese tasting and classy music."

"When did you decide all this?"

"When I was thirteen."

The momentary silence between them ended when Jake popped the truck's hood and that summer flashed all over again. They stood in a dank reflection pool until a mockingbird zoomed over and missed squirting one of their heads with the drop landing between them. They both checked their heads and then Jake grinned. "That's good, Bruce. I want to be there for you."

"That's my Buddyrow." Bruce's chest heaved as his grays locked. They stared at one another as the neighbor lady across the road pulled her mail from the box at the end of her drive. "I hate you moved when Dad died. It was a long year for me, Jake." Tiny blonde curls rounded over his scalp making his eerie gray eyes stand out against his tan. "I spent all my time making wine, turning those Muskies. Thought I'd turn into an alcoholic, be a thirteen year old drunk. Carry on that Lum tradition, too."

"Sorry. Dad had me busy here, getting the yard done. We built a storage building." Jake pointed it out. "They kept me busy that year. What was it, maybe three times at best?"

"At best. Thelma did it, too. We took out all the furniture, cleaned it. Washed walls and painted. Put up new curtains. Thelma runs a tight shift, a real tough lady."

"To deal with you, she'd have to be." Jake cocked his head. "She did something right. You're going to college."

"Thelma's a tough one. Says she's got radars on my scheming. Reckon she knows I turn, but won't mention it on account of I don't ask for any money long as I got some. Don't think she really knows how much or she'd be needing this and wantin' that. And she'll slack off on the cleaning chores, but pushes me on school, manners, stuff you've been doing all along, momma's boy." They chuckled. "College'll make a big difference for the Black name." They agreed. "You still going?"

Jake studied the tops of his shoes. "Yea and no."

"What's that? Part time?"

"My plans minimized from veterinarian to vet tech. You going to Lee County's campus?"

"Yea." Bruce studied his friend's face.

"Me too. That'll be good. We haven't been in the same school district since the move."

"Robin's going, too." Bruce piped.

Jake's greens dug into the news. "You still keep in touch?"

"Ran into her in Jonesboro. I was paying the light bill. She thinks about me." Bruce beamed.

"Dah, everyone remembers you."

"No. I mean thinks about me as maybe we'll date in college. She's taking restaurant management."

Jake huffed. "That's a waste of money. Robin'll always have a job. She'll own Gili's."

Bruce leaned back against his truck and looked up into the bright sky. "Liable ta give it up and work with me."

"I wouldn't wait on that." Jake gestured in large open swoops with one arm.

"Don't swing your arm like that. You look queer."

Jake's ears framed out in red. "You dating anyone special?"

"No time. I was steady three months this year with one. I messed up. Don't call your girlfriend's co workers to check up on her."

"Stupid. No girl is going to cheat on you. Your body's a rock, Bruce. Look at you. Weight lifting?"

Bruce's sly smile suggested covert weight lifting. "Lift a lot of product."

"How much?"

"Moving forty to sixty gallons a month. January and February are nil. You know that. I hold enough back to keep a supply."

"Dang, Bruce. That's a lot of money."

"Can't spend it on anything that shows. Got an undercover who won't take a bite. Yankee from hell."

Jake bit his lip. "Better be careful. Jail is no place for a perty boy."

"Jail? It'd be prison. With the sums I'm bringing in I could do two to five or more." Bruce quipped. "I keep it coy."

"I hope so." Jake's chin bobbed. "That Scarecrow sure got Dan the Man. I'll never forget that. Lord was watching over us, Bruce. As many times as we met up with Scarecrow,

Wart and Fisk, and they didn't get us; wasn't dumb luck."

"Wart and Fisk are cooks. Scarecrow's the only one on duty. He's alone now. But he's got a dog. Don't think he ever brushes it. Looks like its got mange. It's a sniffer."

"Drug dog?"

"You're really out of the loop. Yea, drugs, guns, likker. They train 'em to find illegal tacos, too."

"I haven't seen Scarecrow in a couple of years. I was at the ball field off First Street. Now that I think about it, there was a dog. It stayed right behind him. He never touched it, through the whole game. Couldn't decide if it was a stray or not." Jake checked the sugar bags in the back of Bruce's truck again. "Scarecrow knows your cooking. Why hasn't he come after you?"

"Money."

Jake briskly rubbed his palms together at the dirty business. "Are you going to quit when you start the winery?"

"Oh, I plan to quit this year. As soon as I sell the house. But I need your help."

Jake's Adam's apple made a loop as his throat tightened. And Bruce stretched out his arm alongside the rim of the truck bed until he could reach Jake's elbow.

"Jake, The Company's got to be moved. Needs to be done carefully. Gotta do it at night and gotta move it clear out of town. My plan is to do it all at once, in one night, the night I know that damn Yankee is out of town."

"How will you know that?"

"Leather likes the girls. But the girls love me. He goes to Surf, that nice one in Southern Pines. And so do I." Bruce sounded just like his dad, conning, cunning, and smooth. And for a moment, looked like him, not his mom, with his usual boyish cheeks up high on their Croatan platforms. His locked jaw strutted up in the air; an arrogant look, like Sinister Minister.

"I don't know." Jake turned away.

"Listen at me. The Company's in jeopardy. Scarecrow said their fixin' ta put helicopters on watch. Too much money going around. Think one of the runners got busted and's keeping it hushed. Worked out a deal for walkin' shoes. That's okay. Can't say I wouldn't do the same if I were them. I checked it out. It's true. County got that helicopter grant and is workin' details. The Company's been there too long. And my name was on top of the list." His jaw dropped as he waited for Jake. "Old Man kept a few on pay off, but Crow's my one and only and he's killing me. Goes up every year. Tells me that he has to pay off others and that by paying him I keep my name out of the loop. But either he's lying or I'm just too big for this little town and it's pissin' off the punk cops they got in D&A." After Bruce licked his dry lips he exhaled and gritted his teeth.

"You're asking me to step into a wad, here, Buddyrow. I can't make college tuition. How am I gonna make bail?" Jake crossed his arms. "This is too big. Too much can go wrong."

"Jake, I don't have anyone else I can trust." Bruce burned red. "I don't have anyone." The hot rushed words were hard for him and came out that way, like a red core of molten steel.

Jake's eye nervously twitched as he responded. "What time frame are you looking at?"

Fervently, Bruce leaned in. "A couple of weeks."

The lady across the street tossed pine cones from her drive, turned and faced them, then scouted out more near the roadside.

"What night, exactly?" Jake softly asked.

"Won't know till I get the call." Bruce cupped his hand up over his mouth. "Then I call you. You'll have to be ready. Think up a reason now to leave in the middle of the night before I ever call. Something your parents won't question you on or you'll give us up." Bruce licked his lips and cocked his expectant grays as his eyebrows danced. The look was thirteen. The look was excited. It was a look of invitation to live to tell the tale. And it was contagious as hell.

"I'll say." When Jake spoke too loudly Bruce motioned for him to tone it down. "I'll say there's an emergency at the vets. No. That won't work. They'd call when I was gone too long. I can tell them I have to help a friend deliver puppies. I can give 'em a name of someone I don't really hang with so they can't check."

"I'll pay you, too." From his front jean pocket Bruce pulled out a roll thick enough to plug a judge's sentence and get the judge's mistress an oceanfront condo.

"Put it back before she sees. She watches me all the time." Jake demanded like the neighbor lady might read lips and it made him appear like he had a case of lockjaw coming on. "She'll tell everyone she sees that I'm selling drugs if she gets sight of that roll."

When Bruce waved the neighbor lady smiled and waved back. "She's harmless. We oughta go help her out. Looks like her yard needs raking." He took a step forward. "Come on, let's do it."

"Really, she doesn't like me."

"Too bad. All ladies like me, especially the gray hairs." Bruce flicked the edges of the bills like he was counting them with his fingertip then tossed it to Jake and he examined the roll of Franklins. It was at least twenty k.

Jake slowly handed it back. "Impressive. You know how to take care of a dollar."

"Just like women. Pet 'em till they purr and you will, too." Bruce's laughter caught the attention of the neighbor lady and she grinned at the handsome young men.

Jake popped the rim of the truck bed. "You charm 'em, all right. Looks like that one wants to call you Sonny Boy."

Bruce's boyish cheeks bounced up. "True enough." Bruce juggled the roll from one hand to the other, occasionally toying with Jake that he was going to toss it to him. "Had dinner?"

"Nope."

"Let's go get a pizza." Bruce pushed the roll deep into his pocket.

"Sounds like a plan."

"You gonna tell them you're with me?"

"Yea. Well, I'll write a note. My phone's out of minutes. On the bargain plan." Jake jogged to the house. When he caught himself swinging his arms he locked them. Jake scribbled out a quick note that he was with Bruce. Then just as quickly wadded it up and threw it in the trash. Then took it out of the trash and hid it in his pocket. He then wrote that he was with a friend and not to wait for him for dinner.

Jake hurried to his room as he peeled off his tee shirt and pulled out a fresh one, navy with a double collar in white. He checked himself in the mirror and ran his fingers through his blonde layers, popped in a piece of spearmint gum and spit it out as he jogged back to Bruce waiting in the truck. Jake lunged in and fastened his seat belt. "My renegade is going legit. Man, this is something to celebrate."

Bruce humbly grinned as he adjusted his seat belt over his full taut chest. Backed out of the drive and checked out Jake. "You were in there primpin', huh?"

"Just changed my shirt."

"Let's go to that hole-in-the-wall place in Dunrovin."

"Hadn't been there in years."

"I have." And the truck rolled. "Like watching that old man whiz the dough around on his finger. It's cool."

"Yea, it is. I remember him. There's paintings on the ceiling, right?"

"Yep, and on the walls. Owners are good people. They knew Mom."

On the highway, Bruce kept his truck in the fast lane, passing the slugs. One hand on the wheel, another on the door's arm rest. "You sure keep the truck clean," Jake tested the ashtray.

"Take care of what I've got."

"I've seen the inside of this truck when I wouldn't let a flea live in it. Must be Thelma's boot camp." Jake slapped the top of his thighs in cadence, "Left, clean, left, clean, left," and laughed.

But Bruce stared ahead. "I was drinking more product than test tasting. I don't now. Drinking made me lazy. I could tell a difference right away. And Thelma had a lot to do with it. She put the fear in me. She's my legal guardian and can make my life living hell. She cares. It's the way I remember Mom."

"That's all right, Bruce. I'm glad. And Mark?"

"Mark's a good kid, the little brother I never had. We fight some, but no big stuff. He's like you, been college bound all along. Got him an account started."

"You're all right. Isn't it funny how things happen? You needed a mom and got one. I moved away, closest thing you had to a brother. And you got a new brother."

Bruce smiled at him. "Thought about that, too. Thelma and Mark are my real family. Guess that's why it's gettin' to me that they're going to have to move. I dread it. Thelma's been my mom. But she's stronger than Mom was. She left her husband after the first slap. Won't take junk from no one."

"Like you."

"Yep, like me. And I did some serious buckin' and kickin' when Thelma first started in.

But she didn't take any of my junk. Tried to run away once and she carried my things to the end of the drive."

"Dang, that is tough love. What happened?"

"Two trucks passed and neither stopped to pick me up. Knew both drivers, too. Got dark and them coyotes seemed to get closer and closer, Know what I mean?" They laughed and then Bruce looked up to the iridescent sky. "Man up there knows. Certain of it. Had to carry it all back in, by myself. Then I had to write her an apology."

"And you did it?"

"I did it. Got up the next morning and stared at that paper like I could set it to fire. Took all afternoon to write that one paragraph. I was burnt slam up, wanted to go in the kitchen and, and hit her or something. But she opened up the oven and her broccoli casserole got the better of me."

"Saved by the broccoli, who'd a seen that coming?" Jake laughed.

"She and momma are two of kind." Bruce swallowed. "I owe her. Know of any nice places for her and Mark?"

"No. What about her fiancé? Won't he move them in with him?"

"That's their future plan. Don't know when. They haven't set a date. She won't move in with him till they're married."

"Tell her you got a buyer. Then they'll set a date."

"Thought about that, but she'll be hurt."

Suddenly, Jake's cross face filled the cab. "You never have a problem with manipulating me."

And immediately Bruce's chin aimed up at the sky. His jaw tightened as he stared straight ahead then took a deep breath and delivered his calculated answer. "What was I going to do, beg? I can't ask anyone else but you."

"Why?"

"You're the only real friend I've got." He eyeballed Jake. "Satisfied?"

"Yea, ditto. After we moved, it just got worse."

"That piece of dirt. I hate him." Bruce declared.

"Don't."

"I do."

"Hate the sin." Jake rationalized.

"You church freak. You're so munked up."

"Am not. It's forgivable ya know, like cooking shine or speeding or anything else."

Bruce passed another car. He went from the fast lane to the slug lane and back again. When the needle hit seventy-five Bruce smugly grinned. "When I get my new place you could live there. We could set you up with a trailer."

"Really?"

"Yea, you could be on dog patrol."

"That won't work. I want to raise dogs, heal animals, all kinds."

"Then you're right. It won't work. I don't want no dogs peeing on my vines, digging up my property or running off with my property." Bruce's hateful words filled the void between them. "Business is business and I'm not gonna let some filthy dogs interfere with my profit."

Jake cooled his hot hand out the window in the cool early evening air. "Police dogs come through the vet's office for their exams all the time. I sit for some. I want to raise German Shepherds. The officers say I'm a natural dog trainer."

"That's a laugh."

"No it isn't. Bet I could even train that mangy dog of Scarecrow's to like grooming."

"You want to raise shepherds because of Miss Scarlet." Bruce's half cocked grin mocked Jake.

"That's part of it. She was a smart dog."

"If she was so friggin smart why didn't she save me?"

Jake wildly blinked. "Dog knew she'd be killed. I don't know. Your dad probably hit her at some point. He hit everything." He sat so still he looked like he'd been turned to stone.

"He didn't hit Mom's dog." Bruce nearly squeaked.

"She always had it in her arms. Petting it or talking to it. Could the dog even walk?"

Bruce smiled, threw his head back a bit and said, "Momma always said Muffin knew words. She had that baby trained. Knew the difference between a wet dish cloth and dry. Put the wet ones in the laundry basket. She even taught it to wipe its feet on a rug before it came in."

"I remember that."

"Dad sort a liked her. It didn't act like a dog."

"He never hit Muffin?"

"Don't think so. Once in a while he'd give her scraps. He'd do it to make up to Mom, for being mean." Bruce swallowed as they passed the restaurant's worn billboard.

"You say the pizza people knew your mom?"

"Mom worked here when she was young. And after she and Dad married they'd come up and they'd always give 'em a deal. Mom said they'd make up a special or say they had a fake call in. Mom would jump in and help. She liked it. Mom liked people. I must get it from her."

"Right." Jake drawled it out into two long sarcastic syllables. "When did you become a people person? You get some cordiality lessons?"

"Naw," he laughed. "I can read people. I get along with anyone, long as they don't misrepresent themselves."

"I feel like I'm living a lie."

"Cause you do," Bruce studied Jake's long chin, "with everyone, but me."

"What stations you got programmed on your radio?"

Bruce pressed the button and fiddles and a dulcimer tinged and pinged while Jake tapped the handrest. When the instruments ceased and a torn up gal singing a sad ballad began Jake popped his thigh. "All we need now is a drink of Muscadine."

"Like this, huh?"

"It's all right. Listen to a lot of country. Like the eighty sounds, too."

"I want to fill the store with this." Bruce changed the station and a Celtic ballad strummed. "Met a dulcimer player at a wine tasting in Southern Pines. He said."

Jake interrupted, "You go to wine tastings? That's so friggin' bizarre coming from you. Gotta admit I never thought you'd be the one."

"Be the one to what, Jake?"

"Make it big."

"That's what I thought. That's what everybody thinks." Bruce huffed. "Well, everybody is gonna be real surprised." His tongue flicked across his full lips. "I'm buying a piece down by the railroad in Cameron. It juts up to the original dewberry patch where they grew Lucretia Dewberries."

"Are they special?"

"Not to most people. They like swampy places like most of 'em and they get fat and sweet and make mighty fine wine. Cameron was once the dewberry capital of the world."

"When?"

"In the forties. Trains loaded with 'em left out every day, fresh and fermented loads. Know what I mean? That's all the sand was good for. Cameron has notorious roots, other than my dad." Bruce laughed. "They'll be writing my name in the books later. I'm going to make Cameron famous again."

"I believe you."

"I want you to be a part of it, Jake." His grays softened.

"How? I want to work with animals."

Bruce's happy face turned solemn. "But I trust you not to cheat me."

"You'll come across someone who wants to work wine, someone you can trust."

Bruce sat rigid. "You can train dogs on the side."

"I could. But I wanna be a veterinarian."

"Then be one."

"I told you, there's not enough money. The economy sucks. Advertising's getting cut all over. And we have too much to qualify for a grant."

"What about a loan?"

"If the economy turns around that'll be a choice. Right now I can barely afford gas to drive to school. It's so bad Dad told me to work this first year I'm out and go to the community college next year. But I found someone who's willing to fund my vet tech degree."

"Who?"

"One of my dad's advertising customers. You know CD's, the spicy corndogs?"

"Yea."

"CD's a friend of mine."

When Bruce glared at Jake with taut lips and tight brows Jake turned away. The evening sky's pink cast blended into the pine's sparkling treetops and suddenly faded to a darkened purple as night called and the methodic rhythm of the tires rolled down the highway mimicking the music of waves. They passed the Vass exit. Dunrovin wasn't far.

"Help me think of a name for the winery." Bruce broke. "It's the only thing I haven't figured out yet."

"Okay. How about naming it Dewberry Winery? Or name it after the kind of berry. What did you say? Laretta?"

"That's close, lil Jakey boy. It's Lucretia."

"Little?" Jake popped Bruce's arm with a full fist and made him wince. "I'm taller than you. I know my shoulders are wider. And you've got little feet, dude. You got your mom's body, lil Brucy."

"Idgit."

"Lil Brucy."

"Lanky Hanky." Bruce's wide open eyes clarified how much he regretted the spoken words.

"No one but you would call me that, to my face. But don't."

"Got it." Bruce waited for Jake to quit fidgeting with the seat belt over his chest. "Hey, we haven't talked like this for what, four or five years. I see you uptown, at a game, that's it anymore. I wonder about you."

"I get feelings for girls. They get me excited. But I hold back. Sometimes I wish my dad would hurry up and die. I tell him at supper to go ahead and eat what he likes, the gristle on the steaks, the pork chops, all the bad stuff. I hope he'll have a massive and leave me alone."

"Does your mom have a clue?"

"I can't believe she would and still be with him. They have bouts where they'll sleep in separate rooms, months at a time. He'll stop speaking to her. Won't even acknowledge her existence in the same room. He tries to run her off sometimes. Mom says he's moody and needs his space. Dad'll get me off alone and tell me that we're going to leave her and move somewhere else. But then he got into financial trouble."

"So CD's funding school."

Jake leaned back into the seat and grimaced.

While Bruce cleared his throat and turned down the fiddles. "Jake, why don't you tell your mom? Stop living the lie."

"She hates fags. And even though I'm only one because of Dad she would still hate me. Besides, I'm quitting all this." Jake's spit hit the windshield. "Before I start wearing plugs."

"Say that again." Bruce squinted.

"Anal retention trouble."

Bruce wore the nasty on his face with a grimace that'd pass for a man lookin' to spit out a mouthful of spoiled pork. "That's not right. Not natural at all."

"Mom wouldn't give me any slack. I know her. Everything is black and white for her." Jake shrunk back into the upholstery.

"She wouldn't hate her own son."

"She might."

"It'd be better than living like you do now. Tell her. She'd help you. Get you some therapy. What you're doing isn't natural, cuz." Bruce pleaded.

"I know. And it's damned. Read The Word, first Corinthians, in chapter six, verse nine. Mom read it out loud in church straight on at the gay florist who's been going there since he was a babe. He didn't hide it. He was like a drunk coming in to church drunk. That man was kai kai all the way." Jake spoke exaggeratedly. "He won't come back. And he'll never give up all his Willy's sweet money. He funds everything. My mom's a witch about gay people."

"Sorry. But you aren't gay." Bruce leaned over determined. "You've just been conditioned. Gay is another addiction, cuz. Something people get into and can't figure out how to get out of."

Jake studied Bruce's profile as if it'd suddenly become the Thinking Man's image, until oncoming traffic lights dispelled the thought. "Maybe so, it's all so friggin crazy," Jake disfigured his face, "like me."

Shaken, with red raging from his flared nostrils, Bruce spouted, "Me, too, then."

"Huh?"

"How could I ever say what's crazy and what isn't?" With a fake laugh he shouted, "Good-gooboly-goo!"

Their hearty laughs lied and ended in simultaneous hushed sniffles as the truck pulled into the parking lot. The big glass window was lit up like a showcase as the pizza dough twirled on the old man's finger like a muted, but very enticing dinner bell. They entered with delight and saliva filled mouths as the browned crusts and piping hot pepperoni scents welcomed them.

The fresh faced waitress sported a pony tail. An apron was over her outfit; black pants and fitted white shirt. Bruce and Jake agreed on an all meat pizza with extra cheese and two large cokes. She smelled like pizza and lemon dish detergent. Jake told her, "You have such fine hands to do such hard work. Someone must be taking good care of you."

Bruce applauded Jake's flirting with a high shoulder and grin that'd tease the hair off a hog.

"Good try." With a short smile she shifted her hips. "Anything else? Side salads?"

Jake answered, "Not this time," while Bruce dismissed her with a flick of his chin. Then Jake looked around and said, "See that painting, next to the door?" It was a black velvet, ten by fourteen or so, the poker playing dogs. "Remind you of anyone?"

"Oh, yea. Dad's the boxer." Bruce centered the salt and parmesan cheese as they broke out in toothy grins.

Black velvets, all paint by numbers and a few free hand paintings were mounted everywhere. They covered the walls and the ceiling. Families with children fidgeting with silverware, couples consumed with one another, and loud old people filled the pizzeria's wooden tables. "Where are you moving The Company to?" Jake blurted.

Bruce's nose widened as the waitress served their large cokes in the thick red mottled plastic glasses, the good ones that hold the cold in the glass, not in your hand. After the waitress walked away Bruce leaned across the table and whispered, "Out of town."

"Oh, got it." Jake looked around the restaurant to see if he recognized anyone. When he was confident he continued, "Is it far from me?"

Bruce rolled his eyes and pursed his lips in the hush gesture. "Out of town, five miles from you. Before you get to the tracks, coming from twenty-four, twenty-seven, take a left. There's no visible road, just a grass path right now. But just wait." Bruce sipped his coke and smiled. "It's like buying back my history."

"How's it your history?"

"My people come from there." He leaned across the table again and beamed. "We're the ones who established the Lucretias."

"How do you figure that?"

"My granddad. His told him. It's tribal." Bruce's chest rose. "All real Lums know."

"Know what? I've lived in Cameron all my life. I never heard anything about Lums settling here?"

"You're not a Lum." Bruce looked around and leaned in closer. "My great granddad was Maynor Black Fox. Granddad dropped the Fox. It was hard getting' work then. Listen at me. The dewberries were brought here by descendents of the Lost Colony, Lums who later mixed with the freed Africans," Bruce brushed up the back of his head like he had a fro, "hence the curls and the Black's section. Maynor's daddy was a Freedman and was given a hundred acre allotment by his owner. He married a Lum and in the deal got a passel of free labor. They lived like Indians do, in units. We'd still have that hundred if Dad hadn't bet it off. But we got the pond and twenty of it. Better than nothin'."

Jake's top lip curls. "I don't smell any liquor. I don't smell any wine." He sniffed at the air. "I smell a story teller." He crossed his legs and loosely pointed at Bruce.

"Straighten up. Don't sit like that."

Jake tucked his legs back under the table. "Lums don't want to be associated with the Lost Colony, do they?"

"I shouldn't even tell you." Bruce swallowed and scanned the other diners and when no one was looking their way leaned up further.

"Don't then."

Bruce leaned back. "Okay."

They took long drinks of their cokes and simultaneously stared at the spinning dough behind the counter until the television in the upper right corner fuzzed up. When a man scooted his chair back and his heavy boots boomed across the tile to turn the channel the people seated nearby said they didn't want to listen to that sport's announcer. The lady with them said she was going to change it as soon as that man left.

"They don't even know we're here." Jake stared down Bruce. "Tell me. I really want to know."

Bruce sported a winning smile. "I know. I know you do. What's it worth to you?"

"Oh, man, you always do that. Okay, how about I help you move?"

"You already said you'd help me move."

"I agreed to help you move The Company. I didn't agree to help you move from the house." Jake's shoulders jutted up.

With his hand shaped like a gun, like when they were kids, Bruce laid it on the table. "You got me."

And he grinned like a six year old kid and confiscated his pretend gun. "So, tell me already." Then he took a drink of coke, but abruptly placed his glass down, tilting it and lost most of it in the spill. The waitress ran over and quickly wiped it up with a thick white towel as she informed them that their pizza was in the oven and wouldn't be much longer, maybe ten minutes. When she walked away, Bruce leaned to Jake, but looked over his shoulder as she approached the counter. And hummed over her healthy hams.

They sat leaning across the table as Bruce instructed Jake. "The Lost Colony was led here by Native American Indians, Cherokees, from Roanoke Island. But White, the governor over the settlers, got the war with the English and the Croatians so volatile the English had to escape. One man was injured, fatally. He had to be left behind. The man watched his family escape knowing he'd never see them again. And he blamed White. White was a hot headed man who was vengeful against the Croatoan. Before White ever left for England to get more supplies, it was agreed to carve the name of the destination if the settlers had to leave. That way White would know where to look. The dying angry man carved Croatoan. He wanted to send White to his death. Only God saved White. The waves made it too dangerous to land White's ships. White had to turn around and leave. Then God punished White. White never saw his daughter and grandchild again."

Jake leaned back and crossed his arms. "You're leaving something out. I feel it."

Bruce sat up straight. "Did you pay any attention at all?"

"How does that prove the Lums are part of the Lost Colony? And just how do you know White never saw his daughter or a grandchild again?"

"White left his daughter here, pregnant. Her blood is mine, Virginia Dare's. Used the White name 'cause it told who we were, where we were from and all." Bruce looked around the room. He tapped his head to the left at a family with Lum traits, the yellow brown skin, high cheekbones and wide nose and wavy hair. "Listen at me. White is in their blood and its proof is in the berries, Jake," Bruce was absolutely vibrant. "Lucretias are the same berry native to Roanoke Island. The natives brought them when they came through with the settlers. They lived here for a hundred years." Bruce smashed his finger against the tabletop.

"Do you have any real proof?' Jake asked again. "I still feel like you're not telling me everything. You have a history of that. Gawd. Just tell me your little special fact already." Flabbergasted and wound up tight, Jake drank an entire glass of coke and waved for a refill. "If only this were beer. Maybe that'd loosen your lips."

And Bruce relished the game. He was all smiles and even rocked a little in his straight back chair. When his cell phone rang he motioned for Jake to hold on. He checked the number and answered, "Go to one." He listened. "Then hit five this time and take your time. Call me when you're tucked in," and folded it back down into his jean's pocket. "Always on duty."

"Not hard to guess what that was about."

Bruce cleared his throat. "Lucretias are in the swamps at Lumberton, too. You see, not all the Croatans' prisoners stayed in Cameron."

"Prisoners?"

"Jake, my people've handed down this story for generations. We all know. Croatans made them slaves and had children with them and some of them married freed Blacks. We just don't have any proof. But the berries trace the roots and I just have to prove it to everyone else."

"That's not how I learned it in school."

"Who wrote our history books?"

"You're exhausting. I guess it was researchers, institutions, businesses."

Bruce's gapped mouth clenched. "The conquerors who ended up owning every freakin' thing. Caucasians, mostly males wrote what we're supposed to accept. And think about it. Schools don't want any riots. Too many Lums around to teach the truth. Schools teach what's politically correct and go on about how Lums're now recognized by the Federal Government and sooner or later hope to get on like the Cherokees with the funding part. But that ever won't happen. We don't have enough red blood or enough money for big game lawyers. But the real trigger is the Cherokees want all the funds for themselves."

"Do you have any real proof?"

"What kind of proof are you wantin'?"

"Tangible proof. Something in writing or an artifact with some kind of certification. Genealogy research. Surely someone out there's traced their roots back to the English."

Bruce's eyebrows jumped. "Yea, that's it. Or get some DNA from White's descendants and trace it back to me. Momma's maiden name was White. I overheard it when Dad was calling her out on a bad night."

"That is something to think about, the Whites prove Lums are from The Lost Colony. Hey, just call some Whites over in England and ask. Or some of Virginia Dare's people. There's gotta be research on them. And there's gotta be at least one who'd be willing to help." Jake rested his chin on his propped hand and rather pleased with himself, smiled and thought it all out. "Okay, that's a long shot. What about the internet? Get on the Lost Colony site. Post your theory and,"

Bruce interrupted. "It's not a theory. I know who I am." And the Lumbee families sitting at nearby tables turned in acknowledgement.

"I believe you, Bruce. It's not me you have to convince." Jake surveyed the restaurant's colorful tables.

As the enormous brick and stainless steel pizza oven opened the heat permeated the entire area behind the counter and rushed up and over the toe tapping waitress impatiently waiting on the other side. The sweltering heat brought out her womanly scents and it fell over Bruce and Jake like a sheet laden with an invitation as she placed the piping hot pizza on the center of their table. She smelled of freshly sliced bell peppers, musky young woman sweat, and bacon. Lots of strong bacon scents like she must have helped chop it and wiped it across her apron like a love call.

The red cheeked waitress served Bruce, then Jake and quietly hurried to the table in the back with the loud toddler in the highchair happily slinging stringy cheese smothered in pizza sauce in all directions. A long string of red cheese landed on the black velvet poker playing dogs striking the bulldog with a haunting gash across the skull. After the waitress carefully pulled it off and wiped the painting free of sauce with her thick white towel the young men turned their attention to devouring their pizza.

With a slice aimed at his chin, Bruce leaned across the table. "You're right about one thing. Lums don't want it known about English blood. They want federal recognition. In the eighteen hundreds they were close, and again in the nineteen sixties with Kennedy. But no one else wants us getting federal funds, especially the big tribes." He pointed at Jake with his slice. "The Lumbee Tribe is right off highway ninety-five and drug trafficking there is already horrific. Fed's won't recognize the Tribe because they think they only want to open big gambling rigs. Majority do. But the wise ones know the Tribe'd be a regular Sodom and Gomorrah. Half of all Lums are drunks, the other over achievers. Know which half I am." He smiled and took in the other half of the pizza slice, all except the stiff outer crust which he trimmed away like a beaver on a log and tossed the crust onto his plate.

"I'm proud of you."

"I remember this trip we took right before Momma died. Had to be in Lumberton. It was real secret like and everyone was touching my head. I don't know. Maybe it was a dream." Bruce folded over the next slice in his hand, opened his mouth like it was a big oven and pushed it in as he placed another slice on his plate.

"You mean they were popping your noggin for mommucking like you always did? You were so rowdy."

"No," Bruce's chewed real fast as he held up his finger. "Don't try to talk Lum if you can't do it right. It was a ceremony. Seems like they gave Momma something or passed it around and Momma held it a long time. Anyway, I do remember what they said about The Society. No one outside the walls could know. Real hush-hush the whole time."

"Could know what?"

Bruce flashed a quick smile then leaned across the table. "This real old guy, bent over, white headed, had Momma sitting in a chair out in the middle and I had to sit on somebody's lap and I really didn't want to. And the old guy said she was a queen." Bruce picked up the red glass hexagon decanter and held it up to the light. Then he shook out the parmesan cheese till it covered his steamy slice and washed it down. "I love this pizza. Makes me think of Mom." He speedily shook out more cheese until the next slice was snowed. Took a sip of coke and looked around the room and strained toward the party room, but it was closed. "You're right about proof. I think about that myself. Proof would be real nice. Maybe God'll give me that next."

"Yea, maybe. If you're not lying."

Chapter 4

I'm Not Supposed to Tell. I'm Not Supposed to Tell.

"I wasn't excepting anyone." The prim lady holds the door open in her faded tee shirt and blue jean shorts. "I've been pulling weeds. Tried crowding them out with radishes, but the weeds won." Her fingertips pat at her forehead down to her neck as if she's damping off sweat beads.

"Someone poisoned my dogs." Jake's eyes are lined in red. "Onacona didn't make it."

"Your girlfriend's dog?"

"Fiancé'," Jake quivers, "vet still has two."

"When do you think it happened?"

"Had to be last night."

"Oh, Jake, I'm so sorry."

"I was worried about you."

She rapidly blinks and asks if he wants something to drink as her gaped face sucks in heaps of warm air. He pulls off his boots and places them on the rubber mat she keeps beside the front door especially for him then takes a seat on the divan. When she returns with two tall glasses of sweet tea with lemon he is bent over with his head in his hands. She places their drinks on the magazine and runs her hand over his back. "I'm so sorry, Jake. This will pass."

"No. We've got to stop."

"Oh, no," she blows, "we've come so far."

"It's just the beginning. Scarecrow told me."

"You talk to this man?"

"He's a friend. Yea. He said there's rumors. Like they've been rumored to make accidents happen. Said that's why nobody's ever made a trip to Washington." He looks up at her like a baby bird from its nest. "It's no secret."

"Those rumors have been around a long time."

"You've heard 'em?"

"In passing."

"What does that mean?"

"I didn't have anything relevant to add to the conversation. I walked away."

"So, you agree."

"No." She rolls her head. "The council is an educated group of business leaders. Surely, they wouldn't dirty their hands with criminal tricks."

Jake springs up and shakes his outstretched palms. "You'll be next."

"No one wants me." She palms the stacks of papers on her desktop and turns around to face him. "I'm invisible, the old librarian."

Jake jerks a crumbled paper from his front jeans pocket and pushes it at her. She stretches it out and her mouth falls open. Red crayon spells out the jagged note: 'Done mommucked up. Lumbees are Indians. Let it be or thoust be next.' "That's ridiculous." As she rolls her eyes the sheers wave and the scent of freshly mown grass sparks concern. "Did you do that?" She stomps over to the window. "I never open the windows. Not with my allergies." When she struggles to budge the tight wooden frame Jake tells her to move over and she does, taking full notice of the outdoor view. "You're coming home with me." His command pleads like his heavy greens. And with the newest revision safely in her arms they roar down the blacktop and Jake calls on his friend, the UC. Scarecrow and Lilly abandon their late afternoon fishing trip and rush to meet Jake and Miss Lucy on the highway and decide it would be best to follow them back to Miss Henrietta Prickenrath's house.

"Don't worry." Scarecrow talks like a cop talks to other cops, short, hushed and deep. "They'll be back. We'll be ready," he assures her. They gather clothes and toiletries, five pairs of shoes, her computer and shut off the water. "You'll be fine at Jake's. The Crowsons always have someone around to keep an eye on things," Miss Lilly reassures her. Scarecrow accepts a key and asks, "Do you have any flour and peanut butter?"

"Yes," Miss Lucy doesn't hesitate. She directs him to the kitchen. And in moments her doorknobs are set and doorways prepared. "Mmm. No recorders or wires, just food staples? Seems like your concern is rather relaxed."

"Old timers knew what they were doing, sugar." Lilly directs her to Jake's truck and Miss Lucy pulls out her car keys and informs them that she must take her car. "I have to get to work."

Jake's little house on the Crowson's farm is all wood and all good. Miss Lucy makes sandwiches and Jake washes dishes. She writes and he reads. Not once does she snub the country dust or bristly German Shepherd hairs. But Miss Lucy's solemn refrain of the evening's endangerment crawls all over Jake from his spine up like a paranoia snake burrowing under for the duration. So while she quietly retires at ten he props up on his bed pillows with her latest.

<u>Lumbees Undone</u>, Jake Wilkes, Co Author H. Prickenrath

Chapter 4, I'm Not Supposed to Tell. I'm Not Supposed to Tell.

On a Thursday night at ten-forty-five, the phone rang. Jake's sleepy eyes widened as he sat up and his dad walked down the hall. He opened the door and handed Jake the phone. "I don't know who it is. She sounds hysterical," Mr. Wilkes grumbled.

Jake swung his legs over the bed. "Hello?"

As Bruce stated, "Time," in a girlish squeaky voice Jake crammed his tongue to the back of his throat to keep from laughing and waved at his dad to leave. When he finally closed the door Jake mockingly whispered, "I'll be right there."

Mr. Wilkes was standing in front of the kitchen sink when Jake appeared fully dressed. "My number got out as someone to call to help with deliveries. Got'ta go." Jake sat the phone back on its charger. "Pups could be in trouble."

"Where?" Mr. Wilkes stepped toward the counter nearer to Jake. "Are they paying you for this?"

"They'll give me a little something." Jake swallowed. "I'll be back."

His dad's wedding band twanged the top of the counter like a snare matching the drum beats in Jake's head. His dad gruffly whispered, "What time should I expect you?" And without a flinch Jake punched his time card, "By day light." Mr. Wilkes slowly sipped his grape juice. "Be careful."

Pulling the door behind him, Jake called out, "I know what I'm doing. Don't worry," as he flicked on the floodlights, patted the trunk and grinned. He slid in and pulled out of the drive. "Come on, Crash," he begged the big old four-door.

Bruce was twenty minutes away so with the window down and the radio up Jake peeled off on his mission of mercy. "The puppies I deliver tonight are gonna be big dogs one day. The business that puts Cameron on the map. Good-gooboly-goo." He sang with every song that blared out of the radio as he rushed, but not more than five miles over the speed limit, to the dirt road.

The badly washed and pitted dirt road took seven minutes to safely travel down to the dead end where The Company was hid. But the seven minutes stalled into what felt like thirty sweltering minutes in the hot ass car. With no wind the heat sweltered up like a barbeque pit. There were washes, some two feet wide and a drop off in a curve that looked like there was nowhere else to go, but off a cliff's edge. Jake put Crash into park and jumped out and shook his damp tee shirt off his chest and tried to move the boulders.

Bruce and Jake had made them, thanks to masonry class during their freshman year when they learned how to make sculptural forms with vermiculite and cement. Jake had taken the class when Bruce suggested that they'd have fun. Making the boulders was the last thing Jake helped with before finally cutting ties with the The Company.

Jake struggled to pick up the big cumbersome boulder blocking the path. It had absorbed some water through the years. But it didn't weigh near what a normal three foot circumferential boulder weighs. Jake rolled the others till he made room to the grass lined path for Crash.

He jumped back in and turned off the headlights. The moist grass reflected the partly cloudy sky's three quarter moon's light, making the sand grass look silver. Jake sat up in the seat straining to see the sandy path then jerked to a stop as he realized he forgot to put the boulders back in place. He popped back out, leaving the car door open and walked back about ten feet. He scanned the area, feeling like he was being watched, but didn't see a thing except dark timberline.

As faint footsteps harkened he jerked around to look and then hurried down the sandy grass path. He lifted a boulder and cautiously turned back around to place it into position. He checked again for the faint footsteps. He placed another and checked again. He repeated the steps until done. A soft wind swayed and treetops swooshed as he hurried back to Crash. He jumped in and slammed the door when something cold pressed against his neck. He clasped his neck then ne'r 'bout sat on the dash as he checked the back seat. A giant dog stared straight on.

Jake leaped from Crash. Flung open the back door. Pointed for the giant dog to get out and was surprised when it did. It had the outline of a German Shepherd. As the dog disappeared into the dark timberline Jake nervously laughed as he wiped sweat from his forehead. "Okay. That was a figment of my imagination." He closed the door, started Crash and eased down the dark tree lined path confident the fright of the night had come and gone. As he squirreled down the worn narrow path the chrome on Bruce's truck sparkled. He pulled in behind, the only place to park, and walked around the bend to The Company.

Lanterns were spaced along on the ground to line the foot path like there was some kind of shindig about to commence. Twenty feet from the stills a ping pierced like a cymbal. And Bruce's shadow became clearer. Bruce had most of the stills disassembled and stopped stacking the stainless steel and copper to wave. Still, metal clunked and clinked as frogs croaked and the wind swept the timberline like a hush over the soft pat of water against the rocks.

Jake carefully made his way over The Company's loose parts. Stainless steel buckets and copper were everywhere, both squirrelly and jointed. He alternately checked for clear stepping and for Bruce as he cautiously managed the strewn path with its grabby thorn bushes and what looked like moccasin tails hangin' from overhead limbs. And just as Jake was about to shout out good-gooboly-goo, a figure in the lantern's light filled the hideout. Fire lit up in Jake's eyes like they had their own lantern wicks. "Behind you!"

But instead of scrambling for cover Bruce laughed, along with the figure. Slowly, the figure behind Bruce grew familiar. Then a dog appeared from the black timberline and jogged straight up to Jake. It sat and whined like it really was Miss Scarlet's ghost. As he bent over to pet it Bruce warned, "Leave that dog alone and get busy. That dog's got work to do." Bruce grunted out a German command and the dog disappeared back into the black as Jake stepped closer and closer.

"What do you want me to do first, Bruce?" Jake examined the figure.

Bruce's smirk hadn't changed a bit. "That's Scarecrow."

"Hey, there," Jake called out.

"Call me Russ. Wan'na hold the light up for me while I loosen this nut?" Scarecrow wore a goofy grin and sweat beads that dotted like glitter all over. He looked like one of those long carp out of the river that'd learned to walk on land and when he talked his mouth exaggeratedly opened real wide gasping for air and closed back again. His boots even set at the end of his frame sort a' splay footed.

"Sure," Jake replied, but as he stood face to face with Bruce he whispered, "Thought I was the only one you could trust." Bruce just shrugged and sucked down a bottle of water as Jake turned and left. Jake carried one of the lanterns lining the path as Bruce directed him to use a flashlight instead. "Good thinkin', but I left mine in Crash. Didn't think I'd need it with all these lanterns," Jake replied as he neared Scarecrow and held the lantern up high to get a closer look. He was older than Jake estimated, maybe fifty. And his tall skinny frame pushed out a flabby knapsack of a belly.

"Surprised to see me?" Scarecrow asked as he strained over a tight three-quarter stainless steel nut and the veins in his long spidery fingers wickedly pulsed.

"Your dog surprised me. Got in my backseat when I was moving the boulders."

Bruce coughed out a guffaw. "Hey, bet the Little People made the dog do it. Sneaky spirits."

"Sneaky shepherds, good watchdogs, but mine doesn't have any bite." Scarecrow cocked a half grin.

"Oh."

"You driving Crash?" One eyebrow lifted up halfway up across Scarecrow's forehead.

"Yea," Jake's response lingered like a question.

"Bring the dolly?"

"It's in the trunk." Jake glanced over at Bruce.

When Scarecrow finally loosened the nut he smacked loudly and it startled Jake. "Nerves on end, huh? Don't worry. We're in the clear tonight. Why don't you go get the dolly? Okay?"

"All right to take the lantern?"

"Yea, but let's not give any teeny boppers lookin' for a place to park a reason to be suspicious. Keep it at ground level."

"Right." On his way down the dark grass path the dog whined. And just as he was about to pet its head Bruce warned, "Leave that dog alone."

"Chill out." Jake's harsh reply barked against the pond's lush nightsongs playing through the dark timberline as the dog followed him to Crash. The moon slit through the sky like an eyeball through a tiny keyhole with little light to spare as the deep green grass hushed against Jake's heavy steps. Then the dog's sharp whine shrilled up Jake's spine like a toten trying to get under his skin. He lifted out the dolly and closed the trunk while the dog continued to whine. As he resigned to befriending the dog and stroked its neck the dog's sharp canines sliced his wrist. When he jerked back cussing Bruce and Scarecrow laughed in the distance and the dog jogged away.

Jake reopened the trunk and pulled out a cloth from Crash's tool box. And as he did spied the flathead screw driver and shoved it into his boot, between his sock and the leather, just in case. Then he wrapped the red mechanic's cloth around his wrist and tied a knot against the hot damp sting. Then he grabbed his flashlight from the glove box and wedged it in his waistband at the back of his jeans.

The dolly had been squeaky, dusty, and unused in his dad's storage building. So Jake had given it a dose of lubricating oil and checked out the solid wheels so it rolled like a new one, fast and furiously over the grassy sandy grass path. Jake knocked the first copper vat he approached with his class ring and it chimed over all the other night sounds.

"Enough of that," Bruce scowled.

"Right," Jake sarcastically sang through his rushed breaths, "The Little People might tell the neighbors," as his dimples dug into his cheeks. Bruce's grays shot a bullet straight at Jake's forehead like a thump against his skull and it made Jake reconsider his tomfoolery. "Aren't you taking a risk, moving all this and don't really own it yet?"

"Nothing to worry about. I own it." Scarecrow dropped the stainless steel buckets into a wooden crate.

"Bruce has it going on. Everything's going his way now, even the law." Jake laughed.

Bruce continued organizing parts as Jake rolled the dolly up to the nearest vat and eased it on. "You got something to cover these with?"

"Got a pull-out cover affixed to the truck last week." Bruce didn't stop working. "Got the best price from a dealer in Apex. Had Cassie run it up there for me."

Jake steadied the vat. "Scarecrow, you got a tie down of some kind?" Jake struggled to keep the awkward turnip shaped copper boiler from sliding off the dolly.

"Call me Russ, if you don't mind." With long rushed steps, he brought over a handful of elastic straps from his tool box. "You think it'd be cooler out at night."

"If wishing made it so, Russ." Jake pulled open the neck of his tee shirt and blew a cool whistle down his damp pecs. "Ya'll got the flake stands hid somewhere?"

"Just drums. Hauled 'em off already. Kept the pipe works though," Bruce clarified.

"We want you to haul the pipes and caps. Don't want all this together." Scarecrow made firm eye contact with Jake. "Anything could happen."

Jake speedily fastened the straps. Then rolled the dolly to the back of the truck as Bruce followed and aimed the flashlight when he unfastened the straps. "You'll follow me. Stay a car or two behind. I'll slow down for you to catch up when we get close to the tracks. If we get separated just remember that the road looks like this one, but there's steel posts with a new gate. And if you can't find it do not drive around looking and back up in somebody's driveway. Come back here."

"Got it." They lifted the vat up into the truck bed and then Jake jumped up and scooted it toward the front. He checked out Scarecrow who was kneeling down dissembling pipe. When Jake jumped down Bruce whispered, "If anything goes wrong tonight I want you to look after Thelma." He held out his hand with the thick roll of bills.

"Like what? You think Scarecrow's going to pull something, double-cross you?"

Bruce held his shoulder. "Just coverin' the bases." When Bruce signaled by cupping his package and darted his eyes. Jake pushed the roll down into his underwear. Then he stretched around the side of the truck. Scarecrow was still on his knees. "Does he help you cook and run too? I thought he just took hush money?"

"You think right." Bruce held onto the side of the truck like he was fixin' to hurl. "I've picked him up and brought him here to help. Runs jars when I'm in a bind. And he's in my pocket every month, but tonight, he showed up on his own." Footsteps gained up behind them, but it was just the dog. Bruce pulled at his sticky wet tee shirt. They made certain Scarecrow was still back there working then Bruce explained, "We agreed to be partners when I start college. He'll distribute. I'll cook. And he gets half."

"Why?"

"He insisted. Made the deal right before you hit that vat."

"Damn," Jake winced.

"I'm startin' ta hate that Lum fool." Bruce rubbed over his hawkbill. "He's too much like my granddad's regulators. Had the balls to tell me he came by to check on his investment. Fool says he didn't have a clue I was moving tonight and expects me to take his jubious karyn just like that." Bruce's knife was still in its sheath. "I swanny. I laughed at first. Sure he was just pulling my chain."

"Where's his car?"

"By Thomas's hayfield. You know the spot. We ran through there a few times when we thought we were being scouted out instead of going straight up the trail to the back yard."

Jake fisted his hips while he spanned the distance between the fake boulders and Crash and then between The Company and the light behind the trees where the hayfield began. "He's probably been watching for years."

"Too late now." Bruce seethed. "Glad I got dad's first still hid over at my new place. His daddy made it. A turnip. Hammered. All copper. Got the cap and worm and the same thumper he used with it. Used to seal it up each firing with biscuit dough and clay to keep it from seeping. Fed the pilings to the hogs." Bruce wiped his jaw. "I'm tellin' ya. If my old man had a caught Crow watching bes a mommucked up UC."

Suddenly, a roaring roll from the dark waters ran up their spines. And like a toten done snatched their throats, in unison they hotly whispered, "A dead UC." Again, the gator hissed and the water rolled.

Jake's eyebrows met with worry. "Gator was comin' up on the bank, wasn't it? How fast do they get around?"

"Cam down. Don't worry. I keep 'em fed." Bruce covered the surrounding ground with the flashlight. "Alice doesn't like undercover meat anyway, just chicken."

"Alice is a stupid name for a prehistoric carnivore."

"Alice the alligator, get it?" Bruce's grays danced. "I was just a kid." When he pointed to The Company they headed back.

"Was it down here when we were cooking?"

"Alice's been taking care of thumper tails and any mash that got scalded. Had to beat 'er back when we cooked nanners. Kept the smells down, too. Well, cooking smells down. Been here since I was five."

"And you just forgot to mention that? Huh? Like you do every other most important detail."

"I did tell you."

"You did? Well we sure were dumb little pricks, then. That thing could a' had us for lunch. Gawd, we were dumb."

Bruce grinned. "We were industrious entrepreneurs."

"Whatever. I really don't think I would've forgotten or blocked out Miss Alice." Jake whined as their pace quickened. Bruce did a good job counter acting their long departure by jerking his zipper like it was stuck. He even had Jake hold a lantern on it right next to Scarecrow.

Scarecrow stood up and hollered, "Spit on it." And all three laughed.

Jake slapped his leg. "Glad it's not my zipper. I'm so nervous my spit dried up. I swear if a helicopter flew over us right now I'd faint. I pure tee know it."

"I wouldn't bet against it." Bruce miraculously got his zipper up and whistled out a relief. "Want a drink?" He motioned like he was going to give Jake a drink of shine from a copper worm's money piece.

"Better not. Underage. The law could be anywhere." Jake joked.

Russ struggled to pull a pipe fitting from a long curly copper coil. They rushed over to help him and Jake grasped it with both hands while Bruce held out his hand to catch the fitting before it fell in the grass. The homemade copper band landed in Bruce's hand and he dogmatically handed it to Jake. "Make sure all these fittings are boxed up together." He pointed to some boxes on the edge of the lantern walkway.

"Always a planner."

As Scarecrow stretched out from his tedious task of dissembling the tight fitting pipes the lantern light highlighted his lumpy mid section down to a small pile of pieces at his feet.

"Scarecr, I mean Russ, don't step forward. You got a pile I need to get squared away."

"Thanks, kid. I didn't plan on working tonight." He said so incredibly distinctly, like he was so tired he had to think to speak.

"Too many characters to play, huh?"

"When I'm not Scarecrow I'm the Wizard." Russ pointed up at the sky.

"I believe it." Jake situated the box off to the side so he wouldn't block the lantern's light. He scanned the immediate area then back to front and center and discovered the plastic bag hanging out of Scarecrow's shirt.

Brrring! Like a shot Jake sits straight up. His bedside phone rings two times while he manages the pages and keeps his reading spot. "Hello?"

"Jake," Robin softly coos, "did Onacona suffer? I mean, I know she did. But for a long time? Tell me the truth."

"You don't want to know."

Her squeal forms Jake into a crunched up hump. His throat tightens and burns and is relieved when she resumes speaking. "Gili wants to know too. You know how she is. She's already talked to someone. If her person finds the one who poisoned Onacona first there won't be any legal proceedings. Do you know what I'm telling you? Jake, she can't stand it when I'm hurting. Should I come stay with you?"

Silence holds the line as their breathing patterns proclaim their intent. Jake kisses at the phone. "Gili said no already. I can't make love to you dead."

"That's not funny."

"I didn't mean it to be funny."

"I don't want a husband who's gonna make fun of me, Jake."

"Look, there's a lot going on, Robin. Stuff going on that you are better off not knowing. I have to protect you and if that means you are going to step back for a while that may be the safest way to go."

"I don't like this. What our relationship has become. It's too scary. This just isn't normal. Dogs don't get poisoned for no reason at all. And it certainly isn't part of a normal relationship."

"Are you rationalizing a break up?"

"No."

"Sounds like it."

"I'm not. I'm just scared."

"My cowgirl, my romping stomping cow chasing cowgirl can't be scared. Pull up the sheets and yer boots, baby. I'll bring you a gun tomorrow."

"I have a gun."

"You do?"

"A shotgun and a twenty-two. And I have a carry concealed license."

"Then what are you afraid of?"

"I'm afraid for you. Jake, they came to your place. Onacona was in your home. I'm afraid of losing you to this maniac or thugs. It could be gang related. One of those Lumbee gangs getting revenge and thought Onacona was one of the Detectives'. I still don't understand how Bruce talked us into robbery."

"Repossession of personal property."

"Sure. Whatever. Just tell me what kind of person poisons innocent dogs?"

Jake's finger still holds his place on the manuscript as he pushes his tongue up against the roof of his mouth before finally assuring Robin that he is safe and she is too. He tells her good night and quietly hangs up the phone and hopes he didn't disturb Miss Lucy sleeping in the far bedroom as he reclines to finish reading Chapter 3, Thicker 'n Thieves.

Jake wiped down the hairs on the back of his neck and pushed his tongue up against the roof of his mouth before aiming the flashlight in Bruce's eyes and then at Scarecrow. His cue worked. But Jake was so friggin' nervous he yelled, "What's the bag for?"

Scarecrow twisted his hand up under his shirt. Pulled out the bag and shook it. "Didn't know if you'd have any gungi growing out here or not."

"Man, I ought'a knock you out. I been scared to death you been setting me up; showing up here. Gawd, Russ, just ask somebody next time." Bruce cussed and returned his knife to its sheath. When Bruce had tuned down the most colorful, charged, and ne'r 'bout musical nasty dialogue The Company had heard since Old Man Black played his pipes up in there Russ smiled from ear to ear and asked, "Well, do you?"

Bruce laughed so hard he went into a fit. He was bent at the hip while he held his thighs and squealed and hissed like a funny monkey. His contagious relief sent Jake and Russ into rolling waves of laughter. And the dog whined. Bruce sat down and slapped at the earth as Jake held his bulge and stepped away to relieve himself at the path's edge. Bruce called out, "Don't pee on my plants. Russ is gonna smoke 'em. He loves some Paw Paw and Thistleweed." Russ told them to calm down, that it wasn't that funny. When they finally did, he captured their funny faces in the lantern light. "Do you have any gungi?"

And the laughing fit resumed. Jake yelled, "I feel like I'm in a time warp, man."

"Yes, we have no bananas or gungi." Bruce managed through his snorts. "That stuff's illegal." He rolled across the grass till he hit a pine tree. "Shit."

"The law, the law is coming." Jake teased as he steadied a box of still equipment on the dolly.

Russ clanged two pipes together and yelled, "Hide the law. Here comes the liquor. If we had a dancer, this would be a reunion."

"I really could take a drink." Jake checked out the chances.

Bruce winced a negative on the drink, and then stood up and brushed off to make eye contact with Scarecrow. "What if I did? You wantin' ta sell it or smoke it?"

"Sell, of course."

"A lot of money in weed, but a lot of trouble, too. You get pot heads around, then addicts want your numbers. I like my old guys, the backyard boys, those that just wanna sip." Bruce patted his knife. "Shiners don't want trouble and potheads are nothing but trouble."

"Don't see too much difference myself." Russ tried to take lead. "Bout the same sentence for selling either. And THC messes with hormones and'll give a man titties and temper. Likker gets tempers, too, but the fat goes all around. Overall though, neither one is as good a high as a long legged woman in a real short dress. Whew!"

Jake quickly filled another box with parts. "Shine is safer." He stacked it on top of the other.

"I concur." Russ clanged his pipes again. "Shine is a gentleman's best choice when it comes to a high. But if you ever wanna deal in big money gungi is the way to do it. Stay away from crack, pills and anything imported. Time is harder on those. Grow your own and hire out the work. It's not that difficult with so many illegals around. They're mean and cheap, better'n any watch dog."

Bruce tossed an armful of clanging pipes to the center of the path. "Have you given any thought about where we stand when I go legit? I'll pay you to do security."

Startled by both the unexpected racket and Bruce's forthcoming, Russ stood like a man called out to a street fight. "Yea, I could do security, part time. Watch the back of my eyelids for three or four hundred a week."

"Security guards get about ten to twelve an hour. You must be planning on retiring to put in that many hours."

"I bring a lot to the table."

Bruce stood back. "Look, I'm buying your land. I'm paying a fair price. You got cash down. And I got a signed note saying you agree to it all and'll sell it to me at that price soon as my house sells. Wantin' to back up?"

Jake did. He backed up against a tree and looked for a clear path.

"Hey, settle now. I'm just kiddin' around and I'm tickled with the land deal." As Scarecrow's long lantern lit arms rose in the dark night the German Shepherd leapt in front of him with his head low and hackles high, ready for a command. But when Crow gruffed out a German command the dog ran off and hid again.

Bruce went back to dissembling and so did Scarecrow while Jake rolled the heavy boxes to Crash. When he finally reached Crash he exhaled a deep, "Oh, Jesus." The trunk was open. After he scanned around he pulled the screwdriver pressed tightly against his shin out of his boot and kept it on top of the hood as he jerked the flashlight out of his waistband and turned it on.

Tree frogs chanted squirrely tunes from the nearby timberline like they were mocking his fraidy cat motions just as Jake dropped the flashlight in the thick grass. It sunk in quick and went black in the grass. He fished for it with his boot while 'fraidy cat' mocked him like a chorus louder and louder until Jake scooped up the flashlight and scanned.

Nothing and no one was outside or inside the front of the car. He grabbed the screwdriver from the top of the car and crept back to the open trunk with the flashlight steadily aimed. When he reached the gapping trunk his shiny keys dangled from the trunk's lock right at his forehead.

With a relieved grin he wiggled them out and poked himself, chanting, "Fraidy cat," and his prize trinket caught his eye. Attached with heavy duty fishing line, Preacher Lilly's pearl onion button glimmered in the moonlight from his keychain. He packed the keys down deep in his pocket, the screwdriver back into his boot, and squeezed the boxes into the floor board before hurrying back. The dolly whizzed without weight and as Jake took a moment to thank God he noticed something else. All the stars were twinkling onto the dew covered grass and they seemed to move little sparkling eyes.

At The Company tension and time grew. It festered and lingered. The sultry summer heat pulled every drop of moisture from their pores. Every turn of the wrench, every pull on the pipes, and all the sounds around them, filled every inch of space until they were crowded with anxiety and hyper awareness of the threat of light. Every single sigh was reckoned with on account of Alice's similar hiss. And to top it all off the frogs were so loud it was maddening. There was no room for talking, or laughing anymore.

Their communication became nods, shrugs, points and gestures until they lumbered into their vehicles and started the engines when each of them recharged for the next step in the night move. When Jake pulled up close to the deceiving ditch on the gravel road, he prayed Crash didn't tip over and in. His car was full, packed to the dashboard, side windows, rear headrests and the trunk would hardly close. Jake had to sit on the trunk to force the latch knowing the copper caps would be bent, but could easily be hammered back into shape.

The worm coils and parrot pipes packed in the seats were draped with sheets, Bruce's pink sheets. When asked about the pink all he had said was, "Washed 'em with a red sweatshirt. Won't do that again." With Crash being factory original sky blue, all washed out and pale, Bruce and Scarecrow razzed Jake about his ride being a pastel blue baby crib with soft pink lining. Bruce said, "Baby want a bottle?" as he held up a jar and Jake replied, "Yes, Sir, soon as this is over."

Bruce's new truck bed cover concealed the five copper vats. Scarecrow rode with Bruce. So there was no room inside the truck. And the dog stayed behind. Scarecrow said the dog would go to his car, not to worry about Napoleon. Bruce planned to drive Scarecrow back to his car later. Jake cringed as they separated and Bruce's big truck barely scraped past. Then Jake eased Crash back to the center of the gravel road, put Crash in park, popped out, and jogged back to replace the boulders. He became alarmed when he realized he forgot the flashlight halfway to the boulders and turned around, running.

He covered the ground with the flashlight, then the boulders, and shoved it into his back pocket. Once he was confident that there were no moccasins and Alice was not around he worked in record time to replace the boulders, then sprinted into Crash and barreled down the haphazard road. The pipes and pieces clanged like a wrecked band as he practically went airborne over the ruts and deep washes. The old shocks creaked and twanged, but held up and made Jake proud.

By the time he reached the intersection Bruce's truck was out of sight. There was little traffic; two cars, one coming, one going. Jake left The Company's road with a swirling dust trail. Crash spun out onto the highway as Jake quickly pressed the top of his head to relieve his stinging tension while the gas pedal took his thrusts. Jake's anxiety peaked not being able to touch base. Bruce was going to buy more minutes for Jake's phone in case of any mayhem, but had decided phones could become something more along the lines of evidence than convenience if mayhem got the better hand. When Jake finally spied Bruce's tail lights, he slowed down from seventy-five.

When Bruce saw Jake in the rear view mirror Scarecrow turned all the way around then conversed with Bruce as his hands flew around every which a way in the crowded cab.

Bruce slowed down and Jake got up to three car lengths behind.

There was no air conditioning in Crash and out fear of discovery Jake kept his windows up and suffered. The pink sheets covered the goods and summer's red hot heat covered Jake. His damp tee shirt stuck to the plastic seat and to his skin. Jake pinched the money wad and was sure it was soaked and staining his whities. He tugged till it didn't touch his stuff, but as soon as he released it the wad bunched up again. He rolled down the window down about an inch and stole a cool breath, but when the sheets shifted he rolled it back up. He reached down beside his lap to get a water bottle, but couldn't feel it. He strained as he checked for it in the floor board. Felt around on the seat again, with no luck. His throat scraped against the back of his tongue as he swallowed a dab of saliva.

As The Company's convoy passed a convenience store Jake nearly waved for them to pull in. He was absolutely parched and so hot he felt like he had a fever. But he didn't dare take the risk. They were nearly done. When the bright store lights shone into Crash he made a quick check for the water again. A movement on the floorboard reflected light. He reached for it as his eyes darted from the road to the floorboard. But it wasn't a shiny plastic water bottle. It was a shiny water moccasin.

Jake bolted straight up and made himself skinnier as he tightened up and for some foolish reason, held his breath till he saw stars. And the pressure of the pitiful little excuse for a weapon in his boot scratched his shin. He screamed like a little girl as he darted from left to right searching for a place to pull over, then back at the floorboard to see if it was still there or really there. Both easements were just grass. No telling how deep or dank the drop off. He was out of options as the moccasin's tail disappeared under the passenger's side. Jake veered onto the shoulder of the road, jumped out and slammed the door as zooming lights blinded him straight on.

The headlights weren't really an issue. He knew headlights would pass. It was the blue squirrelly one. Jake's mind worked faster than a nerd's calculator in honor's math. He removed the red cloth from his dog bite, so as not to draw attention. And thankfully, in the moonlight it was no more than a scratch. But his mouth was so dry that his tongue was sharp enough to peel a pineapple when he swallowed. He cautiously peered inside Crash. The sheets were secure. And he repeatedly whispered, "Don't ask. Don't tell." Then boisterously, Jake called out, "Hello, Officer, a moccasin got in my car. Know any good snake charmers?" Then he remembered to politely smile.

And the hefty Sherriff's Deputy politely smiled back. "Mon, that's a new one." He adjusted his belt, or rather pulled it out from under his dunlap and held onto the top of his club like a cave dwelling Neanderthal hugging a drumstick as he licked his lips. His thick tongue reached and stretched but could not remove the breading and cole slaw crumbs from his prickly double chin.

Jake nervously laughed. "There's a guy in Chatham County that does pest removal. Bet he handles snakes, too. I petted a dead beaver in the bed of his truck once. I don't know if there's anyone around here, a snake charmer that is, not a beaver, Sir. Hey, what about the park's wildlife rescue? Don't' they have a group of activists or advocates or something like that? Seems like I read in the paper when they protested draining the pond on account of fish fatalities. They said the fish had feelings. Wasn't that Chatham County?"

He shifted the club around in his belt's holster while he shifted gears from friendly to drill sergeant. "State your name." And he chewed up the remains of something and swallowed.

"Jake Wilkes."

The officer stepped closer and a foot away stretched his neck out to see through Crash's windows. Then rolled his eyes at Jake and checked him out from head to toe, "Ever think of painting this ride? Might wanna go with maroon to match the interior." His tongue punched his cheek like his joke punched Jake. "Can't believe your dad lets you out in this thing. Looks like something a fairy'd drive." When he laughed his belly lunged up over his belt and back down. "Tell him to trade out with Jonesboro's Tire and Body Shop. They could use some advertising. His wife's hung up again. Number four. And you might wanna check on tires, too." He grunted as he walked around the entire vehicle with the flashlight outstretched and leaning so far back he looked pregnant. "Swanny, I wouldn't let my dog out in this."

Then a slow moving truck came up behind them and Jake's armpits flooded a stink that'd piss off a skunk as Bruce passed. Jake licked the sweat from his lip as he prayed all mayhem had been completely doled out for the evening as the officer leaned so far over Crash's driver's side window he lost his balance. In his struggle to keep balanced he ended up tap dancing across the pavement like an awkward ostrich with his club stuck out like tail feathers from behind. "Sure there's a snake, boy?"

"It's a moccasin, Sir."

"What else you got up in here?"

Jake's pecs tightened and his dry tongue up and grew two big horns that scraped across the roof of his mouth as he swallowed and reckoned on a good enough lie while the officer busily zoomed his flashlight over the pink sheets. Abstract forms, shadows and lines begged for definition. The copper worm coils were outstretched in the floor board with the other pieces on top. From where Jake stood the front section suddenly formed an abstract sculpture of a giant officer with a rifle in one hand and in the back seat, the outline of a jury box appeared with twelve finials pokin' up like real heads.

Without further ado, Jake explained. "Propane equipment, a lot of copper, some advertising client of Dad's. I got the short end of the stick and look at me now. Helping in the middle of the night moving this big job they're trying to finish up before a new work week starts over."

"Pink sheets?"

"Don't want thieves seeing it."

"Washed red with 'em, didn't cha?"

"Yea," Jake tried to look ashamed.

The Officer poked his flashlight at Jake like a teacher's pointer. "Thief take anything copper. Honest man ain't got a chance." And with that took his phone out of the snapped black cover and identified his whereabouts and asked for his buddy, Roe, "Got anyone from the station which can remove a live moccasin tonight from a working man's vehicle?" He winked at Jake as he held the phone away from his ear. The laughter boomed. It spurted and hackled and blared in all degrees. The officer rolled his eyes. "Jerks," he told Jake. Someone yelled that he should use his whistle. Someone else said to call Fisk and Jakes eyes popped wide open.

And they widened even more. "Fisk lives off Old Plank Road. Bes ten minutes away, but don't know what level bes in. Got his number? Call back." The officer put his phone back in its cover. "Well, we got a feller, a snake procurer, who can do it, Jake. Dispatch'll call right back. Don't worry. Be back on the job in no time."

"Thank you, officer." Jake kicked the small stones out in front of him on the side of the highway into the grass just like a child innocently does when he's out playing in the wide open outdoors all carefree and without a lick to worry on. The dark timberline lined both sides of the road some forty feet back with a chorus of critters, known and not. He listened intently for a bird, a holy sign, and when he didn't hear one attempted to whistle, to perhaps bribe one into the area. But his mouth was so dry his lips threatened to crack when he puckered up. So he just listened to the frogs calling for mates. And was certain one croaked, "Jailbird."

As the hefty officer headed back to his patrol car he called out for Jake to come sit, too.

But Jake informed him that he was just fine out there. From behind the wheel the officer unwrapped a snack cake and pushed half of it into his mouth as Jake took a seat on Crash's hood. Jake sat there for only a few short minutes due to the problem that he imagined the moccasin seeking out his body heat, as if the hot car wasn't steamy enough. When Jake jumped off he slid in his slick boots across the pavement making quick distance from Crash and its moccasin.

While the officer chewed down his snack cake and made his eyebrows dance as he held onto the steering wheel with his elbows raised up stooging around like he was going to race Jake approached. "Do you have an extra water, Sir? I sure could use it."

"Sure, son." He quickly opened his cooler on the seat and gave Jake a water bottle and he drank it in one long continuous gulp. "You just saved my life. Thanks, Officer."

"Anytime. Keep a-plenty. Ne'er know what'll happen in a night. Don't want to be left high and dry." The Officer winked. "Get it? High and dry?" He laughed and choked up cake and when he spit it out the window, just missing Jake, he lurched out of range and hurried back to the grass.

Jake paced from the grass on the side of the road to the gravel and back. He finally locked his weary legs and folded his arms and in a kinetic exercise tightened and relaxed his aching muscles while he prayed with all his energy that Fisk the feller was out cold and they'd have to call Chatham County's snake procurer.

The hefty officer maneuvered out of his patrol car and marched over to Jake in the grass. "Your lucky night. Mr. Fisk bes on his way. One of his friends bes driving him. Need to warn ya, kid, Fisk drinks. Well, he's a drunk. Know you're dad wouldn't appreciate a drunk being called to help, so, let's not breath it. Deal?"

Jake stood up straight and tall as a heap of grief rushed up into the air. "Good idea, Sir. Wouldn't want Dad to skip this year's free advertising for the Sherriff Department's Benefit up at the Meat Pit and Pie Palace."

"Naw, we need all the sponsors we can get. It takes a lot to keep a town safe ya know. We've even got undercovers and trained dogs now." He rubbed his belly. "Pit and Pie's my favorite."

"Naw?" Jake fought the grin till he had to look away like he heard something in the distance.

"That's just a frog. We've picked him up before. Fisk, that is. He's like a regular, in and out in a couple of days. He cooks a lot. Good meatloaf and hashbrowns. Never burns nuthin'. Serves me extra. Good ol' Lum. Bad luck tho. Fisk grew up in Lumberton with a litter of little sisters. They went to selling themselves and got famous around there and Mr. Fisk took off. He was a teacher at one time. Oh, he's a character now. A few scraps. Mostly drunk or petty theft. Been known to hold up his poker buds with poison snakes. He pure tee ain't afraid a' snakes. Some say he eats 'em." The Officer contorted his jaw in wait.

And the frogs off in the timberline grew louder and louder in their competition to mate. Then one of 'em won and croaked this real long drawn out croak like it was doing orgasms and the officer made a most unexpected uncouth comment along the lines of it being a good night for lovers. It took Jake totally aback and he became even more relaxed. "Heard they taste like chicken."

"Hain't wasting my time cleaning frogs. Not enough meat to keep up a man's strength. Slimey, too. I won't bother with frogs." The Sherriff's Deputy clapped his hands. "Shut up. Stop it. Go courtin' somewhere else you stupid toads." Then looked over at Jake real annoyed like. "Can't hear myself think with all that."

Jake played fool and closed his gapped trap.

But both jumped as if a lightening bolt struck fire to their boot soles when a bumping thumping hissing grabbed a hold of the night stage. They stared dead on at Crash from where they stood. And they stayed there, too, frozen, checking Crash from the distance for snake leaks when it thumped again. And that time they saw it. Its nose wickedly bumped up against the front windshield, wide as a soda can.

The officer aimed his flashlight as he grasped his pistol. The light zoomed across the windshield as the big thick moccasin coiled and curled onto the dashboard and it popped the glass. His long forked tongue flickered. Then his light brown belly stretched up stiff as it glided against the incline of the glass.

"Damn." It burst out of Jake as the moccasin's mouth opened against the windshield. The moccasin's mouth was pink and white and sharp and fangy. And he was trying his darndest to bite a hole in that glass, so much so that his mouth flattened out against it as he arched up and pressed down till it popped closed and like a toaster kept popping up flashing its fearsome fangs. It tried and tried to bite a hole in that glass. Then it coiled up and slapped its tail as it gapped its lethal threat.

Then a car pulled up. No. It was a truck. No. It was a car with the trunk cut out and a truck bed welded on. The ramshackle vehicle backfired as it came to a jerky stop and the officer's jaw twisted in a gross configuration. "I hate snakes," He said as he ferociously waved.

Mr. Fisk and Wart tried to get out. Their heads wobbled out from the doors first, then arms, trying to balance their heads. One leg, then the other followed. Jake cocked his head at the officer and he squinted as he bit the tip of his tongue. The pair wobbled up to Crash with a sack and a shovel. "I'm doing this free tonight, my good officer." Mr. Fisk announced with a tuck of his chin like a gentleman would do if he was meeting special folks. He pointed at the officer while Wart held out the heavy cotton sack. Two cords hung from its hand stitched top. Wart opened it up and looked inside.

"Knew we could count on ya, Fisk." The officer's fat cheeks bounced. "You got one in there already, Wart?"

"Look 'n see." Wart drooled from his snaggletooth gap.

Mr. Fisk angrily pulled Wart's sleeve, "Swanny, you toss one a' awers in thar?"

Wart looked into the sack again and his hat fell off. He tried to pick it up, but couldn't. Even his fingers were likkered up.

The officer laughed through his nose, then collected himself and pointed, "Bes up here, Fisk, in the front windshield." But Fisk was too busy watching Wart. "Fisk, Fisk, the snake is on the dashboard. He's biting at the glass." Wart moved real sudden like and the sack wagged and he dropped it. So Wart jumped on the sack and stomped it good then picked it up and shook it again and looked in. Satisfied, he fetched his hat and squished it over his greasy gray curls.

Mr. Fisk kept the shovel over his shoulder and fashioned his free fingers into a snake snout and snapped at the air. "Fisk, Fisk, Fisk, knows where snake bes. I smell him. I taste him. Fisk knows where all kinds a snakes is." Fisk scowled at Jake and gestured a snake bite then wove and wobbled around to the front of Crash. His shoulders were up so high he had no neck, but his humped back still humped. And his wire rimmed glasses hung off the end of his red tipped nose, so close to the nub, they could fall. Fisk flung open the front door making the old hinges gnarl as the door bounced and the snake coiled onto the dashboard ready for a strike.

He held the shovel out in front of the coiled moccasin like he was going to train it to walk the plank. "Come on, Buddyrow. Oh, yese a bigun." Then Fisk hollered to Wart, "Get up here with that sack. I taint carrying him all da way back thar. Why he might jump off dis shovel here and squirm up dat boy's leg." When Fisk voraciously grinned at Jake his big thick lips formed a big black hole and it was clear he had only a few molars left. "Gid up in here, Wart."

Panic stricken, Wart hurried with the sack. "Bes all de sorry in de world dat snake gid up yer pants." His motions were so exaggerated his hat fell off again. But this time he didn't stop to try to pick it up. Wart ran with the sack held out in front of him like he was already totin' a live wriggling moccasin.

A laugh welled up in Jake till he plum jittered. And as the officer grabbed Jake's shoulder they realized that both of them were enjoying the fiasco. The officer leaned hard against Jake's shoulder as his rolls lunged up and down in sequence with his heaves, so much so that Jake had to brace his legs to keep from falling. Jake struggled to hold in his own laughter so he could concentrate.

When the snake and the shovel met, Fisk didn't cut the snake into a gazillion tiny pieces. He scooped it up like it was a delicate little creature right off Crash's dash. The giant shiny viper weighed so much Fisk groaned for help as he backed up out of Crash's door. It stretched out its big ass head at Fisk and wrapped its tail around the handle, one lick at a time, all the way down to Fisk's bare hand. And Wart did his best to talk it into the sack.

The officer released Jake's shoulder to secure his unsecured pistol. "That's a poisonous snake now, boys. Not a kitten. Got that, Fisk? Don't cuddle up and try to kiss 'er now." The officer kissed at the air as the viper's tongue tasted.

Jake stepped back. "That thing's ten feet long."

"Least," the officer gasped, "and you were in there with hit. You got angels wid cha, boy. That moccasin's mouth'd cover yer entire hand."

Fisk slowly twirled the snake covered shovel over Wart's open sack. The moccasin's mouth slimed over Fisk's shovel bearing fist as he shook harder and harder when the moccasin refused. Then Fisk heaved up and blew a rotten stinkin' stroke of stench right into that viper's snout and it dove inside the sack unwinding its tail from the handle as it raced in. When Wart looked into the sack with his face so close he could've counted its scales Fisk hollered. "Bes in dar. Close da sack, Wart. Tie 'er up." In three licks Wart knotted the cords and held out the heavy sack as high as he could, which was close to three feet off the ground before his balance was tossed. Fisk proudly thumped the side of the sack and the moccasin pummeled around in thick waves like a cat daddy does when it rolls a bream. "Swanny, thoust eat like a King for a week on this 'un." He glared at Wart. "I get the choppers first." Wart just shrugged and Mr. Fisk continued his victory speech. "All we need bes a few hot ellicks to wash 'er down."

With that, Fisk stabbed the shovel into a crack on the roadside's worn pavement with a victory ping that rattled everyone's nerves and then shot Jake and the officer his best grin. "No moccasins running loose on yer highway. No, Sir, Sirs. Cameron bes all cleaned up, officer." He spit when he laughed. "No, Sir. No moonshiners, gun runners or nuthin' illegal like dat with our fine officer on duty." Fisk nodded bye and rushed back to his truck, car, car, truck, whatever, pulling on Wart's arm as he hurried.

The officer called out to Jake to drive safely and not to stop anywhere and then added, "Don't drink n' drive, son. And don't tell your daddy 'bout these two. Promise?"

"I won't. No sir. You can count on that. Thanks again," Jake called out to the officer who then hurried after Mr. Fisk and Wart. Jake thanked his little good luck charm with a kiss as he jumped into Crash and right away noticed the gleaming copper beside him. The sheet was peeled back just enough to see the two inch diameter pipe. And a rush of angst, fear and that damn thrill to live to tell the tale filled his blood with vinegar again.

And the moccasin's sharp musky scent squirreled up his nose till it twisted his guts. He guided the front tires onto the highway. Locked in with stink and good deeds gone dirty in what had to be one hundred and twenty degrees and just then a water bottle bumped his foot. He pulled it up and drank the warm water in one long continuous gulp. Then he checked on the action in the rear view mirror just in time to witness the officer directing the snake charmers to his patrol car.

The officer pointed his pistol at the pavement directing the moccasin sack to the ground. But Good-gooboly-goo, with one swift jerk Wart emptied the sack into the back seat of the patrol car, propelling the moccasin inside. The officer screamed as Wart and Fisk darted back to their truck, car. And Jake laughed out loud as he peeled Crash out onto the black highway sort of singing, sort of shouting, "I'm not supposed to tell anyone what I'm doing tonight. I'm not supposed to tell anyone what I'm doing tonight. I swear. I swanny even, not to tell anyone what I'm doing tonight," as he cranked down the window.

Chapter 5

Totens and Little People

Steel posts and a new gate easily identified Bruce's new place just off the railroad tracks on the back road behind Cameron's one man post office where the paved road's ruts are as big as fresh tilled baccar rows and it's rumored they aren't repaired on account the law likes the way they slow down the local jar runners. Jake slowed to a mere crawl at the entrance as his heart thumped against his sternum and Crash putted over the pushed down grass path.

But not before he rolled down the passenger side's window. The cooler night air purged Crash's stifling hot vapors and viper juices as the radio announcer's deep sultry voice shared the time, two-twenty-two, with a cheatin', drinkin', don't-come-back-no-more-love song. Then as Jake spied Bruce's truck parked by a newly built shed a bright super powerful spotlight blinded him. And as the light x-rayed the sheets covering the copper pipes he held one boot on the brake, the other on the gas and thought up some more good lies as the light edged closer. The closer it got the stronger it became fully blinding him as a figure filled the driver's side window.

"Sorry 'bout that." Bruce turned off the spotlight. "Just verifying it's you."

"Shit." Jake turned off the engine. "Where'd you get that?"

"Raleigh, an outdoor sports store. Keep it in the tool box. Come on. Get out. It's gettin' late." Bruce called for Scarecrow as Jake stretched out, leaned against Crash and took deep breaths of the crisp clean night air. Then Bruce and Scarecrow demanded Jake tell them what in the hell happened.

Jake gathered his wits and pipe. "Am I the only one working now?" He bent over and eased the pile down next to Bruce and as he stood face to face sternly stated, "I'm not supposed to tell anyone what I'm doing tonight. Remember?"

But Bruce threatened to tie Jake to a tree as he aimed at the swamp. "I'm gonna let the moccasins poison you and the skeeters suck out whatever life is left."

Before Bruce could finish Jake grabbed a hold of Crash's hood, slapping, spitting and hackling out one giant, "Good-gooboly-goo!" Bruce smiled at his hysterics. "Why'd you get stopped? That's all we wanna know." Intoxicated with delirium, Jake propped up on the hood, locking his arms out straight so he wouldn't fall over. Scarecrow called him a goof and it gave him the giggles and it spread to Bruce as he seriously tried to tell him to shut up. "We're too tired for this." Bruce kept laughing. "Tell us already."

"A water moccasin got in Crash. It went under the passenger's seat."

"Holy Moly," Bruce declared while Scarecrow gawked, hardly breathing at all.

"A cop saw me. He called dispatch. And they sent out Mr. Fisk n' Wart," Jake's story rushed out. "Did you know they're the county's snake trappers?" Bruce rolled his hand around and around, urging Jake to tell the tale so Jake did, emptying the entire snake sack as they took turns popping the hood and busting a lung.

"That made my night," Bruce said. "Perfect. Perfect ending to a nerve killing night. I swear it couldn't get any more perfect than that."

"Yea. That one'll get around quick." Scarecrow rubbed over Jake's head like a grandpa does a little one. "Glad it wasn't Alice."

"Geez, me too."

They finally finished unloading and covered The Company's parts with a thick camo tarp, securing it to the ground with large steel stakes at the edge of the swamp in a thicket so thick they had had to carry parts up over their heads with flashlights gripped between their teeth. And in some places were on their hands and knees to scoot the parts along in front of them. The dirty work disguised them as wild boars gaumed up in black swamp dirt and its dank decay with briar scratches spurtin' fresh blood each time they swat off the feasting gallanippers.

Bruce insisted they toast their grand deed with his most potent Muscadine wine. He attached a pulley to a concealed heavy duty metal ring. Threw a rope over a limb and pulled up a four by four patch of ground to reveal his bounty. The clever earthen cellar held countless jars. Jake took the narrow earthen steps down and began counting rows. "Damn, Skippy. Regular fox den, huh? How far back does it go?"

"Fourteen feet. Had the old man's last two pallets down here, but his lids were no count. Swamp land ain't like the clay. Moisture eats the pallets and those cheap lids. Stainless lids on mine."

"You sell his?"

"Never. It's in a pit over at The Company. Off the timberline overlooking the water. Up high about ten feet from the top of the hill. Clay there's like brick." Bruce aims his light at a row with plastic wrap askew. "Bring up a jar and we can celebrate proper."

"In a couple of years," Bruce held up his plastic cup to theirs, "we will do this again with my Lucretia Dewberry Wine. Thanks you two. And even though I am so looking forward to going legit and putting this town back on the map I have to admit I'm gonna miss this. And I sure regret I didn't get the chance ta mommuck up that damn Yankee."

"Think of it this way; you've increased your chances of living long enough to have kids to tell your stories to one day." Scarecrow toasted and poured the burning potion down his throat and held out his cup for more.

They each relished the burn while they slowly allowed their stinging highs to loosen the last knots in their tight tongues as they continued the toast of living to tell the tale and beamed like they were heroes. They relived the night with their, "When he did this," and "When you did that," and slapped their thighs and one another's backs and got all toothy and drunk with both endorphins and likker. Round after round until Bruce's jar was empty and they stood shoulder to shoulder like comrades after war.

"I love you, man," Bruce told Jake. "You're the brother I never had."

"You too, Buddyrow." Jake marched off behind the shed to relieve his bladder letting go of some powerful gas pains and petting the German Shepherd along the way. And it wagged its tail and disappeared while Scarecrow covered their newly made trail using a hardwood limb to scratch it all up. Then Crow put on gloves and scattered pinecones, straw and his special nasty mixture of wild critter scat. Bruce inverted his empty jar on the freshly pruned scrub oak and thanked the guys repeatedly then asked Jake if he needed to take a nap or wanted to stay the night in the shed. "There's a couple of sleeping bags for occasions like this. Slept out under the stars till a cooter came up. Didn't wanna risk my nose again. It's cozy and no law'll be looking for ya in there."

"No. I'll be fine. I'll go real slow."

"Well I'm gonna follow you home and then I'll take Scarecrow to his ride, just to be safe."

"That'll work."

Then Bruce told Jake to tell his parents, "The puppies were packed tight, had to wait over an hour for the runt."

"I'm no runt. You're the runt. Runts are always the trouble makers."

"At least it's airish now," Scarecrow blew down his damp tee shirt. "Lost five pounds tonight."

With jelly legs and a humbled head, Jake fell into Crash and switched on the engine, "Sweet Jesus, keep me around to watch over Mamma." The headlights shone on Bruce and Scarecrow as they climbed into Bruce's truck. With eyes burning for sleep Jake opened them wide and yawned as he fished for another water bottle. He downed most of it and splashed the rest over his face. When he finally got Crash turned around he took a deep breath of sweet swampy summer night air, full of pine and Bermuda grass. He stuck his arm out to wave it in the cool air and pure joy covered him. He was singing when the gunshot pounded, "Boom!"

And instantly, Jake was sobered. From the rear view mirror hope was dashed. Bruce's truck was surrounded and Bruce was flattened into the grass while the German Shepherd held Scarecrow spread eagle by the upper thigh. "That damn Yankee!" Camouflage and aimed rifles filled the mirror. "Good God, get me out of this!" Jake peeled out from the slick grassy entrance with squealing tires and went airborne over rut traps. Almost at the end of the haphazard road he met Old Bucky. But he didn't slow down. Oh, hell no, Jake calculated impact with the legendary eighteen pointer. Swerved to miss the thick ass buck and missed his fluffy white flag by inches as he managed Crash over the rutted road at ninety. His head twirled to check traffic as he slowed at the stop sign. Then Crash lurched onto the highway. Thirteen miles later at the Tramway intersection he checked the rear view again.

Chapter 6

Momma Always Said

"Driving Crash?"

"Crash is gone. Block cracked."

"Didn't update me. Doesn't matter. Drive a tractor if you have to." Bruce vibrated with excitement.

"Do I need to bring you any clothes, your boots? Or are you gonna start a orange jumpsuit trend?"

"No orange. A decent shirt would be all right. I've got jeans."

"At nine?"

"That's what bossman says."

"Good bossman. Sending you come home early, too. Can't beat that. Call if there're any changes."

"There won't be. Thanks, Jake. I can always count on you."

"Sure. Glad to do it, Bruce."

After the phone call Jake set to worrying. Jake was sure Bruce had read all the papers, but he hadn't mentioned a thing about the slasher or Bobby Long's murder or Glennie's attempt, or about Jake living on the Crowson's farm with Glennie's sister, Exilee, who had taken Bruce's place as his best friend. But that part wasn't in the papers. And it didn't have to be for Bruce to learn it. Prison made communication from the outside one of the most precious contrabands and therefore, the most common.

There had been comments that suggested Bruce had knowledge of the horrors Jake had survived: The scar on his face from the slasher who was hired to kill him by Glennie because Jake had had an affair with her husband. But that wasn't something that affected Bruce like Jake dating Robin or their unofficial engagement.

The morning Bruce was released from prison Jake awoke to a surreal world. After a threatening drought July's downpour had burst like an overfilled water balloon leaving wet sparkles on Ginger's Columbine off the front porch of the cozy farmhouse at the Crowson's farm. The farm spread over five hundred acres. Rich in both history and busy farm life. Jake leaned against the counter and sipped his coffee and smiled as his roommate, Miss Ginger, left to walk next door for work. She was Exilee's childhood nanny and became Exilee's and Ken's little boy's nanny. The Crowson farm, which had the only section of authenticated actual underground and above Underground Railroad used by runaway slaves in the eighteen hundreds, meant double duty for Miss Ginger. She was the beloved nanny and also gave readings from her historical journal, 'The Black Purse Papers' during tours of the Underground Railroad.

Miss Ginger, a dark skinned petite lady was quite active for a very mature woman. After a lifetime of spinsterhood she started dating her lost love. It was all quite romantic. During Exilee and Ken's wedding a tall unknown man in a good suit and hat had mysteriously appeared at Miss Ginger's table. No one had a clue who he was, except Exilee's dad.

Many years before he had argued with Miss Ginger during her tenure as a nanny for the girls about her dating and trying to provide adequate care after the girls' mother's death. Miss Ginger was expected to be on duty like a real mother so David Sheffield, a busy high school principal, had run him off. And then after all those years he was the one who brought him back. It was an act that brought them all back together and Miss Ginger couldn't have been happier. If she wasn't singing she was humming.

Jake checked his watch as the sun lit the sandy plot calling him to plow. But it was time to go pick up his best friend. Exilee appeared as she made her way to the ponies in the nearby lots, but this time Jake just waved instead of jumping off the porch to help. She was the one who had suggested Bruce live with Jake and Miss Ginger. She had done the same for Jake; moved him to the farm for life adjustments after his life threatening experience and that had worked out splendidly.

Bruce liked the idea of being on a farm for a while with his old best bud and had said that the prison authorities and probation officer thought it would be a good way to adjust. But Miss Ginger had said, "We'll see what kind a man he is first time you kiss Robin in front of him. Don't care how much explaining you do. Man's bent on marrying someone and been cooped up doing nothing but dreamin' about her there's gonna be something between ya that wasn't there before. Don't get your hopes up." And when Jake had explained that they had always competed for Robin and that it didn't undermine their friendship, Miss Ginger had asked, "How long will it take for Bruce to set up living quarters at his new business? Did you say he had a shed?"

The ride over to Beacon Prison in Richmond County took two hours, but it only felt like a few minutes. Jake sang the entire trip, sporadically shouting," Good-gooboly-goo." But Jake's happy expression was soon overcome as the reality of prison socked him in the nose. The heavy smells of prison; disinfectant, stale and sour humans, pungent food odors and strong stale piss was unescapable. It hit the pit of Jake's stomach as he was instructed to wait near the entrance and was thankful they had a window open. But it didn't help all that much. The painted cinderblock's pits held in the stale funk as Jake held his upper diaphragm.

Fast footsteps beat back the nausea and Jake smiled at his dear friend hurrying straight on and then smiled down at the bundle on his lap. The bundle held a tee shirt with a pocket. The kind he liked when they were kids. Jake's mom would put a dollar in his pocket when he spent the day with them for a candy bar and coke for when they went to the store. But Bruce wouldn't spend his. Put it in his jean pocket and saved it. So Jake couldn't wait to give Bruce the bundle. In the tee shirt pocket was his banking investment's statement. The account was in Jake's name, but Jake had marked over his name in thick black marker: BRUCE BLACK, DBA LUCRETIA WINERY.

The guard patted the tee shirt for contraband and took out the slip of folded paper, but didn't bother to read it. Then waited with Jake at the end of the long hallway. Bruce's footsteps quickened when Jake's dimples appeared over the guard's shoulder. And the guard stepped aside. "We all like Bruce. Guys call him The Prince, even us. Got a smart head on his shoulders."

"That he does." Jake clapped with a grin so white and shiny it could've fooled a dying man into thinking he'd seen the holy light."Buddyrow!"

"Brickhouse," Bruce drawled it out, still five feet away. Then, at only three, light flooded his face. He was carrying six haggard years under his eyes. The black half moons under his eyes aged him. The old jeans he wore in six years before hung on his lean hips. The tennis shoes were plain white, newish, from the state. The guard mechanically handed him the bundle and Bruce didn't miss a step as he pulled off his thin assigned tee shirt and slipped on the new one.

Then the guard reached out for Bruce's hand, much less mechanically and shook it as he handed him a suit on a hanger and a sealed envelope with the standard mediocre allotment and release statement. They each said good bye and the guard opened the glass steel bar reinforced door and Bruce stepped out into freedom under the hot Carolina summer sky.

His eyes adjusted and wandered over Jake's scared face as he reached out and gave him a manly hug. They each patted the other on the back and grunted and made comments on it being too long. Jake had become a strong example of healthy living and was every bit the sexy country boy. Bruce was not.

Bruce's full hand softly patted Jake's scarred cheek. "On you, it's just a beauty mark."

Jake absorbed Bruce's knowledge of the scar along with his friend's pale gaunt reflection.

"It was in all the papers." Bruce explained as they stood toe to toe.

"Yea. Half the time, don't remember it's there." He blinked through the lie as he held Bruce's shoulders. "You need to get some rest and some meat on your bones." When Bruce didn't respond, Jake asked, "How much do you know?"

"Cells are like echo chambers, fools talk all night. Glad your dad got time too." Bruce tried not to stare at the scar. From the corner of Jake's generous mouth to his cheekbone and back around it formed a hoof print. "Is it quiet at the farm?"

"Yea, real quiet. You're gonna love it. Night is nothin' but crickets and frogs. In the summer we get the whole band and in the winter you can hear snow falling. Most any time a cow and a pony have a little something to say. But that's all the racket you're gonna get at the Crowson's."

"Sounds perfect. You sure the Crowsons don't mind?"

"Don't mind? They were excited to be helping you. In fifteen days we put up another new room on the house."

"Another?"

"Yea. First one went up after the basement was taken for the Underground Railroad Tours. That room took a month and a half, with three of us. It's Miss Ginger's room. But your room, Buddyrow, when word got out, we had to turn helpers away. Mark, Edge, Scarecrow, Dodger, all your jar runners showed up."

A smile spread over Bruce.

"My little house only looks little from the front. Around back it looks like a two story condo with the stairs and sign and we got the path from the road leading up to the tours in the basement framed with that split rail fencing, first class. It's plain around front, just a sign that tells people to go around back. Let's go. We'll talk in the truck."

"Truck? What about your neon green thing?" Bruce squeezed his shoulder then turned around and looked back. They both studied the forms steadily approaching from the cinder block building's fenced exercise pad. Projected from deep shouts they chanted, "Brickhouse." Outstretched waving arms pushed Bruce's chest like they'd actually touched him and propelled him backwards a step.

"You okay?"

"Yea. Drive me across the river, cuz." Bruce threw up his hand and spun toward the road. "So where's the green thing?"

"I needed a truck. Green thing's gone."

"Good. Truck looks great on ya." He laid the suit over the middle of the seat. Then pulled his seat belt over his chest and the rigid folded statement in his new tee shirt's pocket crinkled. Bruce stared at the figures and fingered its coma's position as Jake fastened his seat belt and switched on the engine. Bruce asked, "Is this a joke?"

"Stock you wanted skyrocketed. Got lucky, that and a smart money market manager. You're rich Bruce."

"Bruce Black is rich." His arm swung up over the back of his head and he clutched it like it may tumble off. "I'm rich. Six hundred k, Robin'll want me now."

Jake stiffened all over as he backed out of the parking lot and eased onto the highway while Bruce stared at the bank statement. When he slapped the dash he laughed and it startled Jake. But Jake laughed along with him and then turned on the radio. Old Country Classics twang out the last of a you done done me wrong love song and up started the next, a how to leave your man song, like they were specifically chosen to poke Jake in the neck. And the poke slowly burned as Bruce sang along with each cheatin' song.

When Jake swallowed the angst his Adam's apple bobbed like a little hand puppet flying up and down his stiffened neck, grabbing his words and holding 'em down while he tried to come up with something good rather than the plain truth. His big green eyes blinked over and over as he struggled to concentrate on keeping the truck between the lines and was relieved by the slight flow of oncoming traffic.

That only lasted ten miles. A twangy tune on taking someone else's man blared out like a Bob White's call from a strutting suitor. It rattled Jake's nerves till he had to loosen his jaw with a faux yawn.

"When's the last time you saw her?" Bruce leaned up.

Jake stared straight ahead. "Robin and I have been dating three months now. We're going to South Carolina in a couple of weeks to look at a horse. Gonna make a mini vacation out of it since Charleston'll be close by." Charleston South Carolina is where couples go to step back in time and allow the architectural ambiance of the eighteen hundreds seduce them along with the natural esthetics like the moss wavin' in the trees and shady lanes with that fragrant wisteria lofting down into their lust hungry snouts."We're practically engaged."

Bruce hastily folded the statement and shoved it back into his tee shirt pocket. And instantly his feet jittered as he sucked in a red hot drawl. Bruce changed the station, going from rock to rap to political talk and settled on modern country. Radio filled the truck with a ridiculous watermelon ruckus as Jake and Bruce swelled up with Testosterone Headiness. They were like toads that had been kissed by a princess and liked it, a lot, but with neither having full and proper mating rights, the truck cab was not nearly big enough for both bloated toads.

"You just forgot to mention that? Oh, that's right. It wasn't on the list of topics."

"I knew it'd be like this."

"Shoot straight with me, on everything."

Jake's eyebrows rose. "I shouldn't have waited. But I didn't lie to you." Jake's stern response bordered on angry.

"Look. People change. I know that." Bruce put on his one sided grin. "You shoot straight with Robin about everything else?"

"Of course," Jake rolled his shoulders.

Bruce lifted his chin and then looked down at Jake. "No longer kai?"

Dogmatically, Jake's ears heated. "Damn it, Bruce, it wasn't planned. We just fell for each other. She was over there with Exilee all the time and you know how she is. I couldn't ignore her." Jake checked his response and blew when Bruce's stiffened. "And no, I am not kai." Jake held the wheel and his stance. "That night when Miss Scarlet was killed, when you stabbed her to death, you announced that you were not gay. You also said I was just practicing what my dad did. You were right. That's all it ever was. I have never been gay. I was conditioned by abuse and then by peers. I didn't know who I was until I was free of him, of all of them." Jake's chest broadened. "Robin and I are serious."

And just like when Bruce was thirteen and stood in the dark with that blade catching the moonlight under his twisted grin, Bruce ever so calmly stated his view. "I'm glad. You've really overcome. Not everybody gets that chance."

"That's true," Jake wondrously replied.

They went on about five miles in nothing but radio racket when Bruce finally spoke. "Aunt Thelma and her husband still doing okay I guess?"

"They're fine. I see 'em out in their yard. I helped with the move. She gave me your old cap guns and some other stuff. She even boxed up your stuffed bear, the ratty one without eyes and your books, even your first tool set. Guess what else was in there?"

"You looked through it?"

"Hey, I saw that teddy bear's ear sticking out and had to see what else was in there. Okay?"

"Yea, so what else?"

"Your Glossy Flossy poster from the closet."

"I'll want that back." Bruce's sly smile highlighted his cheekbones.

"I know."

"Thanks. Where'd you put the rest? I know she wouldn't throw out Momma's things. I had her boxes in the storage building and some under my bed."

"I put 'em up. There's safe and dry. Don't worry."

"Did you go through her stuff, too?"

"What's wrong with you?"

Bruce gazed out the window and slowly leaned back, closed his eyes and did his best to allow the highway's worn waves to hypnotize the paranoia and anxiety into acceptance and hope. His concentration was broken when Jake swerved to miss a squirrel. Bruce looked at his statement again. "This is from the home place, a third with interest alone, plus the stocks I wanted and market accounts?"

"Yep, just like you wanted."

"What about the cash?"

"Safety deposit box. We can go now if you want."

"Now's perfect. I missed the smell of money. I love its stinkin' old paper, nasty fingers all over it. I love money."

"I know you do." Jake bobbed like an excited kid.

"How much did you pay yourself?"

"Damn it. We went through this on the phone. Played it out like I was selling puppies in that conversation. Remember?"

"Course I do. But it's only human nature. Have that much cash at your fingertips and not borrow some, it's not natural. How much?" Bruce smiled. "One, two thousand?"

Jake pressed his head against the headrest. "I told you. I didn't. Knew you'd need it more than me. Never took a single bill."

Bruce's smile faded into a queasy frown. "The whole wad is in there?"

"Hey, you wanna roll down the windows? I bet you missed the smell of fresh air, too."

"Sorry. A hundred years of fresh air and honest faces that'd be good, real fuckin' good. Sorry. But yea, real good." Bruce held his arm straight out the window letting it hover through the streaming rush. "It's gonna be an adjustment, Buddyrow. Hope I can do this quick and get on with my life. Got a lot of work to do."

"You'll have help." Jake patted Bruce's shoulder.

And Bruce's eyes welled up. "I'm beginning to see that."

"You've always been there for me." Jake softly reminded him.

And Bruce let the tears fall. "I bes mommucked up. Hope you can stick with this silly chauld Lum. I don't usually get so tore up." He wiped his cheeks and sucked in the fresh air. "I missed a lot in there, Buddyrow. Missed pickin' on you."

"Good. I did, too." Jake inhaled one of those deep breaths drawn before a shout. "This is a wild and jubious world, Buddyrow. Welcome back."

Radio's mindless bliss and wind gushing in from the open window purged the truck cab as they reached the edge of Cameron near Bruce's land for his new company. Jake stopped at the railroad track instead of just easing over, but Bruce signaled to just go on down the road like he could wait. They turned onto the back road that lead to Jake's bank. Jake told Bruce to open the console and get the key. "There ya go. Already signed the box over to you. Ask for Mrs. Parker. She has the papers. Just sign your name and show 'em your I.D."

"The statement says it's with Federal Credit. What are we doing here?" Bruce held out the key and read the engraved number.

"This is my bank. I just put the cash here 'cause I was here. We can go switch names on the investment account after this. Okay?"

"Why isn't here, too?"

"Investor over at Federal Credit knows his stuff better than the eye candy here. Look, Buddyrow." Jake pointed at the hot doll opening the door for the wheelchair bound gentleman. "Ah, I'd let her open my door. Hey, pretend like you're retarded and she'll hold your arm when she walks ya into the vault."

"Idiot."

"Hey, wait a sec. I've been holding on to this." Jake grabbed the token from the cup holder and jutted it out the window at Bruce and he licked his thick red lips. Wiggled it like a cigar and slid the perty pen in his shirt pocket. "Sounds like a side trip, Buddyrow. Miss those silky thongs and dirty songs." He whistled and shivered. "Man, we can stroke on by this weekend."

"Ladies are waiting in line for you. On poles. All slick and shiny. Screamin' for Brucey." Jake back whistled the saliva like he'd been at a pig-pickin' barbeque contest where all the juices linger in the air and you can lick your arm and taste the sauces.

As Bruce returned with a grin and a fat envelope sticking out of his front jean pocket, Jake turned down the radio and yelled out the window, "Hope you're up for a party. Got a few friends coming tonight."

"Who's friends?" Bruce pushed the envelope down into his pocket. "You doing this at the farm? The Crowsons'll call the law." Bruce plopped down on the seat and gave Jake his full attention.

"Not that kind of party. Some of my friends, and Thelma, Mark and her husband, of course, and Exilee and Ken, no jar runners invited, just in case."

"Believe me, they'll come if they get wind of it; a party and their old boss with rumors of a fine winery going up?"

"You're right, but," Jake whined.

"I know what you're thinkin', Mr. Fisk and Wart."

"Why would I be worried about them? What would they want with you?"

"Oh, they don't want a thing." Bruce's grays darkened. "I do. I want my money."

"What are you gettin' at?"

"The night we moved The Company and the law called for our good buddies to get that moccasin out a'Crash, I figure that's when those pallets of Dad's shine that got missing. Idiots probably been watching me since Old Man Black sucked his last molecule. God knows how many times I was out there diggin' and hiding dirt piles under leaves and pinebeds and felt like I was being watched. I was. I carried every jar down there on a separate day. And they're the only ones stupid enough to dare Old Man Black's kid. Don't cha reckon?"

"I'll give ya that."

"Will ya? Look, Mr. Fisk and Wart took a big risk running from that fat daddy. Think about it. Fisk threw that poisonous snake in an officer's vehicle, was DUI and running from arrest. Serious stuff for two drunks who stay over so much at the county hotel they cook for the fat daddy and his brothers, huh? I could see that in the winter when it's too cold to turn and they're out of cash. But it was cookin' season and Fisk ain't no dummy, ya know. Used to be a professor. He took his chances that night when he figured we'd all be busy, including Scarecrow."

"No way, they've fried their brain cells. They slur everything. Never heard 'em say anything intelligent. Ever." Jake cussed. "Are you sure?"

"Fisk got a look at that copper tubing, didn't he?"

"It was partially uncovered when I got back in. It's likely. Yea, he probably did."

"Well, I got the word they bought a second still a month after. A big honkin' copper vat, looked to be big as a baccar barn. Had Crow go check my hidey hole and pure as goanna on a hawg's ass it was gone. Didn't even put my cedar slabs back. Shitheads."

"Can't be. No way that'd ever get through town unnoticed." Jake scratched over his head and down to his neck.

"Twelve by fourteen sheets on a flatbed covered with a tarp."

For the first time in a long time Jake grinned like he did when they were kids, yurkers who taint got no business with shine, and shouted, "Good-gooboly-goo!"

Bruce guffawed, "That's what she said!" And laughed again followed by a deep gruff hasp and slapped his thigh. "If they can't get my money up I'm confiscating that vat."

"I know you will!" Jake was all teeth.

"You mean, we will."

"Oh, shit."

Traffic was slight on the two lane country highway. Its forests, fields and homesteads lined the road like rich oil paintings and Bruce studied each one. Jake commented, "Nothing like the country, huh? Freedom and sunshine."

"Damn skippy." Bruce inhaled a passing farm's odoriferous cow manure, its earthy plowed scents, and exhaled a little sigh of content. "Beautiful. My farm'll smell like fruits of the Gods and goat."

"Goat, huh?"

"For the cheese and eyes. They're cute little boogers."

"Their cute enough I guess. You'll have to keep 'em off cars. They climb. You'll spend a fortune on fencing alone."

"It won't hurt too much." Bruce patted his shirt pocket.

"That's right, moneybags. You got it all covered."

"That's right." Then Bruce rubbed his palms while his tongue poked his cheek.

Jake passed a vintage setting; a three story white plantation set back with a row of granddaddy oaks on a rich black section of earth with a pond all of ten acres. "Know what I missed? Those naps under that granddaddy oak after fishin' out on the back ponderosa."

"The ponderosa," Bruce sighed. "Long spell since I called it that. But you won't miss it now that I'm back. Liketa get a stringer a' pumpkin seeds and fry 'em in cracker crumbs. Um-mm. If the cooters and Alice haint et 'em up."

"New owners won't care?"

"I only sold the house and the road frontage. That back section was in my family before I was a spark. It's like it's in the Trail of Tears, man. Got stories tied to it that are tribal and sacred. Have to preserve it no matter what. Section was deeded over to my people after emancipation."

"Incredible. Maybe you can turn it into a park or something. Wouldn't that be a come back?"

"From Old Man Black's piece a' ground with gator dogs and toten haunts? Never happen. And booby traps still hanging, and who knows what else, yea, that'd be a miracle."

Jake pushed back against the seat and his green eyes glistened like an angel just perched on his shoulder. He shivered and turned away the air conditioning vent. "Never say never. Anything can happen."

Bruce contemplated as he scanned Jake's face and the scar pit against his stomach like a punch. "You're right. But that's way on down the road. I'm set on getting my business off the ground. That is, right after you and I catch up. Can't tell ya enough how happy I am right now that you're okay and we're headed off to start over together. It means everything. I've thought about this for six miserable years, Buddyrow."

Jakes turned off the radio. "You're gonna love the farm. It's awesome. My life is nothing like it used to be. I get up every morning to do something different. I see what I've done. David's gradually retiring, so I do most of it. His son does some, too. David gives a lot of the tours. They run Fridays and Saturdays. The schools make appointments for their tours. We do those on Wednesdays. Most of the time it's just me out there, the ponies and cows. I've got three rows of tomatoes, two hundred plants, green beans and twenty-five acres of corn about to tassel. Some of that's for feed. And okra."

"Feeding the county?"

"Wholesale and retail and put up a lot. Can and freeze."

"You ever whoop okra?"

"Missed that. Say whoop?"

"Whoop the leaves off before it buds and it'll produce double the pods."

"Whoop it? Like hit the plants?"

"Take a baccar stick and knock off the leaves. Do your plants have buds yet?"

"Nope."

"Good. I'll do it for you."

"Better work or David's gonna be real sore. He'd eat okra for breakfast if Miss Sarah'd cook it. And it turns more per pound than tomatoes."

The Gamecocks

"Trust me, Jakey boy." Bruce drummed the dash. "Hey, did you get the Lucretias?"

"Got 'em planted, too. Was hoping to make that a surprise, but you know me. Exilee and I pick early in the mornings. Miss Sarah freezes 'em. Got a freezer full, 'nugh to make a batch. Then we start on the farm. We're all rootin' for you, Bruce." Jake smiled over at Bruce and discovered his hard core business buddy all red faced.

Bruce coughed out the lump in his throat. "I'm going to pay you for those plants, Jake," in that soft Lumbee tone.

"David bought 'em for you. They're a gift."

"Mr. Crowson? He doesn't even know me. Why would he invest in my winery? What does he want?"

"Nothing. Not all people are like that. Crowsons are good old Baptists."

"Baptists helping turn?"

"They don't see it that way. Believe me. They do not condone drinking. They're just trying to do what God would have them do."

"One God comes to many people." Bruce announced his faith like an old best friend. "Do they know about me? What I was doing?"

"It doesn't matter. You're my best friend. That's good enough for them."

"So that's how Exilee can be your friend and work with you every day even though her sister hired a hit man to kill you for being with her husband and even moved you in next door." Bruce's grays moved like loose marbles. "You could write a freakin' novel."

"Her sister killed our dogs, too. Little innocent babies, she poisoned them."

"Sounds like a woman." Bruce stared dead ahead. "They must be total opposites."

"Yea. Glennie'll be in prison a while. But she didn't work alone. That piece of shit who slashed my face, the one Glennie hired out of Black Ankle where those redneck thugs live under the Confederate flag, he'll be in prison for good." Jake steamed.

Bruce leaned back in his seat and bit the end of his tongue.

"So you heard it all in the prison walls, huh? Did it ever get around about Long's part?"

"There was something about Glennie being caught when she was at Long's office. He hung himself in there, right?"

"Not sure. They believe Glennie hired it or she did it. But the courts couldn't prove it. No one believed Long would hang himself. He loved self. That was what he was all about." Jake paused. "I went to therapy. And he loved power and loved getting away with his secret life. He got off on it. It was never about us. He just liked the nasty and the sneaky. Long was a pitiful human being."

Bruce noted Jake's sunk shoulder, "Evil is a force as strong as good. Let it go, Jake. Focus on the good. Push the evil down and when you feel it risin' up think hard. Concentrate on living right, being good and trying to get to Heaven." Bruce preached like he'd thought about that very thing time and time again. "Think about Exilee. She has a gracious spirit. The way you talk about her I don't believe she's even human. And you talk about her all the time, in every phone call. And to tell you the truth, I'm jealous. She took my place and I want it back."

"Exilee didn't even know who it was bleeding all over the place when she first found me. And even after she did she saved my life. We've talked about Providence, fate and the unbeliever's luck theory. No one who knows about our history believes she and Ken just happened to be trail riding in the same spot I was in the Uhwarrie Mountains, all set to bleed to death, or that Misun found me first."

"Who now?"

"The wonder pony. He's a handful. He's mine now, but still lives in the lot with Choctaw, Exilee's horse. Can't separate them."

"Ahw, I remember now. There was something about that pony in the paper. You and animals have this bond."

"That's right. So does Exilee. And when the pony got near me and I grabbed its leg I could read it and her and somehow. I knew she was going to save me if I could manage the words. She'll do it to you, too."

"Do what?"

"Get in your head. You won't realize it either. She's just like that. Reads people and loves 'em anyway. Just look at what she did when she did realize it was me about to die, she still saved me. I believe. I really do, that God took us both to Uhwarrie's woods that day, to find each other. And she does, too. We talk about it. Exilee says without the experience she wouldn't know how to forgive, how to reach out and put others first. I don't believe it's in our nature. I think we're all just looking out for ourselves, trying to survive. Exilee struggled all her life, being mixed, in the South and without a mother and with a mean ass dad. She's had a rough one. Makes me think that we were put together because she would be able to understand. Ya know what I mean?"

Bruce smiled at him and directed his attention back to the road.

"After she saved me, she says, that's when she knew why she was created. She says that all her ancestors' knowledge was called on that day, African American, Cherokee, the Croatans, the English settlers, she says they're her Lum blood, and even her White dad's German blood. She called it psychohistory."

Bruce cleared his throat. "That's something man, to hear you talking like that."

"Like what?"

"Like Lumbee Indians. You have a big spirit. Exilee can call it what she wants. We'd say she has an old spirit." He waved his arms up and down at Jake like he was getting a fire to spark. "You came into her life to take her sister's place."

"That's awesome, man. I think about that, too."

Bruce's mouth tightened as his face plumped up red. "I love you, Jake. You're my brother. Don't ever forget that." He quickly turned away and looked out the open window.

"I love you too, brother. Hey, that's why we spent our childhood turning Muscadines." Jake's shiny smile was so large it filled the dark gaps between them.

"I want you to be a partner, a real one with a monthly deposit."

"That'd be great. But I don't have time, the farm, sometimes tour guide and the dogs. I spend two to four hours a day working dogs for police training. That's where I make money."

"You're joshin' me, right? I have a fat wad ready to share with you and set you up for easy street and you're gonna tell me no?"

"What about the dogs? I really want to work with dogs."

"We'll see what happens down the road. You'll want on once I get the store front up and music and wine flowing. You'll change your mind."

"I don't know, Bruce."

"Oh, tell me, man, what happened to Glennie's money? I know she had it. A picture of her mansion was in the paper."

"Lawyers in the civil suit, Exilee got some and an account was set up for me."

"Oh, that's it. Well, how much?"

"A full hundred thousand." Jake beamed. "At first, I thought I'd run away and go to vet college in the Midwest. But now I've got other interests."

"Robin."

"I want a normal life. That money could set us up with a nice spread. The money's safe until then. Letting it grow. It'll be good for something sooner or later."

"It doesn't make up for it, huh? An attack like that, it'll haunt you forever." Bruce's full lips pouted like a child's.

And Jake read his forlorn look. Without skipping a beat, Jake silenced the radio. "Tell me the truth, about that day, I mean, have you ever talked to anyone about that beating you took? I mean professionally?" Jake's soft words were softly sliced.

"No. Uh, what's the use of that? They'd just try to label me. Right? Give me medication to deal with it. I don't need that." Bruce's eyes darted from the road to the sky to his lap while his fingertips rubbed together like he was sanding off his prints, hard enough to hear. "What doesn't kill you makes you stronger."

"You're the strongest man, and kid, I've ever known. That's for sure. But what you said about the attack haunting me. You said that like you relate." Jake checked Bruce's profile. "Because I think you do."

Clearly annoyed, Bruce's nostrils flared. "In a way, yea. But it's 'cause I don't want to forget. No one's gonna get me again. Not ever." His jaw jutted like a bulldog's. "I won't play victim."

His crass words hushed Jake and they each took turns changing the radio like they couldn't get the music to block out the memories.

Five year old Jake had walked the wood's narrow path between their houses like he'd always done, but only different that day because he didn't have a grown up to watch over him. His parents had decided he was responsible enough to go on his own. He had gone over to play, but stopped cold. Blood trickled from Bruce's cuts, like ticks burst when you stomp 'em; fast little splatters. Blood was smeared across Bruce's hands from trying to protect his bare legs and back. Blood even colored his blonde curls and cheeks like an ice cream cone drizzled with strawberry swirl and then thrown out a vehicle's window, abandoned, alongside a dusty dirt road.

Between thrashings and cussings Bruce had carefully kept watch on Jake who hid just inside the timberline. And Miss Scarlet, the German Shepherd, had sprung up growling from the clearing on the other side of the timberline and made her way to Jake in silence like a grunt on the front line ready to defend and protect when Old Man Black's terrifying voice warned of more impending blows so Jake pulled her up close.

Bruce began to methodically rest his arms down at his sides as everything seemed to move in slow motion. Even Old Man Black, vicious, still wild drunk from the night before, streaking Bruce with the switch and name calling so sorry in the world nothing could ever take it back, moved across time like drips from a leaky faucet. "Youse a Lum. Youse a Lum. Youse never gonna be more than a loggin' likker Lum! Say it, boy! Say it!" And when Bruce refused, "You Momma's boy, you fairy tale prince, you slimy little shit! Say it! Youse a Lum!" With Old Man Black's characteristic gentle Lumbee voice long gone from a lifetime of chain smoking, the nasty names crashed over the child. He pulled Bruce's arm up over his head, jerking him off the ground as the switch cut through the air in jet fast cuts at Bruce's fair legs. And Jake covered his mouth so he wouldn't scream while Bruce gasped for breath.

Jake was just on the verge of running home for help when Bruce's dad finally flung the switch to the ground. Old Man Black lit a cigarette and blew a hot suck of smoke right into Bruce's little face, but the brave young boy didn't flinch. Old Man Black jumped in his rattletrap pick up. Slammed the door and with full Lumbee headiness ordered, "Gyet that grass mowed for dark or you'll know all de sorry in the world cross da rest a yer hide." His yellow teeth filled his face like a nasty cheap circus clown's entering the Gates of Hell as his truck spit out a dash of hot oil.

Jake took a deep breath as he relived that day while Bruce wiped his wet palms across his tight thighs and glared out the window. It doesn't seem that long ago. But even with his mouth gapped open Jake held in his confession. The confession he had kept for over twenty five years, the confession that he'd secretly wished he'd sicced the snarling dog on Bruce's dad, let him rip his leg off and pull him off Bruce before he'd been so tore up, damaged, ruint.

Instead sweet young Jake had hushed Miss Scarlet's whining with kind words as she tucked her muzzle under his arm and she faithfully waited. He stroked her smooth ears. Then when the truck was out of sight Jake went to Bruce, but Miss Scarlet didn't. Poor Miss Scarlet, Jake had warned her, "Go home." And Bruce had hated her ever since.

Little Bruce's white underwear was peed yellow and dirty brown from where the wobbly legged five year old fell to the ground unable to balance with his jeans shackled at his ankles. But what stood out most of all was the bright blood trickled lines. His quiet tears dried instantly when Jake touched his shoulder. Jake had to zip him up. Had to work the metal button into the hole. Bruce's hands hung at his sides. Bruce was quivering, shaking. Streaked from tears, red from blood, white in shock. His gray eyes locked. Bruce just stood still, practically lifeless, in a catatonic state for the longest time while Jake spoke kindly and softly, like a Christian does for ailing kin.

Jake told him that they were going to be okay now. Told him that he could come spend the night and his mom would make beef stroganoff and they'd eat cookies in bed. But Bruce only blinked. A few minutes later Bruce walked over to the garden hose and wet his jeans down, gritting his teeth to bear the pain. When Jake pointed to Bruce's head he held the hose over and the weight of the water flattened his curls into long strands. Jake mowed while Bruce wandered through the timberline till he discovered a jar of pure medicine as the moon's clock threatened and his mother's blood stained the kitchen. He got drunk and sick and stayed sick for three days, long enough for the cuts to scab over good.

At his mother's funeral, Bruce was rigid against the hugs and polite words of his mother's church people. Bruce blamed them. His mother would have normally been at women's circle meeting that day his dad had come home mean and mad after losing big on card night. But she didn't have a clean dress and didn't have any offering. The power'd been cut off for weeks. Bruce said not one of those church ladies had been by to see her. Several years later when Jake had said, "No one gets that hurt from falling off a step stool," Bruce looked like he could've stomped a feral bull into a hamburger patty, but he never said a word.

Bruce still looked like he could stomp a feral bull into a hamburger patty, so Jake licked his dry lips before bravely asking, "Do you think about her?"

Nearly alarmed, Bruce darted his chin about the truck's cab for a way out, steadily blinking.

"Your mom shouldn't a died that way. She was the most gentle person ever. It was so wrong."

"I don't talk about it."

"It's eatin' you up. You need to get it out."

"Can't change anything about it. Leave it alone." Bruce's leg jittered. He noticed and stopped. "It's not like your deal. You've got a scar you'll have to look at every day for the rest of your life."

"It's like a flag."

"How's that?" Bruce rolled his eyes.

"A victory over evil."

"Do you think you'll ever forgive Glennie?"

The question startled Jake. "Oh, Glennie has real regrets. After she was incarcerated a while she wanted me to come talk to her. But not yet." Jake fingered his scar, tracing it from his mouth around its circle up to his cheek while Bruce watched.

"Shape of a hoof print."

Jake smacked. "Yep. The slasher also cut a chunk of tongue off. They sewed it back on. Lots of speech therapy. That's why I sent the note that I wouldn't be calling for a while. Had a lisp. My taste isn't the same."

"One God knows and sees all. I believe that's why I was incarcerated. I would have killed the bastard. Slasher got it, Jake, bad. A he-she now. Can't hold his crap."

Fully aghast, "And what about Dan? Is it true Dan the Man is at the mental hospital? He really went crazy?"

"That's what they called it. Went to talking to himself, then yelling and trying to save food for his invisible friend."

"Really, an invisible friend, like a little mouse or maybe one of his cats, like a ghost cat, huh? He had way too many cats on his place, mean ones. Probably just all those years of drinkin'. It accumulates. Or maybe it's the Little People."

"Naw. Little People do good. A toten got him."

"A toten got him." Jake softly mulled it over. "How do you know? I mean, Bruce, I really believe your people's stories. They're like the Bible."

"No stories. It's just the way it is. You touch something with a jubious link, something that don't belong to you or someone leaving and their spirit jumps in, that's toten work. Sure as I'm in this truck taking in all this gorgeous land and talking to my best friend in the world, I am certain it was my old man who took up inside that murderer's head."

"Could be."

"Could be? Nothing. My old man hated me. He'd a been after me every minute making the rest of my days headiness, pure stinking mean. He chose to get revenge on Dan."

"You really think your own dad would've done that to you?"

"What? Don't you remember anything?" Bruce scowled. "He was jealous momma loved me and did for me. He wouldn't even let her read to me. Said I didn't need school smarts. He was gonna raise me to be a real Lum and make my way in the world like him, a shiner. I had to play dumb whenever I had words to say or he'd slap me or Mom or both of us. Called us wannabe brickhousers. Said we'd never leave the swamp."

Jake slowed down. "He was a son of a bitch all right. I hope he does spend eternity in Dan's head."

"He got in there at the funeral." Bruce stoically stated. "When he lifted him up out of the coffin and his head went back and everyone fainted. That's when he got in there. I know it 'cause I could feel my old man's spirit like a rabid black dog gnawing on my bones up to that very second. He made me pure ache all over from the moment he died out there on the job cutting logs. He was on me every single day up until the funeral. He barely let me sleep. And there's no way I believe Dan would ever confess to anything. He made him do it. Got in his head to make him confess and stayed. I know it." He seethed.

"Did you see his ghost?"

"Why?"

"You seem convinced, so sure."

"I saw something. Momma said I was born with the veil. Seen all kinds of haints in my childhood. Try to block things now."

"Damn, that's cool."

"Not so much." Bruce tapped his fingers and fidgeted with his seatbelt. "You know he took Dad's money roll and that that money roll first belonged to Dan?"

"No way?"

"Those two stole it from each other. They were a pair."

"A pair, all right."

"Dad would a' stole it back. I know. Wonder how long that went on?"

"The stealing from each other?" Bruce calculated. "Long as I can remember. But they'd still play poker. Recon it was their kind of bingo?"

"The stealing?"

"Yea."

"They liked it or they wouldn't 've kept playing. Only them, the ugliest puss and the meanest Lum."

"Oh, man, even with the new tooth and hair, yea. You know, I figured Dan must've got his hands on that roll, but never figured on him murdering his only real friend. 'Cause he didn't have anyone. I mean Dan had no one. Zilch. He looked up to Black. Everyone else was too afraid." Jake's eyes peeled back. "I remember the first time I saw him. It was that bad summer. Just a few weeks afterward and we were coming back from fishing at the small pond and had three bream. Remember?"

"Yea, he was just waking up. Bet he'd been sleeping there all night. Probably heard every word we'd said. Bet he didn't mess with us 'cause he knew who my daddy was." Bruce snapped his fingers. "And I bet he's wished a thousand times he was still napping on that pine straw bed 'cause he's paying now. They say his eyes roll around in his head 'till all the nurses can see is white and he screams bloody murder till they have to sedate him. His shirt stays wet from slobbering all over himself."

"That's gross. Who tells you about him?"

"Lum's stick together. One word, you name it, Lums'll do what it takes to make things right. Nurses from Beacon's mental unit treat some of the birds at Beacon Prison. Lot of 'em are Lum."

When Udda whines and noses his leg Jake abandons the manuscript and hurries to follow. As Udda leads the wooden floors of his small country home gently creak like a well worn flywheel. With his flashlight Jake checks the chalk mark near the basement door. Creeps down the hallway and aims on Miss Lucy's closed door and finds that chalk mark missing. Jake pets Udda's head and she leads him to the living room. Udda noses Jake's notebook and using a pen opens it to discover the string he trapped it with has been disturbed. He rubs her neck and returns to his bedroom with the string.

The clock illuminates eleven thirty so Jake turns off his reading light and rolls to his side. At twelve, after tossing and turning long enough to make him frustrated, he turns the light on to finish this one chapter. And Udda stays in wait just outside his open door.

"You have two families then," Jake smiled, "the Lums and mine."As Bruce's teeth shone his pronounced cheekbones puffed up so high you could pitch pennies off the edges so Jake went on. "I bet if you hadn't been in prison you would have hunted him down and cut him to pieces. Left him for the buzzards."

"For sure. A Lum or two on Dan and your slasher." Bruce's ears were tipped red. "And Glennie. How did a spoiled rich lady ever sink so low? Hiring a hit man for someone that's practically a kid is seriously low, cuz. She could've just sued her husband. Had all his money, the CD business, and humiliated him in the process."

"I'm not a kid. Look at me. I've filled out a lot. Don't act like you didn't notice." Jake reached up to adjust the rear view and in doing so tightened up so his veins protruded from his firm farm chiseled frame. When his tan line was exposed on his upper arm a blue vein threaded across like an outstretched kung fu fighter. "Exilee thinks Glennie lost it when she discovered her husband had homosexual tendencies. Then when Glennie found out she wasn't going to be Clan Mother and not in charge of Miss Ginger's 'Black Purse Papers' Glennie lost all control. Of course, Exilee and I becoming such good friends didn't help anything."

"You know about Clan Mothers?"

"I live next door to her."

Bruce was totally taken aback. "How's that?"

"Really, I'm surrounded. David's wife, Miss Sarah is full Cherokee. She was in the room when Ginger handed it over to Exilee."

"Handed it over?"

"The black purse, the papers, it was in the newspaper." Jake paused, but Bruce continued the perplexed stare. "Exilee and Glennie had a nanny growing up, Miss Ginger. Exilee grew up trying to figure out who she was all the time, racially and socially. That's what makes this so ironic. Their mother was half Cherokee, half Black. They call their dad an Irish mutt. Their mom died early that's why they had the nanny. But before she died she taught them a few Cherokee beliefs, one was about the woman being wise and the leader of the family. The nanny didn't tell anyone back then what all she knew. Ginger looks like a regular little ol' Black lady. But she was really like their mother, half and half. Anyway, Ginger's carried this family secret around with her all her life. Ginger spent her life researching the genealogy of slave children sent to freedom, without their parents, through the Underground Railroad. There's a cemetery next door to my house. Most of the graves are empty. The babies sent to freedom had fake funerals. Ginger and her sister kept the secret all their lives. Her sister held the slips of paper with the children's name, some without last names even, the parent's names and who they belonged to at the time. The secret slips were kept in their King James Bibles. If you remember, in school we were taught there's no written history of the Underground Railroad as it was occurring. It was too risky. But there is. Our little nanny, Ginger, carried it around with her wherever she went. It is the only written history recorded as it occurred. Her great, great grandmother wrote it, in broken English and Cherokee. It leads all the way back to Croatans taking in the English off the coast. How they slaved some and married some and how they turned Christian. Ginger kept it in a big black purse, the kind you see old women with, like an old timey doctor's bag. The woman who wrote down the history was Onacona." Jake exhaled.

"Have those papers been checked out, yet? Verified by the State?" Bruce asked.

"Oh, yea, historians from all over came and Exilee and Miss Ginger went up to State and to South Carolina and met with the Lumbee Tribe and had names and dates checked and everything. It's real. That's where we're going, to live on the Underground Railroad. Makes ya think about totens, huh?" Jake smiled.

"I'll say," Bruce rubbed the top of his head. "Gives me chills, man. This is awesome. You know what this is, don't you? This is a link to the proof."

"Could be. First time I heard it I thought about you and that night we had our last pizza and you got so fired up about being from The Lost Colony. Wouldn't that be something if you really could say your proof is in the bag?"

Bruce wiped his tongue over his dried out lips and slapped his palms together. "The proof is in the bag! Like that?"

"Just like that."

"Might be more proof than you realize. And my Buddyrow picks me up and takes me to it." Bruce cocked his head to the side. "But Onacona is a man's name. You said it was a woman."

"Well that's what I was told, a she."

"Maybe she was the only child. Sometimes they'd do that to get more respect."

"Don't tell Robin."

"Huh?" Bruce's head popped up.

"Robin named the German Shepherd I just gave her Onacona. They're just alike.

Onacona is loud, showy and demands attention. Onacona's locked up in a kennel with the others during operating hours. She whines this sharp whistling call at tourists. It's like she's telling them to come talk sweet stuff to her."

Bruce grinned and nodded. "Sounds like dog and owner are a lot alike."

"When Robin howls it drives Onacona wild."

"Exilee's wedding made headlines." Bruce stares out the window. "The press fed off that Underground Railroad and mixed blood theme. It's a hot topic. At the prison, we got papers from all over the state and it was in all of 'em. Exilee married the Crowson's only son. Right?"

"Ken, yea. He's great. Ken used to teach middle school. His dad needed more help. He's not rickety, but he's slower. And he always wanted Ken to take up the farm. It's all worked out. I wanted more time with the dogs and he wanted more time with his son. Ken always wanted to work the farm. But there hasn't been money in it for years. His dad's been selling cows and doing pony rides. Sells some. Exilee and I train them together. Oh, and I've got my own horse now. But I rode a pony to begin with. He follows us like a dog. Exilee found him for me. We checked out a lot of horses. But after riding her Walker, nothing else would do."

"What's a Walker?"

"A smooth gaited horse. I have a mix like Exilee, half Tennesse Walker, half Appaloosa. They're smart, always trying to figure out how to do what they want, like take hay from ponies. My horse and Misun, the pony, are a team. Exilee says that it used to be her horse, Choctaw and Misun. But she says Choctaw grew up. Mine is only five. Hers is seventeen. Misun and Pebbles break out and jump the pony fence."

"Pebbles? For real, you ride a horse named Pebbles?"

"Belonged to a little girl. It comes to Pebbles so Pebbles it is. Looks like a handful of pebbles were thrown up over his back. And his face is dotted, too. He's a darlin'."

With his elbow bent, Bruce's limp wrist twisted over his lap. "Only you, Jake." Bruce's voice was tenor and ridiculous.

"I'm not queer anymore. I never was," Jake adamantly fumed.

"Sorry. I shouldn't have said it that way. Prison life messes with you."

With taut brows, Jake asked, "Did you get in trouble, get, you know, jacked?"

Bruce's chin darted up to the sky and without a grunt, sigh or word, looked back down at Jake with his steel grays, locked on for one second and then back to the highway's charming rural landscape.

"My roommate, Miss Ginger, is gonna be at the party tonight. You'll love her. She's like everybody's grandma. Her fiancé is coming, too. They stayed single all their lives and they're finally talking about tying the knot. Did I tell you Exilee's dad reunited them?"

"Yea, believe you did. That's something. I've never met a real life hero." Bruce popped the seat with his full hand. "How's your mom?"

"She's stable now, still medicated. There was one incident. She and Mrs. Long had it out in the grocery. Mom thinks she knew and should have told her. It was bad. Mom was throwing boxes of cereal at her. Mrs. Long just stood there and let the boxes ricochet off her. One of the bag boys told me. Mom sees a psychologist. Dad messed up everybody."

"Prisoners hate child abusers. Most of 'em have had it in some form or another. They get 'em."

Jake stiffened. "Did you ever hear anything about Dad?"

"No." Bruce licked his lips and turned away.

"Oh. I'm sure he's been beat significantly."

When Bruce nodded his entire upper body rocked.

"Mom doesn't talk about it. In fact, she doesn't do much of anything. I've asked her if she thinks she's up to church, that I'll take her when she's ready. But she dismisses it."

"That's serious."

"She was blinking erratically for a while, a nervous tick. I couldn't stand to look at her, like she couldn't stand to look at me, just different reasons. But the psychologist got her to quit."

"The body tells on us. Watch people. They tell on themselves. I read about that, too. There wasn't much else to do in prison. Read every book on business. Every book on wine. Every book on Native American History. You can ask me about engine repair, raisin' bees, raisin' vegetables, children, especially grapes. And there were tons of books circulating on sex, even homosexuality."

"It's a choice." Jake shrugged.

"Sure?"

"Sure."

"A lot of fags sound like women, act like 'em, even look like a woman. Can't a person be born that way?" Bruce pushed.

"No. I don't believe that. It's a choice, like drugs, lying, meanness, anything. People get conditioned. God didn't put peters on men and a place to put 'em in women for nothing. We're supposed to be dads and leaders. Who's gonna line up and follow a fag in drag?"

"Other ones," Bruce quipped and they both laughed.

"See a lot of that in prison?"

"Fraid so. I'd like to forget it. Can you make yourself forget things?"

They were both looking straight ahead as Jake slowed the truck onto the dirt road where the Crowson's property begins and Bruce belted out, "Good-gooboly-goo," as the tires crunched against the gritty gravel road. Yellow ribbon streamed from the wooden fence line and cars filled the Crowson's drive. "They put up a lot of ribbon for you, Buddyrow."

"Holy Moly," Bruce checked out the Crowson's pristine spread and when a million little butterflies tickled his head wiped them away.

"Indeed. This is blessed land, Bruce."

"Like a picture. Why didn't we ever cruise through here?"

"Cause runners don't cruise."

Bruce tilted his head back and guffawed. "That's right."

Calves were jumping and butting heads. And horses neighed and ran to the barn as Jake pointed out Miss Sarah and David Crowson's house, the main one, then Ken and Exilee's and then his. "Biscuits and gravy Sunday mornings over at the big house. Then Robin and I go to church, same one as Miss Sarah and David. We both believe in raising children in church. It doesn't matter what kind. And I'm okay that she wants to keep up with her Cherokee beliefs. They're a lot alike, Christians and Cherokees."

Bruce rolled his eyes. "Already talking children?"

"Dating is a step in finding a life mate. And you know Robin. She likes things her way and has some strong opinions. Better we get it all out front." Jake's diplomatic response left Bruce with a cold expression.

"Well, since you're being up front about it all. Know that I'm ready to handle her if you can't."

"I pick my battles and I know how to compromise and she loves me. She's told me so."

"When did she say that? When you gave her the dog?" Bruce's coy response made Jake slow down even more when they passed the dog kennel. As Jake's truck nears Onacona barked with the other three he had in training. The runs are adjacent to the shed which once housed pigs, set about three acres from the houses. It has cement floors and sturdy walls. But to be German Shepherd proof he had to use heavy duty galvanized dog fence wire. It was four hundred dollars for a two hundred foot roll. Then the entire kennel had to be tourist proof for insurance purposes. Jake also had a no trespassing sign made in large letters. "Do not feed dogs humans." Bruce snorted at the sign as they passed. "Humans, huh? Do Wart and Fisk qualify?"

Jake raised his eyebrows at the suggestion. "One of those dogs is for the Feds in Raleigh. The other two are gonna be sniffers for Harnett. Something happens to any of them and there'll be big trouble."

Bruce scanned over the farm. "I love it. This place is all the fine in the world, Jake. The way the three housen face off, it's like an old plantation."

"It is." Jake pointed through the row of barns and sheds on out to the field. "MacGregor's Crest is over there. We put up a post and beam over it. Used rough cut lumber, wide floor boards and have big lit up shadowboxes with Underground Railroad information hanging on the walls. There's a heavy glass panel over the opening in the ground so you can watch as the other tourists leave the underground passage out in the field. The tours begin in the basement of our house."

"Say that again."

"The tours begin in the basement."

"How does that work while you're living there?"

"There're two doors to the basement. The inside door near the laundry room is kept locked. We don't think anyone would do something stupid. But you never know. The other is the outside door. The basement had sliding glass doors that went to the patio. Exilee made the patio years ago. Now it has primitive looking wood doors. The entire basement was made to look old. We even painted the cement floor to look like the clay in the passage. There's a picture map for children and one for adults and there's some life size cutouts of people dressed in vintage eighteen hundred's clothing. That's one good thing Glennie did."

As soon as Jake pulled in under the unattached carport Bruce hurried around to the front yard and absorbed the view. The Crowson's house was a larger version of Jake's place and the one squared up next to it. And they were surrounded with vintage farm.

"Glennie made the cutouts?' Bruce asked as Jake stretched out next to him.

"She sent Exilee pencil sketches from prison. She taped 'em together and they laid out perfect like those standup movie star cutouts in the theatres. Exilee had a print shop transfer the sketches. Glennie used prisoners for models. Real hauntin' faces."

"I know the kind." Bruce rolled his lips like he was working out a sour taste. "Do you think she'll recover? Get out and be rehabilitated?"

"No. She had temporary insanity when she was caught poisoning the horses and trying to kill anyone in her path with those traps and the shears. She nailed the law and her dad with those things. Attempted murder. She got forty years."

Bruce whistled. "Yea, that was in the papers. Slipped my mind. She had a pit dug. Wonder who that was for?"

Jake stood statuesque. "For me. When I trail ride I usually stop right at that area where the pit was discovered. The sunlight gets in there. Makes a good napping spot." Bruce questioned him on whom and Jake clamped his lips and then spit it out, "Illegal Mexicans. She hired them to build and set the traps."

"Glad it's over."

"Yea. No dreams, nothin' now." Jake lightly punched Bruce's arm. "Hey, don't talk about it too much. I'll start dreaming again. She was freakin' mad, ya know. But she was normal as you and me the day she hired that slasher. Glennie's as recovered as she'll ever get." Jake unlocked the door and held it open for Bruce. "Welcome home, Buddyrow."

"Cuz." Bruce entered like a child discovering a candy store. "I love your place. It even smells country. Smell. Smell the walls." Bruce was close to hyperventilating as he toured around. "Country vittles and a granny's dusting powders, tonic and dog." If Bruce had had a tail it would've wagged.

"Onacona lives in here, too, when I'm here. When I've got one in training it has a time period for indoor behavior and discipline training. You can keep your door closed."

"Hey, I'm not complaining. I love it. Even dog smells don't bother me." Bruce wiped his palms over the furniture, outlined the lamp and went over the top of the kitchen table with his open hands. "It's amazing what you miss. The little things, the sounds of the birds outside. Love the open windows. The wind, smells of normal life, not two thousand people crammed into one cement hole." Bruce opened the refrigerator and looked inside. He opened the stove, the cabinets under the sink, the cabinets over the coffee pot. "I haven't seen a normal kitchen in years. I might be in here a while, do all the cooking till the new wears off. That okay?"

"Good with me. Do anything you want." Jake's orders poked Bruce like a hit in the chest.

Bruce held onto the back of the kitchen chair and tried to hold back the raw emotions as his face twisted. "Anything I want. Sorry," he added when Jake reflected his angst. "It's just so good here, so good to be out. I couldn't even sit without permission."

"You can be yourself with me, Bruce. I know who you are." Jake's soft words pushed out everything else till it was just the two men.

"Who?" Bruce's face was so distorted. "Who am I? The son of a con, a Lum who got caught selling shine? I'm a loser. An ex con, a man who served time, that's all people see." He took the statement out of his pocket and shook the crap out of it up at ceiling. "Even with money that's all they'll see."

"Not your friends, not mine either. You're a hero, especially to me. Bruce, don't you know that?"

"I don't have any friends. Just you. Everyone else just worked for me." He ripped paper towel from the roll next to the sink and blew his nose. "How am I your hero? Tell me that one."

"You won your war with your dad." Jake's nostrils trumpeted like he'd just declared a country's victory then deflated to normal as the two men lamented.

Bruce acknowledged Jake's statement with a bit upper lip and admired the cozy kitchen and dinning room that adjoined the small living area. Everything was brown and orange except the yellow curtains that hang tied back with strawberry print ribbon above the kitchen sink. Even the worn throw pillows were orange. But a warm orange, the kind that comes from years of use. There was one picture on the wall. It had a black frame. But the picture was brown, too, a tired early eighteen hundred's sketch of cowboys taking saddles off their horses in front of a barn with a nearby two story clapboard house. A young child played in the dirt yard with a stick as an attentive chicken cocked his head at him. Holstein cows were in a side lot. In the kitchen window a woman wearing pants and oversized shirt with long locks escaping a haggard bun told of the drudgery as her hand swept over her brow. The scene held Bruce like he was trying to plant himself there, in that time, when life seemed simple.

"He beat you. Your old man was a monster, the worst kind. And he dragged you into the dirt with him with that church. God hates that kind of thing. But you won, Bruce. You're smart. You even educated yourself. That's real ingenuity, took a lot of self discipline. Your dad didn't have that. He didn't have nothing on you. And now you're going to have it all and I believe that's God's reward because you're going legit. You're going to be rich and famous. Remember, you're going to put Cameron back on the map. That's who you are, Bruce Black."

With his face still planted in the picture, Bruce inhaled the picturesque scene and Jake's speech just as it was presented, with deep pure honesty and his shoulders dropped. "Thanks, but that's only how you see me." Jake lowered his head as Bruce neared. "What do you have to drink?"

"Sweet tea, Miss Ginger sees to that. The water's good, too. Well water from right out there." Jake showed him the well house through the open kitchen window. "I keep a jug in the fridge."

Bruce opened the cabinet above the sink and commented on his glass collection. Chose a blue glass and poured the cool water from the fridge and sipped and savored it. "Pure. No after taste." He poured another and enjoyed the cool water with his eyes closed then held the glass to his chest. "Ahh. It's amazing what you miss. I feel silly. You want some?"

"Sure. Pour me a glass." After the cool water Jake excused himself to the bathroom.

"Hey, can I take a whiz off the back steps?"

"Just make sure no one's around."

Bruce searched for a good spot through the screened back door and then gleefully stepped off the back porch. There was no one below the elevated steps at the entrance to the Underground Railroad, so he went down the thirteen steps to the grass. He bent over and ran his hands over the blades then briskly rubbed it. Pulled up a handful and sucked in the crisp earthy scent. He briskly approached the old pine trees, a pristine bunch, some so old their tops were twisted with curly limbs and gnarls. Pulled down a limb and sucked in its sweet pine tar perfume and rans his hands over the trunk's rough bark and flaked off a chunk. Crumbled it and marched through the thick sand grass. Over a thick blanket of pine straw and maneuvered through the scattered thorn bushes and willowy mimosas flocked in fluffy pink. He leaned his head back and inhaled the fresh hot summer pine thicket's disturbed floras. Then with full sunshine in his face he unzipped near a significant prickly pear outcrop.

The indigenous cactus was one that Lums knew as edible, medicinal, as a base for likker, and used its leaves' pectin as a binder in plaster. Prickly pear cactus was a symbol of transformation and strength to Native Americans. The outcrops' yellow flowers and red fruit also attracted bees and the yellow jackets which busily hummed near Bruce's knees.

Bruce zipped back up immediately, when less than fifty feet away through the old growth Longleaf Pines, Robin's hair caught the sun like black silk and glimmered as it swayed in cadence with her song and horse's rhythm. And even though all the words were not clear the ones that counted were. Still as a fox on a quail, Bruce went unnoticed, until Jake let the screen door slam. Robin reined in her horse and smiled. Bruce appeared trapped in the blooming prickly pears. She urged her mount forward as Bruce pulled up a bloom and offered it. "It's yellow," softly, but testosterone driven, his symbolic gesture reddened her cheeks as Jake stepped off the back porch.

"Like a ribbon." Robin backed up her mount a couple of feet away.

And Bruce emerged from the prickly outcrop. "Should I hold it between my teeth?" He dared her as he tapped his front teeth together. "There aren't any big oaks."

Jake's lengthy steps depicted a soldier on ploy. "Did you say oaks? There's some small ones." Jake pointed. But neither Bruce nor Robin looked.

Bruce folded the slick yellow bloom down into his palm and turned to Jake. "Is it okay if I take a shower, Buddyrow? I'm all hot and sticky now."

With his hand gripping Robin's calf, Jake caught his breath. "Ya don't have to ask. This is your home long as you need it. You're free to come and go as you please."

"Thanks," Bruce humbly replied. "Good to see you, Robin."

"You, too. See ya later. Mrs. Crowson and Exilee've been cooking all day." Robin's head was tilted so far her long hair tickled her mount's side and as the gelding vigorously twitched her deeply cut tee shirt deepened her valley as the mountains quaked.

"Sure I'll pleasure it, ma'am." Bruce abandoned the couple with a quick wave as he hurried back. Once there, he unfolded his other palm and held up the slick yellow bloom over his hot face sucking in all his dreams of his sweet dear Robin.

Chapter 7

Irony Under the Twinkling Weeping Willow

Miss Lucy went to work on schedule without a morning coffee, water, or hello between her and Jake as he slept on and on until Ken bangs on his window. "Hey, city slicker. Get up." Udda whines and Jake busily sweeps his hand past her busy nose to stroke her as Ken sings. "Get up. Get up. The sun is up. The bird is on the wing. No it's not you crazy thing. The wing is on the bird." And Jake sits up. Throws his pillow at the window and looks around for something else to throw as Ken smiles through the curtain's slit. "Open the door, busy boy."

Ken follows him to the kitchen and repeatedly taps the counter. "It's too early," Jake groans then chugs a glass of sweet tea.

"Tell me that's Robin's car and I'll quit." Ken's clownish grin wears on Jake like a spider up his arm and he swings. "Damn it, it's a old lady from the library. She's helping me get Bruce's people together."

"How's that? She Lum?"

"No," he pours another glass and drinks half wiping cold slobber across his forearm. "I mean I'm telling her my story about growing up with Bruce. I'm going to use it to flush out the thief or thieves and try to get their group to see the truth and stop with the Tribe quest. Do you know what I'm saying? It's too early for me to be talking much less explain."

Ken's half grin and loose meandering walk to the front door put Jake on guard. He slaps the glass down on the counter. "Don't start, Ken Crowson. It's too damn early. I'm serious now."

"A librarian? They're those quiet types, dangerous." And Ken rushes out the door. "Don't primp on account of us, Jakeypoo."

"Us?" Jake grimaces out the screen door. "Hey, Exilee." He folds his arms over his nipples. "Be there shortly."

Jake manipulates his routine chores to avoid Ken and Exilee. And whenever Ken nears

Jake shouts, "I got it," taking the bulk of the chores like he holds the heavy thoughts. But when the screen porch door slams several times Jake does not linger behind. Miss Sarah and Exilee bring out red cabbage slaw, green beans and fried chicken with fresh sliced peaches on the side.

Jake has his napkin on his lap first. "Man, now that is a spread. You ladies are angels. My belly is rubbing a hole straight through to my backbone." Miss Sarah asks David to say a short prayer and as soon as he is done Jake chows like he'd been hemmed up in a dry well. Ken pours Jake another glass of tea. "Wanna tell Daddy about your new girl?" Jake places his bowl of peach slices on his empty plate. "You tell 'em." And by the time he sucks down the last slice Ken's silliness is forgiven.

"She's a suspect." Jake rises and takes the binoculars hanging from the slanted nail and steps to the screened in porch's door and looks through. He scans from his house to the cemetery to Ken's. "Scarecrow and Lilly helped. Got wire on her phone and background. I mean background. She's a old country gal like this town has never known." Jake places a gentle hand on David's shoulder and bends over face to face. "You ever heard tale of a Prickenwrath from England?"

David works his palms together and when he cocks his head down to the left his long curly ear hairs twitch like the wisps of white covering his slick white head. He drawls out the napkin tucked in his overalls and wipes his hands clean.

"It's on the deeds. Old land grants have Prickenwrath as owner all over the Southeast." Like Jake jerked the chain on the fan chills whiz across the porch. "Crow thinks she came here originally to do land research."

"Can't be," Ken plants his back against his chair.

"The old land grants, you got 'em here?" Jake spreads his open hand out toward the living areas. "And where's Luke and Miss Ginger? There's no tours till after one, right?"

"They're at your house by now. Well, in the Underground's office. Tomorrow there's a private tour. Some bigwig up in Raleigh and his special group. So Luke is helping her clean up after the second graders. Popsicle sticks, gum, you name it. It's on the floor and since he's closest and will take a penny for each piece he got the job." Exilee lightheartedly laughs as Miss Sarah returns with a large clear plastic encased envelope. "You know Miss Ginger isn't gonna stop to eat and risk him gettin' sleepy."

"Smart lady," Ken kisses at Exilee and she leans over and gives him a nice one.

The hearty envelope is ecru and browned at the edges with exaggeratedly looped handwriting spelling out Colonial Land Office Patent, 1629. Further down in fine filigree is the verification, Lord Henry Prickenwrath. David taps over the Prickenwrath name like he was smashing a spider. "We were the planters. He paid for us to come here and improve the settlement and he got the land. But before it was all done he made some bad errors and was hung. That's how I heard it. His own people came over here and saw about it themselves."

"So how did we get the land?" Ken's bright blue eyes sharpen.

"Marriage. His daughter and one of my uncles. Have to look at those genie papers to tell ya 'xactly which." David chews at the inside of his mouth and then stirs up Jake. "Hey, she mention any a this?"

"No. All new."

Miss Sarah urges David to share Lord Prickenwrath's errors. And when he waves her off she hisses, "Don't try that with me."

"It'll just put more oil on the rag," he shakes out his worn cloth napkin over the tabletop.

"The truth'll do that," Miss Sarah snatches his napkin and pushes it in her apron's smart pocket. Her apron is blue with little white checks and red birds like North Carolina's Cardinals flying from the hem upwards. Her sleek black hair is braided down her back and her Cherokee cheeks are bright red with fury.

"What Dad? We're all grown ups here. Go ahead."

David peers down the pasture like something caught his eye and stays there. "Lord Prickenwrath burned a house down. The English sent their army people over to talk to him when word got to England that he'd taken up with Indians and had children and sent his white wife to a city up in Virginia. The English were gonna take his land if he didn't send his children away and live proper with his white wife. Prickenwrath said he'd meet these people at that house and give over his children." David's chin quivers. "They say the army men cried. It was horrible. The children were half out of the windows and he ran 'em back in with gunshot. They hung Prickenwrath right there." David points at the pasture down by MacGregor's Crest where they plan to dig the well. "Seems like history's a little ripple in the river. Just keeps on. Wind blows. That doesn't change. Water beats down the rocks. That doesn't change." He looks up at Jake and sniffles. "Maybe your book'll change it, Jake." As David grasps Jake's hand he hugs the aged wise man like a teddy bear.

"I wanna read that manuscript." Exilee's back is cocked like a rifle. "Is it here?"

"Yea, and a copy at the office."

"You are concerned," Miss Sarah takes the peach bowl and asks if anyone needs more. When no one responds she clears some dishes and says she wants to read it, too and to invite Miss Lucy for dinner. "I need to see how Miss Ginger and her new man are doing. Hope they don't have plans." After she's in the kitchen she yells, "Put down that chicken leg, David and no, you don't need a cookie." She sniffs, "Seven. I'm making," her sweet voice tears away into sniffling silence.

David lists off several chores including a trip to town for Exilee and tells Jake, "First, I wanna look at your book. That okay?"

"Sure," then at the steps Jake asks, "What is it you're looking for? Something worries you about her having my information. I mean, what could she do to you?"

"Jake, it's not just me. Don't you know you're one of us now?"

David Crowson reads all afternoon. The first hour in the hard chair at the table on the screened in porch. The second in the living room recliner. Then back to the screened in porch in the hard chair, but with a pillow on Chapter 7, Irony Under the Twinkling Weeping Willow.

The party was held on the Crowson's big screened in porch overlooking the pastures that lead to the creek in the dark timberline. By seven thirty the summer sun eased down behind the timberline and what was left of the bright Carolina blue day burned out in the thick treetops smeared in scarlet. Surreal, like a painting on the ceiling of one of those holy churches, Bruce breathed it in with a heavy dose of fresh farm air heavy with pony. Curious ponies twisted their heads out the fence boards to greet him from the nearby lot while those in stalls nickered and neighed, "Hello."

"Been a while since you've seen one of those, huh?" Jake startled him. "You've got a lot to look forward to. In the morning we have coffee on the back porch and watch the horses run up to the barn. Ken's geldings do it every day like clock work. There's two red headed cockaded woodpeckers, a hawk and blue birds that get all stirred up when they leave the timber. Then the purple martins when the horses run in the barn." As Bruce stretched to see down into the timberline Jake shook his head. "Ken's geldings are in the barn by now. Put 'em up at night since Onacona was poisoned."

"Oh."

"Look, rabbits." The two rabbits circled and leapt over one another. "We've seen red pheasants strutting around doing mating rituals and turkeys leading their chicks, always lots a' rabbits, and foxes playing. Not at the same time. There's binoculars on the porch. You can have first debs on 'em in the morning. Never know what we'll spot."

"Love it. Need to overdose on this ta get rid of all the, all the other." Bruce's full lips pouted with the kind of sweetness a child has when a rabbit gets real close for the first time and discovers the innocence and wonderment of creation.

"You might wanna build your mansion next door to the Crowson's." Jake teased.

"He won't want me that close. I'll visit though."

"Give these people a chance, Bruce."

"I am." Bruce scoffed. "Lums can be real charmers."

"Good. Now chill."

"Chill? Better catch up or you'll just be eatin' my dust, Buddyrow." When Bruce exaggeratedly waved for him a bawling bull jerked him to a stop. "Gawd, he sounded like he was right behind me."

Jake busted a lung. "He's in your back pocket. Just passed his lot. He's on the other side of that shed."

"Is he sick?"

"Lovesick. We call him Two Tails." Jake caught up. "We'll feed him in the morning." Only a few steps from the screened in porch a waft of Brunswick stew, cornbread and sweet pies lured them like a fisherman's jitterbug cast out across a still water teasing with its soft easy chatter.

"Two Tails, huh?"

Jake opened the screen door and Bruce stepped up. Already seated around the small table and leaning back in the rockers on the far side nearest the weeping willow out in the back yard were Miss Ginger, Exilee, Ken and both Magee boys with their parents. They all exchanged quick hellos. The boys were eighteen and twenty something, sat tall and handsomely, too. The Magee family looked like kin of Sidney Poitier, that famous perty Black and Native American Indian man who took on timely acting jobs pertaining to racial injustices during the nineteen fifties and sixties and won himself an Oscar, like he was born to do just that very thing.

The Magee family is like that, too, descendants of the very Eber Magee who's foot is buried in the Underground Railroad. They own the property on the other side of the timberline. The fifty acres was signed over to them by Mr. Crowson's great granddad when emancipation was declared some two hundred years ago. Every generation of Magee's been proud workers and successful entrepreneurs. Mr. Magee didn't get high school finished for working day and night, but his wife went back and taught school for pert near twenty yeas and his oldest son got college in the Army and his youngest will be going to the community college. The boys hardly had enough spare time to wash their cars much less see about keeping the legendary Magee recipe in circulation or fetch a dollar jar running for Bruce.

When a loud diesel truck rushed up and blasted its deep horn Exilee laughed, "Robin's back, ya'll. We can eat now." And she nimbly lofted from her chair to greet Bruce. Her curly black hair was in a long thick braid down her back with a cute curly tip just above her lean waistline. She wore tennis shoes, blue jean cutoff shorts with white cottony threads teasing her tight tanned thighs, and a baggy tee shirt that gripped the girls despite the extra fabric. "Hey," she hugged him hard and smacked his cheek with a surprising damp pucker. "Welcome to the farm, Bruce."

His cheeks bloomed as dark red as the plum jelly sitting on the table. "Glad to be here, real glad." Bruce nodded at everyone and the Magee boys twice before totally letting her loose. When Exilee raised her eyebrow up at him with a cocked grin he finally let go of her hand too. And his ears redden to match.

Exilee poured him a glass of sweet tea from the pitcher on the table. And he finished half while everyone else on the porch welcomed him and then Mrs. Crowson, a petite Native American Indian woman who barely looked forty came out of the kitchen with little four year old, Luke Crowson, her grandson, Ken and Exilee's boy. Luke was a pale child with orange cheeks. His build was square and solid and had soot black hair, straight, not curly like his mother's Lumbee Indian hair and had his dad's English jaw, a strong wide one. He approached Bruce and lifted his open arms and Bruce didn't hesitate. "Hey, there. This your farm?"

"Yes. Are you gonna work the tractor with Papaw or help Jake and Mommy get my ponies walkin' the line?" Luke leaned back from Bruce's arm to check his expression and grinned with Bruce.

"Whatever you tell me to do, Sir." They all laughed with Bruce. "What time does all this start anyway? I'm used to first light hittin' the floor runnin'."

"Hear that, Papaw? He's just like you!" Luke leaned in to Bruce's chest and then checked for Jake and when he saw that he's outside the porch walkin' Robin inside, said, "We have ta go get Jake up sometimes. He goes city on us."

"City, huh? I'll fix that," Bruce chimed as they all enjoyed the newcomer.

Luke squirmed down from Bruce and eagerly opened the door. Robin was wearing one of her many white western tailored blouses, tight from the ribs down, tucked in deep, and unbuttoned so far the valley girls shone when her black satin hair swished across them. And she was wearing skin tight hot pink jeans. "I got a chair for you, Robin, next to mine." When Luke beamed up at her she squatted her six foot five inch height down and kissed him. "Mmm-mm," she smacked his cheek and left a glossy red pucker. "You got that right, little man. When are you gonna let me take him riding, Exilee?" Robin towered over Luke. He looked like a penguin wagging its tail because of his dark hair, black jeans, yellow faux alligator boots and black tee shirt, other than the printing on the back. "Kiss me. I Rode a Pony over the only Authenticated Patch of Underground Railroad – and Survived." Robin's booted foot reverberated like a bouncing ball irritating Exilee until she threw her head like a mad mare.

"When I have time to go too. Just 'cause Luke can ride that pony in the round pen doesn't mean he's ready to go trail riding with you." Exilee fisted her hips. "You don't even stay on the trails."

"I ride with you on tours, Momma. I wanna ride with Robin." Luke rationalized.

Exasperated, Exilee led Luke from Robin and guided him to his papaw. "Robin's trail rides don't have prepped trails. You know how we drive the tractor over the paths and put down fresh sand clay and scoop the poop? Well, real trails don't have maintenance. They have limbs in the way and holes in the ground and yellow jackets. There's just so many things out there, honey. We'll go as a family sometime."

Luke armed one hand on his hip and the other on his papaw's leg. "What day?"

"We'll get it in next week, somehow. Okay?" Exilee promised as she tried to smooth Ken's grimace with a wink. Summer is a busy time for any farm, but for one giving tours it was hectic. Ken told Luke, "I'm gonna get you up early this week and we'll put you in the round pen with some obstacles. If you pass all the tests we'll take you into the timberline on Still Pass Trail. A deal?"

"Deal."

Exilee pulled Robin into the kitchen. "Come here and help me in the kitchen, Miss Restaurant Lady and let Bruce get to know everybody." And Jake followed.

Luke told his papaw, "I don't ride a pony. I have a horse."

Mr. Crowson pulled him up onto his lap. "That's right. You sleepin' with me tonight or in Daddy's old room?"

"With you, Papaw." When Luke squeezed his papaw Mr. Crowson told him that he was gettin' a grip like his and would soon be strong enough to change the three point hitch on the tractor. Well that just spurred Luke on to drill his papaw on when and if tomorrow was a good day and if not could they do it the next. And everyone laughed in good cheer.

Ken's bright blue eyes stood out against his dark farmer's tan as he greeted Bruce with an outstretched hand. Ken wore his dark brown hair in a crew cut and mirrored a primed drill sergeant or hellish jail guard, depending on the mindset, as he reached out for Bruce's hand.

"What's your schedule tomorrow?' Bruce promptly inquired.

But Ken's humble smile and shrugged shoulders answered the real question. "The farm perty much tells me what to do. I look at the garden and know what to pick, or if it's time to till. The animals fuss if we don't see about 'em. We do a lot of mowing. Biggest thing going on right now is trying to figure out where to dig a well."

"I can help with that." Bruce was still shaking his hand when Ken gently pulled away.

"You wanna dig or carry rocks?" Ken's eyebrows danced.

"Shoot, I'll be glad to do both. I miss workin', getting dirty and sweaty. I even miss the smell of it. But I was really talkin' about witching the well with a divinity branch," Bruce explained. "Grew up witchin' for spring water."

"Yea, that's right. I mean, well, everyone needs good water. You can show Dad." Ken's hands were flying. "You can show all of 'em. We'd all like ta see that."

"Ya'll have water trouble?" Bruce asked Mr. Crowson and he just gestured no.

"Nope." Ken's hands gently waved about. "We want a hand dug well for the tourists. We're gonna cover it with acrylic glass housing and hang a stainless steel bucket over it for making wishes. Hang it about knee high. Tourists can get a drink of water out of a fountain spigot next to it. Rock it up like the well to match. Wanted to the old timey thing and let folks drawl the water up with a wooden bucket. Insurance rep says not to." Ken gestured for Bruce to take a seat. "We're going to cover it with a gazebo. Thinking about a post and beam or logs with dovetail joints and a wood shingle roof. It'll match the post and beam we put up over the passage. Run electric to it and have a recording from the Black Purse Papers. There's a lot of good stuff in there. I like the part where

Onacona explains that the baby they're sending to freedom is being born again and will have a new life and new family on the other side. It always tears me up when Miss Ginger reads those parts." Ken leaned to the side and his scrumptious thick black eyelashes created a sexy shadow and made his deep blue eyes an abyss any woman would long to dive into.

Miss Ginger, seemingly resting in the high back rocker, winked at Ken. "You could talk a squirrel into selling his nuts." She had slick short black hair, curled and set, brown tennis shoes and a soft blue cotton pantsuit.

"That'll set the stage for old timey." Bruce peered up at Ken from the white wooden chair with his pale tired grays. "Sounds good. And you're gonna hand dig the well and place the rocks by hand?" Bruce stretched to check Mr. Crowson's face, but when he didn't stir rest back against the chair. "You'll have to use a corbel placement or they'll collapse into the well."

Mr. Crowson's blue eyes flashed. "You dug one, have ya?" His dark worn work jeans were thinned to light blue along the sides of his thighs, knees and the hemline. And his plaid blue and brown short sleeve shirt was also thinly worn and one sleeve was ripped and stitched. He was wearing worn tennis shoes and his cowboy hat hung behind him on a hook next to binoculars. While the smooth darkened areas on the arms of his once white chair claimed his grip.

Bruce wiped his sweaty palms down the sides of his jeans. "No, Sir. Six years of reading." He quickly answered Mr. Crowson, then back to Ken. "I can make a lot of things," Bruce slightly cocked his head, "A solar water heater, house out of dung or straw. Wire a house to meet inspection. Read about raising goats for cheese and how to do it. You can ask me anything about Lucretias or dewberries in general. Can tell you about grapes, too. Got big plans for The Company." His words whisked out like they'd been hurled off a broom. "Already have an order list prepared for the equipment, storage, even the bottling procurement. First, I want to contact a metal building dealership, find the best deal." Bruce made firm eye contact with Mr. Crowson. "Can't say thank you enough for those vines, Mr. Crowson."

Mr. Crowson didn't push him further, but politely smiled. "You can call me David."

Ken slapped his hands together. Reached over to Bruce and held his shoulder. "You'll meet that steel building dealer in just a few. He's looking forward to meeting you, Bruce."

"Naw?" Bruce's lips rose up. "He's coming over now?"

The two Magee boys smiled at him. The youngest, Thomas, gave him a flick of the hand, like the kind used in town to signal the store church had a load to go. And Bruce caught the cue straight on, stepping back in time like it was just last week, and flicked his pointer finger up and down, the need more shine motion, and then pounced up from his chair with a "Good-gooboly-goo!" It was so loud and unexpected that everyone except Thomas and his brother were wide eyed. Bruce and the Magee boys met in the middle of the porch to shake hands. But Bruce surprised them with bear hugs.

"You know you're famous, right?" Thomas asked Bruce.

"Hope not," he grumbled with a wide smile. "Kid, you look great, both of ya. All cleaned up and spit shined."

"You, too. Get cleaned up and all kinds of good things happen, huh?" Just like that, young Thomas set the dinosaur in the room loose and it took up the entire screened in porch like a real horned triceratops.

"It's looking that way." Bruce gripped his jaw like a man pulling out that dinosaur's tooth, real stringent like. Then, as if huntin' season on triceratops opened that very second Bruce covered his eyes as headlights rushed him.

Cars pulled in all over the place, parking every which a way, and all at once, like they were precisely summoned right on up to the farm. It was as if the fence lines were runway lights leading to a shindig held in one of those city coliseums where people pay to see famous folks.

Most of the arrivals were invited. The crowd from Sunday school meandered up the walk followed by staggered guests including the post master and his seven boys who own small businesses, most of 'em in town. They all bustled in and wandered the cozy country home as they filled it with an abundance of homemade goodness. Biscuits and several pones of bread, pintos, tater salad, pies, cabbage with bacon, two big platters of middlin' meat, apple fritters, creamed corn, coleslaw, casseroles and cheese grits, fried chicken, barbeque chicken and roasted chicken and a ham slathered in pineapple juice passed and teased and filled the country home with the kind of goodness imagined in Heaven.

Bruce took it all in like a child at his first big birthday bash. Only Bruce was still so chauld up he shook a bit. It wouldn't have been noticeable at all if he hadn't picked up his tea glass. He put it back down as several of the post master's sons put an eye on his stress. He rubbed his hands together like he was trying to keep warm in between greetings and handshakes. It dispelled the shake and he continued with a fine job of greeting, all cleaned up and respectable like, like he'd done that kind a thing all his live long life.

After that group mingled past, Ken gave Bruce his finest smirk, "Surprise."

"Pyert me right up. Jake said it was just a few of his friends. Where we gonna put all these people?" Bruce shared a smile with Ken as the summer night's stars began to show themselves and the pond's frogs chirped for mates.

"Ah, we got tables under the porch, here." Ken aimed at the willow tree down behind Miss Ginger and when he did she hooked onto Bruce's arm and with her sweetest Southern drawl said that she had a date with him for breakfast and that she was gonna work up a mess of biscuits and gravy. Then she pulled him in closer, "Bes chicken bog in the fridge and I'll keep a cup of ellick hot for ya, chile, if you bes sleeping in." After her surprising Lum vernacular warms him she lets go.

Bruce grinned like a wildcat. "I swanny, I see right here youse gonna be my slam favorite roommate, Miss Ginger." When he winked at her she gently squeezed his hand as another group filled the screened in porch's doorway. "Hope there's enough chairs."

Ken told Bruce, "We'll have the lights on in a minute and you can see better. There's tables and chairs we got from the church fellowship hall out under that tree by the pond. Momma likes it out there."

Ken's former co workers were hard to miss. The teachers flocked in like geese, honking and snarking and causing such ruckus they drowned out the bawling bull in the back lot, while researchers from up at the university eased in quietly. And everyone was carrying covered dishes. Robin's parents', Gili and Little John were loaded with various forms from their family restaurant, Gili's.

Gili's long gray bob bounced like her fast steps as her petite frame kept pace with her tall husband's long stride. She was pale as gardenia blooms with bright red lipstick and carried cake boxes. She seemed every bit the prim English lady while Little John was a giant dark skinned Cherokee, handsome in every way and walked like a buck, stealthily and assured even with his arms stacked with covered dishes. As she stretched her neck out to yell, "Don't piddle, now." Little John lengthened out as he adjusted his long arms around the carefully stacked covered dishes threatening to tumble.

"Don't you dare drop those." Gili screeched as she reached the steps and Ken eased her load. That's when Gili locked onto Bruce and pinched his butt cheek. "You sweet little Lum, give me a kiss."

"You know how to treat a Lum, Miss Gili. All those sweetnins gonna spoil my figur'."

"Bones. You need one a these lime pies to keep for yourself. I'll put it up for you, Hon."

Bruce thanked her and Ken steered Gili and Little John into the kitchen. Ken hurried back to Bruce. "They're always entertaining," Ken chided, "Gili is a descendant of Custer, General Custer," he whispered, "the Indian killer." When Bruce didn't flinch Ken went on. "Little John was ostracized from his tribe for marrying her. He's full Cherokee." Bruce bit the tip of his tongue then sizzled a smile. "No wonder Robin's so hot, all that war pumping in her blood." Ken's exaggerated nods matched his goofy grin, "Put a bull in a head vice, I'll tell you that." Then he looked around to see who may have overheard and relaxed when he was assured his wife hadn't.

But her daddy had. "Gili'll snap your hand off, boy." Little John excused himself and went to scout around the pond. The screen door stuck open when the worn metal spring cinched up in the stretched out rusty spot. Ken told Bruce that there was always something to fix and went on to say that rust was common in high humid areas while Bruce stared up at the rust on the ceiling fan until he was diverted by more headlights. The stunning bright lights spotlighted the rusty spring on the screen door. "Wouldn't take much for that ta snap in two," Bruce squinted. Ken agreed and then stepped out onto the steps with his arm up over his eyes as he inspected the curious mix of vehicles joltin' and slidin' into the farm.

The seventy's chromed caddys and equally aged four doors to haggard sport trucks to shiny new bugs, were marked in Bruce's memory like the dared cigarette burn scars on his forearms. He braced himself against the door jam with his arms crossed over his chest and everyone on the porch stood straight up for the real surprise guests.

As vehicle doors were slammed the passengers united like soldier ants and charged the screened in porch in scattered formation. They were not carrying covered dishes, but toted pokes and jars. Snap, that's Jimmy Bean, a long lean handsome Lum with suntanned skin and gray eyes and mostly gray hair, reached the steps with a full smile, a jar dangling from one hand in a spider like grip over the lid and with his other, offered his poke. "Bes your favorite. Know'd you missed hit up in dat Beacon Hotel." His minty fresh breath eased Bruce's fears and he was delighted when he realized that the jar was empty. Snap held the bag open. "You're favorite, orange pop in the bottle. Glad you're out, Buddyrow." He smiled as Bruce inverted the empty jar. "We all brought jars for ya. Minders we got debs on yer first batch a' wine." And that's when Snap sparked Bruce straight on.

In fact, that fire sparked like he'd never walked out a' likker's flames. Bruce pulled Snap and the jar close and they gripped one another like a chain holds a gate closed as Bruce quietly confided, "Can't wait to get started. The Crowson's even planted the vines for me. This is it, Snap. I'm gonna make it." When Bruce's head tingled he rubbed it down and Snap wiped away a fast tear. And everyone on the porch took their seats.

"Always knew you would, you stubborn cuss. Come fishing wid me after youse settled and no more cold biscuits and hot soda. I'm got a wife now cooks a spread that you'll set you for a two hour nap, straight on." Snap patted Bruce over and over and then waved for his new wife who was busy talking to Edge. When his wife didn't pay him any mind he told Bruce, "Runs that mouth like an outboard: leaves me in da wake." Bruce shared the laugh. "Sounds like a match made in Heaven. How does Edge like her new step mom?" And Snap smiled real wide and told him that he should a' took up with her a long time ago. "Took kin so fast I didn't count for nothin' first year. Whadaya 'xpect? Edge was fetched up on the edge, ya know, those low downs. I took her in and did what I could. But she was longin' for a mother." Bruce agreed and commented on how things seem to work out for the best. Then asked Snap to take his orange pop to the kitchen and to hurry up and meet him back out on the lawn.

Bruce placed the jar alongside the wall and stepped out onto the thick summer Bermuda lawn and as he neared his old pals sucked in heaps of honeysuckle and cantaloupe from the nearby melon patch and they contentedly settled on his lips like watermelon juice and sunshine, all nice and easy, like he was already pleasured up drunk.

Five more jar runners rushed to greet Bruce and joined in on the tail end of the conversation between Bruce and Snap. Someone spat out that Snap hadn't caught a single fish since he'd married due to the racket he and his old lady made. And more excuses followed: "Like two politicians."

"Weren't that. Bes two crickets!"

"Bet they'd talk da hide off a beaver." His wife, only five feet away, was still busy filling Edge's ear and clung to the longing girl's bare arm as she stared after Bruce.

Edge held her chin down, head slanted, and boobs up or maybe they'd just grow'd up with the rest of her that way, perky as hot peppers. At twenty-four she cleverly turned around and shifted her firm hips. Edge's short shorts had red bandana trim that matched her petite bandana blouse making her look like she was wrapped for something or another with the bright white bow tying back her curly light brown locks.

Edge toted a poke for Snap's new wife. And Old Rodger Dodger who had lumbered before suddenly scurried to speak to Pig Pen and the two stepped off to speak in private. Scarecrow's lanky frame was followed by the lovely Lilly. Bruce and Ken melted and drooled like Lilly was waltzing into their arms as Pig Pen and Dodger filled their mouths with chewing gum. Dodger discreetly emptied his half full jar by bending over and coughing as he flushed its contents into the tall grass by the fence post and Pig Pen kept watch.

Pig Pen was Cassie's oldest boy who was twenty at the time. Cassie was only fifteen when he was born, so they had perty much growd up together. His real name was Lassie Ben Deere. But with all his name conjures up speaking it aloud was shut down, prohibited, outlawed, deregulated, and punishable by all sorts a' authority figures, when he was only in second grade, on account of fights. Pig Pen slung a rock with his juvember with such accuracy he'd knocked bulls out cold for as long as three seconds. From third grade on school records had plainly identified him as Ben Deere, but even at his high school graduation, when Pig Pen was called up to the stage, it was Lassie his classmates resorted to. They cheered, "Lassie, come home," and "Yea, Lassie," as Pig Pen had only one and one half arms. And with those same limbs he had saved the football team's beloved mascot, an aged ram named Horny.

The newspaper article had gone viral up and down the East Coast. Horny had climbed the stadium's outdoor bleachers and challenged an opposing team's audience member for their CD. CD's are those crispy fried versions of corn dogs made in North Carolina by Exilee's ex brother in law who had an affair with Jake which sent Exilee's sister, Glennie totally raging mad to the extent of hiring the hit man later called a slasher to kill Jake. Anyway, Horny just loved those CD's. And when it wasn't offered he butted the stingy man's chest. Well, the man stood up and proved himself to indeed be a large piece of a man, like a six foot niner with shoulders you could stack a record breaking brick bat on. He picked up Horny and dropped him down into the open area between seats where all the steel beams zig zag. Tragically, during the fall the ram's horns got stuck and he was suspended there like a goat on a rope.

Pig Pen was on the other side as all this went down with the binoculars he used when the cheerleaders squatted or bent over. Good thing it wasn't half time. Anyway, Pen ran to help while the opposing team just jeered and cheered so loudly that Horny's wails were drowned out. It was just awful. In fact, that was the newspaper headline, 'Awful Horny.' Everybody read it.

Pen sprinted up the bleachers with his stump popping out of his shirt sleeve till he reached Horny. Horny had rubbed his horns back and forth over the metal till he'd worked one side slam off and was dangling by only one half of the set and was screaming just like a baby cries. So Pen lunged down into the metal abyss catching on support beams with his legs and his one good arm as he descended, just like you'd see a monkey in the jungle swinging on vines. But Horny got all excited and broke himself loose just as Pen reached him and they fell to the ground together.

A crowd of concerned classmates and their parents had gathered. They witnessed the fall and good thing they did or no one would a' believed it. Pen had got himself under the goat and cradled it, taking the brunt of the fall. That's the kind of kid Cassie fetched up.

Bruce grabbed Pig Pen's hand. "So glad you came. Read about you in the papers. Maybe you can help me with my goats. I plan to have a goat dairy with cheese on the winery's grounds. Say the word and you're my man."

"Horny," Pen snorted, sending bust-a-gut laughter over the group and the nearby ponies into blowing and nickering fits. It gradually settled and they caught up a little on Pen's life and his brothers' and Bruce learned that the economy was wearing 'em down like hard rain and no rain. Even with the butchering Cassie and her boys did it was not enough.

Tale was butchering was how Pig Pen had lost his forearm. Summer between his first year of seventh grade and second year of seventh grade there was a cow not prepared to be sacrificed under the guillotine they'd rigged up over the draining ditch. In fightin' the creature for its life he had lost one forearm. Pen had made do with one and one half arms, but it was not easy. They lived on a farm, rent free, in exchange for keeping the place mowed, and general maintenance, including anything with wheels, just outside city limits. They turned a dollar with outsiders' vehicle repairs, too.

From feeding to mucking to hauling and killing and running down a yard chicken for supper, they took turns with all the chores. They also took turns taking classes at the community college. Taking turns meant one took the class the first semester then the next in line so he could share notes and use the same book, when not updated with another, same with clothes and some girlfriends.

The aura of mystique and rawness and that kind of plain dirt farmer charm that only comes from livin' it oozed from Lums. But this bate had even more than that. This bate had roots in jar runnin'. And that meant they'd all run from the law or been caught and jailed and some'd even been shot.

Bruce's toothy grin and busy arms embraced them in delight when not a single one smelled too much like likker. And sweeter still, their pokes were filled with store bought goodies they'd shared in by-gone days just like they'd gotten together and planned their purchases. But when over zealous Bruce grabbed a hold of Edge's waist to swing her around like he'd done since he was six and she was all of three, the chickens roosting on an overhead limb flew over, squawking and flapping and shedding feathers and fluff till she squirmed loose. A large Americana hen and her mess a' dibs chirped after the flying flock in a yellow streak. And everyone around was wiping their heads, checking for chicken drop when one second later, the bull bawled and the ponies in the lot neighed and nickered. Scarecrow hollered, "Let that filly loose, boy!" as Lilly pierced the air with a sharp whistle. Two ponies reared up on their hind legs and bit at one another's necks. It was like everything on the farm was 'gainst the swinging.

The tracked wheels creaked as the big heavy barn doors opened and the orangey yellow light outlined Robin's curves. With one hand on her hip and the other waving the chickens waddled inside. A minute later Robin called for Jake to help carry buckets. After he gathered two armfuls Jake yelled, "Got your chair, Bruce," as he held up a wee three and half pound stainless steel bucket. And they all laughed when Bruce wagged his tiny tight tail.

As Snap proudly stood next to Edge she confidently stepped up toe to toe with Bruce. "That how you gonna treat your employees? Swing 'em around and scare 'em half ta death? Every one a' us needs a job and plan on being in on your winery, Mr. Bruce Black."

"Mister, now, is it? Good thing I didn't get you too high off the ground. You're stacked up tighter than I thought." His red ears and lusty eyes were hard to see in the dark, but his mommucking up was real plain like. "You're all grown up, Elizabeth."

Edge leaned back a smidge. "Yes. And I'm serious 'bout that job. Only reference I got is you. How's jar runner gonna look on my resume? You made me, so you're responsible."

Dodger hollered, "She's a-gotcha now."

"Well, I'm sure we can work something out." Bruce told her real loud and sarcastic like. Then he mischievously grinned. "Can you read yet?" And she slapped his arm. "That's not lady like." Bruce cocked his jaw and slyly grinned while he held her slim shoulder. He scanned the bate a' them and hollered, "Bes be a great day, huh? To make Cameron revenue with the likes of us old likker head Lums, I swanny that'd be too good."

Edge fisted her hips. "I'm in my second year of college, who you calling likker head? I'm aim to be your bookkeeper."

Scarecrow stepped backwards and coughed, turning his back in a not too non obvious manner, as least for Bruce, and did his best to check out the wheels parked along the fence line and caught them with lightening flash clicks of his camera. Lilly called in plates on her cell phone and in one, two, five minutes slipped it back into her front pocket and smiled up at Bruce addressing his jar runner's.

Bruce straightened up extra tall to pay both Scarecrow and Edge some serious mind when Ken stepped up to bat. Ken cleared his throat. "Bruce'll have plenty of positions available. I'm sure he'll be taking applications, soon as he gets a building up."

"Thanks, Buddyrow." Bruce ran a hand over the bank statement in his back pocket.

When Cassie pouted her plump lips extended past her gums. "Bes ritin' tests to work likker, just 'cause youse puttin' up a building? Dat's some jubious crap I'm ever heard. Brickhouse Bruce," she spat as her curly orange bangs bounced against her sun damaged forehead. "You know taint one a us, ol Lums other 'n Edge and my boys who writes." Even in the faint light her blue eyes pierced like marbles tossed across glass, threatening to shatter anything in their path.

Dodger belted out, "I don't want no reglar job. Bes a-bench warmer and batch taster, right chere. I'm da man for that and youse pay 'nugh my boy'll be done right. Gotdat, Jack!" His front partial loosened, but with his two first fingers dodged them back in his white bearded face. Disgraced and humbled, Bruce agreed, "Whadever he needs. It's covered."

Cassie got right in Bruce's face. "We all been praying for you. All our regular jobs closed, left town or the illegals took 'em. We's livin' off butchering scraps and whadever we get out a da ground. I won't take nuthin' from the state and kin only sell part a what we growd or we won't have nuthin' ta put up." She clamped down before slowly looking back up at him. "Can't come up with 'nuff for car insurance. We's all that way. Ridin' hot." Cassie's anguish deepened the lines in her weary face. "Lums been put out here in Cameron and were all countin' on you. Bruce Black, say you're gonna do that for us, one time," she breathed the words like she'd prayed 'em over and over, "just one time, say it out loud."

Bruce clutched at his throat. "Swanny, Cassie Locklear, I bes real overwhelmed right now. I'm tired as hell. Don't think I've slept in two days, too excited, but I can tell you that as far as I'm concerned, you're family." Cassie looked about fifty, but was only thirty four, with a passel of seven yurkers from several different men.

"You bes that for us, too," and she drew in a deep breath and quietly mouthed, just for him, "and more." And Bruce felt her passion, her strength and need and hugged her and held her by the shoulder as he turned to his friends. "One thing I learned in prison, wherever there are two or more Lums you are on the swamp." He scanned the faces of his fellow Lums. Made eye contact with Cassie and took the paper napkin she held up to him. "My vines need fertilizing. Need to do some tilling and mulching, too. Show up Monday we'll get at it. Cash paid daily." He united them in Pow Wow fashion as "Yee-yee-yee-yee!" pierced the air.

As they calmed Ken said, "I'll haul a tractor over." And Bruce quietly accepted.

Cassie roughly wiped away her fast tears and then kissed Bruce as he flagged for the crowd to stop still. "Wait. Who needs car insurance? I'm not having illegals working at my place." And he pulled out a roll. Hands flew up to mouths, popped chests and waved over heads and within minutes his hands were empty. "Come on." Bruce waved. "They're gonna have my party without us." With cash in their pockets, socks and bras they stood a bit straighter and walked a bit taller. And again like soldier ants, only this time with a bust-r-go-broke Master of Ceremonies as their king, they all headed up to the screened in porch.

As Bruce held the door open for his fellow Lums he was handed the symbolic empty jars with gutsy grins and gratitude as he stacked the tokens along the wall. When Cassie handed him her empty jar she palmed his chest. "Bes yer mother's heart dere." She curiously shivered, but quickly reclaimed her stoic demeanor and toted her poke of saltines and chipped beef into the kitchen.

Bruce's chin was up in the air, struggling to keep together, as he twisted around and settled down on Miss Ginger, still in the big rocker. "I'm waiting for a full jar myself. Helps with the joints of the morning, a hot tea with honey and whiskey'll do the job." "I'll be selling wine, Miss Ginger. Oldest pain killer around."

"Well, I can take ta uppity spirits, too. Whatever does the job best, right chile'?"

Bruce beamed over at Miss Ginger like he used to do his momma.

Scarecrow and Lilly held out to be the last guests through the opened door. "Add ten pounds and you'll be up to mixing crete with a shovel. Boy, yer skinny." Scarecrow pulled up Bruce's bicep and pinched it too hard. "Hey, easy now." Bruce rubbed down the spasm. "I'll be hiring that done. Looking for a contractor."

"That how it is? Well, start with your jar runners. Half of 'em been throwin' up buildings without licenses for years. Bound ta know a legal contractor." When Scarecrow set his empty jar beside the others Lilly tapped him on the shoulder. "Who was that big guy in Robeson County that just got the Lowry's out on bond? He's a contractor and he's a Lumbee."

"Ah, that'd be under Deese's jurisdiction," Scarecrow told her then back to Bruce, "I got Deese's number in my friend's list." He pulled out his cell phone. "Get ya a name and number in just a few." His bony fingers set to punching and in seconds was chatting, then slid the phone back into his shirt pocket. He pulled out his pad and pen from his back pocket, tore off the top page, and pushed it into Bruce's hand. "Call him first thing and he'll be over to take down details."

"Thanks, but what's in it for you?"

"This time, nothing. Guess I'll spend the rest of my days trying to convince you that me showing up wasn't setting you up." Scarecrow leaned into Bruce and whispered, "Fisk sent you up. Called that Yank and he was sittin' on go with a posse." But Bruce was still hot, so Crow made it light with a snarky smile. "Yank was on his way out and wanted ta claim a victory 'fore he went north. Or he'd a never took the word of Fisk. Yankees think they got something on us. Gawl dookie, their fat egos rub me wrong every time. I hate we didn't ship 'em out ta France when we's setting up the states. Some kinds just don't belong anywhere though." When Bruce was still rigid Scarecrow got rigid too. "Been wantin' to tell you, but knew I couldn't say any names on visitation. Too much ta risk."

As Lilly circled around them with wide open arms she exposed her pistol. "I'm so glad you're going legit, Bruce. You make us so proud to be your friend." She kissed his cheek. "And we're gonna get Fisk."

After the trio disengaged Bruce guided them outside. Five steps into the grass he faced Scarecrow. "What's with the camera?" But he eyed Lilly.

Scarecrow's big brown eyes doubled and his lean pale face lengthened like he'd been stretched out on a pole. Then as his lips came back together he grinned like a dog over a half chewed ham bone. "I'm on the job. Even when I'm not. Fisk and Wart haven't been seen in months. But there's smoke coming out of their barn where they got that city block of a still going. Thing is all copper. Figure they're stockpiling, an outsider's running their jars or they got an unidentified."

Lilly checked around and stepped closer. "They bought that big copper still after stealing the last of your daddy's goods."

"And I say they're gonna pay me back or that still is mine."

Like a crawling caterpillar Scarecrow's thick black eyebrows met. "That'd be stealing."

"Repossession," Bruce calmly quipped.

Lilly flicked her long brown hair and her D cups perked. "We never had this conversation."

The gentlemen faced off fully loaded and neither backed, so Lilly detained Scarecrow by the arm down to the food filled tables.

After greetings with the kitchen ladies the jar runners also tracked down to the tables under the weeping willow. It was lit up like a Holy Christmas tree with tiny white strings of twinkling lights braided down its long thin branches. Twinkling stars danced across the rims of platters, plates and bowls as the dangling strings ever so softly swayed, like little spirits blessing each morsel. The scents of warm comfort foods filled the cooled summer night's air as Mr. Crowson announced above the salivating crowd. "We need to bless this food before we get started." Frogs chirped, distant birds whistled, livestock's heavy steps slowly neared and horses restlessly pawed and blew while ponies puffed. But when a rooster crowed and chased his strayed cackling hens a whippoorwill pierced above them all and silence swept like the ocean's wave over the Holy Christmas Weeping Willow.

"They're done, Papaw," Luke explained followed by the crowd's hushed sweet laughter.

"Heavenly Father, you've blessed us with another foundling and we ask for wisdom and success as he makes a new life. Bruce is a smart man and we are so glad you chose us to get him off to a good start. May all his friends, new and old, join Bruce in his new life and know that God's Grace and mercy is the only treasure we will know on earth to see us over to the other side." He raised his head and spread his arms across the crowd. "Hope to see every single one of ya in Heaven." After a short pause he tucked his head and said, "Give us two stomachs and pig jaws. We've got a spread here that'd choke a crew a' hay balers. Pass me Momma's tater salad first. Amen."

As laughter and Amens made rounds a lone slow moving vehicle sounded alarm. Rough metal scraping metal followed by a booming backfire set all eyes on the newcomers. One headlight was higher than the other. Jake fled from Robin's side to grab a hold of Bruce who was three yards away munching on a strip of cracklin' as he made fast tracks toward the rattletrap's ruckus. As a larking voice heralded from the opened door, "Mon, ain't you a-making tracks!" Jake and Bruce kept marching straight on. But their lips formed fat circles as Mark propped against the hood and posed real purty like he'd popped a slug in a prize size bobcat.

"Gotcha, huh? Man, the look on your faces." Mark busted a gut till he spit on himself. "Knew I would. Delayed getting' here long as I could." He hissed, spit and hissed some more while Bruce and Jake awkwardly smiled at one another. Bruce's beefy top lip curled. "What in the world made you buy that junk jalopy off a them? And how'd you ever talk your momma into riding in that thing? Good Gawd." He peered in deeper. "You talked her husband into the back seat, you rascal." Bruce opened Thelma's door. She said it wasn't necessary, but thanked him. Then he raised the seat up and helped her husband squeeze out. And other than the grunting and growling was real polite and quiet about it.

"Have to wax her car." Mark's slender arm reached up for the tennis ball, blackened with soot and road grime, slowly bobbing on the CB antenna welded onto the running board and whacked it. When it zinged back and forth on the hefty steel rod threatening to raise a bruise on his noggin he stepped back. "I'm making a float out of it for the parade. Got it cheap, well, with a trade."

"Trade for wooden nickels, I hope." Jake swung a hard left at Mark and the boy ducked. "Hey, you got a hair cut. Joshing about you looking like Jesus paid off, huh?" Then Jake told Bruce, "We're in the same class at church."

"That was the trade." With bright blue eyes, tawny skin with high cheekbones and chiseled features Mark was the most handsome Lumbee.

"Say what?" Bruce stood back.

"I grew my hair out while you were gone, grieving thing I guess. Cut it off the day I heard you were getting out early. Fisk and Wart were up in town and heard about it. They came to the barbers and offered the car and everything."

"No telling what they're gonna do with it." Bruce's brows met while his jaw hung in suspension. "How long did it get?"

"Long enough we couldn't tell if it was a he or a she walking at a distance. He swings his hips." Jake mocked Mark's gait.

"Do not."

"Well you did."

Thelma was busy admiring Bruce's lean build and how his cheekbones were more astute and his nose less wide and short crew cut a dirty blonde. When she commented that he looked healthy Bruce explained that he went on a Mediterranean diet after reading how it promotes longevity and it made him lean. And his aunt said that it brought out his magnificent features. "Mark bought this thing 'cause the senior girls said they'd ride in it. He called and asked before he ever handed over his money. There's a parade now in downtown Cameron on their graduation night. Then a dinner at the Thomas's. The girls love Mark." She ran her fingers up the back of his new short hair do. "He's so handsome."

"Quit, Momma," Mark's shoulders rolled her arm off.

"I missed you, brat." Bruce and Mark embraced and popped one another's backs.

"I missed you, too."

"Well, you got me now." Then Bruce sighed down at petite Thelma. "Well, do I get a hug?" Moving his dear Auntie, out all of a sudden like, from the home place after he'd just been incarcerated had made prison visitations limited and awkward. The less the better for each of them as the fresh cut between them needed time. After a lengthy embrace Bruce and Aunt Thelma walked hand in hand while her husband walked ahead carrying a large black kettle of chicken bog by its wooden handle. "I knew you still loved me when I smelled that bog, Thelma."

"Course I love you, like my own." She looked up at him and was delighted he was all chauld up. His strong wide jaw was clenched down like he was gonna crush rocks for the foundation of that building a' his any second.

Jake and Mark lingered over the jalopy. And Jake told him that if he stayed late they'd be over at his place for drinks at the after party and that he'd tell the story 'bout the night he and Bruce moved The Company. Mark said he wanted to hear the entire low down of what went on the night his step brother got sent up. "Sure," Jake replied, "We can tell you everything now."

"You'll have ta give me a ride back tomorrow or at least by Sunday. I'm a greeter this month." Mark leaned over the hood.

"No prob. But what about your parents?"

"Don't let her fool ya. She can't wait to drive it. Even mentioned when I get a real car maybe I could paint this pink for her. Thinks it'd be cute." Mark made an idiotic face and rubbed his gnarling belly.

Jake threw his head back. "That'd be perfect, and a yellow daisy on the tailgate. Yep, that'd crawl all over Fisky boy. Come on. Let's eat." Jake thumped the hood of the notorious ride and they sprinted off to Bruce's welcoming home party.

Chapter 8

Turquoise, Hot Pink and Orange Make the Colors of Fire

Young Thomas Magee and his brother rationalized that they were grown and could handle a late night party and still work the next day. Mr. Magee reminded them they'd given their word to help dig post holes the following day. They left around ten. At eleven tables were stacked up against the house under the screened in porch and those not attending the after party headed home. The post master's son with the barber shop and steel building dealership agreed to meet Bruce for breakfast and then drive over to his property. Then Miss Sarah and David waved bye to the last of their guests and David warned the kids, "Still got to feed up in the mornin'."

Jake set up the counter. He pulled out the likker jar he'd been saving especially for that night from behind the surplus sauerkraut in the pantry. He encircled the prize jar with thick glass jiggers he'd purchased at the dollar store and set a bowl of pretzels on the side. Then at eleven-thirty, way past regular hours, Miss Ginger poured half a glass of buttermilk and sat back in her rocker and sipped as Mark eagerly poured the 6 jiggers of Old Man Black's finest.

Miss Ginger stopped rocking as they belted it down with gasps and fast hot ears. When nary a one a' them choked she resumed rocking. Scarecrow, Ken, Jake and Bruce held their jiggers out for seconds. Mark and Robin set theirs on the counter. Robin got all the attention when she suddenly held down the girls like they were gonna bolt out of their stirrups and knock her in the chin. Then she threw her hands up over her head. "Hot damn! I'm ready to ride now!" She stomped her boot against the wooden floor and when she posed like a Native American Toy Doll all juiced up and ready for positioning in her hot pink jeans Mark got real still and quiet.

Jake calmed Robin and schooled her on safety and said that it wasn't a good idea. "You'll get hurt out there in the dark." Mark flipped his glass jigger upside down on the counter. Robin squirmed away from Jake's tender grasp. "It's half moon. There's plenty of light. Come on, ya'll, let's have some real fun." Robin's long black hair shimmied across her long back and teased the crest of her firm seat. "You can ride, can't cha, Bruce? Exilee, we can put him on Choctaw." Robin pulled Mark up to her side and embarrassed him as she held him real close. His eyes were level with her valley. "I'm gonna let this boy ride pony style with me." Mark was all too willing, throwing his arm up over her shoulder, "Okay!" as he got an eyeful.

Then Miss Ginger's hard soled shoes tapped like a judge's gavel against the wooden floor. "Put that jar up for one of you breaks a leg. Why don't we do something we can all do?"

"We?" Jake's head tilted. "We'll probably end up outside, Ginger. We'll be out of your hair soon. Anyone need to use the bathroom first?"

Lilly and Edge were pointed down the hall as Exilee said, "We can go to my house to sleep. We won't bother you, Miss Ginger. I promise."

"Oh, no bothering about it. I'm with you." She stood a foot shorter than Exilee, but it didn't matter. Miss Ginger seized command with her crooked pointed finger. "See, I missed my youth, chile, busy raising you. I'm what you call, a retroactive senior." She mischievously smiled and proclaimed, "Read about it in a magazine, how women like me is called; dating and working. That's what I am, retroactive."

Exilee sucked in what had to be two full lungs of fresh oxygen before releasing. "All right, then. What do you want to do? But remember, this is Bruce's welcoming home party. Don't make us play bingo, please."

Meanwhile, Jake and the boys, including Mark, had another jigger lined up at the kitchen counter. In sequence, they threw it down. Mark held himself steady against the counter and brazenly ogled over the ladies and attempted to discreetly undress Lilly.

"Like melted butter right down ta my toes," Ken's Southern drawl melted Exilee, but she told him not to have any more that she had some real butter for him later. The men poked and hammered Ken that maybe Luke needed a little brother.

"Oh, my word," Miss Ginger slapped her palms together and threw back her head. "Men ain't got enough blood for both heads." The guys hacked and laughed as Miss Ginger bullied between them, but when she hastily snatched up the lid and screwed the devil's loose lip juice closed the boys ceased. Lilly and Edge cheered on Miss Ginger as they returned from the living room. Exilee shouted, "I can't believe she said that. She's not herself tonight, really."

"Oh, you don't know the half of it," Jake yelped. "I live with her. Never know what she's gonna say."

"I'm in a dangerous state, old enough to know better and young enough to do it." And they hysterically gawked at the prim little nanny in the blue pantsuit.

Ken wrapped his arm around Exilee's shoulder and warmly whispered, "Any chance of getting a tour of the Underground Railroad tonight?" in his deepest bedroom voice while he grinned and winked over at Miss Ginger and most everyone returned his goofy grin.

"No more likker for this boy. Over," Exilee shrugged out from under his sexual connotation. Then she steadied on Miss Ginger, "Good idea, that's something we could all do, Miss Ginger." And smiles ignited. "You give the best tours."

"Something's not right," Mark squinted.

The manuscript quivers when Miss Sarah raps the door jamb with a wooden spoon handle, but David keeps reading and tells her to wait. "This is interesting. Kids got into some shine. Let me see what they do." She returns with tableware and proceeds to set the table and asks him to at least change his shirt before dinner, but he waves her on.

Luke runs ahead of his parents and Jake walks with Miss Lucy. "Do you want me to introduce you formally or regular?" She keeps her eyes on the big house as she tells Jake that she can do it herself.

Butter in an old burnished saucer serves at the centerpiece. The tan saucer is rimmed in black whirls, dots and triangles. Miss Sarah brings out a large platter and demands David change his shirt. She arranges it on a side table. The pile of corn on the cob waits decadently on the tan burnished platter rimmed with fine sienna red birds. The other has Miss Sarah's much loved Cherokee bean bread sandwiches filled with poke salad and chicken. That platter is much older, not burnished, and has a large chip where crushed white shells are visible. David stops reading when Miss Ginger sets down that platter and he grins like an opossum. "Feeling retroactive tonight?"

Miss Ginger tsks as she hunkers down over his shoulder to read a few lines and gasps. "She wrote that?" Her fiancé smiles at the pair and takes a seat across from David as Jake opens the door for Miss Lucy. She nods at everyone and walks straight on to Miss Ginger and holds out her hand. "I've heard so much about you. Miss Ginger, right? I'm the one writing Jake's story."

David eases the pages under his overall bib and declares he'd better change his shirt or he'll have to eat in the barn. While Miss Ginger compliments Miss Henrietta's nice dress and suggests a seat. "I'll be right back, hon."

Miss Henrietta's library work and her home invasion and friendship with Jake are all lighted on throughout the beginning of the serene summer supper. Then as eight thirty brings dusk and more mosquitoes Exilee lights a few citronella candles. "Too bad it's dark out over MacGregor's Crest. Love ta point that out to you, Miss Henrietta. Won't be long we'll have the well house up and a security light and we can have a little party." Exilee favors on Jake. And they are all rather surprised as Ms. Henrietta says, "How nice."

Nods and smiles make their way around the table and Luke wants to know when. Ken tells Luke to help his grandma so they can have pie and Luke wants to know if he can have ice cream. Then Ken tells Exilee to take Luke in the kitchen and get him ice cream. And as Exilee hands her son the generous bowl of the vanilla ice cream he had chosen Luke throws himself onto the old linoleum. "No! Like Ginger makes it. Hot pie and ice cream." His pennies scatter and roll out onto the screened in porch. "He worked himself into the ground today." Miss Ginger picks up the pennies and hands them to Luke who counts each one. "Exilee, you want me to take him to bed?"

"No, I need to get in early, too. Had to go to town and get, get some things done and didn't get my list done here. Good night, everybody. Thanks, anyway, Miss Ginger." As Exilee kisses her cheek she holds Luke by the shirt collar. "And I'll be seeing more of you, I'm sure, Miss Henrietta. Just let me know if you need anything. I'm usually around."

"Thank you, sweetie. You are the most gracious family. I'm sure I won't be here long. The detectives already have a lead on the suspect."

"That's what I hear." Jake excuses himself and says that he needs to help Exilee bright and early and Ken jeers the city slicker and rolls his eyes behind Henrietta Prickenwrath's back as they leave.

As soon as they are out of range Miss Ginger tells David to go find those pages that she gets 'em next. David brings them to the table, but lets her know she can't keep 'em till he's done. They'll be in the drawer. He aims his white head at the serving table. "You can get 'em 'round lunch tomorrow."

Miss Sarah tells Miss Ginger and her fiancé, "He'll be up at four reading. Haven't seen him this fired up since, well, I don't know when."

And at four David rises and looks out across the road to Jake's and when no lights are on turns on his lamp beside the recliner and begins where he'd stopped in Chapter 8, Turquoise, Hot Pink and Orange Make the Colors of Fire.

"Tours don't come wid sugar tits and baby wipes. You wanna see the Underground Railroad sober up 'n come on," Miss Ginger whisked out her palm sized flashlight from her polyester pant's pocket and plotted toward the laundry room. At the basement door she turned around. "I'm not carrying you babies down the stairs." She slipped out the key tied to her wrist and unlocked the heavy duty lock from the sliding Dutch bolt on the basement door. As it scraped open she clicked on her flashlight. "Jake, get a couple more." And she creaked down the stairs.

Lilly was first in line as Jake took Robin by the hand and Edge stalked Bruce like a fox on a pheasant. Her red-tailed target was midway against the counter. And predictably, she followed Bruce as he followed Ken and Mark, but then Bruce managed to get between them. Mark foolishly grinned like a chicken lost in a fox's den as he clumsily followed Edge down the stairs while Exilee grabbed a flashlight from their bedroom. Scarecrow had stepped outside to take a phone call and suddenly appeared in the hall. "Geez. I didn't see you." Exilee braced the flashlight like she'd cock it against his jaw. "Sorry."

"No, I'm sorry, Exilee." Scarecrow lowered his arms. "I should've let you know my whereabouts. Just making sure the home is clear. Gonna lock up?"

"No," she shrugged and hurried to catch up with the others who were already in the basement. "No one ever messes with anything around here. Come on."

"Bruce's door was the only one shut." Scarecrow didn't budge. "Shouldn't we at least close the entrance doors?" He insisted as she hurried down the steps.

"Go ahead. But you're gonna miss the best part. Ginger gives a dramatic introduction." She projected from the stairwell.

"Comin'." Scarecrow took a mental picture of the cozy home; its horse and cowboy statue on the table next to the recliner, the red pillow on the worn orange and brown plaid couch, the sketch on the wall, the likker jar, the glass jiggers, and exactly how he'd set the bedroom doors. Bruce's door was closed and Scarecrow pushed the others closed only halfway with a sock in front of Jake's door. Miss Ginger's door held a wedged slipper.

The basement's staging for the Underground Railroad was like a real movie set. Like it'd been professionally staged with life size fiberboard cutouts of slave families and farmers and Native American Indians with pieces of European clothing over their crafted animal skin shifts. Wall mounted oil lamps with electric bulbs replicated shadows on the rock walls just like the runaways would have experienced.

But the door to the Underground Railroad was not to be seen. The room appeared to be a food cellar with jars of beans, tomatoes, corn and kraut. A wooden barrel with a tight fighting lid and piles of potatoes and hanging braids of onions. Exilee pointed above their heads to the Leather Britches. Hanging across the low ceiling in row after row, were dried green beans. She explained that Leather Britches were best cooked in a dab of bacon fat and water in an iron skillet and were delicious. Then the guests sought out the door again.

Miss Ginger held up a candle to the right of her jaw. "Tonight you will be taking a tour of the Underground Railroad. It is the only authenticated passage in North Carolina. I will be your guide. I'll be quotin' from The Black Purse Papers as well as telling you things I know and left out, if you prove yourselves trustworthy. The papers have been studied and verified as the only written history of the Underground Railroad written in time as it was happening. Names, towns, rivers, 'long with facts on the true beginning of the Trail of Tears, facts on trading with the Croatans and their light skinned prisoners and the exact origins of Black Indians."

Jake and Bruce simultaneously reached out to tap one another's forearms and jumped. Jake whispered, but everyone heard. "Welcome back, Bruce." Jake and Miss Ginger exchanged sheepish smiles as Jake kept a firm grip on Bruce's arm. "This is your proof, Buddyrow."

His gap grew into a smile when Miss Ginger said, "Hope yer sober. This took some plannin'."

"Yes, ma'am. Thank you."

Edge pat Bruce's back, but when he didn't acknowledge her quit. Robin, on the other side of Jake smirked at her attempt while Mark glared at Robin's backside.

Miss Ginger examined faces like a school teacher. "Before folks and babies left here they prayed. All kinds of danger was ahead for 'em. Devil Masters, that be the slave owners, hired bounty hunters to bring back their property. Sometimes they'd be ordered to be kilt if they'd took a likin' to running away over slavin'. Bounty hunters were the worst and did whatever it took to track 'em down. They'd question any folks along the way, all peoples who did any trading, and especially slave owners who had been tolt on for being easy on their slaves. Not only did they question people, they tortured people to get word on where runaways were hiding.

One of the things many don't know is that Devil Masters even paid slaves to track their own people. Many believe the enslavement of Negroes is when the derogatory slang, nigger, originated. Others believe it began as term for slave traitors." Miss Ginger placed the candle on the simple wooden podium holding a stack of leather string bound papers. She unfolded the mini reading lamp from under the podium, clicked it on, blew out her candle and the original Black Purse Papers radiated.

She kept eye contact with Bruce. "The Black Purse Papers were written in Onacona's time, in her language. The professors from the state college said it is called pidgin. I told them I call it half Cherokee and broken English, 'cause that's 'xactly what it is and they laughed up there for a minute at that fancy college, but agreed with me one hundred percent. Over the course of two weeks, I read it to them and deciphered it. They had me on recording and everything. Now any student can go to their library and view the tape there at the media center. Imagine that? Been kept secret all these years and now the truth can't get out fast enough."

With spread eagle hands she hovered over the pages. "I spent my life studying it, every single word. If it meant four months findin' a ninety year old Cherokee or spending an afternoon with a crogedy Black man, I fount out what each word meant in their time. My reading for tours is from the translations or you wouldn't understand it. And this one tonight is not my regular. It's for Mr. Bruce Black."

Her crooked rigid finger followed the line on the page. "This is what Onacona writes about the Underground Railroad passage we are standing in right chere: Pox saved our Negro babies. When pox came to nearby farms a plan was made with White women in nearby towns who wanted to help runaways. They got pregnant right off. When de mid wife came, who was commonly a Negro house slave, she gave her a small gourd with pokeberry juice. In the gourd's tiny opening was a cloth rag. The new mother was schooled on when to give her newborn pox with the stained rag. Then the mid wife would return for a doctor visit and claim to take the baby to the specialist who had been tolt ta clear up pox from other babies.

The specialist was a doctor who was also a big time conductor. The law had fines and prison and even death for those who helped runaways. Slaves were valuable property and helping one was looked upon like helping thieves. The doctor risked his life, his wife's and their own children's to save these babies. He'd have as many as five pox babies in his house for his poor wife and older chidrens to tend to. Course there weren't pox, but there was still bottles and butts 'round the clock for that poor wife a his. Dere'd be a few mothers who'd have to take on the pokeberry pox and put on suffering like with the babies at the specialist's house from time to time to ward off suspicions and to get some help for his poor wife. Cause no one else wanted to help with the quarantine sign hanging on the front door.

Now this plan started on 'count when a Negro slave had a baby the owner could decide whether or not he wanted to keep his property or sell it and that new mother had no say at all and the White mothers saw their pain.

The Lord works this way still today. He gives us suffering so we will know why, when and how to help others. It's a terrible pain to lose a child, a pain that leaves a hole inside that can't ever be filt.

The slave mother was schooled on the pokeberry pox, and then often as quick as a few days after birth, she'd give her baby the pox. The master'd be told and he'd come down to the slave house or send someone he trusted to check and decide if he wanted to let the baby take doctoring or just risk it dying on his property. This is where the biggest love you ever learnt comes in. Knowing she'd never see her baby again, the Negro slave mother let her baby go, to live in freedom and most likely never ever see again. She handed over her new baby to the mid wife who took that precious chile to a station where the Underground Railroad's Pox House started. That'd be right chere!

As the Negro baby traveled the Underground Railroad he went in many clever disguises. The baby'd be on wagon rides in barrels of grain resting on the bottom in a hidden compartment and in hat boxes and cloth bundles. They'd be in saddle bags strapped behind saddles on slow walking mules and Onacona writes that a baby in the mountains was delivered to freedom up North in a fine cherry dresser drawer. And they were all delivered to houses where babies with the pokeberry pox had been sent to White Doctors. The White mothers took those Negro babies onto their swollen breasts like they were der own. Doctors as far away as West Virginia and New York became specialists for sake of freedom. The specialist would fatten up those White babies with goat's milk and bread pudding and those big enough were fed creamed corn and mashed taters. And there was always a gourd hid for case a stranger checked in, but with the pox scare, there were hardly none. It was the plan of all plans. Everybody gained somethin'.

But the Crowson's specialist was 'ventually fount out. A husband who didn't pacify like his wife turnt the specialist in when he came home unexpected and saw his wife caring for a Negro baby. There's no other words on that family.

When pox was wiped off babies with a wet rag the specialist was fined many thousands and imprisoned. Prison was wood floors, no air stirring in summer and no fire in the winter, pure de hell in the South, with the foul stink of a life rottin' chained to a wall. They didn't kill him. They tortured him. They gave him the slave pacifist's punishment, torturing him just like a slave. They whipped him out in the street, branded him, stretched him and cut off toes. They did all 'cept cut off his tongue because they wanted to know who was helping. His wife moved to Canada with their children where she schooled Negro children and he starved himself to death.

The mid wife got sold to Mr.Crowson's farm, which was a slave working plantation. And after a couple of years when word had settled, they went on just like before. Gourds got passed around the nearby plantations and when a new momma wud 'cept the fact the only way her chile would ever know freedom and loved dere chile enough to let go, she gave her baby the pokeberry pox.

Only this time, the baby suffered. To keep the red pox marks from washing off on the checker's wet rag, hot wax was doted directly over the pokeberry pox mark. And not only did the pox stay red it welted up like a mosquito bite so it looked like the baby'd been infected for several days. And everyone knew the pox was most contagious when the pox burst and the puss run out. So the baby was even a bigger threat than before.

The master'd rush his slave baby off for doctoring here where slaves were watched over real good at the Crowson's." Miss Ginger flashed her showy grin. "It didn't take long for this very house to be made the Pox House and no bounty hunter dared enter for fear of pox." Miss Ginger swung her arm behind her to the primitive 'Pox House' sign hanging beside the entrance doors. "I love that part, those smart Blackies."

"Sometimes a master wud allow a mother to bring her baby to the doctoring mid wife herself. And there'd also be a few here with a case of pokeberry pox, daddy's too'd make it here, even a brother or sister, to keep down suspicions. Parents would go through with the sufferin' death of their innocent chile' and a funeral, of which were fake. They did it to for two reasons, to help themselves let go and to make their baby's death look real. Oh, they didn't put on for the good owners of the plantation here, but for bounty hunters laying in wait on the edges of the property. Their campfire smoke trailed in the skies like dark devil tails. That's what they call 'em here in these papers, too, devil tails. The Negroes were always in danger as long as there was White men owning slaves.

But the mothers' mourning was all too real. They'd be sick with grief. Onacona writes of songs sang to these merciful mothers, slave songs, as she combed out their knotty braids and greased them up again. Peoples on the Crowson farm ended up with one song in their heart. They'd be every which a way doing chores and any one of 'em could be heard singing as the sweet baby was sent to freedom from down here and an empty coffin was put in the ground up there. There is a cemetery, Bruce," she pointed, "between Ken's place and Jake's with near a count as possible of three hundred sixteen little coffins. Only a few real burials up there."

Miss Ginger slipped her hand under the podium and pressed the recorder's button. Wind stirred the fields to sing as grains tapped and stems swooshed. The faint voices of playing children became clearer and clearer, until one distinctly said, "Momma." An ax split a log, cracking and falling to the ground. Chains rattled in the distance as a crow cawed. Reverberating claps beat against the walls, as if in rhythm with easy ocean waves and the welcoming home party gravely absorbed the Underground Railroad's true history.

A woman's mournful wail, then a man's angry moan, then the clapping again, and just as the hairs on the backs of their necks tingled, out poured the mournful yet proud voices of a complete robust choir.

"OH! Freedom, oh! Freedom,

Oh! Freedom, over me;

And before I'll be a slave

I'll be buried in my grave,

And go home to my God

And be free."

It played three times, bouncing off the stone walls from a loud eye opening blare down to enjoyable to retrospectively low and then as faint background music. Miss Ginger cleared her throat. "Now the mid wife had to keep a few babies back or the whities wudda come suspicious and not lowd her to doctor any. But over the course of her work and the work of seven other known counts of Pox Houses, there were thousands of Negro babies sent to freedom." She paused a good long while. "That is love."

Miss Ginger leaned over the podium toward Bruce who was front row center in the dark orangey basement. "There are five Onacona's. Onacona is a man's name. The first was a man. Onacona means White Owl to these Cherokee and it is like a title and a name. It was given to those who showed themselves as wise leaders or who were expected to be wise leaders. The second and fourth were also men. But the third and the one who wrote The Black Purse Papers was a woman, my great, great grandmother, rest her soul. Yes, leaders were both man and woman in both Indian and African history. It is a White man's fault that women been put back." She sort a' growled and all the men leaned away.

"Tracing back with the State's professors her times were eighteen hundred twenty to eighteen hundred sixty. She died a terrible death. She got caught helping the runaways and got what was worst for women. One of those men carried that copulating sickness and it traveled to her mind. In prison she lay in sweat and puss sores for months before she died and then they took pictures of her in her coffin and put it in the paper. They did it to two more conductors working mid wifery and shot one dead after she let her wolf dog loose on a bounty hunter and it took his hand off. As punishment those bounty hunters axed off one hand of each of her four childrens. Their pictures were in the newspaper with warnings to slave pacifiers. The Pox Houses closed." Miss Ginger heaved as the background chorus sang, "I'll be buried in my grave."

"But runaways kept coming." She grasped the podium. "They kept running. And they kept singing for Freedom, Oh, sweet Freedom." As Miss Ginger sang tears ran down her neck and no one seemed to breathe.

Miss Ginger slowly exhaled and her audience followed. "Onacona writes here that the Cherokees met first the Croatans on the Neuse River in the sixteen hundreds." Her eyebrows raised. "Bruce, here's your some proof now." And he warily licked his lips. "The Cherokee met them while on a trading trail to the Coast carrying buffalo knives and turquoise. This time the Croatans led them to a large settlement on the Lumbee River. They feasted and rested for several days and on the last night traded for two Croatan wives with the gray eyes. They wanted the gray eyes because the Cherokee believed these women to have more medicine. The gray eyes had blood with the powerful Portuguese and blood with Whites so they were special to the Cherokee. They had many kinds of medicine." Miss Ginger swung her head to Exilee.

"Medicine to the Cherokee meant a special way with nature, maybe controlling it, but for sure knowing how to make nature work to get what they wanted or needed. And the gray eyed Croatan wives promised to teach their new Cherokee family how to talk in a book and how to write like their mothers. The Croatans showed them a stow of treasure books and they took some for trade with a buffalo knife with a turquoise beaded sheath.

Some of the first words taught were at the wedding party. Man was called 'mon'. Measure was called 'mension'. Ask was called 'ax'. Knowledge was called 'wit'. House was called 'hosen'. And love was called 'lovend'. Onacona did not know when she wrote these papers that the words were old Anglo-Saxon words from days of Raleigh and his mighty mistress, Queen Elizabeth. And Onacona did not know what she wrote then would solve a twentieth century people's crisis, a people who've wasted days upon days of trying to convince the world what blood runs in them, like it makes any difference.

But she did know that the new words were White words because the Croatons told the stories of how their people took Whites from the Coast and made them slaves and married some. That is why they had Indians in their tribe with the gray eyes."

Miss Ginger's crooked finger ran with the page's words and Bruce followed it like a mule on a plow line, heaving and urging. "This tribe's settlement was in a low woodland, a swampy region, what Croatans' called pocosin land. It was plenty in whortleberries and black berries. Croatans traded them. The Cherokee's traded for berry wine which they drank mostly there during the feasting and marrying of the two wives." She stretched her neck. "The Croatans lived in settlements on the Neuse River, on the waters of Black River, on the Cape Fear, Lumbee, and be as far as the Santee in South Carolina. But the main one covered what we know as Robeson and Cumberland Counties, and Averysboro. And they shared trails with the Cherokee up to the mountains eastward. The three counties had trails that come together and became what we call Lowrie Road today.

Bruce Black, you and your kin and all da jar runners with a dab a Lum been runnin' the same berry juices and runnin' the same trails from as far back as the sixteen hundreds. Whadyasay 'bout those apples?" When her eyebrows danced so did his.

He clasped the back of his head with an outstretched hand and heavily sighed. "Honestly, I'm about dizzy." Both Edge and Jake reached out for him. Edge kept a hold of his firm narrow waist while Jake held his bicep.

"Do you need to lie down?" Edge pleaded.

"No, really, I'll be okay. A big day. New everything, all I've ever wanted, just rushing up at me. Don't stop."

"I'd say you have an angel guiding you, Bruce Black." Her honey smile melted them. "Bes too jubious not to be supernatural, boy. Not only do you have the blood right and the time right, and now some proof, here's your proof for those vines."

Dogmatically, Bruce scorned Jake because he knew he'd told the secret, but was instantly forgiven. Then Bruce rubbed down the bumps on his forearms and Edge grinned over at him and rubbed hers too. Robin gnashed her tongue in her cheek and stepped back as if she couldn't bear to stare any longer. And when Mark nearly fell over trying to get out of Robin's way Exilee pulled him to her side. And Ken peeled him off.

"My great great grandmother, Onacona, writes that our people received dewberry vines as gifts from the Croatans. And the Cherokees promised to plant them only on the other side of the mountain so other people could not make their wine for trade. She writes that the Croatan told the Cherokees that the vines had come from the Whites they took prisoner." Her crooked finger aimed. "I got this page copied for you 'long with da two on when they met and their Queen words. The professors and I agree that in the papers White doesn't always mean color. And one more thing, Bruce, your name is most likely from the Croatans from the Black River settlement. Onacona has every name of the people her people traded with and writes that they named one another from where they lived more than, like us Cherokees, from who we show ourselves to be and sometimes who we are to become.

Come here. I want to give you the necklace. You will give it more honor than any glass case ever will." Miss Ginger pulled out the long turquoise beaded necklace and Bruce leaned down while she slipped it over his head. "You can wear this now. You are Master of Ceremonies." The glossy organic beads were about a fingertip wide.

Bruce fondled the large palm sized effigy hanging from its center and held it up to the flickering bulb's orange glow. The well-worked stone shone even in the dark. "It's a bird." Jake aimed his light and agreed. The bird was about two inches by three, simple, but grand and made of a green turquoise with a golden brown vein.

"Let me see." Edge stepped within an inch of brushing against him and examined the beads and effigy, shivering as Bruce breathed, "It's either a raven or a crow. What's holding it on?"

As Miss Ginger answered, "Intestines," Edge backed. "Strong stuff, probably buffalo or big cat. They had black cats on the prairie. Onacona has charcoal sketches of all kinds of animals they dealt with. There's prints for sale in the office shed. Samples in the frames behind the register and the ones for sale rolled up in the basket. Miss Sarah and I have a few more we keep to ourselves. There's some gruesome things in those sketches. People being eaten by dogs. Slave families thin as floor boards squattin' over a single bowl of sweet taters. White men'd bet over mean dogs and one of those wild black cats they had tied to chains. General public don't want mean things up on their walls.

Onacona seen a lot a hate in her times and also a lot of love. There's birthing sketches and momma's nursing and daddy's gnashing their teeth at fake funerals. You can tell it's a fake due to the background fiddlers. They're all Negroes. Fiddlers were for funnin', back then. To me, the pages are all priceless. But you can pick one of the copies for just five dollars, honey."

Exilee squirmed between Ken and Jake to get closer to Edge. "We're opening a gift shop next year. Working on sculpting babies for the shop and trying to figure out how to make 'em faster. My first weren't saleable. Miss Sarah loves them. But who's gonna pay forty bucks for a rock baby souvenir? And forty is cheap. That's paying myself four dollars an hour."

Jake and Scarecrow strained to see the turquoise bird as Bruce held it up. "I'll show it to you when we get done." He carefully gathered the strands and allowed the weight of the effigy to ease it down under his shirt. "Know what I'm gonna wear to the opening now." Bruce smiled and as he did caught Robin smiling back.

Exilee gently pulled on Bruce's arm. "I put it on once and got a rush. Really, I felt something and had to take it off." Her dark pools of light permeated his grays as he agreed that the necklace must be attached to the spiritual world.

Jake poked him. "Hope you plan on pants, too, Naked Chief Tonka Wonka." They all giggled. "Or maybe you'll sell out if you're naked. Label a batch, Naked Chief Wine."

From out of the laughter, Scarecrow called out, "How about Looseleaf Chief?"

"Well, I'm not wearing a suit. They're for funerals." Bruce declared. "But for sure pants."

"And weddings," Robin casually added as Bruce and Jake locked grays and greens. Until Bruce disciplined himself away from striking up a fire with Robin's hot pink jeans smoldering like red hot coals under the dark orange light.

Edge drew attention near the shelved fruit jars. "My daddy and I put up apples every year. They're best turned out with nutmeg in the sugar water." Her backside formed a nice blue heart trimmed in red right at her creases as she bent over the jars. Still under the influence, Mark goofily gazed and stepped closer. "You ever go out dancing, Edge?"

"Turned out?" Robin's hushed fuss silenced everyone as her shoulders swayed and Edge popped back up. "You're a Southern farm girl?" Robin's arched back and hipped hands hollered 'chick fight.' "I thought you were doing time in college now." Like she was selling life insurance to shipwrecked bachelors, her cheesy smile and sweet tenor oozed. "Girl, that bandana trim is perfect on you. Is that what you wear on campus?"

When Exilee jumped between them Lilly tapped Exilee's shoulder and she quickly turned to see who touched her. Lilly's calm repose instantly eased her. "What kind of medium are you using for your sculptures Exilee?" Robin and Edge did a bad job of acting interested while the guys looked down at their feet.

"Soapstone." Exilee answered Lilly while she told Robin to behave with a dash of her evil eyes. Robin rolled her tongue across her teeth and jutted her butt off to one side like she was cocking a loaded gun. So Exilee turned her back and blocked Robin's aim at Edge.

"Thought about making a mold?" Lilly suggested. "I took pottery class when I had some medical desk duty a few years back. Shot in the calf. Not serious. Get my hands in the clay every chance I get."

"I bet that is fun." Exilee's big brown eyes danced over to Ken. "But if I used a mold I couldn't sell the babies as hand carved."

"That's true."

Edge flagged Exilee. "They won't care, hon. As long as it looks like the real one and it's cheap. People just want a little souvenir. They'd sell."

Miss Ginger waved her flashlight across the overhead beams spotlighting Ken. "Get the door. We have a load for a friend of a friend."

"Huh?" asked Edge.

"Underground Railroad talk for sending a slave station to station." Miss Ginger explained.

"I love it. That's so clever. I can't believe this wasn't taught in school." Edge declared.

"It was," Robin huffed.

Mark held up his hand and when Jake laughed at him put it down. "Habit. Anyway, the papers should be in the classroom. Some teachers do delve into the specifics on the Underground Railroad. But I never heard a lot of this and Mr. Chavis, you know how Lums talk."

"That's why I'm in their surrounding counties," Scarecrow mumbled. "Call me Scarecrow."

Mark boyishly grinned and tapped his fingertips together as he surmised the group. "In the ninth grade I wrote a sociology report on the Negro slave before and after emancipation. About your papers, Miss Ginger," he pointed, "in the research arena there are correlating dates and books, like, 'The Croatan Indians of Sampson County, Their Origin and Racial Status' by George Butler. It was his summation for separate schools. Indians thought Negroes were dumb and dirty and they wouldn't go to school with them. On the sociology path, my report covered the ladder of status and how there's always been prejudice. There's also the newer work of Adolph Dial, 'The Lumbee' and Karen Blu's, 'The Lumbee Problem.' After the English married natives they picked up on their traditions. But when that mix married the emancipated slaves, they picked up a few of theirs, like their knowledge of natural medicine and religion. The language anomaly is as much of a barrier as any for us Lums to make it into college much less a West Side housing division. But the Lumbee vernacular is also what keeps the tribe. That's why it sucks sometimes being Lum. You can't please everybody."

Bruce clapped twice. "Give you another shot and we'll learn how to create atoms with our bare hands, huh?" He ruffled his hair and Mark just grinned. "You always were a smart ass."

Robin wrapped her arm around Mark. "We don't care about bloodline. Okay?" She got right up in Mark's face barely missing his lips as she spoke, but capturing Bruce's eyes straight on. "We love you just the way you are. Right, you guys?"

"Mixed mutts are the smartest anyway, right, Mark?" Exilee chimed.

"I guess so," Mark put too much thought into it while Edge proclaimed she was a proud Lumbee Indian.

Lilly tapped Mark's shoulder. "So, in your report, what was the final decision on the psychology of the Lumbee?"

"The wave of history of the mixed race follows a self existential crisis pattern as the people try to label themselves and can't find their box. They'd be better off on an island if they can't be happy just to be." Mark whitened every single smile in the dark orangey basement. "Humans want labels and add levels of importance to those labels. Just the way it is."

"Zoom Zoom, aren't you on the ball?" Bruce proudly smiled. "Maybe you oughta be Master of Ceremonies," Bruce suggested to his cousin as he held his hand over the effigy tucked under his tee shirt.

"You haven't called me that in years," Mark sheepishly smiled.

"Zoom Zoom?" Jake asked.

"That's how he did everything when he was a kid." Bruce gripped Mark's shoulders like they were a steering wheel. "Zoom Zoom. Zoom Zoom." And Mark revved up his pretend boyhood engine and when he backfired everyone guffawed.

"Thank ya, Zoom Zoom. You're very bright. If you boys are done now let's get on with with it." Miss Ginger aimed her light on the wall behind the shelves of fruit jars as Ken and Jake pushed back the primitive heart pine shelves. On rollers for ease of movement, but still heavy with jars, they strained over the cement floor. The floor was painted to look like packed clay and finally a curious small door appeared. The door was three slabs of thick heart pine with a slab across the top and one across the bottom. It was short, real narrow and very old.

Miss Ginger curved her index finger into a black hole near the top left of the door. "This hole was kept plugged with a pine knot." When she pulled the door open it creaked as the cool damp air rushed out over them. She swept the entrance with her flashlight, first up then down and up again to dirt walls with wood ledges and thick overhead beams. The pine was almost scarlet in places. "This is heart pine." She exemplified it's density as she fisted the overhead beam and it barely made a sound. As particles sifted through the light beams she consoled them, "It's just dirt."

It was very apparent the measurements between the overhead beams were not in equal increments. "Use your indoor voice," she whispered. "Vibrations make the dirt fall and it ain't just dirt. It's soot, from lanterns and oil lamps." She bent over at the shoulders and tucked in. Her steady pace left them with the threat of being left behind to creep alone into the dark passage.

First thing they did was clamp their bare arms around their chests to ward off the chill as their hot breath steamed. Crouched over and cramped in slow steady steps, they crept deeper and deeper as their lights bobbed from wall to ceiling to floor. "Boo," Ginger unexpectedly blasted as she turned around with her light under her chin and held the bold enunciation on her lips. And they all told her not to do that again.

"Effigies fill holes all 'long this underground passage. They were carved by parents of babies sent to freedom." Miss Ginger shined her light on a depression in the wall about six inches long and three inches wide into a shadow box with modern plexiglass protecting a primitive rock sculpture. "It's a man." The brown rock had been crudely chiseled into the cookie cutter shape of a man.

They studied it in wonder as they absorbed the underground. It smelled like pure dirt. Any area not marked by light was pitch black. And the passage was narrow while the ceiling was low. And the floor wasn't smooth. So with dubious footing the newcomers either slid along or barely lifted their feet. But they were all stooped over and searching for whatever there was to see on full alert.

Edge traced the outline of a hole while Jake aimed the light. "Looks like the baby is sleeping. I wonder if it died before it could make the trip." And Miss Ginger moved ahead until her light was swallowed by the cold black path.

"Isn't she going to tell us about it?" Edge asked after Jake said something about it being a day past Ginger's bedtime. "Ginger has her ways." Ken's lighthearted tone lightened their dark moods. "She lets the passage do the talking for the most part. We'll catch up with her and you can ask her about effigies then. All right?"

"Here's two more." Jake aimed his light on the sculptures; a dog and a baby.

Edge had to touch the glass. "Babies and babies."

"Miss Ginger and I counted them. There's three hundred sixteen, just like Onacona wrote. It was a major wow factor for the professors. Course they took every rock and loose chunk of heart pine up to the college and tested 'em out with archeologists up there with lab equipment. It's all good." Exilee assured them.

"Archeologists exclusively? I'd love to read their papers and any anthropologists', too." Bruce told Exilee.

"Man," Jake huffed, "you did some reading, didn't cha?"

"Read and excercise," Bruce laughed. "Best thing ta do in there. All shut up. Habit now ta read endings first. Know what I'm getting' into. Wish life was like that." And Jake whistled, "Say that again."

"I've got their numbers and one sent me a report. I read some of it, but after about the nineteenth hundred time of reading about the same rock and its iddy biddy centimeter gouge that surfaces like another rock hit it, I got bored and put it back in the envelope. There's close to a hundred pages on the effigies from just one professor." Exilee theatrically yawned. "Come on, you two," she told Lilly and Scarecrow. "You don't want to miss anything tonight."

"Got that right," Scarecrow projected and it echoed repeatedly until it reverberated back, "God at light."

"Indoor voice," Exilee reminded. "We don't want to get covered in this stuff, ya'll. You can't wipe it off. It just spreads. You'll have to shower."

Lilly and Scarecrow caught up with the others and then all three girls sighed over the baby effigies. Some were swaddled. Some were carved with caps indicating a boy. The uneven skull caps with rounded outcrops indicated hair and thusly, female. Some had open eyes. Some closed. And all had at least one letter carved into their backside.

Jake pushed his flashlight into Bruce's hand. "Focus on the support beams."

"Why?"

"You count 'em to keep track of where you are."

With a half smile Bruce faced him. "Like counting the cedars."

"That's right."

Robin gently elbowed Jake, "What's that about?"

Jake waited for Bruce to speak before answering and when he didn't Jake obliged. "When we were kids we worked a still in his daddy's woods and we'd count the cedars we planted to keep track of where we were. We were always moving it. Cedars lined up like graph lines."

"Oh, both of you were shiners? That's what you have in common." Robin jittered.

"We're like brothers. We grew up next door to each other, hon." With a gentle touch Jake rounded over her shoulders.

Bruce counted the beams aloud and on number seven stopped. "Yurkers in my momma's hair till she passed. Then we ate at his momma's all the time."

"That's right," Jake smacked. "Old Man Black never cooked, did he?"

"Oh, he cooked every night." Bruce chuckled. "But you can't feed a first grader shine and send him to school the next day. I ate with the Wilkes for eight years. They're like family." Their hushed conversation sounded like possums hissing and chewing in a cabbage patch.

"I can't hear the train. Ya'll be quiet." Exilee's projected hushed voice was almost manly.

"There's no train around here," Scarecrow deduced.

"Not physically," Ken heightened their curiosity.

Bruce's and Exilee's lights shined on the plexiglass and new wooden support beams made to look primitive. It stood out against the ancient black passage. The passengers of the Underground Railroad huddled, fitting their bodies together like chicks around a hen, tucking limbs to fit as Bruce aimed on the plexiglass protected overhead beam adjoining the new ones.

"An inscription," Edge excitedly pointed. "That's old English." She told Bruce to aim his light at the beginning again.

"It's broken English," Robin hastily corrected.

"Same thing," Edge's head teetered as she leaned up closely against Bruce.

Ken kept his light on the inscription as he slipped on his teacher's hat. "Slaves weren't routinely taught to read and write. They were self taught."

"Read that loud enough so everyone can hear," Jake said and Bruce squeezed around till he and Jake were nose to nose. "You a teacher now, Buddyrow?"

"Just thought you'd like to read it." Jake shrugged. "It's your party. Do what you wanna do."

"Don't sing and I'll try to translate." Bruce licked his lips as his brows hunched. "It reads: Debl Massa tuk my Fut, selld my Son Den Debl Massa suld me ta Massa Crowson, Gud, gud sah. Lord hurd de cry an de fits en Pryres - Run Lady Run Git ares Son Sleep dey Run all de Nyht I see alhs de Chile's at de Lords Gate - Eber Magee." Bruce's deep quick breaths sliced at the light.

Robin offered her interpretation as she stepped next to Bruce's raised arm. "I've done this before." She wiggled in closer until she felt what she thought was Bruce's leg and let her hand slip from her own thigh. But Edge grunted. So she just clamped her arms around the girls. "Devil Master took my foot, selled my son. Then Devil Master sold me to Master Crowson, Good, Good, Sir. Lord heard the cry and the fits in prayers. Run lady, run. Get our son. Sleep in the day. Run all of the night. I see all of the children at the Lord's gate. Eber Magee."

"That's real," Edge whispered.

"That's what they all say," Ken replied in his long drawn out way.

"Yea, it is." Exilee refrained.

Bruce aimed his light near Exilee. Found her face and then clipped her shoulder. "Magee like Thomas Magee?"

"That's right. David's people deeded the land over after emancipation." Exilee told Bruce.

"That's awesome, all this history under your feet every day. It's so inspiring." Lilly rubbed her arms.

"Freaky. Bet your daddy has some ghost stories, huh?" Scarecrow widened some eyes.

And Ken gasped, "Ghosts? Heck, yea, but we're used to 'em. They're everywhere. Luke was three years old and made his way into the cemetery after dinner one afternoon and Mom and Dad and Exilee and I were all watching him hop from rock to rock and stand on headstones. Didn't think anything about it. Dad asked him what he was doing and he said he was playing keep away from the ghosts."

"That is so weird," Lilly enunciated with clear distaste.

"You ever seen one?" Scarecrow asked Ken.

"Yea. Don't keep count. They're everywhere." Ken nudged them forward. "Lead on, Bruce."

Bruce aimed from the ground then up the wall as the passage narrowed. Robin and Exilee could no longer squeeze next to one another. They all followed single file. Edge followed behind Bruce. Mark was right in front of Exilee. Ken was still last. And Miss Ginger was out ahead.

"I'm cold," Edge whined.

"Rub your hands together," Bruce suggested.

And Robin hissed to Exilee, "If she'd pull her shorts out of her crack she'd get another two inches of coverage." Lilly giggled and when Exilee told her to hush Robin turned to Lilly, "You know she's not wearing any panties for them to crawl like that. She's a thong frog." Lilly gasped and clutched her mouth closed as Exilee pinched Robin's arm. "That hurt."

Mark turned around to the ladies like a little boy with a squirt gun and squeezed. "Underwear for women should be outlawed." Jake and Bruce laughed as the echo traveled into an indistinguishable mumble as dirt and soot particles drifted down. Then Robin told Mark he should go tell Edge to pull her shorts out of her crack. "Just leave it alone," Exilee stomped and more soot dripped. And when that crazy Ken dared Mark to do it everyone hooted and soot washed down till there were sneezes and complaints.

A few feet later when Lilly discreetly told Exilee, "You know, my UC work requires them," Exilee urged Lilly not to tell too much. That Jake had filled her in on the dancing details and that she was not being judgmental. Lilly huffed, "I can see what's going on." And at that, Scarecrow told the brood of biddies to stop pecking. Ten feet, then twenty passed. Then up to a thirty-four support beam count they focused on warming their arms and keeping their footing in the cold damp earthen walls.

Exilee's flashlight made overhead circles as an updraft of air blasted toward them like a train running downhill with an 'ugg-gg-uggh-uggh' purr as their steps crunched against the gritty ground. Ken's footsteps went down flat, not heel to toe. Robin's steps were faint while Exilee's made a definite hard heel to soft toe. Jake's steps were that of an old man, contacting the ground with a flat force. His steps paused in cadence with Bruce's as the 'ugg-gg-uggh-uggh' purring equalized with a cool shaft of air level with their heads. Shoulders raised and chill bumps tingled as their temperatures shifted with the ice cold breeze. Edge reached up for Bruce's shoulder and slid down onto his bicep. And the crouched group huddled closer like a clutch of biddies as they eased down the cold dark passage.

"Do you believe in ghosts?" Jake tried to whisper.

"Who're you asking?" Bruce whispered back.

"Robin. I know you do."

"I believe in spirits," Robin clarified.

"Then what's that?" Jake suddenly stopped.

"What?" Robin's startled whisper spooked Exilee as she grabbed onto the back of her shirt. Bruce aimed his light. A fluorescent yellow line was painted on recessed bricks on either side of the earthen floor. As Bruce's light shone on a wooden framed box recessed into the earthen wall Robin firmly squeezed Jake's arm. "Good try. Is this new?"

And they all sighed, except Ken and Exilee. "It's been up a couple of months. Had to wait for the state to turn it back over. There was some quibble about burying it even after the Magees signed it over." Exilee explained.

Packed together at the new find they stretched as Bruce aimed his light on the metal plaque. "Eber Magee. 1836-1838, one of the babies." Then as his light hit the glass they gasped. "Oh man, a foot." Inside the shadowbox rested one adult size skeletal foot. Its brown and yellow bones were held together with steel pins."

"He buried his foot down here two years after it was cut off." Robin projected. Mark cleared his throat. "Gross, but common, I'm afraid."

"Yea, I remember that in class." Edge chewed on her finger.

Bruce turned to Exilee. "Any more surprises?" And she laughed, "Scared of ghosts, Mister Master of Ceremonies?"

"No. Just don't want anyone getting hurt." Bruce remarked.

"Uh-huh," Exilee tossed her ponytail. "Don't worry. No one will get hurt. The ghosts around here are like your Little People not like your big bad Totens."

Intrigued, Bruce's on guard demeanor dropped. His chin tucked a bit as his eyes softened and he unconsciously outlined the bird effigy under his tee shirt. "Little People does not imply stature."

"I know. Your Little People help others, like our ghosts. But let's say you get someone to shout 'haunt' down here. Then we're gonna be on guard like you are for your Totens." Exilee's Southern drawl charmed him. "Do you know where the beliefs originally came from?"

"My mother was always talking about Little People, saying they moved things around the house, playing tricks on her. Once swore she saw a pair keeping the clothes on the line during a wind blast. Old Man's work shirts would've hit the mud hole, that kind of thing. All Lums got a story on Little People. It's a Lumbee thing."

"No, a Portuguese, African, Middle Eastern, thing," pausing between each then added, "Totens, too."

"But tokens is an Elizabethan word that means the same as toten does now," Mark clarified. "An old Shakespeare play I read."

"Oh," Exilee studied him best she could in the dark.

Bruce leaned to her then suddenly jerked up his chin and tilted his head back like he was reverse parking. "Oh, is it the papers, too?"

"Some. Came across things researching. Like you and I are distant cousins." Exilee announced as she aimed her light in his face. "Oops."

"Can't be too related, you're a half and half."

"Who told you that?"

"Don't know when I learned it. You know how things get around. Your dad's the white principal, blue eyes and curly white hair, and your mother was Cherokee." When Exilee pulled back with half a smile Bruce asked, "No? Then where does your kin go to?" Bruce shone his light on her face and when she squinted he kept it just under her chin where it exemplified her thick lips, strong jaw, full forehead and full nose.

"Mom looked Cherokee, Star Locklear Sheffield, half Lumbee. The Blacks, your Blacks, married into the Locklears three generations back. Before they kept records it's known that Cherokees owned the most slaves, half breeds and blacks. Before Africans, they took the first explorers as slaves, the Spanish then the Whites. Anyway, Mom was a Lum Cherokee."

"Are there any Blacks on your side? I mean black colored?" Bruce asked.

"In the late eighteen hundreds. That's in the Black Purse Papers, too. When a Black Freedman married an Indian he usually got the rest of her family to help work the land. Same for Indian Freedman. It was a win win."

"I got jipped," Ken yelled and soot shook down over him till he had to spit it out. "All I got for marrying this squaw was a boney backed mare." Ken laughed and Jake nudged him on, begging, "Hey, I'll give you fifty bucks for the mare, but do I have to take the squaw?"

"They go together, mister, sorry," Ken snorted. "Got a triple C breast collar that goes with 'em, for plowing."

Robin and Exilee sarcastically laughed while Scarecrow and Lilly lingered at a baby rock sculpture in the passage wall.

"My dowry'll be so significant every educated Indian in the state'll be asking for me." Robin teased. Then she squeezed behind Ken to follow behind Jake and Bruce. But Ken pressed his backside against hers to aggravate her. "Your husband has a big butt."

"Me? Let's measure, right here. Right now. Who's got a boy scout survival knife? Why I do. And it has inches and centimeters right here on the handle. Whadoyabet she's a thirty incher? Is it legal to keep an Injun with butt that size or does she need to grow a little more?" Ken pulled her by the waist and she whacked him so hard it echoed up and back down the passage while soot sifted down and Ken shook off the burn. "Why can't you ever play along with me?"

"Cause your ideas are stupid, stupid."

"They always end up like this," Exilee huffed at Lilly who was right behind her. "Indoor voice, you two." She gritted her teeth as she wiped soot from her eyes.

Scarecrow's light zoomed. "Ya'll expectin' company?" All the flashlights darted behind them. The creaking ground to a stop and the door to the Underground Railroad closed. The cool air grew cooler and their hyper aware heartbeats drummed in their ears. Their footsteps gritted as their breaths pitched from soft nose whistles to open mouthed panting. And the purring chug of wind over their heads ceased as silence rang like a haunting ghost story.

With Edge pressed up against him, Bruce tugged on Jake's arm to follow and he did, as he wrapped his full hand around Robin's and she jerked on Ken's as he held Exilee's shoulder and Mark, Lilly and Scarecrow followed the train ride out.

Chapter 9

Slick, Slide and Alibi

"Besides, the escape door is kept locked from inside the house now that it's public. Its purpose was to bring up a slave when its master sent someone to check up on his pox, like a bounty hunter. The parents went all the way to the opening at the base of the hill to let go of their children under the Freedom Train's sky, but would come running if they heard the signal. It echoed down the whole passage. "Here, boy," followed by a whistle, just as if the family's beloved pet was being called home."

The group crept along taking the long way out to the opening at the base of the hill, a good twenty acre pass from Eber Magee's skeletal foot's grave. A few feet from the opening Ken instructed them to turn off the flashlights. So near sober they peered out from the cold still black earthen embankment for the same eighteen hundreds view.

Tucked only a few feet behind ancient Longleaf pines and father Oaks, the trickling creek splashed over rocks as mini waves crested. The trickling creek partnered with the summer foliage chanting a comforting blanket of, "S-Free, free, free," as it rode the soft wind up the hill like it was purposely blown to entice the timid. They stood completely enchanted as "S-Free, free, free," chimed over and over from the timberline seducing the entire group like they just might walk into the dark timberline.

In unison, they even stepped forward in an attempt to see. When they strained real hard the shiny silver creek twinkled through the still darkness. And satisfied, they politely smiled at one another and without a word looked up into the dark night sky at the steady North Star. They stretched and swallowed the past's nasty reality like bad medicine then scattered to roam and run the hillside checking for Miss Ginger even though Ken advised them to stay on the foot path. "Ya'll need to be quiet. My parents have the windows open."

"They can't hear us," Edge sassed.

"Everything carries up to the screened in porch." Still in teacher mode, Ken directed with an outstretched arm. "See, no trees between here and there. The porch was the look out. Still is some days."

"Don't they have central heat and air?" Mark cocked his head.

"Nope. Attic fan and fresh air. And their phone's in the pantry." Ken grinned and Scarecrow agreed that was the way to live. Ken explained, "They visit people when they want to talk. Phone is for emergencies. Ya'll be quiet now."

They headed back toward Jake's house scattering like guineas once onto the open terrain and then flocked together again, recounting the Underground Railroad party as the most educational party they'd ever attended, everyone, except Bruce. At the top of the hill Bruce lingered over the timberline view. He stretched out his arms as his dark shadow lengthened forming a long cross out from behind him. And with the crescent moon above Bruce wore a crown in the dark blue night sky.

As Ken guided Mark, Scarecrow and Jake to Two Tails' lot Mark said, "Yea, mon, I'm whiffed goanna many days. Gaum up my sinuses." And Jake tells him, "Mark, I skinned a stillborn calf to save this one, Two Tails. That's how he got his name," Jake explained.

"You skinned it?" Mark asked. "Did ya make a gambrel or just nail it up by the shin bones?"

"Neither. Had it all over the ground. Mostly held it between my legs. Really, I was a wreck. The newborn was born dead and Two Tails' cow had refused her. I called my vet and he said that the only thing he could recommend was an old cowhand's trick. Tie the skin of her calf over the orphan calf. Well, she stopped bawling and now we have a big pet." Jake snapped his fingers and Two Tails cooed a soft moo.

"Regular cowhand, what this farm needed. But Two Tails is ruint. What are you going to do when it's trailer time?" Ken leaned against the rail.

"He's staying, Ken." His greens pinched. "He does tricks," Jake told Mark. "He counts and he'll pull treats out of my back pocket with his tongue. Watch." Jake snatched a wad of grass and put it in his back pocket and climbed over.

"That's sort a' gross," Mark told him. "Doesn't your butt get all wet and slimey?"

Scarecrow laughed as Two Tails looped his tongue around the grass and Jake checked his butt for a wet spot. "Trailer him over to Lumberton. They know what to do. Hell, they eat anything, even butchering horses."

"Good Lord," Ken spat, "now that's perty low. Like eatin' a dog. Can't you put a stop to that?"

"When we catch 'em we will." Scarecrow begrudged. "Usually find the entrails and skeletal remains after the fact. Don't waste much. Make craft crap for their Pow Wows with the hides and hooves. Don't know what it's gonna take to end that mess." He sighed. "Well, till they all get sick. France issued a urgent call for the CDC to start horse meat inspections on account of deaths. Horse meat is full of toxic meds and parasites. Get Alzheimers, cancer, worms, just a mess what these ignorants are eatin'. If, and I mean a big f-ing if, horse slaughter is outlawed the Feds might send us some more UC funds. We can't be everywhere."

"That's just sick," Jake stomached.

"They steal 'em, too," Mark said. "Things are bad for the people right now. Illegals took their jobs. They're back to their old ways like they've got a real reservation. Gamecocks and gambling fetch big dollars and so much homegrown half the kids in elementary school been exposed to it and gang activity. Horse slaughter fits right in. No ethics. No honor."

"Lums need to stick together. I know that. But gawled dookey, there's no excuse for that gyarb. I got an education and fought my way out. I don't see why they can't." Scarecrow spit. "They keep it up and there won't be a swamp. They'll all be in jail and we'll only exist in history books." Mark's brows met as they each summed in agreement with tsks and quiet reflection.

Out of concern that Miss Ginger may be wakened Exilee led Edge and Lilly to her house for a bathroom break while Robin peed by a tree. As they reached the hill's plateau Lilly remarked, "Hope Miss Ginger is okay. She just disappeared." And Exilee assured her that Ginger was probably tucked in like a lamb. Then Robin cantered up acting like she was roping a calf which she pretended was Edge. Her imaginary lasso was right over Edge's head when Jake bellowed out a wailing calf's moo.

Robin dug in her heels and ran straight on. She dropped his feet out from under him with one swift toe tuck and hopped down to her knees at his feet. "Hold!" she hollered as she stilled his kicking feet.

"You're a wild woman! And Black." He sat up and held her by the shoulders as she wrenched back and forth.

Exilee shouted, "She's incorrigible."

Jake fussed, "Stop. You're getting it all over me."

Robin shouted that she didn't care, that cowgirls take the dirt and Jake yelled, "Okay! We cowboys like doing it in the dirt," real deep and coy like. Then he pulled her down to his impatient lips.

From his sanctuary on the hill Bruce opened his eyes as the tree frogs chirped and a whippoorwill called. He mimicked the whippoorwill and in a few moments it called back. He whistled for the Bob White. A Blue Jay's shriek. And the soft Bluebird chant, "Cheer, cheer, cheerful, charmer," the ones his momma had taught him. He repeated the delightful call. And on the third a mockingbird replied, "Cheer, cheerful, cheer." He laughed out loud and was in the middle of his Bluebird refrain when the moment was lost.

Ponies nickered at the chatty bunch of ladies as they neared Exilee's drive and Two Tails the bull bawled like he was in pain when Jake passed his lot. Bruce jogged to join them and was halfway there when suddenly Miss Ginger ambushed them, "Stop right there." Bruce's heart jumped as they all balked and gasped. "I've never had such a lollygagging group. What are ya'll doing down there, making babies or what?"

"Good, gawd," Scarecrow chuckled. "Did she get into that jar?"

"Did you close the door on us?" Ken snapped and Miss Ginger laughed so hard she couldn't talk.

"You scared the daylights out a' us. Why'd you do that?" Exilee asked Miss Ginger.

"Thought it'd be fun. It was." Ginger wholeheartedly laughed and they joined. When their giddy fit wore off she told them, "Wait there. No. Turn around. To get the full effect we oughta be up here where we can look down over it all. I want ya'll to 'xperience what the real runaways did." And they simply obliged.

Miss Ginger's arm stretched out and the group followed till they had to turn around to see the timberline again. "The light was snuffed out as soon they felt the temperature change. The baby chile was kissed good bye and the Freedom Train made its way into the timberline, hidden by the slope of the land from bounty hunters. Then slaves made their way to the cliff, the one that butts out over the creek, gathered supplies left for them and entered the cool creek with its spring fed tributaries. Sometimes, there was rafts or hand dug canoes to make their way to the next station. Mostly, they waded and swam in the deep places as the baby was rafted on makeshift tree trunks or bamboo rafts. It was scary and dark and the only way to be free."

"A storm's comin'." Miss Ginger stiffened as she checked the sky. "Listen. Must be way off, but it's comin'." She was still questioning the numerous stars blinking back at her when distant beats pounded like drumming thunder lettin' loose for a summer downpour on the hot July night. It grew clearer. Louder. And faster. When the thunderous beats vibrated against their soles they curiously looked about then Edge squealed, "What's that?"

Misun's white mane flashed in a light beam. "A pony's loose," Robin huffed sarcastically and marched toward the runaway's hoof beats, but stopped as numerous distant eyes glowed. "Stampede! Get to the barn or get run over." As she sprinted to the barn she told Exilee, "Your pony's a freakin' mess, girl," then to everyone, "He does this all the time, like he's freakin' starved for attention. But this time he's not alone. Come on."

Exilee broke away from the group hurrying to the barn and Jake was right with her. "Misun?" he called out. "Misun, is that you?" In full throttle he turned to Exilee, "Well?" Their eyelids ridged up against their disbelieving eyes when not one, but all three of Jake's dogs led by Misun rushed up in a barreling jog. They slowed to a pace then a fast walk and sought out the hands that taught them.

In sequence, they all obeyed, but anxiously spun their ears back from where they came. "Exilee, whadaya thinks going on?" Jake asked as they panted.

The agitated pony backed away from Exilee and jerked his thick neck back and forth and when that didn't get any response, spun around and blew. "He's beautiful," Edge awed and Lilly agreed, "Look at his eyes."

With all the light beams his brilliant blue eyes sparkled out from under his long white forelock and his paint coat created a pleasing pattern of brown river rocks and black pebbles against his white coat. "Pretty is as pretty does," Miss Ginger quipped. "He's for sale," Ken called out as Exilee neared her Misun. When the pony trumpeted a back tingling squeal Exilee signaled for everyone to stand where they were as she got closer and he did it again. He reared with a mighty trumpet. "Quit! I got it," Exilee scolded.

Exilee aimed her light toward each of the three houses and barns, the fence lines and white sandy road, and all their dark hidey holes, but when nothing stood out, she stroked his neck. As he jogged away Mark laughed and Exilee cussed. And again, she scoped out the perimeter's dark hidey holes.

"Don't think your pony knows German," Mark told Exilee as they noted the dogs on guard.

"He's trouble," Lilly pouted, "but he's gorgeous."

"This is going on video." Edge aimed her cell phone's video recorder at the dog and pony show as Exilee aimed her flashlight all around. "This is so funny."

"It's not funny," Jake reprimanded. "These dogs are priceless." Misun kicked up his heels toward the dogs and swung his neck for them to follow. "Crap," Exilee hurried.

"Sitz," Jake's deep voice pulled a smile from Robin. But Exilee grabbed Jake's shoulder,

"No, make em' track the trouble that started all this."

"Are you sure?"

"Yes! If they take someone down it's their problem."

"Such! Such!" Jake's German commanded the dogs at a sprint with their snouts to the ground. Then down to a pace. Then a walk as they checked scents. Robin ran off in the direction of the flatbed trailers' barn where they had all parked. "I'm getting my rope! Hold on, ya'll."

"Bring your flashlights. Something's wrong." Exilee waved for Ken as the group cautiously followed Misun.

"No gyp is priceless," Bruce mumbled.

Ken tried to sneak up on Misun, but every time he would fart and dart away. Exilee stomped toward her husband. "When are you gonna learn to listen to me? Just follow. Misun's fixin' to lead us right to it."

"To what?" Edge worried.

As Ken took heed and cautiously followed the pony with his flashlight the pony sniffed at the air and puff talked while the dogs sniffed. "Rabbits is all," Miss Ginger tried to remain calm. "There's enough folks out here. No one'll bother us, honey." But Lilly pulled up her jean's pant leg and held out her once concealed hand gun. Miss Ginger tapped Edge's shoulder and pointed. Edge zoomed in on it and then back to the animals' hind ends. "We'll, stay here," Miss Ginger told Lilly.

"No. Stay close to the group. Don't want to lose anyone." Then Lilly signaled Scarecrow as she went around to the screened in porch and he followed the dogs. His large handgun shined silver when Miss Ginger's light ran over it and Edge zoomed in with her phone's camera. "This is gonna be so hot. It'll go viral."

The pony twisted his head at Scarecrow as he approached from the left and blew a wet hippo blast that startled a, "Shit," out of him. Edge zoomed.

"The sound on?" Mark whispered to Edge and she affirmed with a shiny white grin.

Exilee mumbled that she was tired of the hassle and approached Misun again, this time, she quietly cooed, "Oginalii, oginalii, do-i-s-di-hi-na?" Misun flung his head up and down and then mouthed Exilee's shirt tail like a foal does a teat. "Someone scared him," Exilee told Ken.

The Gamecocks

"Hush," Ken flashed his palms as Scarecrow pointed out an odd figure and the dogs whined as they rushed. A dark shadow drug itself along the road. Jake yelled, "Such! Pass auf Wache!" And the dogs bolted like feral badgers.

But Misun outdistanced the dogs, jumping fences and clearing ditches, before they even reached the pony barn as the shadowy figure lurched with arms out for support in a hop-jump-run. The lightbeams flashed over the dogs, neck in neck and in noses and hooves. While Ken, Jake and Scarecrow did their best when Mark disappeared behind the big barn. Ken sprinted down the sandy two lane path. And then it was just Jake and Scarecrow against the pack ripping the stranger apart.

In a dead run Exilee yelled, "No, Robin! No!" as her lariat hovered over Misun's ears. Robin hastily jerked back and fell. And Misun farted and darted away then spun around to blow contempt. And the harried stranger sliced through the jet black night with a shining machete. Jake signaled and the dogs backed up and surrounded the stranger with raised hackles, snarls and snaps.

Scarecrow commanded the stranger to drop to his knees with his gun at his back and the stranger threatened with his machete. Crow jammed the barrel between the stranger's shoulders and the machete spiraled down in a silver sliver and barely missed Exilee as it twanged into the earth like an arrow. And the stranger raised his arms in defeat.

Instantly, Misun pinned his ears and joined the pack. "Pass auf Wache!" Jake commanded. Their necks swelled with heated threats, raised hackles and swollen necks. And Misun pinned his ears flat and lowered his head. Pawed and snapped in a motion to charge as the dogs' fangs shone white against their dark coats and a chorus of trembling growls encased the stranger as Scarecrow holstered his gun and dove into the snarling pit.

Just as Scarecrow was about to pull the thick man to the ground the stranger screamed, "No-o-oo!" Misun snapped the thick man's thigh. And blood pulsed in long streams up over the pony's white writhing mane as the pony jerked the screaming man three feet off the ground.

Women screamed and the pony ran away dragging the thick man's upper body across the grass as the snarling German Shepherds' snapped at his head and flinging limbs. Onacona hung on by a mouthful of hair as the stranger reached for her ears. Jake and Exilee ran, commanding the pony in both English and German to drop it and the dogs to guard it. The wailing man jerked on the dog's ear and she released only to snap his ear and he screamed again as he covered his bloody ear. "Help!"

From the edge of darkness Bruce charged spread eagle at Misun and growled like a primal beast. Instantly the dogs gained on him while the pony darted off with his prize to the left. One dog lunged at Bruce's outstretched arm, but in mid air Bruce stabbed it in the neck with his rock rigid bare hand and it retreats. Jake sprinted, shouting, "Hier!" But the dog went back for more, with the pack. The dogs snapped at Bruce's flying legs as his pants ripped up the sides and fangs lunged for skin. Bruce kicked dogs straight in the snout. Elbowed another and then whacked the pony across the neck.

The dogs lunged again in fierce rage and were hurled to the ground as Bruce seized the floundering man from the pony's gapped jaws whipping the stranger's thick body against the dogs. Bruce pinned the man under his boot right over his gushing flesh. "Arghh," he cried and Misun returned to sniff. "No!" The stranger threw a handful of sand in the pony's face. "No." And to Bruce, "Youse gonna be all the sorry in the world. You son of a bitch."

"Pfui," Jake commanded the dogs not to touch the nasty man. And Bruce pressed down even more against the round man's severed femoral. Bruce pressed and the man screamed again and again. Finally pulling himself up over his severe gut with his mouth wide open like he was fixin' to bite and was served a swift kick to the jaw. And the man fell unconscious.

Scarecrow blew, "Didn't think he'd ever shut up." He told Bruce to stay on the look out while he searched his pants pockets and when he said he didn't find anything cussed. He scoped out the area. Told Bruce he'd call for EMT and was going to check out the house.

Robin took her time dusting off her butt and swooned as did Edge while the two dreamily gazed at Bruce. Robin gazed through her lusty Cherokee brown eyes. While Edge lusted through her camera lens at the brute of a man who in less than twenty four hours had become a primal mystical powerhouse. Edge zoomed in on his thick honey lips. On that soot stained boyish face, then down to his tight hiney and his barren thighs scratched with fang lines and dripping dots of blood as his jeans' legs flapped open against the cooling night wind.

Edge zoomed out for a full view of his heroic stance over the pinned man then aimed back up at his mysterious gray eyes and zoomed back to other places. Edge licked her lips over the primal heat he'd stirred as Robin finger combed her slick black hair up over her gracious bosom. Every flashlight was aimed on Bruce as his gray wolf eyes drawled the two ladies like doe in rut over the horned ornament. Bruce's chest heaved up and down, expanding over his small waist as he glared out into the darkness.

From discerning views the rivaling ladies unabashedly curved their mid backs and sashayed over to the heroic scene where Misun blew and pawed near the unconscious man. Bruce told the pony to back off, but Misun continued. Exilee marched over and commanded, "Check his pockets. Take his pants off. He's got something." She rubbed Misun's withers and he tucked his head up under her arm. When Bruce stated that Scarecrow already had a clean search she stared him over and then pried his mouth open with a stick and checked his nasty snaggletooth mouth to no avail.

The dogs paraded like a pack on wait for a meal, whining and sniffing at the man, the air around him, and Bruce. "Onacona," Robin kissed at her dog, but it did not obey. "Lass es," Jake signaled his dogs to leave the men alone and then hand signaled them to be at rest and they restlessly circled around and one by one lay down in a loose huddle. "Good Lord, you make a scene, don't cha, Buddyrow." Jake stared at the sight: Robin gawking over her hero and Bruce pressing harder and harder against the unconscious man's wound. "You don't have to keep pressing. He's not gonna struggle. He's passed out," Jake told him. But Bruce's locked jaw prevailed as he continued pressing.

"Is he dead?" Edge asked as Miss Ginger eyed the scene.

Jake dropped to his knees and checked the pinned man's carotid. Then took off his sooty tee shirt and told Bruce to get off so he could put on a tourniquet. Bruce took a breath and said, "Work it under his leg or he'll bleed to death. I'll keep some pressure while you do it." Jake assessed the possibility aiming a light all around the bloody wound site. "You're right." And Robin swooned. "You saved his life. I thought you were just being mean."

Edge kept the video running as Jake worked his wound up tee shirt under the thick man's big upper thigh while Robin aimed a light. Jake's biceps pumped the hardy blue veins under his white shoulders as he strained to tighten the tourniquet. "Let off easy now and let's see if it stops the bleeding." Jake studied the tourniquet as Bruce eased off and blood pulsed over his shoulder. "Put it back." Jake grabbed Bruce's bloody boot. "You're gonna have to keep it there."

Ken rushed back from the sandy two lane road. Ten feet from the group he hollered for them to get their lights out of his eyes. "Just me. It's Ken. His ride just tore out a here. Looked like a girl, long hair, yellow sports car. Certain of that." Ken got closer. "Not a very good get away car." Ken grimaced over the scarlet sight. "That pony. I'd a never believed it if I hadn't seen it." Then Ken looked up at Bruce. "Man, whadathey feed you in prison? I need some of that."

But Bruce was still checking the perimeter and barely grinned.

Scarecrow called for Ken, "Get up here," from Jake's front porch just as Lilly rounded the corner of Ken's house with her drawn weapon. When Scarecrow signaled for her to watch over the group she relaxed her weapon. Lilly quickly sized up the scene with the unconscious man, asked if anyone knew him and when no one did told them that rescue was en route and to hold tight. "Keep that video going," she informed Edge. Then to the group, "May be flushing more perps. Keep alert."

"But the getaway car just left," Robin perplexed.

Lilly spun around. "How long you been on the force, girl?" The words jerked out. And when Robin speechlessly gapped Lilly simply said that no one wants to get caught. "They'd leave their own momma at the crime scene. Help me keep watch." She affirmed with a pointed finger.

"They're after Bruce's cash." Exilee rubbed her arms. "One of his friends probably went blabbermouthin' about how he gave out some cash tonight and they came after the rest of it. That's all." The bloody man's inverted pockets shined like flags.

When Bruce finally unclenched his jaw he gained everyone's full attention. "Jake, where'd you put Momma's things?" He held his hand over the bird effigy under his dirty sweat soaked tee.

"In the big barn." When Jake stretched out his arm all four dogs honed in on the big barn. "On the flat bed trailer with the busted axle. No one knows about that stuff. It's just toys and pictures, things from your momma's room, isn't it?" Jake told Robin, "Woman kept everything. Covers a twenty foot flatbed." Robin just shrugged.

Bruce breathed like he'd bust wide open any second. "Where's that rescue squad comin' from?" He spat. "Glad it's not one of us bleeding to death." His angst showed all the way down to his bare blood dotted throbbing thigh as he pressed into the wound even harder. "Turn that damn thing off."

"Okay. No prob, cuz," Edge flipped it closed. "The video's only a couple minutes. Mostly still shots," she mumbled to the others as Bruce directed Jake to hold his foot down on the wounded man, but Jake refused. "I need to get in my house and see what's missing." His arms cut through the dark night. "And we'd better wait for the medics and do this thing right. The Law's tricky. We don't want him suing us later."

"Yea, we better wait," Exilee calmly advised and the others agreed. "Call again and see how long they'll be," she instructed Robin.

Robin quickly made the call while adjusting the girls and demanded logistics then relayed the information that they were enroute less than one mile from destination.

Then she lingered over Bruce. She studied his muscular neck and back up to his mysterious grey eyes and then to Jake's jealous greens. When he winked at her she sheepishly winked back.

Unexpectedly, the pony nudged up against Exilee from behind and she jumped with aimed fists. But Misun puff talked like pony's do and she embraced the little charmer while breathing in his musky grassy scents. "Do you have more cash here, Bruce?"

"Not worried about it," Bruce moaned. When he quickly cupped his package the ladies looked away in giggles, except Exilee. She stared him over. The two locked down until Bruce finally gave. His eyes rolled and chin stretched out like he was changing faces and even in the challenging darkness the change was significant enough. His stoic poker face with the deep set eyes and elongated cheeks were gone, replaced with a round boyish face and friendly eyes. But while she was entranced with inspecting Bruce her pony rubbed her till she lost her footing.

"Here they are." Edge's neck stretched out like a Thoroughbred's on guard. "Yep, that's them." The big white hood charged the corner. Passed the hay pastures and roared toward the houses with a cloud of spewing sand. The ambulance's blinding lights held them as Edge resumed recording. "Just this part, Bruce, I promise."

"Damn, this is gonna wake Sara and Luke. Get prepared, ya'll. David'll wanna know the whole shooting match," Exilee cracked her knuckles.

First thing EMT had to say was that Bruce saved the man's life. Then after a speedy assessment, a rushed EMT punched needles as another capped his face with an oxygen mask. And even with their bright spotlights no one could identify him. They called in stats as Robin spilled out the entire pony dragging karate chopping dog whopicodling heroic fight. "Is that what happened to his ear?" asked the EMT checking his eyes and reading his pulse.

"No, that was my dog," Robin proudly answered and all four EMTs dogmatically checked behind their backs. "Oh, they're on rest command," Robin assured. "Don't worry. They know a bad guy when they see one."

"This must be one bad dude," replied the EMT reading the blood pressure monitor. Another guided the EMT with the tourniquet cuff to lock it down as he added, "Baddest man in the whole damn town. Geez." The EMT with the tourniquet monitor justified that it was locked down and directed Bruce to slowly ease his boot off from the toe to the heel in slow increments. When no blood seeped they reflectively sighed.

But Miss Ginger and the others cringed at the gooey red blood, the purple clots and thick caked blood covering the chunk of missing flesh from the man's thigh. Bruce scraped and rubbed his boot across the grass while the four EMT's lifted the man onto a stretcher. As they hopped into the ambulance the last one in told Bruce, "He could've easily had a heart attack from the shock alone. Knocking him out saved him from that. But your boot did the trick, preventing death by exanguiation."

"I don't know what happened." His statement took them all aback. "Well, it went down so fast," he rationalized as he squeezed his palms together. Eyebrows danced. Doors closed and sand spun. And the tour group checked one another's soot covered bodies in the orangey red tail light.

"Barn wired for light?" Bruce asked Exilee and she explained where to find the switch. Edge offered to take a flashlight and Robin honed in like a hawk. "Just what does Bruce have to do to prove he's a big boy now, scalp somebody?" She rolled her shoulders in conjunction with her hips leaving no doubt she was the princess on petty as Jake stroked the dog's ears nearest him.

Edge shined her light over Bruce as she recorded his stealth toward the big dark barn. When Exilee called out for them to tell Mark it was okay to come out now if he was still in there hiding Bruce sped up. "Wait for me," Edge urged. Then when she matter of factly announced into the mic, "Bruce Black in action again to find his step brother" he laughed. "You haven't changed a bit, you little pest."

He wedged open the huge double doors. Felt for the switch and flicked it on. Suspended fluorescent bulbs flickered and dinged until darkness was snuffed and the edges of the loft glowed. At once, the disturbed yard chickens peacefully slumbering in their dark barn clucked and chattered. When Bruce and Edge sought out the middle aisle and didn't near the roosting chickens the chatter ceased as their footsteps gritted against the sandy dirt floor. And from above the occasional flutter of a purple martin's wings filled the big barn.

The mid section of the big barn held two humongous tractors, mowing attachments of various sizes, hay baling equipment, and two rows of more farm equipment. Stacks of drying lumber posed in the loft. And up against the back wall were two flat bed trailers. One was empty. The other held Bruce's beloved cardboard boxes. Mark popped up near a disheveled box sitting open on the earthen floor and gasped at his find. "Mom took this game when I was just a kid."

And Bruce streamed down the aisle. As the item became clearer at ten feet away Bruce stated, "It's a war game." And Mark's dry mouth choked him as he shook the shiny black laminated box. It was no larger than a shirt box, but screamed as large as a tattle telling teenage sister that Bruce's stepbrother was pilfering. With eyes as wide as a tot's over a daddy's belt, Mark squeaked, "Mom doesn't like violence."

Two feet away, "What else did you find," Bruce cocked his head, "Buddyrow?"

"Nothin', I swear."

"You snuck in here soon as ya got the chance."

"No. It wasn't like that." Mark stammered. "I thought if somebody was in here I could chase him out. That's all."

"You tell people about my things being stored in here, my old toys? They're worth something for a collector." Bruce breathed hot bull steam as he peered over Mark's shoulder at the rummaged boxes. Several on the front row were wide open. "Or are you lookin' for something more valuable?"

Mark sidestepped out of the way and told Bruce to look for himself. "Nothing else is missing. I swear."

"Don't run off."

Edge began another video. "Yea, stay right there."

"Give me that." Bruce snatched at her phone, but she jerked it away and hopped backwards like a crow with a stolen trinket. "Okay, I'll turn it off." And Edge slipped it into her short's back pocket. Then as Bruce inspected his boxes she tucked it into her bra, tightly against the left cup. "You lookin' for anything particular? I can help." She flipped open a box and before he had a chance to answer was turning pages in a picture album.

Bruce rummaged through the open boxes. "Did you even think about closing 'em so barn dirt doesn't get in everything? It's all I've got left of my family." He swallowed the anger and heaved. "When are you gonna grow up?"

"I swear. I didn't open any. These were already open." Mark tapped at a box on the front row. "There's one in the back. Check it. It looks like it's been opened, too."

Bruce carefully stepped onto the flatbed trailer and eased boxes aside until he stood over the box with the flaps standing askew. He glanced back at Mark. "There's dirt all over it, 'cept where someone just opened it." He glared down at Mark. "Scarecrow will run a set of prints for me. All I got ta do is ask." Mark didn't flinch as Bruce laid back the flaps. Lifted up his momma's old jewelry box and fought his burning eyes.

The dull finish had old nicks and alarming freshly cut grooves. Bruce freed the jammed crooked drawer sticking halfway out and Dime Store earrings and tarnished silver costume jewelry fell out into the jammed open drawer beneath it. The drawers were as plain as the outside of the box. No velvety red lining, but the box had been well crafted with dovetail joints. He carefully scooped up the jewelry and placed it into the top drawer which held a simple gold chain.

"What'd you find?" Edge tried to see.

"My mother's jewelry box. It's broken." With it clutched to his chest he faced them.

"Damn," Mark winced. "I'd love to know who did that."

Bruce climbed down and sat on the edge of the trailer and his bare blood dotted legs shone under the florescent lights. When he gently manipulated the drawers closed a square chunk from the bottom fell and as it landed dusty barn dirt flew up. Bruce's weary red eyes welled up as he held the box up to his chest. One leg uncontrollably vibrated while the other twisted around its blood stained booted ankle.

"Maybe we can fix it." Mark warily observed.

Edge picked up the wooden chunk. Dusted it off and placed it on Bruce's bare thigh and when she did allowed her fingertips to linger long enough to feel his heat. Bruce inspected the piece and then tilted the box in varying angles as he inspected the damage underneath the box and dry dirt splashed up again. Bruce cradled the coveted box up to his chest. Held his breath and let out a resounding sigh over the sight of the fallen chunk. It sparkled like the Little People had lit a thousand tiny live fires.

"Oh my God, look at this." Mark held it up to the light. "It's beautiful." Edge reached up for it as Bruce sat spellbound. "This light is pitiful." Mark stretched the piece out of her reach. "Shine your flashlight on it." As Edge aimed the light Mark blew on the golden filigreed cross and the black stone center blinked. "Wipe it off, Mark," she nearly whispered. Diamonds encircled it.

"It's the real thing." With eyes as wide as silver dollars Mark held it out by the edges. As Bruce beheld the unbelievable bejeweled cross Mark stood extra tall. "Kind of thing royalty wears, huh?"

Bruce marveled up at the cross with the same serendipity smile his momma had. And Mark wiped the dusty cross with a clean spot on his sooty tee shirt, but it was still hard to determine what the other stones were. So Edge told him to spit on it and when he did the rubies shined.

Bruce grabbed it as he sprung off the flatbed, "All those years ago, in that chair," Bruce softly palpated, "this is what she was holding." With both hands he held it up to the light as the serendipity smile returned. But it vanished after he jammed the cross down into his front pocket. "You two are in jeopardy now, like me."

Mark backed up as Bruce seized Edge by the arm. "The Society won't let this happen. Everything that's gone on tells me that." He panted and she winced. "No way, never, The Society won't let this happen. You can't tell a soul. Understand?" His fierce penetration frightened them both into silent agreement.

"The secret council, it's for real?" Mark's quickened hushed words spread chill bumps.

She rubbed them down as her nostrils flared. "That's all rumor," she cried, "Some stupid teenagers started that junk at a Pow Wow. There's nothin' to it. It's in all the schools now. We're from the Lost Colony. Heirs to royalty. And we'll never get federal funds. It's so stupid. Who cares?"

Bruce jerked Edge up by the shoulders and shook so hard the white ribbon holding back her long brown curls fell to the dirt. "You got it wrong, girl." She tried to jerk away but he jerked her back square into his glaring grays. Scared a squeal out of her and clasped his hand over her mouth. "This is the last time I'll tell you. Not another word. This never happened."

The chickens chattered as the trio left the barn to its dark and Bruce palmed the turquoise effigy hugging his swollen chest. "I'd say I'm lucky to be alive, but I believe there's more to it."

Mark secured the big barn doors and the trio walked in silence until they reached Jake's front steps. Edge said she didn't think she should drive home. That she was too tired. "I can sleep on the couch."

"That's where I'm sleeping," Mark informed her as he cautiously peered around the dark corners of the house. "Wonder if those dogs are put up?"

Edge said the dogs wouldn't bother anyone unless they ran. Then said she can sleep on the floor. That she'd make a pallet. But Bruce told her to drink a cup of coffee and that she'd be fine. "Just don't stop anywhere." He held the screen door open as he told Mark, "If anyone else was with that fool he's long gone." Indoor voices merged into a dull roar and amplified toward the open door. "Get inside. Sounds like everyone else is."

The trio stepped inside and Edge went straight to the coffee pot. Bruce to the hallway and Mark squinted through the screen door. When Miss Ginger asked, "Who's out there?" Mark jumped and flashed a wild smile. "Oh, just telling the farm animals good night is all." Mark plopped down on the couch and leaned over the arm rest nearest her rocker. "Isn't that how ya'll do it?" Onacona was curled up on the floor between them. She raised her head and Mark reached down to finger her thick coat. Then firmly rubbed her eager neck.

Miss Ginger winked. "You stay all weekend, chile. We need to get you city boys straightened out. Okay?"

"Plannin' on it." Mark swung his legs over the couch cushions to recline. But in mid air Miss Ginger yelled, "Uh, uh, uh, pull them filthy boots off. Youse covered with soot. Get up." She threw him a blanket from beside her chair. "Wash a blanket lot easier than that couch." As Onacona sniffed his boots Mark tightened up all over. The large German Shepherd's ears flattened back, then one pointed toward the hallway.

"We need your office, Miss Ginger. Yurkers taint got no raisin' these days." Scarecrow stretched out behind Mark as he pulled off his boots. Crow ruffled the boy's hair and then lowered his towering frame over the back of the couch and coyly cuffed Mark's ear. "Whadcha find out there, boy?"

"Nuthin." When Mark clamped his lips like he was fixin' to be spoon fed sulfur Onacona whined at his knees, but Mark hatefully told the dog to go lay down.

And Scarecrow remarked, "Never send a boy for a man's job."

Lilly pressed her finger into the dented door jamb before she opened the passage door. "They succeeded. Russ, look at this." Scarecrow shook his head. "Claw marks." Lilly examined Scarecrow's growing fury. "Fisk and Wart," he seethed.

Jake's eyes whitened. "Those dents tell you that?"

"Hammer claws; their signature," Scarecrow blew. "Been closing the bars on 'em for years. You'd think they'd smartin' up and use something else."

"Well tell me how you know how each door was?" Ken warily asked. "You set 'em like that?"

"I did. I propped 'em. I'm on county's time tonight." Scarecrow led them back down the hall and on the way swept down over the couch and popped Mark's crossed arms a loose. "I told 'em Bruce might have a little trouble with some old jar runners or a shiner. And I was right. Someone went through Bruce's room."

Scarecrow opened the door to strewn clothes and Bruce rummaging in dresser drawers on the overturned mattress. Pillow fluff scattered as they inched through the mess. Jake picked up Bruce's clothes halfway folding them as he layered them across his arm and scornfully surveyed the ruined room. "They must've searched everything." They all pitched in and when Bruce simply asked for a trash bag the monumental tension threatening to burst swished all the way out to the little square frames in the screen door.

Chapter 10

Straight Back Chairs and Copper Stills

Summer's stinging yellow slit pierced the edge of the gelding's pasture holding Bruce captive as if a bold beautiful woman were undressing before him after his long cold and disciplined years of celibacy. Propped up on his elbow, in the twin size bed, he cupped his jaw and gazed spellbound out the dark early morning window as his pinky finger tapped at the delicious curve above his full top lip. He admired the bright slice of dawn until it thickened and the light sparked like fireworks in long jagged lines against the black of night trying to hold it down. But that burning urging dawn rose and boldly broke free spilling over the hill.

With morning's orange light he carefully went through the bundle of clothes Jake had purchased for him until he found a new dark blue pair of jeans. He pulled the jeweled cross out of his decimated jeans and held the precious token up to the window where the yellow light lit the twinkling gold filigree like fire. Yellow streaks glazed straight on to the corner of the dresser mirror where his turquoise bird necklace hung. The minute indentions signifying bird eyes blinked with life.

He slipped it over his neck and checked his reflection. Summer's yellow orange light highlighted the dark circles under his eyes marking him as aged and weakened. Still, he exuberantly smiled like a child with the winning ribbon. He ran his hand over the nest of curly brown hair between his pale pecs and placed the bird effigy in it like it was a fur nest. He tightened his abs and palmed his rock hard core then counted his ribs until seduced by the breakfast sausage.

His barefoot steps went unnoticed. The only light on in the cozy kitchen was the bare bulb over the golden stove top. Miss Ginger's honey brown skin glowed orange under the burning bulb as she tended a black iron skillet of sizzling sausage. Everything else was either black or hazy orange in the omniscient smoke. Bruce blinked at the clock on the coffee pot's base. It was ten till five. "Morning."

"Sit down and I'll get your ellick, chile."

Bruce warmly smiled over her accommodating reference as he chose the straight back chair facing the front door. After she turned the patties she poured two cups of coffee.

"Pour your own cream." She positioned the half and half pint container in the middle of the round table. "Never can tell how much a man wants." She didn't say a word about him sitting down at the table without a shirt. Not a word. But behind his back, cringed.

Bruce poured enough cream to make his ellick the color of brownstone in the sunshine while Miss Ginger added none. "I like mine strong and black like I like my men." She grinned as she took a seat across the table.

"Then why'd you ask me for a date?" When Bruce leaned over the table her grin faded. "You know more about me than I do." His hot words rushed as his bird effigy tapped the table. She leaned up closer and whispered. "Mark's on the couch."

"No. He's going through Momma's boxes in the barn." Bruce leaned back, pulled the jeweled cross from his pocket and put it on the table. "He thinks there's more."

"Lord Almighty," she ogled. "It's true." She studied Bruce then spryly scooted her chair back. Flicked on the light and hurried behind him. When she flapped Bruce's ear back and with her fingertip traced the deep lines she sent shivers over his bare shoulders.

He turned around and looked up at her with a grimace. "You better tell me something." His wide palm covered the jeweled cross as he tucked it back into his jeans' pocket and she instructed him to get their coffee. She turned off the light and led him to the back porch. She aimed her cocked head at the deck area overhanging the entrance to the Underground Railroad Tours. The early morning summer dew rested on the wooden deck like it'd been pressure washed. When its slick surface caused Miss Ginger to slide Bruce all but dropped the two cups onto the railing to catch her. "Never know when the Lord is gonna call you up. Do we?" She was not smiling.

Bruce handed her her coffee cup as she sat on the top step and he slid past her to sit below, situating himself so he could lean back against a spindle.

"Spill it," he smiled. "Like you just said, we never know." His coffee went down in one long gulp. Then he held his empty cup at his chest like he was waiting for her to fill it with treasure.

"It's all like it's supposed to be, I reckon. Presbyterians call it Providence." She took a sip then leaned into him. "Your ear is marked with the cross."

"That's a birthmark. A defect."

"The natives had odd ways about 'em." Her head stopped bobbing back and forth. "When they took the Whites they marked 'em and each of their childrens so they'd know where they came from. Each generation is marked." Her eyebrows stood up.

"That mark is for the leaders, the descendants of Governor John White's daughter. He was given the cross by Sir Walter Raleigh." She cocked her head down at Bruce's front jean pocket. "Queen Elizabeth took it straight off her bosom and gave it to him for finding the New Lands." She gasped up at the dark shadowy sky as the orange and blue gleamed its edges. "I don't know if they believed it had powers or not. But they knew for sure it didn't belong to them."

"Is that in your papers?"

"No, chile," she whispered over him. "It's too dangerous."

Bruce looked away out into the timberline where he'd handed Robin the yellow cactus bloom then back to Miss Ginger. "Are the Crowsons in danger?"

"Don't imagine so, but you've got to claim your heritage so all this can stop, you hear?"

When the bluebirds sang their morning cheer a hunting hawk swept in and they dove into their hidey holes. The hawk, too low and too close to stop, landed on a split rail post. Stared right at Bruce. Opened his sharp bill and showed his tongue. Then ejected upwards like a rocket on fire hurling fluffy little scrap feathers that slowly stilled on the dewy grass.

"The Society, are they the ones who killed my mother?"

"I don't believe that for one second." Miss Ginger's entire body quivered. "The Society wants to fight the Lums for English blood rights. It's an honor issue. There's no money in it, no funds gonna set 'em up like The Lumbee Council keeps hopin' on for the feds to do with Indian rights. Government says the Lums don't have enough red to have to pay 'em. I know. I talked to them face to face. I been in the beltline, boy. Take a switch ta me if I get that notion again. Snake pit of damnation! I never!" She jabbed at the air. "I was right there in Washington and spoke with representatives who'd been pissed off at one thing or another and was willing to give me a word. Most of 'em thought I was just a simple minded old Negra woman." She guffawed then quickly focused back onto Bruce's eager eyes. "Oh, chile, I been all over, up and down the East Coast visiting retired Congressmen, Chiefs on their death beds and shriveled up Negroes who tell it like it is and like it was when it was all going down." She cautiously stopped when Two Tails bawled in the distance. "Someone's out. You said Mark was in the barn."

"Yea, that kid," Bruce sighed and looked down into his empty cup.

"He knows something's up. Maybe you oughta warn that boy 'fore he talks to the wrong folks. This is serious now. The Lumbee Council is in Washington right now looking for more votes to get on board. They're not gonna let The Society get in their way, if they can help it." Miss Ginger backed off and pulled her lips together like she was fixin' to dare the truth out a' somebody.

"You believe that thief or would be thief here last night was sent by The Society or The Council?"

"You don't really need to ask me that, do you?" When Bruce shook his head she added, "They're regular The Second Society now, aren't they? Bruce, you been protected for years by The Society as much as possible without giving away who you are. Lord knows they pulled some fast ones to keep you from gettin' kilt or beat to a pulp being in the middle of all that likker business all your life."

"Who told you that?"

Startled, Miss Ginger held her cup to her lips and studied him over the rim. After it was empty she asked for his hand. "Bruce, I lived a long time and seen what makes folks do what they do. I just know, okay?"

"Don't play games with me." Bruce's baby face begged. "I need to know everything. I gotcha on the Crowsons. So they know and you, but who else? I can't stand not knowing who is in on this, who's a part of The Society, who to trust." He seethed. "I can't stand it."

"I know. But I don't have those answers. When The Society opens itself up to you, and they will, be open to the truth."

"The truth? I thought you just gave me that, Raleigh's jewel from the queen and the mark and the fight. God knows, what else is there?"

Miss Ginger grasped his forearm. "People been waiting a long time for you to be ready. I'm sure of that. And I got a strong feeling they know you're 'bout as powerful as a bull after last night. If not, they'll know by lunch time."

His quizzical expression begged. "Just tell me." He huffed. "What else is there? Powerful for what?"

"Easy," she sternly warned and he took it well. "You just watch. This little town'll have every ear bent down to the Coast and back before noon over your welcome home visitor last night. They ain't stupid. Someone come in here like that knows you got some powerful medicine worth risking their life for." With her chin tucked down and nostrils flared, "Keep an eye out. Be aware of everyone and everything as it happens. It'll tell you the truth faster than folks will. Understand?"

"You're right." The bird effigy tickled in its fur nest. "They want the proof. Me too. What I've waited for all this time." Bruce ran his palm over the jeweled cross deep in his front pocket. "The proof, and the truth. It's not my cross, is it?"

"No. I just feel that there's more. I told you all I knows." Miss Ginger took in a deep breath. "This thing is bigger than what all we seen. And chile, when the truth comes out, embrace it, no matter what. Your momma would 'a wanted it that way."

Before he could open his mouth Mark hopped up the steps. "I knew it was you, early bird." He lightly swatted Bruce's big bare toe. "What time we meeting your building dealer?" He sniffed up at the open kitchen window. "Sausage? I thought we were meeting him for breakfast. You buying? I think we should go to a buffet."

Bruce couldn't help but grin, like Miss Ginger, as she stretched and surveyed the little back yard up to the side of the house where the split rail guided the tourists. "Do I hear those dogs? Or something else out?"

"It's the dogs. They been out all night." Mark called for them. "Onacona started whining and when I opened the door to let her out these guys greeted me." He took turns playfully rubbing their necks. "They're so big. Glad they like me."

"Did they follow you into the barn?" Bruce asked and Mark's shoulders twisted like a child's twirly bird toy, "Naw."

Miss Ginger laughed as she headed back inside. "Exilee counts those birds with Luke every morning. His favorite is Chirper." From the doorway, she turned around to face Mark. "Luke's chicken only got one wing with feathers. He wore the others off. How he carries it around."

Mark scratched his neck and swatted at the no see ums. "I didn't see where they messed with any chickens."

"Come on," Bruce stretched out like a slinky across several steps and when he stood stretched some more. "Let's eat."

Mark reached out to pop his cousin's concave abs, but Bruce was too quick. "You need a few pull ups over at Dunrovin's Pizza." Bruce released Mark's wrist. "And have the milkshakes." But when Bruce squinted like he'd suddenly got a headache and squeezed the railing Mark asked if he got into the likker jar after everyone went to bed. "No, kid, but I might today."

"All right," Mark played the railing like he was jamming drumsticks. "Knew I'd have a good time this weekend."

The old copper hinges creaked so loudly the dogs rushed up the steps and whined up at the kitchen window. "Bet she's hiding your fun right now," Bruce bantered.

The stealthy German Shepherds took turns circling to rest on the deck. Their dark brown eyes glimmered with the morning's gold sun. The brilliant ball of orange fire lighting up the dew covered Bermuda lawns and the fescue and orchard grass pastures defined day from night as it highlighted the Alpha's golden undercoat. Onacona was the last to circle. As she surveyed her pack and rested her head on her front paws her rich dark sable coat parted in folds like shimmering golden silk.

But the dogs didn't rest for long. As soon as they heard them they ran with sharp squeals of delight as they greeted the young family. With soft strokes and Luke's tail teasing the dogs escorted them to Jake's front door. Exilee knocked once then told Luke to take off his dew soaked boots and let them dry on the porch.

"Papaw doesn't put his on the front porch. He has a rack." Luke fisted his hips.

Ken signaled the dogs off the front porch while blocking them from knocking over Luke in their excitement. "Better put 'em on the rail or a dog might drag 'em off." Ken instructed as he hurried to take a seat at the kitchen table and Bruce asked, "Ya'll this early every day?" When Ken's poster boy smile assured him that early rising taint never killed a soul Bruce let out a little whistle, "Can we catch a nap under a shade tree then?" And Ken popped the kitchen table, "We do that all the time."

"When you're at Papaw's you can do it like him. When you're at someone else's house you do it like they do." Exilee firmly explained as she finally guided Luke through the open front door.

Jake sleepily stumbled into the living room. "Let's eat." And the dogs happily cried for their master.

"I thought you took 'em back to the kennel last night," Exilee asked Jake.

"Was going to, but Scarecrow told me to leave 'em out. Said they'd keep anyone else from comin' up. Least slow 'em down."

Miss Ginger filled the brown earthenware bowl with steamy scrambled eggs. "Better fill up, busy day comin'," and after she placed the bowl on the table gently squeezed Bruce's bare shoulders. "Put a shirt on."

Jake sported a grin. "Knew she was gonna getcha. Hurry up."

Sausage with eggs and Miss Ginger's pan bread fried in the rendered seasonings with apple butter topped over it like icing set Bruce up for a nap. But he just yawned and threw back another ellick. Then left to help Ken and Jake make rounds and feed up. The dogs were fed and kenneled. The ponies were greeted and fed, then cows in the calving lot. Luke spread pieces of broken bread for the chicks and Miss Sarah tossed a pan of scraps. Water troughs were topped and Jake promised they'd get the beans and tomatoes fertilized and weeded, soon.

The heavy breakfast under July's humid sky, and metabolizing likker, soaked their backs and underarms, so they changed shirts before piling into Jake's pick up. Jake fondled his gold luck charm wiggling from his keychain. And smiled when Lilly's pearl button sparkled.

As they left to meet the steel building dealer they waved bye to Luke standing on the furthest slate slab of Papaw's walk. The kenneled dogs wagged after Jake's truck when it passed and then cried in vain as it turned onto the graveled county road and was enveloped by the pristine Longleaf Pines.

"Ya'll were gonna eat at Crossroad's, right?" Jake asked as he turned onto the pavement.

"Yep. I'll talk him into a biscuit to go." Bruce opened his eyes and covered his yawn when the truck stopped. Then felt for the jeweled cross deep in his pocket.

After Bruce went inside to greet the metal building dealer Exilee wiggled out of Ken's lap out into the parking lot and stretched. And it quickly became apparent the restaurant's glass front made for good viewing. Exilee's signature blue jean cut off shorts were very popular with all the old timers and farm hands. Ken wisely waved her back into his lap as Bruce exited the restaurant followed by the salesman and then Edge. She grinned and waved like a child on parade wearing a fresh white blouse, but the same hot red bandana trimmed shorts.

"Think that's a coincidence?" Ken talked through his smile.

"Be nice," Exilee did it, too. And Jake just grinned.

Forgotten in the bed of the truck, Mark suddenly slapped the roof of the truck. "I like short shorts," he burst into song, "girls who wear short shorts. Give me those short shorts."

"Shut up," Jake yelled over his shoulder out the window while Ken and Exilee snickered.

"I'm gonna ride with him," Bruce called out and Edge rode with Bruce in the salesman's car.

As soon as they arrived at Bruce's land, Jake pulled up close and unlocked the steel gate's chain. The existing shed was a post and beam structure with tough heavy tin siding and rain washed rust stains. Wildflowers and somewhat sad pear tree with long draping branches and squirrels feasting on its fallen fruits, stood tall and humped over next to where the makeshift road ended. The dark pond reflected the tips of trees in the timberline and they waved hello when a crane launched from the bank where the pussy willows waded. The picturesque setting was so surreal with the flock of bluebirds dashing this away and that and charming little bunnies circling about the tender young vines that they all quietly absorbed it like it was an assignment to remember every little thing about Bruce's promising vineyard. Jake shook hands with the salesman as Bruce counted rabbits. "I'm Jake Wilkes. Too busy last night to introduce myself."

"Mike Kendall, nice to meet you." He was a slender man, middle aged, with barber's eyes; sizing him up for when he needed another trim. He wore a light blue dress shirt, short sleeves and no tie and had on light weight navy dress pants and smart brown loafers.

Ken told him good morning as Exilee and Edge ventured off to check on the Lucretia vines. Mark introduced himself and went on to ask if Bruce had told him about the after party. But Bruce gave Mark the look and he smartly diverted the subject towards short shorts. And that's when Ken gave Mark the look. But not before Mark spoke. "Isn't Edge wearing the same shorts she had on last night?" When no one acknowledged Mark he asked for a bandana, a red one, and complained of being sticky. And Bruce finally gave him the tap and the eye.

Bruce led the men to a hill overlooking the young vines encircling the large dark pond. "This is where I want the distillery. It needs to go up, pronto." A rabbit ran right between them and another threatened to follow. At the timberline a white and gray tail slipped into the thicket. Bruce grumbled about getting rabbit traps, even though Jake offered to bring a Bassett hound from one of the local rabbit hunting sheriff's deputies. And all the while a rabbit family played gleefully at the pond's edge.

He turned his attention back to Kendall and informed him that he wanted a cash price on his quote. "Gonna ship in grapes until mine are mature and get my recipes down. The grape vines will encircle the Lucretia's. An aerial view will look like a jewel," he paused and sternly smiled at Mark, "like a big brown pool jewel circled with diamonds. It'll be gorgeous." They agreed and talked on about who could take them for a plane ride to get an aerial photo and Kendall informed them that one of his brother's had a pilot's license. "Well, I know where to go if I need something. Your daddy knew what he was doin' to have all those children. Huh?"

"He's a smart man."

"And he's got a smart son," Ken piped. "How many men you know with two jobs? That's smart. All you Kendalls are bright like that."

"Wonder if the girls need any help?" Mark jeered as he began to sprint off, but Bruce grabbed the back of his tee shirt and told him he'd better stick around. "What if something happened to me? Who's gonna carry on the Black legacy? Make fine wine and handle all my money?"

Mark's gums were thinned pink as he accepted the responsibility and Jake just tried to hold back his laughter. Bruce discreetly winked over at Jake and then with his arm firmly around Mark told Kendall more. "I'll add on to the steel structure, so when you price out grading go ahead and include the showroom area, too." He let go of Mark to walk out the dimensions and then swung open the imagined showroom's front doors. "Got it all drawn up just gotta get a blueprint run."

"I can handle that, if you like. Cost ya between four and six if the architect doesn't have ta make a lot of allowances." Kendall offered. "This is a great spot. You can see everything."

"Just to run a blueprint? You don't understand. Those drawings are designed by a professional engineer." Bruce caught Jake's questioning eyes. "Brother Lum up for fraud. He spent twenty for it and lost his house, wife, kids, but the guy who ratted him got it." Bruce read Kendall's embarrassment and held his shoulder. "Hey, I'm not him. I don't hold a grudge like that. In fact, I'm thankful for the time I spent. I don't have a grudge against any brother Lum or whitey or any others. I can tell you're a Christian, Kendall. I am too. What do you think of dropping that expensive claim to get federal funding?" Kendall didn't budge and Bruce had his full attention so he went on. "We don't have enough Indian blood and I believe it's more important to be true to who we were originally destined to be anyway."

"Who's that?" Kendall's dry lips formed a circle.

"You're Lum. I can tell that much."

"Yea, Dad's on the council." Kendall stiffened.

"No problem. It doesn't matter. This is just business, right?"

"Right." His relieved smile plucked Mark.

"Kendall," Mark stepped up to him, "are you on The Lumbee Council?"

"No, not on it. Been to meetings. It's important to know what's going on, on the swamp."

Bruce surveyed his property again. "Yea, spent a lot a days here, daydreaming about this," Bruce scoped the area like it was the first time and as he rounded the Lucretias encircling the pond smiled over at Ken. Then back to Kendall he said, "The showroom will be a two story deal with rustic cedar siding and old bubbled glass paned windows like you'd see a hundred years ago. It'll be wider than the steel structure. Don't want the manufacturing side visible from the entrance."

"So do you want me to see about the drawings?" Kendall asked.

"Yea, I want to get this up pronto. Need to work on my recipes. Make sure I haven't lost my touch."

"I can start today. My wife can handle the barbering and beauty departments. No problem." Kendall checked his watch as he pulled out his electronic tablet from his waistband and activated the internet. Punched in the dealership and stated that they can handle it all online with a simple signature as he held up the vivid images sequencing across the screen.

"Technology grew overnight, didn't it?" Bruce observed the small three by five display screen. "First time I've seen one of these other than the in the tv room."

Mark squeezed in shoulder to shoulder. "You can play games, too. Poker, Bingo, even watch a show. Know what I mean, a show show." He grinned like he's just seen a show show and looked around for the girls. While Jake and Ken agreed that the tablet was going to save forests, but hurt local pulp tree farmers. "Plymouth is laying off fifty workers. It was in the paper last week."

"I hate driving through those paper mills. Smells like septic," Mark frowned.

"We can make it any way you want." Kendall held up the screen for Bruce. "Have kits ready to ship. Know which one you want? There's ridged steel and arched and slab, and colors."

"I have a vision," Bruce mumbled as he took in the sliding images. "There, that's just like it. It was in one of the brochures I ordered."

"You could mail yourself things in prison?" Mark asked. "Why didn't you order yourself a file?"

"Are you planning to work for me?" Bruce shot his grays as one eyebrow furrowed.

"Yea, at some point. I'm still in college."

Edge returned smelling a tender limb. "What's this? There's a city block of this stuff growing over there." Her thumb jutted out over her shoulder.

"That's sassafras," Exilee told her as she smelled its leaves. "It's an indigenous plant. Was there anything else there or just that?" Perspiration dotted her temples and purged the baby curls napping tenderly along her forehead. She wiped them down, following the length of her thick black braid, pulling it over her shoulder.

"Just this, like he's growing it," Edge puzzled over the limb and chewed the severed end. "Tastes good, this for your wine?"

With a warm smile and grays darkened under the shadow of his hand held over his brows he assured the young trees were cultivated. "Add sassafras and chocolate and strawberries, all kinds of natural flavorings." Bruce plucked a leaf tangled in Edge's fly away light brown curls.

"Where's the chocolate patch?" Edge's hips shifted as she batted up at Bruce.

Mark pointed out past the pond. "Go look over there." His opossum eatin' grin announced his intentions. "Check if the seeds sprouted. You'll have to get up close. Just bend over. Don't get all dirty on your hands and knees, unless you don't mind that kind of thing."

"Pig." Edge pulled down on her short's red bandana trim and huffed.

When Bruce told Kendall to order the plans for the steel building image on the screen the ladies instantly became interested. "That's a church," Exilee exclaimed.

"I know," Bruce affirmed. "It'll be perfect, the rustic showroom and the shiny chapel where the grapes are crucified into wine." They all sighed. Then Bruce turned to Kendall, "Can I get a dark purple roof, Lucretia dewberry purple?"

"Yes, sir, just sign here." Kendall held up the tablet while Bruce looked for a pen. "You use your finger."

"Amazing," Bruce signed for the metal church structure with a deep purple roof and then tapped his chest and when he did felt the bird effigy and clasped it. "Momma would a' loved this place."

"Now, what about equipment, Bruce? I researched wineries and found major satisfaction with this manufacturer." Kendall held up the tablet for Bruce as miscellaneous forms flowed past. "Any tanks, bottles, and other distillery equipment we can get from Bavarian dealers in steel or copper."

"Got that all squared away, Kendall. My Lum brothers will be commissioned to make most of it. Even got a glass blower in mind for the bottles. Thinkin' about settin' him up on the property." When Bruce's chin darted toward Jake his arms flew up to the top of his head as Bruce clarified. "Got my heart set on this big honkin' copper still from another set of Lums. You probably heard of 'em, Fisk and Wart."

Kendall's eyes 'bout popped out a' his head. "They lookin' to sell out?"

Bruce winked. "Well, Jake, think I should make an offer on Fisk's big copper momma? Or should we just go get it?"

No one moved. Ken's eyes were as big as white biscuits. "Heard it took up the whole baccar barn." It's like the bate of 'em were stuck. Their shoes were cemented into the shifty sand and legs locked down straight over 'em.

"I'm not helping you steal that thing. I'm not." Jake closed his eyes and turned his head.

"Who said steal? Did anyone hear me say steal?" Bruce confirmed with each of them and Edge especially when shook a negative. But Exilee serenely smiled and surprised Ken when she went on to say that they'd be glad to help. Why he couldn't even speak.

"Well," Kendall stepped off toward his car, "we done for now?"

Bruce brought Kendall back by the elbow and sincerely conveyed to the group the terrible injustice of Mr. Fisk and Wart stealing the pallets of likker from his daddy, who was then Preacher Black, after Bruce had worked so long and so hard, digging and hiding dirt piles and luggin' each jar on a separate day or night into his specially hidden pit to save a little piece of his family history and how that big copper momma was rightfully his. He explained there was no way those slime balls would own up to the theft. And went on to say, "Never in a pine tree stump turned ta lighter will they come up with the money they made off my daddy's likker and pay me back."

Then Bruce daringly pulled Kendall up so closely he could've kissed him and whispered so lowly no one else could hear. But what was clear was that Bruce was enthralled with the dark insignia sewn onto Kendall's shirt. Bruce nearly ripped it off tugging on it. But Kendall held it down. "This is not The Society they had in mind."

In those few minutes, those few short zingin' minutes, Bruce convinced Kendall that he was not planning to steal anything, but repossess. And not only that. Bruce convinced every single one of them to help repossess the big copper momma and to do it in the light of day when he was sure Mr. Fisk and Wart would be sleeping off the night's drunk. "You tie and I'll hold 'em," Bruce told Jake. "Know you'll want a front row center for this." Bruce's teeth shined like white blinds.

"Oh, no I don't," Jake spat. "I don't want any part of this. I'm going back to college. I'm gonna be a vet. And you just said they'd be sleeping, so you sneak in there yourself."

"They'll be asleep when we get there. But we don't want to take any chances. When those copper sheets start falling they'll be ringing like bells." Bruce tilted his head back and laughed like a crazy man, barreling it out until he had to hold his knees before he was ever done with the laughing fit. Then with all the seriousness of a caped heroic cartoon guise, his gray eyes set in deep. "I can't wait to see their filthy faces."

"Oh, man," Jake rubbed his forehead then slapped his thighs. And Mark, why that silly boy, he lit up just like Jake had done on that fateful night when The Company was moved. He smiled from ear to ear.

Ken and Mark worked together hastily removing the boxes from the second flatbed trailer and hooked it up to the transfer truck brought over from Kendall's brother's garage for Bruce and Jake. While Bruce and Jake convinced Mr. and Mrs. Crowson that if there were any damages to the trailer, and swore that there wouldn't be, that Bruce had enough funds to cover it. The borrowed truck had to be back before morning at ten when Kendall's brother returned from the men's retreat. (That time the Methodist men were learning 'Forgiveness in Families and Why it Matters Most.')

Jake drove the borrowed truck because he had a license. He had to get a CDL for hauling hay with the Crowson's pristine thirty year old big rig. Bruce sat co pilot and Kendall straddled the console. Then Ken, who was most familiar with his aged farm rig, drove it to haul the other flatbed to Bruce's old stompin' grounds, from where The Company was moved six years before. And the entire time Mark questioned Ken on married life.

After being dropped off at Crossroad's Restaurant, where Edge had left her sporty red two door, she spun out making a doughnut in the middle of the road. Well, with the charming jealous petty waitresses bitching out the window as the pretty young smarty pants got all the attention, it took all of eight seconds for 'em to call the law. Edge sped up the road. Turned around and made two more doughnuts, reveling in her position on the repossession team. She was as good as those stunt drivers on television in those competitions making figure eights.

When the first red light whipped around Edge reined her horse to the center and spurred like the world was on fire. "Hot Damn!" She checked the rear view. "Harnett County, too. I love you Harnett County, boys. Those roads flat as your stupid heads.

Come on." She did not give them the pleasure of reading 'Kiss This' plastered on her bumper. But anyone could've read her flagged finger.

Exilee's position was to notify as many jar runners as possible. Bruce needed all hands to dissemble and haul in jet speed. First, she called Robin to assist her. People in the restaurant business get to know people, so Exilee was sure she'd know how to reach Bruce's people who had showed up with the empty jars.

Exilee told Robin, "Do not under any circumstances tell anyone." And the entire time Robin was trying to concentrate on the phone her momma, Gili, was bellyaching about being short on help. Robin begged. "Exilee needs me today. Just today, Momma. It's important." Gili gave in and said that whatever was so important had better make her some money because she was not getting paid for her time off gallivanting. Robin slipped the memo pad used for take out orders into her pocket book and with the names and numbers of Lumbees, specifically jar runnin' Lums who ordered half price specials, she fired up her diesel to meet Exilee.

The two ladies excitedly conveyed to the jar runners that they were to bring screwdrivers and crowbars, five pound hammers, rope, blankets, duct tape, any available dollies and anything else that they believed may be needed. And Pig Pen was told specifically to bring a pig, a large hungry pig. There were few questions. No hesitations. And they were so excited to be included in the repossession not one asked for monetary compensation.

Mr. Fisk and Wart lived and operated only twenty or so minutes away right off a major four lane highway where the exit into the sleepy town of Siler City slopes off. There was usually a highway patrolman or two scouting around for an intoxicated taco. They abounded in Siler City, a rural farming area with chicken plants and horse farms where cheap labor was easily exploited. However, there happened to be a run on jar runners that day.

In the newer rig, Jake, Bruce and Kendall passed two rip roaring Mounties as Jake casually obeyed the speed limit and casually pulled into Mr. Fisk's and Warts' unleveled clay and rock drive. The tractor trailer's air brakes shooed and shooed as it slowed to a stop near the unassuming tobacco barn just before the little ramshackle once white house.

The old baccar barn that housed the big copper momma radiated the kind of sweet yeasty scents a bakery emits only there was corn sprouting up all around the barn like something'd been crapping it. Bruce marched right through the erupting piles and with a crowbar pried off a board from the barn's back wall. The black fabricated insulation board was thin and light. Then Ken pried off one end of a six by twelve heart pine board. And they all peeped like school boys ogling over a show show.

Meanwhile, under Mark's guidance, Ken pulled onto the dirt road that ran behind Bruce's old home place that had been sold six years before. Mark strained out the windows checking for witnesses. "This orange giant is extra loud now, huh?"

"Yep. Double that." Ken prayed aloud that the ruts weren't deeper than they looked. "Dad liked the bright color 'cause he drives as slow as Christmas Eve, especially when he hauls the boys who help with hay on the flatbed. But you're right. Right now it does seem extra loud, in every way." Ken opened the door when they reached the road block boulders and Mark waited anxiously in the transfer truck. "How long are we supposed to wait?"

"We're not. Get out and help me." Ken closed the door and studied the large boulders flanking the drop off at the end of the dirt road. "They don't look fake," he yelled.

"Well they are," Mark gripped the lip of the window with his chin just over the edge.

"Aren't you something," Ken barked. "Come help me before someone hears this truck."

"Not with alligators out there. Hurry up." Mark leaned out looking.

Ken groaned as he rolled the water laden vermiculite boulders to the wayside and looked down the drop off. "Good Lord." He worked up a good sweat and climbed back in.

"I still don't see how this is gonna be an alibi," Mark called out.

"The trailers are identical. Everyone knows this truck belongs to my dad, best man in town. Bruce and Jake are going by Kendall's brother's loggin' site to get logs. They'll stack 'em around the copper sheets. It's right down the road from Fisk's. Fisk uses same outfit for logs to cook with. We'll say we unloaded logs or switched out trucks 'cause this one gave us trouble. All we gotta do is confuse the law if one of us gets pulled. That shouldn't be too difficult." Ken winked. "But pray anyway they don't get caught in the act. Don't believe we could get out of that."

"Hmph," Mark pondered, "what about serial numbers?"

"Nope, Dad and I made 'em. Did all the welding, the floors. The axles were bought used. No serial numbers. Just tags and I don't have 'em. Jake's got 'em."

"Shit. And exactly what are we going to tell the law when they ask why it's here?" Mark sassed. "You know someone's gonna call this in." Mark was truly clueless to the exact details of their position in the plan as he had to walk off into the woods and take care of business while the plans were doled out.

Ken told Mark, "Be still, Mary Lou. You worry too much," and parked parallel to the big dark pond. Rippled waves rolled the old john boat tied to the rinky dink pier. It was missing an oar and was heavily littered with leaves and pine straw.

Mark blew up like a teenager. "So, already, what do we say? One could show up, ya know?" Mark studied the tall grasses as Ken got out. This time he left the door open. "You're gonna overheat. Better get out." But Mark yelled, "I'm not kidding you. There's gators out here. Totens and haunts and probably some skeletons, too." When he couldn't see Ken he panicked. "I'm tellin' ya, Old Man Black put 'em here to keep away instigators. Hey, get it, alligator, instigator?"

"Koom, ka boom," Ken's three fifty seven echoed as the alligator hissed its last.

Simultaneously, back at the sight of the repossession, the July sky burned bright red stripes down their hairlines. By the time Snap, Dodger and Cassie with her seven boys showed up, the entire back side of the baccar barn was laid open. They smiled up at the big copper momma. "Fisk and Wart secured?" Snap asked.

Bruce sucked the salt from his beefy lips. "Well, they're tied up somewhere."

Cassie scowled, "Explain dat."

"They weren't here. Went inside. No sign of 'em." When Bruce didn't ease her concern Cassie hunted about like a yurker with a fishin' pole going to snag the rumored granddaddy bass. Bruce asked her, "What are you so fired up for? If we see 'em are you running out on us?" And Cassie scowled, "Our guillotine's gone. Bolts, too. Fools set on dying." Cassie's youngins cussed like everyone else, but Bruce had said the f word first. "I'll help ya' look. But it probably isn't here," Bruce fumed. "They'd a takin' it to the scrap yard. Paying good on steel." And Cassie agreed, but didn't stop searching.

After Bruce and a few others had searched the back Cassie went around front and came back around cussing. "Keep your eyes open and put the word out." Cassie tucked her chin and aimed. "Bes a mommucked up life take our token. Bes a family thing. Ain't gonna have a bit a peace till its back wid me. Gotdat, Jack!" Snap assured her they'd get it back. "Lordy, we's not all de sorry in the world got thieves on the swamp take yer tools of trade. Bes a price, Cassie dear. Heads will roll." And everyone got the picture as Stink dropped a big rock from a dirt mound and it rolled to his momma feet. And she glared at it like she already had the thief's head. "No peace for any a-us." She stood tall and rigid as she caught each eye.

"Where's that pig, Pen?" Bruce adamantly asked Pen.

Without so much of a grunt, Pen jogged to his momma's pick up and pushed and pushed the wooden crate down the planks. He lifted the cage door and guided him. "Where you want him?"

"That's no pig." Jake exclaimed as he backed up into a tree. "That's a hawg!"

"Figure the snakes are by the fixin's. Ya'll help herd him inside." Bruce directed as he warily followed. "Can't believe Scarecrow's late. He's never late."

Snap stepped inside the barn scoping the walls, the junk, the crates and all the nooks and crannies. "Crow won't answer his phone. Must be his day off. Laid up, ya' reckon?"

Bruce squinted. "Poor Lilly." They quietly giggled as the huge hog's gonads bounced in conjunction with his aggressive rooting. He rooted and dug until his snout was covered in orange red clay and had dug a fine hole next to the fixin's barrel where a sheet of tin was secured with two large field stones. "Stay back. Won't take him long."

Some swallowed their spit while others spat at the hawg. Dodger caught his teeth after an especially aggressive kapooey splat on the voracious beast's butt. Someone got its ribs. Spit spun down its spine. And someone else crouched down and whizzed a line straight at its gonads while its head jerked up the tin lid over the snake pit.

The slithering mix squirmed and hissed. And Pen warned Dodger not to mess with his hawg as the hungry beast blissfully chomped with crunching grunts. Slimy wiggling sections slowly stilled as nasty red snake blood streaked the earthen clay floor and the hawg. Several grown men held their mouths shut. Some leapt about the baccar barn as snakes escaped the hawg's lethal jowls. Brazen Cassie stood firm with her legs braced for stompin' and Kendall held a garden hoe up like a dagger.

"I'm gonna vomit," Cassie's youngest told his momma.

"Gyet," she pushed him out while Dodger argued that the hawg would clean it up.

Then Snap asked Pen if he wanted a picture? "Yea, get that. We can sell tee shirts, Mom. Whadayathink?" Pig Pen clapped for his snake eatin' hawg as Snap took pictures with his cell phone. "Looky, he's got two and there's one biting his belly. Get that, Snap." Snap took the pictures and then ran at the hawg with an old baccar stick and batted the snake that was wrapped around its head, but its fangs were lodged like a fish hook. "I can't get it off. That moccasin'll kill him."

"Not Snowball, Ma," Cassie's youngest scrambled toward the hawg as Pen snatched him up from the back of his jeans. His legs thrashed in the air. "Not my pig." His red afro shook like cheerleaders' pom poms.

"Get back, Snap. Move," Cassie commanded as the beast spun in rage at Snap who, from the pig's point of view, was a competitor for his snake dinner. As the hawg spread his jowls to bite Snap snake chunks fell from between his giant crusty canines while smaller chunks stuck. So with one coiled snake atop his head with imbedded fangs and another still lodged to its belly it snorted twice before lunging. Snap sprung up the side of the baccar barn clinging onto an axe hewn log and shimmied up into the rafters like he still had a lot of yurker left in his fifty year old bones. Then the threatening hawg rooted up at Cassie. She voraciously clapped as it neared. And the clapping spawned, diverting the hawg back to the pit for more snakes.

"Snakes don't kill pigs," Dodger plainly spoke up at Snap in the rafters. Then explained, "Bes fat ta take in da posin."

"Ohh," Snap climbed down.

Bruce checked out the cooking pit. A suspended black iron hanger held an old black iron cooking vessel. He heisted the lid. Dropped it and coughed like he'd hurl. "Snakes, snake stew." He stepped out back and was quickly freed of his heavy breakfast.

Cassie was first to mention that there should be some concern over whether the humongous copper vat was full. She panged the side with her open palm and when she couldn't determine pulled a flathead screwdriver from her painter's jean's loop and gave it hard knock. The big copper momma sloshed just enough to tell. The smile on her face grew until she looked like the kid on the snack cake packages, full of sugar and spice and freckled and nice. Only she had a wicked little laugh.

"Should I mension hit?" Pen wandered about the vessel with his finger up like he's bound to find an inscription with increments. "Snowball's probably thirsty now. But not that thirsty." Cassie's other sons scrounged up several Styrofoam cups and chipped bowls and hurriedly rinsed 'em with the hosen off the other side of the baccar barn. When the youngest one held up a pitcher without a handle to Pen he discreetly told him not to let Ma see, but she was already on to 'em and hurried around to the hosen. The various vessels cleared the boys' heads as she flung them into the woods and Pen shoved the pitcher into a mess of jars with his boot.

Kendall chuckled as he used his electronic tablet to calculate figures as he paced of the vat's circumference, "one hundred two," then guestimated height, "one hundred fifty ish." The big copper momma moaned. Kendall anxiously looked for Bruce and he told him to hold on, that it was too late. The zealous helpers had already unscrewed bolts from the highest areas they could reach without a ladder as Kendall announced that the big copper momma will hold five thousand gallons. And then they all learned the snake pit was deep.

All kinds of snakes spewed out of the pit when the yeasty half brewed likker gushed from the four by eight gapping hole. Big fat brown ones with hexagonal designs on their backs, yellow bellied, those perty red, black and yellow ones that are poisonous and the same colored ones that weren't, washed up onto the clay floor and went crawling up anything and anyone. And poor Pen's pig was full as a hawg. He grunted and groaned as Pen pushed his bulging balking ass back toward the snakes.

Then Pen screamed like his butt was on fire. One hand held his left cheek and his other swept with the wind as his hawg proved how fast he could run. Cassie told him to turn around and hit him in the snout as she chased after them. While the men in the barn fought off snakes with rakes, shovels and baccar sticks, stabbing the wet snakes crawling all over like they were in a tizzy. They dumped the dead snakes at the edge of the woods where there was a mess of metal and engine parts, pure tee junk and a few good grocery carts. The snakes hung over and on in every which a way and Snap took their picture. Then they got seriously determined and knocked some snakes off some tall metal parts in the pile and hauled them into the baccar barn to stand on while they dissembled the big copper momma.

Back at the alligator hidey hole, things were stinky. Ken showed off his hand gun in a most threatening manner and Mark whined, but pinched his nose and obeyed. The dead alligator had released a belly full of the nastiest, rottenest, most sulfuric and almost silent gas imaginable. The two hurried past the stink and Mark lunged to the john boat. "Oh, my gawd. Oh, my gawd." He jumped in with both feet making the boat jar from side to side as Ken struggled to untie the seasoned rope's knot.

"What are we doing out here?" Mark cried as he sat down on the small plank seat and the little john boat shimmied. Ken kicked the boat from the pier and it rattled off uneasily as he took up the only oar and explained the most pertinent part of the plan Mark happened to miss out on. "You're gonna pull up a prize and load it on the flatbed." With the oar in one hand and gun in the other Ken exaggeratedly grinned from the rinky dink pier.

"You're freakin' crazy. You're trying to kill me off. You know all about Bruce being the one, don't cha? You know I'm next in line, don't cha?" Mark ranted. "And I don't believe Bruce told you to do this. Did he?" Mark attempted to stand in the small craft and it dangerously tipped. "You'll get caught. My momma'll search the ends of the earth for her boy. She'll never stop, I tell ya. We're royal blood, Ken Crowson. The Society'll come for you, too, and your boy. They'll want an eye for an eye. That's how they are. They're not that different from all the other Lums. We're cut throat." Mark took in a deep breath and Ken finally blinked just as Mark became determined and paddled with his hands.

"Keep your hands out of the water," Ken warned as the rolling black waters propelled the little john boat. Mark grabbed a hold of his seat. Stiffened and tried his best not to breathe. And just in case the alligator sensed his heartbeat drumming acid rock through his nervous ass he braced up off the seat. And they both gawked as the lumpy back surfaced. Ken nervously aimed and ally got pissed.

With its giant white snout snared open it rushed the bank toward Ken. "Koom, ba koom," the three fifty seven did not echo further for the bullet lodged deep in the abyss. Ally's middle suddenly blew up like a balloon with the echoing charge and deflated just as suddenly. The alligator closed its mouth and slowly rolled and sunk. One big bubble later several little bubbles spawned and what seemed like hundreds of little baby alligators swarmed from the banks into the water as Ken squeaked to the end of the rinky dink pier with both the gun and the oar. As the gentle undertow of the water lured the john boat to the dam and within reach of reeds, Mark prepared.

"Do you see a chain? There's supposed to be a chain over there. Look for it. You gotta pull it up before you get out. Bruce said you'll never reach it from the bank. That's the way his old man did it." Ken yelled the instructions as he kept watch.

"I see something." Mark took off his tennis shoe and gently paddled.

"Just let the boat wander over on its own. It'll go straight to it, according to Bruce." Ken blew and Mark fumed, "Well fuck you. He also said only one gator was left." The water calmed as the trees held their bird songs like cork lined walls. And their heartbeats drummed like the firing squad's death march to the boat's hypnotic rhythm.

"Must be the water inlet." Mark looked over his shoulder to Ken. "What am I going to pull up? I have a right ta know."

Ken studied the perimeter. "Look for a jar inside another jar."

"A jar? That's it! Bruce can do this himself. He's always Tom Sawyering some idiot into doing his mess. But it won't be me. Not this time." Mark reached for the reeds on the bank and was about to step out when Ken fired a shot. "You didn't!" Mark trembled.

"I don't know why I care or what all this is about, but my dear wife thinks she's gonna save the world if we can help. Now pull that damn chain up right now!"

"You stupid hayseed. We'll both end up in jail over this. Stealin', or attempted stealing anyway. Crap. They can book us on killing endangered species, too." Mark hit the boat's rim with clenched fists. "How were you ever a teacher? You can't teach shit. I don't see anything."

Ken did his best not to impede the insipid punk or shoot a hole in the john boat by keeping aimed at the ground in case of an accidental reflex. "Boy, we tell the law we're waitin' on Kendall's driver to deliver with his loggin' equipment. We got yellow tape to string around the loblollies and any oak under three feet around. That's one alibi. And we can kill any alligator that threatens our lives while we're doing business. It's legal. Got it?" he paused. "Now get the damn chain so we can get back in the truck."

When the logger's diesel engine putts and purrs down the rutted gravel road Ken shrugged and headed back to his truck and Mark cried like a little girl. "Get back here with that gun. You better watch over me." But Ken kept walking. "You better not let anything happen to me," Mark cried. Ken waved for Kendall's brother to come on down the grassy path. "I mean it," Mark yelled. "Okay, I'm pulling up this stupid ass chain!"

It didn't take long for the swarm of young alligators to finish off the other freshly killed mature one when they hadn't had any fish to eat and all the frogs were et and there's nothing left except extremely thirsty birds and occasional squirrels, feral dogs and regrettably, an occasional stranger. Not long at all.

Mark noticed their beady red eyes blinking up at him as he nervously grasped the slimy jar and quickly unclasped the steel clasp from the chain. And made quick notice of the steel guide line attached to the water inlet and john boat and went starboard to work his way back to the pier. And when he did the jar rolled against a sharp shim and it broke open exposing the clear jar within containing a hand written paper. Words flashed like blinding camera bulbs.

Back at the snake ranch, Mr. Fisk and Wart were mentioned so often during the dissembling of the big copper momma that the jar runners began to tease Bruce about actually caring to their happenstance. "Even if they're sober by now, they'd be in our way. And they're gonna be awful mad about those snakes."

Kendall finally loosened up enough to laugh with the wiry group. And right then, the bright yellow sports car like the one that was aiming to be the get away car at the Crowson's the night before zoomed up and they hushed up. Bruce pushed his screwdriver into the back of his jeans and marched straight on. The long haired driver did not notice Bruce because he was too busy checking out all the vehicles and the transfer truck.

One by one the jar runners peeked and peered from the baccar barn at the he she. The glasses covering its eyes were the comeliest thing about it. Bruce and the he she faced off as a lollygagging passenger slowly emerged from the back seat. Wart purged from the back seat like a sloth, an obese sloth, as his signature wart covered face hit the light of day. He wiped his eyes as he took in the bate of 'em and got back in. He sat down on the passenger's seat, wobbled from the far side to the near and one foot at a time managed both onto the floorboard and closed the door.

"I know that hair." Cassie's boy with the lisp whistled for Bruce. "That's your cuz's hair." And Bruce gapped, "Mark's?" And the yurker declared, "He sold it. I was there." Cassie looked back at her boy like she's fixin' to whopicoddle his yurker tail, but instead just gave him the hush signal.

Bruce chuckled and shoulders danced. "Mr. Fisk, you've changed."

He jerked off the badly made homemade wig and spat a wad of black nasty and a stream of brown followed down his chin. "Swanny, you'se a jubious sight on my side a' da swamp." Mr. Fisk flicked his wrist over at his barn as his face grew good and hot. "Think I don't know what yer runners are up to?" Then he spat out a yellowish brown drizzle daringly aimed at Bruce.

"I'm taking the copper vat and all its parts as payment for the pallets of shine you stole." Bruce stepped closer while Snap took pictures and Kendall took video with his tablet.

"You think I won't steal it back?" When Fisk grinned like he's got the game by the tail his mostly toothless gap sucked in air making him whistle. Then Wart mumbled from his seat somewhat safe in the yellow car that Bruce had something in his pants and Fisk licked across his toothless top lip and panted. "Too hot for this today, Buddyrow. Let's make a deal."

"No deals."

"Bes dat charm on yer a-neck? That'd make it even." Mr. Fisk's thin eyebrows danced.

"Shit," Bruce growled and pulled down his neckline and Fisk's face faded white as his once white house. "Only way you'd know about that is if you had eyes on me last night. Is your grunt gonna make it? He lost a lot of blood."

"Bes a tuff un," Fisk growled back. His beady eyes all but disappeared under his swollen lids. "That Indian trinket da only charm you wearin' dese days?" Fisk trembled.

When Jake sprinted toward the porch and told Fisk to stay out of Bruce's business Dodger told him to stay out of it. And with a stern squint, so did Bruce. Just as Wart opened the glove compartment and Bruce's chest heaved up like it did the night before. "You gonna die today?" And Wart closed the glove compartment.

Fisk scanned the bate of 'em. Lowered his head like he was gonna pray and his bald spot shined up at 'em from between the two un kept piles of gray curls at his ears. As he looked back up he pushed his glasses up and took a deep breath. "Thoust may have it." His humped back lowered in a slight bow as his outstretched palms shone up and he mumbled, "Your Highness."

Bruce leaned back ever so easy. "Whad you say?"

Fisk slyly grinned as he straightened as best he could with his hump. "Get it outa here 'fore I change my mind."

Cassie's youngest yelled, "Hineys. That weirdo called Bruce a hiney, Ma," as his red afro cheered.

"Git over here." Cassie pointed down to her side like she possessed a telekinetic ray and slid the yurker in and held him by the afro.

"You need that still, Mr. Fisk." Bruce rubbed his backside and then his head. "You can't just give it to me." As Bruce focused on Mr. Fisk's beguiling smile he fully recognized Fisk's mumbled words and was instantly paralyzed like he'd been snake bit by a mighty moccasin.

With a sweeping hand Fisk dismissed him. "Well I am. Hurry up with it and get out a here. Still's got a Toten on it. Taint made a good batch in her yet. Just get it out a' here." Mr. Fisk's back humped over like he was plum tuckered out as Wart slithered out from the car and went around the front of it keeping contact with the hood. Safely at the once white house's rickety front porch they woke the sleeping coon hound with a booted nudge so they could open the front door. The dog managed two steps and threw itself back down when suddenly Pen's hawg jogged past. The dog did keep one eye on it before flopping its head back down onto its clay encrusted paws. "Ya got my snakes?"

"What'll we do for dinner?" Wart cried.

"Jus be," Mr. Fisk patted his old friend's shoulder. "We bes all right." Then he whipped around to Bruce. "Throw out my snake stew?"

"Didn't touch it."

Fisk curled his top lip up at Bruce. "We'll get a bog together." Then Fisk comforted Wart. "Come on, now. A few ellicks and we'll hit the creek up for a nice moccasin or two and raise another mess. I'll let you stomp 'em this time and I'll hold the sack. Would you like that?"

"Oh, Fisks," Wart's lisp was so bad it was more difficult to understand. "Bes all de sorry in the world you bes bit by a posnis un. I holds de sack. I dos it. Okay?" Fisk agreed as he held the door and Wart wobbled inside.

"I swanny, boy," Mr. Fisk flanked the front porch like he was fixin' to declare war. "Thoust more trouble now you got all brickhouse. Mess easier when you was no more'n us'ns." He let the door slam and the coon hound stirred to stand and finally took notice of all the trespassers and wagged his tail before tucking in for another nap.

Snap took a picture of the sleeping hound with Bruce in the foreground. Then turned to the runners and took a shot of them as they threw their hands up in disbelief. Even Bruce. "Well, you heard him. Let's get 'er done. Don't rush too hard, now." He trailed off in thought as he whistled a light hearted tune.

"Yes!" Jake's joy sent him practically skipping back to the baccar barn like a yurker after a candy. "Hey," Bruce pulled on Jake's arm, "Get your phone and try Edge before Snap breaks my legs. Lord, I hope she wasn't pulled."

"I bet so." Jake asked Bruce for her number and then realized that his friend wouldn't know it either. "Should I make Snap think I want a date with Edge, or what?"

"I don't care. Yea, say it's a date."

Snaps' callused hands were thick and burly like he'd been turning wrenches or turning tractors inside out. He snapped out one bolt after the other in the time it took Jake to unscrew one. "Hey," Jake casually called to him down from the ladder, "can I have Edge's phone number?"

"Naw." Snap climbed higher and snapped out another and it barely missed Jake's head. "Edge is at home. Busted out a' folly's ditch."

"Oh, no, she wrecked?"

But Cassie sashayed over and patted Jake on the back. "She got away." Cassie winked. "Bes brothers on the swamp. Nuttin' goes down we don't know." She gently palmed his scarred cheek and then boldly reached down into his front jean's pocket. "Thoust pearl token for instance." Cassie dangled it over his head.

"I was a kid, Cassie. It was nothing."

"That's enough," Bruce told her and then to Jake, "Call Ken now and let him in on the news. No worries, Buddyrow."

When Miss Ginger fishes for the pages in the serving table drawer and is angrily disappointed she scouts through the big house and discovers Miss Sarah in the quilting room, "David fell asleep reading. He's in the bed."

"David, David," when there's no response Miss Ginger wiggles his foot. He sucks in a snore and she picks up the pages and starts out the door, but his baritone beckons. "No details on where." Miss Ginger grasps his socked foot, gives it a firm shake and David opens an eye. "Jake doesn't know either, least that's what her pages say. Not sure 'bout her box either. Hasn't asked about it. Thinkin' I'll fill in those gashes. Keep it safe over here."

"Yes, but give it to Jake or he'll get suspicious when he sees it at your house. Like a prairie dog been popped on the head out a' every tunnel he's dug, poor Jake keeps a dog in the bedroom and another one a' those beasts in the basement."

Chapter 11

Say that Again, Boy

Nearly a year and a half later an officer shifts into the corner again and this time his badge catches the light like the prim lady's silver slippers. She shuffles her feet then signals the genealogical society's president to commence. "Prove your psychohistorical theory, Mr. Jake Wilkes." With one arm cocked off his side like a Cardinal's flapping wing he motions their guest, Mr. Jake Wilkes, to the podium. The president pushes up his thick black rimmed glasses with the tip of his trimmed fingernail, "We can't stop talking about this, the Holy Grail and our neighboring county's Tribal Nation being linked and all with documentation." He coyly looks down and over the rim of his glasses to the prim lady seated near the podium before sliding his bright red pants onto a seat behind the desk alongside the wall.

The desk is stacked with three rows of Jake's updated controversial articles and his new business cards. And over the desk is a new banner; 'North Carolina's Royal Lumbee Indian Heritage,' the title of Jake's book co authored by H. Prickenwrath. And the officer in the corner is a fed with a rifle. So is the one on the podium's far right. But the deputy is there. Out in the parking lot sharing his donuts with the other visiting feds.

The prim lady rises and with her hand over her heart projects her soprano like a bell leading the Pledge of Allegiance to the American flag which stands right behind Jake. A short prayer commences the program during which the prim lady admires Jake with a most discreet grin. "You've caused some excitement. Out of North Carolina's fifty five thousand registered Lumbee's we could only make room here tonight for fifty and still maintain fire code." Her molars' cusps outline her gauzily cheeks threatening to pierce one of the spidery purple veins. "It's a first. Congratulations." She's so uptight and in need of some good grease, her knees squeak when she resigns to her seat, but it goes largely unnoticed as the thick tight rows before the podium rise with rushing applause.

Even if Jake didn't have his dusty albeit respectable light gray cowboy hat resting in his chair and scuffed cowboy boots and the kind of jeans loose only in the tail where you can tell a man is used ta' struggling with heavy equipment like tractors and wrestling cows and such, any woman would say he's a hardcore cowboy. His neck and forearms, all tanned and muscular, have veins like heavy duty power cords pokin' up in 'em each time he taps the podium to still the applause. The prim lady stares up at his bright green eyes and layered blonde hair, silky as a show pony's mane, as she twirls a pencil in her short gray page. The eraser pulls strands into a knot and she awkwardly chirps as she yanks it out.

"Hello and thank you. I can tell by looking out at this fine audience, hi there," Jake returns Mrs. Thomas's giddy wave then takes up the microphone and walks to the center of the aisle, "that most of us know each other. A lot of you know me as the kid with the scar on his cheek." The overhead lighting highlights his cheekbone and pronounces his dark scar. But it doesn't curb his raw appeal. It accents it. "Some know me as the kid from Beaver Bridge Baptist Church." The last of the standing, sit. "To others I'm the guy who used to work at the vet clinic, the one who restrained nervous patients and cleaned up their pee." Pleasant laughter spills across the rows of metal folding chairs as he throws down a paper napkin and pretends to clean up an accident as he returns to the podium.

"I was on my way to State. Wanted to be a vet and now I'm pushing thirty and the owner of Lucretias's Winery. How that came about is exactly how I learned about the link between North Carolina's Lumbee people and America's first pilgrims. It's how I learned to listen with my heart and my head." Their eager shoulders recline as Jake lingers over his note cards before he solemnly continues. "Before I ever got out of the truck I prayed ya'll would be open to this. I'm asking a lot. I realize that, for you to risk your most cherished treasures, for our Lumbee guests here, the very core of their self existential beliefs. My best friend, my buddyrow, died in my arms. It made headlines. I'm doing this for him. It's all he ever talked about." Jake sips water from his favorite cup and when he sits it down on the small serving tray it sings, "T-t-tink," from its fine silver fluted form.

As the lights are dimmed a single shaft of light filters up through the suspended royal blue carpet fibers to the overhead projector's screen. A powerful image of an aged Indian in a mixture of Native American Indian regalia and pioneer clothing sits in an Early American spindle chair. "Chief Sitting Bull, speaking at the Powder River Conference, in 1877 made the following theological statement concerning the pioneers: "Hear me people: We now have to deal with another race, small and feeble when our fathers first met them, but now great and overbearing. Strangely enough they have a mind to till the soil and the love of possessions is a disease with them. These people have made many rules which the rich may break but the poor may not. They take their tithes from the poor and weak to support the rich and those who rule." His life was so inspirational an entire group of mixed race people wake every day hoping to be fully recognized as Native American Indians, North Carolina's Lumbee's Indians, who are officially recognized only by the state. But the Lumbee Nation should be seeking honor in other arenas, like as America's original pilgrims. And I'm going to tell you why tonight."

The officer steps out from the corner as the back rows stir, but the hushed words are nothing, but cocky remarks.

Click. The screen lights up with an enchanting dark skinned woman. "The Croatans are defined as the South's mix of White, Black," Jake directs them to the woman on the screen, "and Native." The audience grins up at the bare breasted lady like they've just won an Island vacation. "A common denominator here is knowing that races blend for survival. A real honorable tie for the Lumbee can be traced to pre-Columbian voyages in the fourteenth century when English Protestants were under persecution. Portuguese were leaders among seaman. They made the craft, the sails and the seas their own and were hired to explore The New World under Columbus. The Portuguese seamen were a rough and tumble lot, hardy as the life aboard ship claimed them, and their language reflected such. And Portuguese settlements were within Croatan range. As we know, language is a strong origin indicator. Scholars point out the Portuguese vowel usage, such as 'oy' in the Lumbee language. The use of present tense such as 'I am' instead of 'I did,' 'I be' instead of 'I have' or 'I will,' and dropping the 'g's' from plurals. An example of common Lumbee vernacular is 'I'm bes fixin' to whoop up a mess a' chicken bog.'" The audience members vary from giggles to dropped jaws to furrowed brows. "So, let's add Portuguese to that Croatan definition."

"Bullshit."

The officer clears his throat.

Click. An image of a pale and so very young queen adorned with a double strand of pearls from which a fanciful cross hangs coldly fills the screen's white palette. Her fire red hair, slicked under a pearl coif, claims her heart shaped face. "Another honorable tie to consider is the result of Queen Elizabeth I, spouted as seeking more wealth and land, and to her charmer Sir Walter Raleigh, a privateer pioneer, who sought glory, gold and freedom from the Catholic rule. He founded a secret society, 'The School of Night,' which was attended by highly prominent Elizabethans. Beliefs were discussed and it is closely related to the mysterious Rosicrucian movement which is tied to the disbanded Knights Templar and to present day Freemasons." He pulls up his favorite cup and rushes a mouthful of water, winks and tells them, "These little metal things keep it cool," and takes another.

"Truth be known, Queen Elizabeth I was as much on fire as Raleigh on religious freedom and condemned the persecution of Christians. She was nothin' like her half sister,"

Jake's arms sweep across the room, "Queen Bloody Mary, who partied over the ordered massacre of Christians. Staked and burned them. And beheaded them." Jake sucks in air and sends a guillotine's whistling strike into the microphone as he chops down at the podium. "When Mary died the citizens loaded tables into the streets and burned bon fires for days to celebrate. She was a monster." Jake's blonde layers shiver and the prim lady purses her lips so tightly the top lip forms a hook over the bottom like a bird's beak.

"Queen Elizabeth I was a Christian pacifier. She never married. A king would have put his interests first and she wouldn't put her people in jeopardy." As Jake's wide palm stretches out to the queen's portrait his finger flicks the screen and it creates the illusion of her majesty walking into the room. "There were many suitors, especially from Spain. And it was no secret she sought out the friendship of her childhood friend she had assigned to royal duties, but she did not fulfill her heart's desire. Instead she directed her passion into aiding the Protestants like she was on a mission from God. The combined forces of the queen and the pioneer, Raleigh, set in motion America's biggest ongoing mystery, The Lost Colony."

Click. Governor John White's watercolor of the original Virginia coastline with an elaborate compass and royal crests, and ships with their bellowing sails plunges starboard over the front of the room.

A gentleman taking notes on the front row leans up as he raises his hand. "I've read several books on the Lumbee and The Lost Colony connection. I don't recall a link to the Portuguese in any of 'em."

"Thanks for mentioning that. When ya'll first saw that Portuguese lady in the first clip did you think she was an Indian?" Jake scans their faces and so does the gentleman taking notes. Several admit to the Indian theory. "Raise your hands if you first thought she was an Indian." Three quarters of the room fills with raised hands, but the back rows still have a slew of tucked chins.

"Did everyone notice the queen's necklace? Bet it's worth every drop a' moonshine and copper from North Carolina on up to Kentucky, huh?" While he wryly grins across the audience, keeping his eyes on the back rows, he takes notice of those who share his enthusiasm. But his grin quickly fades when the umpire glares up at him. The back rows huddle into a fast roar looking put out and fired up.

Click. The screen displays a sketch of European fashioned men around a tree with the word 'Croatan' carved on it. "Governor John White, a leader for the English pilgrims, told his colonists to leave word on their whereabouts should they have to leave their stake. He had left to bring more supplies and when he returned he found this inscription. Years later a missionary's interaction on the largest Croatan settlement with blue and gray eyed Natives is documented. They were described as yellowish brown and had curly hair. And they could 'talk in a book' and spoke English. Their English words were most curious to the missionary because they were of the Royal European vernacular, like 'thoust.' Along with this documented eye witness account behavior indicators dictate the English blended with the Croatan over time."

The screen displays a large golden filigree cross with a white rose at its center and in bold print the Rosicrucian statement, which Jake reads aloud: "What think you, loving people, and how seem you affected, seeing that you now understand and know, that we acknowledge ourselves truly and sincerely to profess Christ, condemn the Pope, addict ourselves to the true Philosophy, lead a Christian life, and daily call, entreat and invite many more unto our Fraternity, unto whom the same Light of God likewise appeareth?" The next image is of an English pilgrim in one of John White's sketches. The White man is reading the Bible to a Croatan. "These, my friends, were America's first Christians."

"One God knows all, like dis bes a-catawampus," a nearly masculine voice from the back row announces.

With a serious, but soft expression Jake holds up the next note card. "This is an excerpt from 'A Role for Sassafras in the Search for the Lost Colony,' by Philip S. McMullan Jr.

On March 25, 1584, Sir Walter Raleigh received a 'letters-patent' from Queen Elizabeth "for the discovering and planting of new lands not possessed by any Christian Prince nor inhabited by Christian People, to continue for the space of 6 yeeres and no more." Raleigh's first expedition was a short reconnaissance voyage between April and September, 1584, by Amadas and Barlowe. Two Indians, a Croatan called Manteo and a Roanoke called Wanchese, came back to England with them.'"

Jake cast his arms behind and bows. "We are in the presence of royalty," and rises with outstretched arms. "We are in the presence of descendants of America's First Christians."

The medieval image that follows sits the audience members deep into their seats as Jake leans across the podium until it tilts. "Put yourself in Sir Walter Raleigh's shoes. He was an intelligent industrious man, a Christian man. Okay, we have to be factual, so let's add that he made some bad choices along the way, such as an illegitimate child and the killing of innocent Natives to plunder their wealth."

He jabs at the audience with a heavy brow. "I want you to think about what drove him to do what he did. Okay? This is the psychological drive. That's what we are exploring, why people do what they did and how it can prove historical theories based on basic human behavior. In 1572 Raleigh witnessed the St Bartholomew's Day massacre where French Protestants were massacred by French Catholics in Paris." The screen's medieval image is an old oil painting of naked Christians writhing in the streets as sleek dogs devour the bodies and lamenting wounded. "The slaughter of Protestants, Raleigh's fellow Christians, spread throughout Paris. It lasted several weeks. Modern estimates for the total dead vary from 5,000 to 30,000. So it was only logical for Raleigh to charm the queen in order to be the chosen one to find a 'New Found Land.'

The ancient Church of Egypt, one of the Oldest in Christianity, St Bartholomew's martyrdom, bloody as it is, is commemorated on the 1st day of the Coptic Calendar, which currently falls on September 11." Jake's rigid finger points at the screen as it clicks to a daunting image of The Twin Towers as the second plane strikes and fires erupt and the structure collapses. "Let me tell you something. The Knights Templar have always been crusaders against Islam. That's why they were organized in the first place. In America, September 11, 2001, will live on in epiphany." His zealous passion spreads out across the room like seeds in a wind gust. "Christians must bring the truth out into the light. Stop being the meek politically correct puppets our liberal media conditions people to be and help end this Holy War."

When the members hasten against the chairs and their eyebrows take flight Jake somberly adds, "How many times does the Bible mention bravery?" The members relax. "A lot. It's a shame that in the land of the free and the brave so many have become afraid to speak up. I understand it though. So if any of you have something they want to share, any little thing, your daddy's daddy told a story about a group of leaders who had a secret meeting, or your aunt told your momma about a heirloom that was handed down through the generations. It was something that proved they met up with the Algonquin Indians or better yet, the Lost Colony, anything," Jake throws an arm back over his shoulder to the desk, "take one of my cards and call me." He offers up the card. "Make the call; a heroic act of valor. You could be the one to save the next generation from more of this ungodly mess."

He twirls the cup by the lips to and fro as he scans over his note strewn cards and suddenly stops twirling as he holds up a card. "I almost forgot, Portuguese seaman worked aboard Raleigh's commissioned trips, but weren't listed on the ships' registers. That's why their DNA isn't included in the studies currently being conducted." The man taking notes who had reminded him of the Portuguese woman resembling an Indian, smiles. "It's only logical. Drop off a group of gentle Europeans in the wilderness and a group of hearty Portuguese seaman. Which group'll have more survivors?"

The man taking notes raises his hand.

"Yes?"

"John White's watercolors are in museums and reference books as chronological markers for Early Americana. I've studied them and there's not a single Portuguese." He taps his pen on his notepad.

"They manned ships and helped build the colonists' settlement, but they wouldn't have stayed on. The Europeans are notorious for beheading those who offend them. And the lot of seaman, as needed as they were, were rough and mean and just as soon cut a man as back down from a fight. Governor John White wouldn't have dirtied his canvas with the likes of them."

Click. Moses, as portrayed in a rich oil painting on Mount Sanai with the stone tablets inscribed with the Ten Commandments roars down to the people on the big screen. "In the Holy Bible, Exodus 34:4 states that the Ten Commandments were written on stone tablets from Mount Sanai. A section of tablet with thirteen symbols was discovered in England near a holy well where a medieval chapel once stood. It is believed to be a section of the Ten Commandments. The tablet is made from the same arenite sandstone as Jabal Musa, near Mount Catherine which is traced back to the time of Helena of Constantinople. Saint Helena, (ca. 246/50 – 18 August 330) found relics of the True Cross while building The Church of the Holy Sepulchre in Jerusalem."

Click. A larger than life image of the Dome of the Rotunda of the Church of the Holy Sepulchre, in Jerusalem penetrates the audience like a Holy presence just set foot in the library's conference room. "The site is where Jesus was crucified."

With his fingertips cupping the edge of the screen Jake gives them time to digest the Dome's splendor. Its light curiously refracts into the room as if they've transcended space and time and the light really is Holy.

"St. Helena built several churches on Holy Land and recovered many Christian relics. She ordered the Temple of Jupiter demolished to build one of those churches, The Church of St. Cyrus and St. John, on the Holy Land of Jerusalem, Temple Mount."

Click. A stone fortress smack dab in the middle of an arid desert city made up of smaller stone structures glares down at them from the screen. Inside the fortress is a large hexagonal stone structure with a golden globe finial. Under the picture is the description, which Jake reads aloud, "The Dome of the Rock is the structure in the middle. It's in the location where the Bible declares the Holy Temple should be rebuilt.

In the early eleven hundreds crusaders were knighted to form unions against Muslims trying to invade Holy Land. For nearly seventy-five years the Knights Templar, Christian

Crusaders, protected Temple Mount." Click. An image of a medieval knight in his tunic, with a sword and bearing the cross interests the members and they whisper amongst themselves calling names of Freemasons in the audience. Several men adjust their seating positions as Jake continues. "The Knights Templar are believed to have been given many Christian relics to protect over the years, including St. Helena's discoveries.

One of those relics is from the Passion of Christ, the tip of the lance that pierced his side to prove he was dead. It's documented that it was taken to St. Helena of Constantinople and she hid it in the church of St. Sophia. Later it was enshrined with the Crown of Thorns in the Sainte Chapelle and in the French Revolution moved to the Bibliotheque Nationale. The Crown is preserved. But the lance's tip is long gone.

Considering the mysterious healing powers associated with pieces of the True Cross, and considering human behavior, the tip was most likely stolen. I suggest it is in the hands of a group known for miraculous healing, a branch of crusaders named Knights of Hospitallers."

Gruff huffs and shuffling shoes spark from the middle rows. And squeaky little old ladies whisper like gossiping Sunday school girls.

"You see, the Knights Templar were not only warriors. In fact, most weren't warriors, but were philosophers, engineers, healers and bankers and formed branches to assign these talents. The Knights Templar had begun as poor Christians and became wealthy as Christians supported them. Soon Kings were borrowing from them and this led to their virtual demise. The rulers couldn't pay back their debts so erroneous charges were made against their threatening dear crusaders. What would have changed in history if the crusaders had overtaken the Royal Kings' positions? Would Christians have complete rule over the majority of the countries? Would Christians have maintained the Temple Mount? Or is our history as it should be, according to the Holy Bible?"

The image of a modest church on a country hillside fills the screen. Then an illuminated tunnel with keystone bricks ensuring timeless arches lengthens over the screen like a slithering snake. "The Knights Templar is credited with building many churches and tunnels and caves with scripted messages on the walls during their openly active years from 1109 to 1312. One such cave is the Rosyton Cave." Click. The screen's primitive drawings on the chalky cave walls depict urgency. "The drawings are medieval and depict Jesus' crucifixion and the two tail stars of the Big Dipper called Benetnash and Mizar. These stars depict the same guardian angels on the lid of the Ark. The Ark of the Covenant is said to contain the tablets of stone Moses wrote the Ten Commandments on. These drawings reappear in church murals and a famed Kirkwall Scroll in the possession of the one and only Knights." Jake's stiff hands jolt up and down over the podium. "The movement and behavior clearly convey the Knights Templar were consumed with knowledge of the Christian treasures and they had an urgency to relay this information, but only to other crusaders."

Jake asks for lights and as the recessed lighting fills the room he takes a folded chair and sits it in front of the aisle. "Who can tell me how the Lumbee are linked to the Knights Templar? Sit right here." He unfolds the chair. "And I'll give a Franklin to the one who tells us which Christian relic the knights protect now." He pats his wallet and walks around the chair like it's a pit he doesn't want to fall into spreadin' out his arms for balance. Several guesses are thrown into the air. A few sound ones. But Jake sits after a grave man states the knights are sworn to secrecy and then asks, "Where'd your water cup get to?" And Jake smirks up over his shoulder, "Miss Prickenwrath, I'm not done yet. Don't pack up everything." Then faces his guests flippin' his perty pen. "Ya'll let me know how you want your books signed."

He grasps his knees and leans toward them and in a secretive kind a' way shares, "There were over twenty thousand of these crusaders, from England, France, Jerusalem, Tripoli, Hungary, Antioch, Croatia, and Portugal. There it is again, that Portugal denominator. Common sense, human nature and the honor these crusaders upheld is enough for me to believe they did not dissolve, but went underground. Some joined military orders, taking their treasures with them, groups like the Order of Hospitallers," Jake's eyebrows dance along with his roping hand like he's got a calf by the hind legs. "This group was previously titled the Knights of Hospitallers." Jake scans across the middle rows. Stands. Makes a quick check on the back rows. Turns his back to them and returns to the podium. "Some were pensioned and allowed to live out their days as commoners. A lot of 'em went to Portugal, because of the Christian persecution in the rest of Europe. It was one place where they could be safe. This is one explanation of the Templars in Portugal. Was another place the NewFoundLand, our old Virginy?"

A hand rises from the mid section. "One of the leading temples is in Portugal. The knights are real proud of that." The middle aged man who passes as Lumbee in a sport jacket and dress pants could also easily pass for a younger version of the Lum two rows behind.

"Yes, sir, thank you for sharing that. And I'd like to elaborate. The knights built a full fledged fortress and called it the Castle of Tomar for the first king of Portugal. Most folks don't help others without wanting something in return. Right?" Jake half grins. "When the King of Portugal, a fairly new country still under attacks, invited the knights it was because he needed their protection. Later, when the Pope disbanded the Knights Templar an intervention was made so Portugal could keep the knight's treasures they had brought with them, by forming the Order of Christ Church. That was a swift one, huh? No one knows 'xactly what those treasures were."

Jake smiles as he surveys the members and takes a seat in the chair again. He leans up from the chair and starts out in a whisper, "Some believe the Templars possessed a fleet of ships at La Rochelle in France, even though there is no proof." Jake claps his hands and the front row jumps. "Is anyone seeing a cycle of secrecy here? The Templars didn't wanna leave proof. They had too much ta risk. They took off to the New World on old Viking routes, making one of the pre-Columbian voyages. And like we were just talkin', on Portugal, the Knights Templar did not really disband. They just changed their name to Knights of Christ. Just like the temple they built was renamed to the Order of Christ. In 1492, this group from Portugal provided the navigators for Christopher Columbus' journey, and the Order's cross was featured prominently on the sails of his ships, however there is no actual evidence. Of course not." His face reddens. "There's too much at risk." He literally shakes with each defiant syllable. "Just like the Lumbee Council has too much at risk."

Jake rises from his chair. "Now, can anyone tell me the link of Lumbees to the Holy Grail? Be specific." Metal chairs strain and clank along with the expected. And determinedly, Jake talks on over the complaints and threats and finally resigns when the front rows rise to leave. Then it happens. From the bowed up back rows a faint glimmer teases like the pokeberry pox when the polite man and his similar familiar, presumably dead for years, exchange hugs as the remaining guests vanish.

Chapter 12

You Were Always There for Me

The never ending ocean wind as strong and busy as it is sends a lonesome longing in its rhythmic call like a lovelorn whippoorwill. Singing its refrain in vain. His curly dirty blonde locks whip about his orange tawny cheeks and his handsome thick lips pout while he scouts for the odd new delights, the spoots. They are scattered in outcrops, like his new family, across the black sandy shore. With his bucket half full he calls out, "How many do we need?"

"O, best get a bucket full. Games bring da players. Thy'll have drinks and eats at it all along. Summer dim 'ere. No dark ta speak of. Be dancing, too. Frances bes calling on tha ladies. Dark hair's comin'." The old man's stocky frame pushes along against the wind until he becomes a darker version of himself outcast beyond definition.

The others are strewn about like crabs each on their own quest, as men do when competing for food, or charmers, or loot. Changing hands when their buckets wear heavy and cleverly counterbalancing wind gusts without falling as shirttails flap like wings. In their thick leather soled boots they walk backwards across the sands at low tide sporting knives and buckets and bellies happy with dark brew. They each check the other's buckets looking over their shoulders and stealing peeks as they kneel down to free the razor clams from their black sandy beds. With brimmed buckets each man finds his way back to the courtyard and rinses his load at the well. "Take mine to the cooks, would ya, Pops? I'm gonna walk on the beach."

"Walk, eh? Keep tha boots on or we'll be packing razor cuts fer sure now. Our Orkney undertow haint fer sissy boys. Takes a man's last chance 'ere."

Past the soft sand he pulls off his shirt and dashes toward the crashing waves. Summer in Orkney is a high of 54 Fahrenheit. But with the cold wind it feels more like 45 on bare skin so the invigoration exceeds to exhilaration as the cold wind washes his tears to his ears and he braves the chilly forty degree splashes. "Good goo-oo!" He doggedly wades in to his hips until the force pulls and tugs and begs. Like a lover from the other side of the world. His muscles strain and sting, but he holds and buries his heavy boots into the sand like posts into clay. The cold ocean slaps his chin and splashes over his curls till he's soaked senseless and numb as a hapless little baitfish. But just before a vicious white wave promises to turn him catawampus or drown 'm dead he jerks free and dives toward the crashing shore.

He lays face down on a pillowy sand bed, thrashed and pecked free of spoots and its kind by the various fowl. His depression had gotten the better of him and his unexpected hot tears wet his forearms as his heaves purge suicide's lure. He allows the ocean's greedy laps to lick over his legs and the force to sway his hips as the cool sand warms enough under him that the chilling wind doesn't sting. The ocean's rhythmic love call seduces him into a relaxed state and he props his head and absorbs the shoreline. Rocky passes with lush green blades whistle over and up to the hardy wild flowers much like the daisy aster outcrops in his pinelands. Busy gulls screech high in the sky and on the shore puffins chirp and purr only feet away. With the only true human footprints being the shingle rooftops, the threat of seclusion in exile screams until his throat burns and the leather boots tighten like irons. When gulls circle overhead and dive closer at his teasing goldilocks he stands and shakes off what sand he can.

All pink and sticky and polka dot black with shiny sand he picks up his shirt and jogs to the stone wall encircling the courtyard and on the other side pulls off his strict boots and wading trousers and tosses them onto the well crafted and well seasoned work bench where fish are cleaned and lies are primed. Protected from the cool ocean wind he gazes past the courtyard's open gateway to the mighty ocean and off to his right spies the sign. The magnificent aurora borealis waltzes across the clear summer dim sky into the open abyss claiming his only thought of happiness, a second chance at love, and warms him enough that the chill bumps calm.

In his soaked tighty whities he bounces through the courtyard to the largest stone house. The island claims forty people when they're not fishing. Half live in the five stone structures making up the men's quarters. Right now, half of those are smilin' wide at Bruce's buck n' hide as he whistles back and cat calls, "Hey, mama's boys, anyone up for a swim?" He politely moons them, politely being that he doesn't bend over, and his numb pink butt shines like bright red rouge on a white whore. He spins back around to his riled mates and pulls at his waistband. "All natural if you can get the dark hair over? Whadayasay, Pops?" And all cat calls cease.

Pops cracks the broom handle against the stone floor and thrusts the bristled end against Bruce's backside as he pasts in the open foyer. "She's me sweet neice. You'll not be showin' 'er dat sport or you'll be danglin' yer dillywhopper fer bait off me rig." And laughter rounds out the parade. "Gotdat, Jack?"

"Yes, Sir, bossman." He hurries to the kitchen where the sweet meat is purged from the shells and the roasting orgasmic aromas clench around the sweet tender spoots like lips.

"Gawl dookie, ya'll can cook. Must be in Heaven's kitchen. I love it!" He opens the half door's base and the ocean wind traps it open. In hurls a gust of salty sea air as Bruce spatters salty black dots across the smooth stone floor and they crack spoots open and boast on their loaded buckets. The large kitchen is already heated with the large dome brick oven's live fire. Hearty garlic cloves roast with onions and they mingle with the sweet rosemary as the scents permeate his pores while he warms up with a whiskey and spins like a rotisserie toasting near the hot dome oven and his manhood is quickly coveted.

Two men cracking their razor clams hold up their pinky finger sized spoots and ask if there's a girl on the island who needs a wee man. "Let us know. We'll take two." One claims it is not size but the action and pushes his tongue in and out of his beer bottle and another follows with a spoot in his. The cook announces that if there's a woman needs to see a real man to come see him. "I be da only one among ya' that's cause fer a, a fight," he lingers over the words as he realizes the true dilemma. Bruce is half erect and half drunk and doesn't feel his engorged endearment. So the cook clues him in. "Newby, lad, be a help and get the pickles out o' yer pants. Silly me. Get the pickles from the pantry."

But Bruce pours his glass half full again and asks where the pantry is as he opens cabinets. When he leans over the large kettle with the creamy sauce he pushes his finger in and sucks it clean and the young man chopping parsley and thyme tells him not to and that he'd better get dressed before the girls come or no one else will get to dance. So Bruce makes his way down the hall and half drunk and melancholy admires the hallway's décor, including his. And laughs.

Curious, if not familiar, portraits in dark walnut hand hewn oil rubbed frames hang in the wide open hall like the oven hot Orkney spoots smothering in the creamy garlic sauce. He rubs down the fresh scar tissue tightening between his ribs as the promising sting of the razor clams' saltwater bitters and sweet meat forms drool pools in his cheeks. The scent is so fresh he can't help himself but to lick his forearm when he is sure the hall is clear. And the act purges more memories. More angst. More thirst the afternoon's drink has not quenched. He closes his bedroom door and dresses in quiet reflection sure his life is in purgatory. He nestles into the quilt covered chair. "I can still kiver up and pretend I'm all the fine in the world." The rattling window panes hypnotize him into a sweet swampy dream when there is a knock at the door.

Pops winks and hands over Jake's smuggled book. "Mail came while you were making it with the waves. They've cherished the photos round and round now and wish to see the films after dinner. What do you want me to say?" The stone wall holds the tall windows. A walnut paneled wall holds the Knight Templars' precious sail's remnant, The Kirkwall

Scroll. And Pops asking Bruce for permissions holds Bruce's tongue as he stands.

"Well? What'll it be, lad?"

"Why here?" When his forlorn gaze and angry jaw make their demands Pops closes the door behind him and motions for him to take a seat and when Bruce obliges with a keen eye he witnesses the transformation. Pops holds his palms up to the sailcloth and proclaims, "We got it safe 'ere. Thar's one fer tourists at the manor." He looks over his shoulder at Bruce, "Don' be touchin' it and such. Yer oils'll take what life's left in 'er, eh?" As Pops drawls the sailcloth's thick braided cord and unveils an ancient rhunestone his tunic shifts and the upper third of a red cross tattooed on his lower hip flashes. "They traveled to Portugal and helped fight off tha dark Islamics and built mighty fortresses and came 'ere to Scotland fer tha same. Whilst I've only memorized tha story I haven't a clue what each figur' says. Story of tha first times 'ere is in this stone. Fine historians, theologians, philosophers and warriors. K'ept records of everythin'." The stone is at least eighteen inches tall by thirteen or fourteen wide and has jagged brown lined figures crammed in neat rows.

"It's like the one in America. There's a museum. Just recently, I think within the last five, a forensic geologist verified it. The uh, Kensor, no the Kensing,"

"Kensington Runestone. O, I know. Norwegian. Tells o' our 1362 voyage. The fishin' trip and comin' in ta find thar fellers slaughtered by tha reds. It was understood. Tha Knights were a threat."

"The same people made this one?"

"Same and naut. All Templar Knights. Ships passin' in tha night on thar separate ways to live and build new worlds, Christian worlds. We protect our own and other Christians, lad. We Knights have a duty. You have a duty." Bruce stands to study the stone's odd inscription and Pops warns, "It comes wid a price. We pray you'll come aroun'. We's plannin' to school ya up 'ere in Kirk and sen' ya back."

"Kirk?"

"Here, thar, all o'er. Kirk bes tha church, tha Word, boy." With his steely hand gripping Bruce's shoulder and his stinging icicle blues alarmingly close, Pops confides, "There's not time fer bargainin' and you're da best choice, ya hard headed lug. Thought you'd drown out dar wid yer curls soaking in da white foams. Had me prayers smokin'. Bout ta call fer help if ya hadn't turn' about."

"I didn't see you."

"Don' be fooled. I'm over me youth. Proud eighty-two and a Knight till I'm under. I'm tellin' ya now. We all are here."

"And the dark hair, your niece? Are the women knights?"

"O, most wicked, lad. Tha bonnies'll kiss and take yer heart an' life an' no back to it till it's out from under ya. Now get together. You've got ta make an impression. Every man here's asked me niece fer a dance."

"And?"

"N', she's been waiting fer a man who'll take da wakes with 'er."

Bruce bangs his chest like an ape and spins a quick twirl to find him opening the door and halfway out when Pops tells him, "Rest yer flippers and clean yer ears. Kate's o lot o' woman fer any man, even a prince." And Pop agrees, without hesitation, to delay dinner so Bruce can dive into his precious book, and the films are chosen for afterward. Predictably the last chapter is devoured first. And like a fine appetizer from the first bite homesickness is fed a heapin' dose of remedy. Chapter 12, You Were Always There for Me.

The gravel's lime dust swirled and settled as jar runners backed up to the building. They jumped out with cash burning holes in their pockets and placed bets on passing motorists having out of town plates. Dodger and Snap placed one dollar bets and when stakes were raised walked. Cassie's older boys were loving South Carolina. They bet between themselves while the two youngest played hide and seek around the restaurant until the six year old chunked a rock and the four year old to fell flat in a muddy rut. The red headed brat swore just like his older brothers as he tried in vain to wipe off the mud and smeared it instead. "Run," his older brothers yelled as Shorty hollered, "Here comes Ma!"

Two fast slaps to the yurkers' tails then Cassie swung them up into the truck bed. She held down the older and secured him with a bungee cord. Then she pulled out a sack of tee shirts from behind the driver's seat and sorted through for one without big holes as the youngest jerked back the bungee cord. "Damn it!" sounded the sting and the bright orangey red afro bounced in a frenzied escape. When Cassie spun around the crying boy's eyes doubled, "Get Stink away from me, Ma! He's got a stick!"

Pen snickered and then asked Snap, "You got a cell phone?"

He flipped it open. "Gambler's anonymous?"

"Very funny. Call Bruce."

"Taint got one yet. Easy, he'll be here. Probably helped feed up or something like that." Snap rested back against the hood of his adored late nineteen sixties pale green boy toy. "How's the bite?"

"I'll have a big dimple where the flesh rots out. But Momma's seeing 'bout it."

"Thought she got you to the doctor?"

"Yea, I got a venom shot and antibiotics. Three refills."

"More hits on you than a ball bat." Snap admired the young man's strong muscular frame and veins like rigid pythons choked up 'round his pit bull biceps. "Bet you'd be a tough'n ta take down." Snap's tee shirt matched both his car and his banded straw cowboy hat. His strong angular facial bones were tanned extra dark while his long rectangular hollow cheeks were lighter. And his full lips bled red while his gray eyes darkened under the shade of his brim. With his jeans tucked inside his fanciest alligator skin boots he was a double for a hottie on the rodeo circuit.

Dodger peered into Snap's nice ride. "Honeymoon over?"

And Snap half grinned. "She's resting. Woman works hard. Said to bring her a take out."

"Oh, she's already got you trained." Rodger Dodger slapped his leg. "Dunrovin here has a large cheese pizza on special tonight. Let her dress it up way she likes."

"Good idea, Dodge."

"Is Edge staying home, too?" Pen casually asked.

"She's already here. Got a early ride in." Snap smiled. "Go tell her hi." His big gray eyes flashed from under the brim of his straw cowboy hat.

"Oh, I can wait."

"Go talk to her. You kin get a beer inside."

Cassie rolled her eyes at Snap and then smiled at her son, "Not yet, Lassie." Pen was rather handsome that summer's eve with his stubble shaved. Even with the large jeans Cassie had rushed in and bought at the dollar store so he could be comfortable with the thick wound dressing Pen charmed the eyes. With his red curls buzzed into a smart crew cut he was every bit a soldier fresh from the heat of battle with his half arm's fleshy scar tissue sunburned scarlet to deep purple.

After Cassie draped a clean tee shirt over Stink, she batted her big bright blue eyes up at the shadowing cloud. As it stagnated over them in a welcoming respite from July's stifling heat in the dusty parking lot it dulled the bright orange in her curls to an appealing red. She wore it pulled back in a short tight ponytail with baby nap curls around her freckled ears. And tiny jade buttons perched from her delicate earlobes adding a touch of class. Overall, in her button down white shirt, clean blue jeans and nearly white tennis shoes, Cassie was very becoming, even with the red headed afro tot wiping boogers on her jean's leg in his mud stained tennis shoes and adult size tee shirt. On to his mischief, she plopped him into the back of the truck and checked for sticks. Threatened him and then joined Snap.

As the cloud covered the sun in its slow descent, she checked across the street for oncoming traffic. At six o'clock on a Saturday night there was little traffic and as the locals passed she called them by name. "Bet Williford is having fish tonight."

"Saturday nights they're trying to use up everything before it times out. Get more that way." Dodger checked Cassie over as she tied her loose tennis shoe strings. When she rose from her squat he asked if she was going out afterwards. "You kiddin', Dodge?" She spat. "Aint you beat? I'm tuckin' in early. Bes a lot to clean 'fore the next round. Gotta sharpen all the damn hand axes and knives."

"We's on ta a name on our guillotine."

"Who?"

"Same idgit took our Book got our blade."

"You sure?" Cassie's cheeks filled.

"Fraid not. Or we'd a-stole it back already. Reckon?"

"We got our Bible back, Dodge." Toe to toe she swore. "And we'll get our blade back and we're gonna keep it fer good. Hear?" Her lips curled. "Do you like lamb?"

"Too greasy. Why? Plannin' on a-thinnin' out the field?" Dodger nervously looked around. "Dear, we're talking about letting go, right?" And Cassie half grinned as Dodger flicked off a chunk of nail along with the black line of filth with his trusty hawkbill. Cassie told him to go wash. "Dose the same overalls you wore this afternoon?" She fisted her hips as Dodger lumbered into the restaurant with a hitch in his giddy up. "Damn, youse a' bossy woman." And Snap hollered, "Whadya do to yer self? Real work get cha' today?"

As the Magee boys pulled up the jar runners tightened up and bowed up. But the Magee boys walked straight on to Cassie's boys and offered their stash on the game as a blinding white luxury car passed. "There's no one around here with that much money. That thing's fresh from Detroit, man." When Thomas Magee held up a five it waved like a flag.

"Thomas's can. They own the whole town. Or the McKeithan's." The wiry and pale, gray eyed middle boy with blonde bouncy curls, Alice, snatched Thomas's five. He held it up to his cherry red lips and kissed it. "Thank you, gentlemen."

"Check it good," Cordy yelled to his younger brother, Shorty, as he strained through the binoculars right next to the highway. "Don't you drop those, Shorty," Pen warned his brother.

Joe Ray flipped the bills in his brother's hand and asked, "How much we got, Alice? Give ya a' pinch for a five." Joe Ray jerked up his gut of snuff and when Alice tried to snatch it he pushed it back into his pocket. Alice bowed up and pushed his brother's chest. "I'll tell Ma if ya don't give me some after dinner."

Thomas Magee nudged his big brother and when he didn't jump on the feminine name young Thomas did. "Alice? What's that about, man? You the mom when Cassie's out or what?"

Pen's chest increased two fold as he eavesdropped on the forthcoming punches. And so did Cassie's. But with her magic finger she drew the circling wand of peace and the boys laughed it off like it was the best joke of the day. With a big smile Cordy informed Thomas that it was a family name and that he'd better call him Al.

"Sure," Thomas's tongue ran his teeth like a motor cross warm up. Like he'd learned right along that a dry mouth was much more likely to get a broke tooth 'cause a fist just don't slide as well. "Alice."

"Shit." Pen rushed as Shorty gave his brothers the thumbs down from the highway and ran for the fun. "Put dat wad in yer pocket, Cordy. Don't lose it!" Shorty slid in and yanked Thomas down by the ankles. Down in the gravel, he took a mou'ful, but it was the kick in the face that cut his lip. Thomas' big brother held back two by the necks in a bear claw as Cassie folded her arms one over the other and whistled a shrill ear splitting yurker call so loud that the curtains in the restaurant were spread wide open. "Bes an index to pizza and all else in two seconds you don't listen up, boys," her red face threatened.

After the boys shook off the fury and most of the dust they had to divvy up the wad over their momma's command and shake hands. Shorty smiled so politely it was sickening, "Good doin' business wid cha." While Cordy waited for his momma to go check on the young boys in the back of the pick up and when he was sure, asked young Thomas, "Where's yer daddy?"

"You know where he is."

"Afraid ta say, boy?"

Big brother Magee was finally ruffled and with red tipped ears challenged. "Your family doesn't want recognition because it knows it won't help anymore than it does now. So what's the difference?" His spicy aftershave mixed with their stale breath. "After all, Universities want English speaking students."

"We's all going to the community college and paying our own way." Shorty snubbed. "Bes pride in keeping the swamp. Our teacher says long as we can, whad she call that word, Cord?"

"Convey."

"Long as we convey the message 'cross it don't matter." Shorty's nose pert ner flattened out. "Your daddy's a traitor to real Lums. Real Lums don't want nuthin' from Whites. No special nothin' and no federal anything." Shorty bowed up, "Us'ns got pride." His fourteen year old chest puffed out like the bon a fide sixteen year old on his driver's license.

"Man, you don't get it. You pay attention tonight and you'll figure out a thing or two. Like, we want to help, Shorty. I like you guys." Thomas scanned their faces. "We go back, all those years of runnin' for Bruce. Man, we grew up together."

"We're keepin' our roots." Shorty strutted like a rooster about to go into the ring for a master Lum's cock fight. "Look at cho, chocolate Lum. Only injun in ya is that ma a yours. If she is your real ma."

Cordy reared up as his dartin' fingers stabbed at the Magee brothers' chests. "You two got all the easy runs."

"No," the elder Magee boy's testosterone drummed. "We got the ones your ma said was too dangerous for her boys. We handled all the coloreds for your own good. There was no favoritism. Bruce isn't that way. And our father is in Washington. Without men like him they'd have the county bulldozed." The elder boy's nose flared as it drew in the heat and his jaw tightened 'till the thick muscle pulsed. "Those people don't get small town ways. My dad does and he cares. Get it?"

But young Thomas Magee's jaw was loose as an idiot clown's jumping out a' barrels in a mad bull's ring. He stepped up real close to Cordy. "Now, can you say, "Who's your daddy?"

Snap cooled his hot face with the brim of his straw hat and sprinted over to the heated group. "We're here for Bruce. Let's go inside and get a sweet tea now. Come on." Stink popped off the truck's tailgate. Ran inside and as the door closed struggled to lock his brothers out while his tongue writhed about like a wet snake over his jaw. He jumped up and hit at the latch over and over until Edge pulled him away.

Shorty walked in record speed to be in front of Thomas and asked Alice, "Who invited them?" With his long arm Snap whipped at Shorty's shoulder. "Bruce did. He invited all his friends." And as Pen's juvember's thick rubber band worked up from his loose jean's waistband Thomas told Snap, "They were lookin' for trouble." And Pen pushed the juvember back down.

When the older Magee replied, "Some things never change," Pen squared up, "We have to change first." And when they all gave him the eye, added, "It has to start with us. Right?" And shoulders relaxed. Heads bowed. And Snap looked to the sky.

Cassie freed her rock chunking son from the back of the pick up and he ran to the restaurant and sought out Stink and right away yanked his ears. Stink's face matched his hair until he became one little hot ball of fire. The two scrapped like hog littermates grunting and biting and kicking. The staff, owner and patrons watched in disbelief as a pitcher of sweet tea wobbled when the pair rolled under a table.

Dodger rose from his straight back chair in such a rush it fell to the tile with a fat clack as he yelled, "Bes all de sorry in de world yer ma sees dat. Help me, Edge." On all fours she jerked Stink by the leg and drug them both out. Stink stayed on top with a mouthful of nose as his brother pulled his ears. Dodge cracked both against their thick heads and immediately they winced and grabbed the fast whelps. Stink stood ready to kick Dodger, but he held him back with a fist full of red afro while Edge shook his shoulders. "You gonna end up in the broom closet, hungry! That what you want?"

Well, they all rushed into the restaurant and the older boys discovered real quick it would be in their best interest to take a seat. Cassie was red as a firecracker. "What are you doing ta him?" She yanked Edge's arms off her baby boy. She didn't even have to touch Dodge. He let go of Stink and the six year old wearing bright red teeth indentions across the bridge of his nose confessed. "We weren't fightin, Ma. I swear."

"Shut up and sit down."

Stink didn't pay his momma much mind for lookin' over Edge like she's an unwrapped candy bar as he licked his lips. "I'm thirsty." Stink clasped onto the red bandana trim on her short shorts as she sashayed over to a table by the window. Stink was on the verge of spanking a cheek when Edge pulled out a chair for him and he climbed up. But the owner came out from behind the counter and directed them all to a large secluded area in the back. The cinderblock walls had no windows and dark purple drapes hung open at either side of the adjoining wall. "We gonna see a movie, too, ma?" Cordy asked.

Miss Ginger rode over with the Crowsons. They picked up her fiancé on the way. Bruce had said he wanted to get to know him if he's gonna be sparking his roommate. Ken, Exilee and Luke drove their own truck because farm life put the child up at daylight or before and that meant Luke could get fussy and they'd probably have to leave early.

That left Jake, Bruce and Robin to ride together. Robin sat in the middle wearing a scent of musky waitress; roasted peppers, beef du jour, and sweet lime sorbet in her turquoise tee shirt and yellow jeans. When she loosened her long black silk from the red band a wave of gardenia blooms threatened to hypnotize each man into proposals. It was like a multi flavored beef brisket in a seductive glaze on a silver platter was between the two twitterpated friends.

Bruce and Jake were so slobbered up they couldn't sing with the radio for swallowing, so Robin crooned right on and bathed in their appreciation and applause. When she sang those crazy for lovin' you classic lines in her deep sultry manner and aimed Bruce's way, he told her, "I'm making time to get my license first thing tomorrow. Break ground and get 'er done. Won't take long. I'll be a millionaire, Robin." And Jake turned down the radio so low there was only a faint glimmer of classic country love crap in the stuffy cab and Robin stopped singing. Jake placed his hand on her tight yellow thigh. "Did Gili find someone to cover your days off for our trip?"

"I did. Exilee's gonna do it. She knows how important this horse is to you." Then Robin told Bruce, "It's his first. Well, the first he's shopped for."

"That's ri-ight." Bruce leaned up and danced his eyebrows at Jake. "Let me know if you need any help."

Jake's tongue dug a hole behind his front teeth. "You read about horses, too? All that extra time on your hands, huh?"

Bruce adjusted his jaw and with an arrogant brow studied the parking lot as they pulled in. "The Belgium can be traced back to Medieval Knights when wars were fought on horseback. Writers called them the 'Great Horses.'"

"I didn't know that," Robin exclaimed. "You must have tons of information. You wanna come with us to South Carolina? You could help us decide. Ya know what? You might want one, too. I can see you now, riding your horse across the vineyard." Her hands waved like she was playing horse puppet across the dashboard. "Didn't he say there was another one, Jake? Two geldings, one was seven, the other a little older?" She swiveled to Bruce. "I know you have the money." She grinned. "Do you feel any different now that you're so rich? You had it so hard growing up. You must be walking on clouds."

"I'll be walking on cloud nine tomorrow when I go to the bank and we get it all put in my name." Bruce slyly held his hand over her leg, about an inch away from her heat. "Feel me and tell me. Am I different good or bad?" One side of his mouth grinned while his tongue damned back the extra saliva before it streamed down his chiny chin chin. But with an elevated shoulder and shameful smile she pushed his hand away and Jake rolled his eyes. "Hon, we can pick out a horse for Bruce, if he wants us to. He'll be too busy next week. He's got a business to set up. Okay?"

"You're right," Robin arched up after the men got out and slid out Bruce's open door. "You trust us to pick out a good mount, right?"

"Course, I do." Bruce closed the door as Jake hastily paced to open the restaurant's door. And Bruce slowly escorted Robin inside, pausing to coyly adjust her pocketbook's strap over her shoulder as it pulled on her blouse and exposed her bra strap. Then with a cracked smile, "There you go." Toe to toe, his nose was just above hers, "Let me know if you need anything else adjusted," and Robin stared straight on at Jake by the open door. "Don't make her mad or I'll make you ride home in the back. Gotdat Jack?"

"Might ride back there anyway," Bruce jested as Robin marched off huffing behind the heavy purple drapes and Bruce detained Jake by the arm. "Stars are gonna be magnificent tonight."

Jake's green eyes darkened under his thickening lids as he grew against Bruce's grip. "Robin and I love wishing on stars." And at that, Bruce let go. "Sorry. And for what it's worth, I'm glad she has you. She couldn't have found a better man." They quietly merged toward the back room lit with wall mounted decorative lanterns and candles on the table. Then Bruce curiously gestured to a tapestry. The long narrow black and white forms and geometric patterns suggested a story being told, much like the creation story at the top of the fabric. Their hot ears cooled as they studied the curious old textile.

The middle depicted a regime or city and then movement. Beside the long tapestry was a coat of arms much like the design on the tapestry: An alter was flanked by a female and a male winged angel with horse legs. A five pointed star and all seeing eye in a sea of clouds were above them. The coat of arms was painted on old tongue and groove boards, unframed and lacking all luster, in simple azure blue lines.

They lingered over the two wall hangings as drink orders were taken, getting the waitress's attention by clicking as if to urge a pony to giddyup. "Sweet tea." Then Jake told Bruce, "Never seen this artsy fartsy stuff before." And Bruce bit the tip of his tongue.

Once drink orders were served and pizza preferences made Bruce told the waitress to keep bringin' 'em until he said whoa. "Wonder what's keeping Scarecrow and Lilly?" Jake asked Bruce. "Think they called it a day?"

"I doubt it." Bruce and Jake sat across from one another at the far end of the table. Robin sat at the end of the table, like a queen fitted between them. Exilee tried to get her to sit next to Luke and her, but she declined, obviously, because Edge was next to Exilee. An empty straight back chair divided the Magee boys from Cassie's boys and on the opposite side an empty chair protected Miss Sarah from Stink. When word got around the table, which was six rectangle tables butted together, that there was no imminent danger at all of the law becoming involved in the big copper momma's repossessioning everyone jeered and cheered.

Mark rose. "It's not that funny." By the time Mark explained the litter of alligators consuming the monster alligator and the gun and the boat attached to the steel lead line the laughter ended with a snort from Dodger then Stink's question on why Mark didn't think it was funny and Luke's question on when could he go see the alligators. Mark answered when he pulled out the letter. Miss Ginger and Exilee both covered their mouths and Bruce firmly pointed. "Now, Mark I just asked Ken to pull up that jar since he was gonna be there anyway."

"Why'd you wait till now? Why didn't you do it yourself a long time ago?" Mark sat back down. "Sometimes I think you're just tryin' ta get rid of me."

"Geez. I didn't even know it existed until last night. Scarecrow told me." Bruce paused at each guest as the letter was passed down. Comments declared its age, fragility and earthy scent. Bruce trembled as he breathlessly unfolded the tight creases. He held it close to his face as Scarecrow and Lilly, dressed in matching blue tee shirts and khakis finally arrived and stood directly behind him. Bruce stoically and carefully folded the letter and placed it in his shirt pocket.

"Can't believe not one a you sorry Lums called to check on me. I could a been dead in a ditch." Scarecrow shook Bruce's chair. "And that's something ta smile about?" Lilly quietly took a seat between Stink and Miss Sarah while Scarecrow looked about the room as if he was considering sitting in one of the chairs up against the wall as he made his way to the chair between Thomas and Pen. Cassie sat at the head of the table where she could keep an eye on all her boys. Lilly faced the dimly lit path from the kitchen to the dining area while Scarecrow faced a set of double doors with an emergency exit sign.

The big copper momma and alligator stories were highlighted, hyped and spread as thick as the cheese on the hand tossed pizza. The stories were told over and over until everyone was full of happy, pepperonis and salads. Cassie's boys rubbed their bellies and burped into their hands as Dodger's heavy eyelids closed when he leaned against his straight back chair. He had guzzled one beer while waiting in the front room and two more with his dinner.

Miss Ginger woke him when she twanged her fork against her heavy ceramic dinnerware plate to introduce her fiancé, Mr. Warren Croom, as a professor of history from North Carolina State University. Mr. Croom stood and welcomed Bruce and stated that he'd waited a long time to meet Bruce Black.

"You have?" Bruce's grays filled out like silver dollars.

"Don't worry, Mr. Black, I won't query about anything contrary." Mr. Croom spoke so seriously alarming the waitress turned around without serving the peach and chocolate desert pizzas.

"So what are you going to ask?" Bruce nonchalantly quipped as he charmingly studied the tall lean professor in his dress shirt and slacks.

"Mr. Black, does this mean anything to you?" Mr. Croom drew out a paper from his coat jacket and displayed it for all to see.

When Bruce didn't answer Cassie's boy, Cordy did, "Isn't she the Queen of England, the old one?"

"Very good. Precisely, Queen Elizabeth I, as she contracted Sir Walter Raleigh." He hands the picture to Bruce. "Is there anything in this picture that stands out to you? Anything?" Mr. Crooms was the only one politely smiling.

Stoic Bruce coyly passed it to Robin. She passed it to Jake, then to the Crowsons. Dear Miss Ginger bit her lips and passed it to Edge. Edge stared at the queen and then down to Cassie and then Edge stared at her silverware as Lilly took it from her. Lilly's eyebrows twitched, but she casually passed it on. When Cordy commented on the queen lookin' like his momma Cassie told him that he's a silly boy. But Mr. Croom locked down on her and then to each of her boys until he hit on Bruce again.

When Scarecrow stared at the page he licked his lips and breathed a bit faster. "I have something on paper, too. Might be nothin'. Came across it when we were, uh, talking to Mr. Fisk earlier." Scarecrow stood and handed the sketch to Mr. Croom and he taps the tabletop. "Let us in on this. It's interesting to say the least. Who is Mr. Fisk?" After noting the sketch Mr. Croom handed it to Bruce.

"He's a Lum with a still operation. I do some work for the county concerning that business and had the opportunity to attain this from him." Scarecrow's cheeks sucked in just the slightest.

"When?" Mr. Croom innocently inquired, "He offered it or you discovered it?" And Bruce dogmatically darted at Scarecrow. "Can't say exactly."

"We were there all day and didn't see no law," Shorty affirmed and Stink grinned. "Only pig there was eatin' snakes."

"Shh," Cassie warned as the boys giggled.

Lilly held her palms up to Scarecrow, "The gig is up." And Scarecrow agreed with a tumbling sigh as she explained, "Scarecrow tracked down the yellow get away car last night and took the two men to a safe place for interrogation. We were up at your barn, Cassie. We walked 'em in by gun point letting 'em think it was over if they didn't tell us something. Said we were gonna feed their bodies to the pigs. They already knew that pigs'll get rid of a body overnight."

"Oh, my gawd," Robin huffed as whispers and hushed tones spread.

Mr. Croom's eyes loosened from their aged draped lids as he took his seat.

"It was the only way," Scarecrow summed. "This sketch was drawn by The Lumbee Council for Mr. Fisk and Wart's operation. They were to find the jeweled cross in that sketch and take it to them. It's proof of The Lost Colony's contact with the Lumbee. It's the deal breaker, boys."

The Magee boys gasped then the elder addressed Mr. Croom, first with his piercing stare, "Are we in danger? What about us? Is there any proof of when Black blood mixed with the Croatans? Is the council after that, too?" Young Thomas' angst powered him from his seat, "Do you know my dad?"

"Yes, I know your dad," Mr. Croom calmly held their attention. "He contacted me after a thesis was published and that was over thirty years ago. We've talked on Congress' floor together. We've traveled extensively." And then anxiously to Scarecrow, "Are we in imminent danger?"

"Until we press charges, yes." Scarecrow scanned the private room again.

"What's stopping you?" Jake ignited.

"In a court of law you'll have to have the proof of the cross." Exilee cocked her chin at Bruce. "This is a win win, ya know. You'll make history, the newspapers and your business will grow so fast you won't believe it. That's what happened when we went public with the Black Purse Papers."

Edge scooted the two pizza crusts around on her plate and then cut them into little itsy bitsy pieces with the side of her fork. Luke whined to get down and explore the room and as he did was joined by Cassie's two youngest boys. On all fours they played hide and seek as pretend puppies, yipping at one another from under the double row of chairs stacked against the far wall.

The waitress's squeaking rubber soles announced her along with the intoxicating sweet pizzas as she entered the quiet private dining room. She asked each guest's preference, peach or chocolate, and served the slices, lingering over Bruce's shoulder and commenting on the turquoise beads peeking from the collar of his tee shirt.

"They're ancient, from a good trade on the Cherokee's trail." As his grays shined up at her so did Robin's scorn. Brightly smiling, the warned waitress moved on to play with the three young pups. She whistled for them, "Good boy," she cooed. "Sit and I'll give you a prize." After the sweet pizzas were served she asked if they'd like a cherry pizza as well, but it was declined.

As soon as her footsteps faded Jake and Bruce stared one another down and just as they were on the verge of leaving their seats Mark brazenly cleared his throat. "Read that note now."

"You already read it, huh?" Bruce rubbed over his jaw as he contemplated.

Ken placed both his hands on the tabletop. "Me, too, Bruce. I think it's important. You should read it."

"My mother wrote it, but Scarecrow just told me about it last night. Jubious, as it is, he came back after everyone was in bed and told me that there was a trip we had to make. But it didn't work out." He shrugged, "Mark got the pleasure."

"You feign," Mark aimed.

As Bruce spread the letter open his face changed from excited to dark.

My dearest Bruce,

Every prayer from my lips is for your survival. I love you and at this last minute realize I need to tell you a few more things. I pray you get this. I'm tucked it in your special place with your dried frog and bug collection. There is only one other person at this time who knows of this letter and its dangers. She will do everything possible to ensure you get it before it is too late.

The many years of ridicule and torment we survived at your father's hands and secretly learning English and yet had to speak the Lumbee vernacular is, in retrospect, the easiest part of our charade. You see, the reason he denied me calling you my prince is because you are. You are the Prince of the Queen's Second Society, meaning the Queen of England. Governor John White was given the assignment to establish The Society in her behalf on the New Found Lands. For this task White was presented a treasured cross. It was to be presented to any new explorers in their settlement to verify their royal assignment.

The safety of the new society upon arrival in the New Found Lands was ensured when they met the Portuguese Knights. Some of these knights had blended with African explorers who had forts along the same waterways. And others had blended with traveling Indians. To the queen's pilgrims, searching for land not claimed by other Christians for a period of six years or more, this was a blessing. Because according to the queen's proclamation they had the authority to claim any land not inhabited by Christians for a period of six months or more. And the closed minded pilgrims could not conceive the natives as Christian.

Should you survive you will learn the significance of this letter and all the stories told you. And know to follow this example.

Behind your ear is the mark of the cross. All of John White's daughter's ancestors are marked with that cross at birth. It is our duty to preserve the colonists' honor by simply attaining to educate ourselves and protect our heritage from demise. That means, Prince Bruce Black, should you be asked to present the cross in your lifetime to America's Federal Government do it. We are to honor Christianity. Mark your children with the cross and tell no one and should you not marry within, not even your wife. As I told my husband and surely ruined your childhood as he hated you for who you really are from that day on. I am so sorry. I pray one day you will forgive me.

I love you so much,

Your Mother

Lizzie Black, married name

Gladys Elizabeth White, birth name

Bruce stealthily approached Cassie at the head of the table on the far side. Bent over her shoulder and down to her ear politely asked, "What do you know about this?" Instantly, she panted. He spun her straight back chair around on one leg as she clasped to her seat. Tears welled. Her freckled face reddened. And her ears stung bright scarlet. She mouthed, 'no,' but Bruce motioned for her to stand. Her boys were frozen in their seats as she sullenly followed Bruce. As soon as he hurled her chair into the middle of the room, she sat. He paced back and forth behind her as Cassie gripped the seat.

"You were the one who cleaned the blood. Her bloody fingers ran down the walls. It wasn't an accident. Was it?" The purple veins in his neck rippled up and shined like writhing snakes. "Was it, Cassie?" Bruce checked behind her right ear. Leaned his head back. Sighed. And closed his eyes. Then behind her left.

When she jerked in deep wails her boys gapped open in awe. Pen's leg vibrated like a revved three fifty engine against the table until the sweet teas threatened to tumble. "No, don't make me do this." She sunk to the floor on her knees and begged. But he wouldn't look at her. When she pitifully cried over her shoulder at her boys Stink threw his chocolate pizza to the floor and hurried over.

Bruce quickly lifted Stink into her lap then pulled back his ears as Cassie quietly sobbed into his unruly red locks. Bruce directed each of her boys to come. Cassie's rock chunkin' son was second.

Exilee called for Luke and Ken met him halfway. Scooped him up and took him back to the table. His grandpa wrapped his long arm around them like a thick road block. And Miss Sarah cooed kind words about his puppy belly being round and full. But Luke asked if he was next. And was sad that he wasn't.

One by one Bruce checked behind their ears. He wore the poker face of champions, the one ingrained from a psychohistorical Lumbee Indian tradition of trading and gaming. The one Kings have worn through the ages when dictating, "Off with his head." The one Negro slaves have worn when facing mean masters and swore on the holy book that they don't know nuthin' 'bout no underground railroad. He wore it so well that when he was done and walked the line of seven boys lined up straight against the back wall that they all flinched when he summoned Edge.

Mark piped up and asked, "You want me, too?" Bruce told him to come on first. He checked and then aimed over at the line and Mark joined them while Stink got a napkin from the table for his ma to blow her nose and climbed back into her lap.

Exilee assured Edge that she'll be okay, that Bruce was only revealing facts and that the truth was the most powerful tool in the world. But Edge molded down into her chair. Snap smiled at his daughter and told her, "We're just laying out some facts, honey. Go on," and then she rose and stoically waltzed up to Bruce and turned her back to him.

He checked behind her ears and twirled her around. Face to face he traced her hairline and the curve of her brows. The way her left ear turned out just a smidge and the dimple in her chin. Then, in one brief moment, as her bifurcated tongue jet between her teeth it was as if they were the only two in the room. He held her face in his hands. "I think," and his smile returned. "Uh, I think you're my sister or a very close cousin." She excitedly examined Bruce as he exclaimed, "Jimmy Bean, tell me something here." Edge checked behind Bruce's ears. "It's the mark, just like in the letter," she hummed.

Snap mumbled, "She's your sister," then looked down at his peach pizza.

"We didn't hear that," Bruce roared. "Move your hands so we can hear you." His sudden intense rage frightened Edge and she hurried backwards.

Snap slowly raised his reddened eyes. "Edge is your sister, Bruce."

"That would make my mother a slut."

"No. Not on my life. Never. Lizzie needed a little kindness." His hands shook out before him. "But it got out a' hand like those things can do. Can't you imagine what it was like for her?"

"My mother cheated on Old Man Black," a crooked smile broke and Bruce guffawed. "She got one over on him. Amen, brothers and sisters!" He wildly clapped.

Snap sat up taller. "It was the year he was up for cutting that UC in Raeford. You were just three, probably can't remember. Lizzie went up to Western Carolina and worked a casino job for the Cherokee last four months of her pregnancy."

Edge's void expression claimed her. "You been lying to me. My momma weren't no drunk. She loved me, didn't she?"

Snap defensively stood, but Miss Ginger and Miss Sarah begged him to sit back down and explain it all out to her and to give her a minute to take it in. Snap took a drink of sweet tea and cleared his throat. "And I am your real daddy, Elizabeth."

"Oh, God, I love you. I'm sorry," she cried.

"There's nothing to be sorry 'bout. Come here."

But Edge stood up straight, straighter than she ever thought she could and it made her so tall and gave her such presence that Bruce rightfully asked her, "What are we gonna do with Cassie?" Edge scowled over her pitiful bent frame like a queen over a thief, "Get the truth out of her, any way we got to, brother."

Cassie attempted to rise, but Bruce quickly bore down on her shoulder. "What did you do to our mother, Cassie? You with the Lumbee Council? Huh?" His grays penetrated like totens' souls were sparking out. "Speak, while you can." The slap startled her. And Edge said she'd do it again.

Cassie took the assault like a logger. Adjusted her jaw and seethed as she aimed her daring dark blues. "No," Cassie kicked as she fought Bruce's hold. "It's not me. That's not it. I swear it."

"The council is behind this. I've figured out that much. But what I don't get is those marks on your boys." Bruce echoed as a customer peeped in through the dark purple curtains, but was shooed away with Scarecrow's long swing.

"She altered their marks," Dodger glared at Cassie as he leaned into Scarecrow's shoulder. "She won't let him go I tell ya."

At first the footsteps signaled the waitress, but they were too hard and tapped like leather. Bruce braced. Then stood at ease when it was just the owner. His arms flew up as he smacked his lips, "Nadie amor el repartidor de pizza." And the ignorant group politely smiled. His greasy apron streaked with yellow butter and red sauce covered his signature red pants and white button down shirt. His thick black rimmed glasses increased the size of his big brown eyes and rested on his thin humped nose. When he removed his apron and hung it on the coat peg flour flaked off like snow. "Ready or not, this meeting needs the moderator. I am Allen Bishop, owner of a Dunrovin Pizza, elder at Beaver Bridge Baptist Church, and a long time member of The Second Society. Presently, I act as secretary, but I'm going to step beyond my assigned duties tonight and make the administrative decision to enlighten you before we're interrupted."

"I know who you are, about this place. I'm remembering it. My momma was right here." Bruce pointed down at Cassie and squeezed her sunken shoulder. "Do you know what this woman has to do with my mother's death? 'Cause that's what I wanna know and I'm not leaving until she tells me." His heavy hand squeezed her thin frame and with a refrained grunt she sunk even lower.

In the most relaxed manner imaginable Allen requested Scarecrow and Lilly secure the doors. Scarecrow drew back the heavy drapes and the front dining hall was void of patrons. Half empty glasses and pizzas littered tables. Crumbs trailed across the tile. And the sign on the front door read open. He pulled on the metal bar and verified the door was locked. Flipped off the front room's lights and returned as Lilly returned from the kitchen followed by another man with red pants.

Allen welcomed him with an open arm. "This is Frank Sheffield, known by most of you as Principal Sheffield. And to Exilee, Dad. He is our President."

"Whoa," Exilee whispered.

"Thank you, Allen." Frank quickly paired up with Bruce. "Exilee's mother was a descendant of the original colony, the Moor family. Out of honor for her I accepted this position."

"How long have you been doing this?" Exilee's words buzzed out like drone bees drunk on nectar.

"Since I married your mother. She educated me and I've been determined," Frank took a deep breath, "to stop them."

Bruce roared and the room gasped. Allen pleaded for Bruce to hold on, but he just grimaced and pulled Cassie up by the neck. "Tell me. Tell me right now. What happened to my mother?" Cassie's boys bowed out from the wall ready to fight, but Scarecrow pulled back the strap on his holster and secured their steps. "Bruce, easy now. Your mother wouldn't want you to do this."

But Exilee cried out, "Was my mother killed by the council? What about Glennie?" And her daddy grimaced. "No. Glennie did that, with her teas." But he didn't falter. "She was coerced. She was just a child, an innocent pawn. The Lumbee Council will stop at nothing to get federal funds, nothing. The boys at the goat farm were schooled, conditioned and persuaded to seek out Glennie, because she was most likely to cooperate. Their dad is on the council. The boys stalked her while she picked flowers in the field and her materialistic nature proved them right. I believe it was candy and a book of rhymes. But she didn't know, Exilee. She made the tea because she was conditioned to believe it would make her mother well."

With Cassie by the neck Bruce demanded Edge to come. "They can have Cassie and then they'll want you." He wrenched Cassie's neck until her pleas were chicken bone garble. But Pen was loud and clear. "Let her go." Lilly and Scarecrow both stood armed at the exits and with a clear shot Lilly drew. But Scarecrow signaled no. "Stay out of this," Bruce spat.

"My son had the mark," Allen pleaded. "He died in an auto accident. It's been 18 years now."

"Well no one's tried to kill me!" Bruce screamed. "I don't believe it. You people are fools!"

"Oh yes they did, over and over, but you outsmarted them. And you've been protected," Allen adamantly explained. "And you have Scarecrow," his arms stretched out across the room, "and all your friends here and the ones you don't think are your friends." His bared hands banged like a diamond hoe. "It is no coincidence for a single one of us to be here. We have saturated the state. The country. We are worldwide, Bruce. With a powerful rein all the way from England, to this very day. For this very moment." As he calmed he clasped his hot hands into prayer. "We want you to go to Washington, Bruce. You. They all say you're the prime candidate and the timing is crucial." But Bruce shivered and stammered and reared back with Cassie like a rag doll as he drew her to his chest like a shield.

David's chair strained as he rose and Miss Sarah clung to his hand until he had stepped out of reach. "Bruce, you are a smart man. Surely you know what we are giving you tonight."

"Giving me? Fuck you!" His passion pulsed around Cassie's cinched neck until her dry gasps and purple lips pleased him and she fell limp down to his hips. With a snarled smile Bruce jerked the jeweled cross from his pocket and slung it across the slick floor. "I have my own plans." As Edge bent to pick it up, Pen clamped his juvember in his scarlet stump, loaded a small steel sliver in the band and whizzzzz, Lilly aimed too. "Boom, Ka, Boom!" Screams echoed as they ducked and huddled and a stream of blood declared the hit.

Bruce held the sharp gapping flesh between his ribs as Cassie gasped and heaved deep breaths. On her knees she squirmed to her boys and Allen rushed to her side. "Cassandra Elizabeth, tell me you're all right, dear." As Bruce smeared the fresh blood in long denying swipes across his chest and his dear forsaken Cassie still reached out for him. Still in anguish and disbelief until her sons fully encircled her and she crumbled. Grappling her dear Lassie's legs, she cried, "Oh, thoust precious, child, what have I done? My prince, my dear, you will suffer too." And Pen stooped down and cradled her while his brothers stood paralyzed, even Stink, until the dense smoke from kitchen bellowed into the room. "Ma! Fire, Ma!"

The extinguisher gushed. Clanged up against the block wall and the waitress exclaimed, "Find the rear exit!" as she rang two pizza tins like tambourines. "Follow me!" Smoke, foam and frenzy filled the secluded room as Allen leapt over flames into dark smoke and disappeared and reappeared with two more extinguishers. "Help me." Ken snatched one and they sprayed floor to ceiling and the smoke slowed to gray puffs. But the fire crackled on from the kitchen like a waiting lion. "We're gonna need help." Allen yelled and Ken yelled, "Wet the drapes!"

Robin wailed when Jake pushed her out the exit door and told her, "Call the fire department," as he lunged back in for Bruce and was enveloped in the gaseous haze.

Smoke swirls eked from the ceiling like iridescent snakes licking at Cassie's head as she stealthily approached Jake. She slicked down her unruly red curls behind her ears and along the way jerked the jeweled cross from Edge. "I was there, Jake." And Jake called out, "Bruce! Has anyone seen Bruce? Gawd! Answer me." And Cassie stroked his scared cheek with one hand and with the cross in her other held her fist like an anchor at his chest. "Lizzie was a tower for her dear Prince. Always. And she taught me everything. She taught me how to protect my own. But I took it one step further." She almost smiled. "Yes, after The Society sent their laymen to mark my newborns I waited and altered them with a red coal, except for Lassie. He was too old by the time I had full knowledge." Jake cried out for Bruce again and Cassie gently covered his mouth and nervously panted, "I helped Lizzie write the letter. I'm the one who fought Old Man Black." She held his forearm and forcibly shook him. "He wouldn't let her go. He was too big. You must believe me. He pulled a knife on her. I did all I could possibly do."

Pen escaped the smoke and heaved. "Jake, be on your way. Forget about us if you want peace. I'm telling you." He panted as Cassie patted his chest and Pen aimed at the exit now visibly lit in bright red. "Out or in? And you've seen in, Jake. So don't claim you weren't warned." He held up his stump. "Things aren't always what they seem," Pen soldiered up, "on the swamp."

"But Bruce," Jake cried as turquoise floated up from fumes on the other side of the secluded room and he started for it, but stopped as Stink neared and dangled it up over his head and proudly slipped it on.

Cassie waved for Edge and when she cautiously neared pulled her in close. Placing Lassie's hand over Elizabeth's while pushing the jeweled cross into Elizabeth's other hand. "I, Cassandra Elizabeth White do ask you to marry and keep yourselves pure for our mother society in Christian martyrdom and for our Second Society here for all Lumbees to come. I ask you to mark your children. School them. And if it's not too late choose one. One like Bruce Black and present the truth." Her lull quaked and warranted. "I ask this of you, as Queen."

The End

On March 25, 1584, Sir Walter Raleigh received a 'letters-patent' from Queen Elizabeth "for the discovering and planting of new lands not possessed by any Christian Prince nor inhabited by Christian People, to continue for the space of 6 yeeres and no more." Raleigh's first expedition was a short reconnaissance voyage between April and September, 1584, by Amadas and Barlowe. Two Indians, a Croatoan called Manteo and a Roanoke called Wanchese, came back to England with them.' Excerpt from 'A Role for Sassafras in the Search for the Lost Colony,' written by Philip S. McMullan Jr.

Cover Image Credit and Content Credits

I gratefully acknowledge the following sources.

Cover Image (1503 copper engraving) in Public Domain.
http://en.wikipedia.org/wiki/File:37_Coat_of_Arms_with_Lion_and_Rooster.jpg
German painter and engraver Albrecht Dürer.

For the authentic Southern Negro Slave song, 'Oh, Freedom', I thank Upton Sinclair, ed. (1878-1968), 'The Cry for Justice: An Anthology of the Literature of Social Protest,'1915.

For the dedication to research in, 'A Role for Sassafras in the Search for the Lost Colony,' by Philip S. McMullan Jr: "On March 25, 1584, Sir Walter Raleigh received a 'letters-patent' from Queen Elizabeth "for the discovering and planting of new lands not possessed by any Christian Prince nor inhabited by Christian People, to continue for the space of 6 yeeres and no more." Ralegh's first expedition was a short reconnaissance voyage between April and September, 1584, by Amadas and Barlowe. Two Indians, a Croatoan called Manteo and a Roanoke called Wanchese, came back to England with them."

'The Croatan Indians of Sampson County, Their Origin and Racial Status. A Plea for Separate Schools' by Geo. E. Butler, Clinton, NC, from The Seeman Printery in Durham, NC, 1916, was especially helpful in placing the Croatans with the English. The English dialect from early Queen Elizabeth and Sir Walter Raleigh's circle were witnessed by a missionary at a significant Croatan Indian settlement. There is no way the Indian people with the light skin and light hair could have been familiar with the very exclusive dialect without interaction with The Lost Colony. The mixed Indians are also reported by the missionary to know how to 'talk in a book'. This also proves the English interaction. Further evidence is in tracing the names of John White's group of colonists.

'The Lumbee' (Indians of North America) by Adolph Dial and 'The Lumbee Problem: The Making of an American Indian People' by Karen I Blu were also helpful with verifying the Lumbees as mixed with English by dating and witnessing of co existence among the races.

The website www.Native-Languages.org provided an informative document. It is titled

'Uncertain/Extinct Algonquian Languages: Etchemin, Loup, Powhatan, Lumbee, Beothuk.' It pertains to pidgin languages that derived from mixing races. Also, this article printed in the Journal of Genetic Genealogy, 5(2): 96-130, 2009, 'Where Have All the Indians Gone? Native American Eastern Seaboard Dispersal, Genealogy, and DNA in Relation to Sir Walter Raleigh's Lost Colony of Roanoke' by Roberta Estes, was the pancake for the pure maple syrup.

'The Lumbees' (and the "Lost Colony") by Julia White is an informative online article. An excerpt: "A professional historian of national respect, after an examination of the oral and written evidence existing, concluded, in 1891: "The Croatoans of today claim descent from The Lost Colony. Their habits, disposition and mental characters (sic.) show traces of Indian and European ancestry. Their language is the English of 300 years ago, and their names are in many cases the same as those borne by the original colonists. No other theory of their origin has been advanced, and it is confidently believed that the one here proposed is logically and historically the best, supported as it is both by external and internal evidence. If this theory is rejected, then the critic must explain in some other way the origin of a people which, after the lapse of 300 years, show the characteristics, speak the language, and possess the family names of the second English colony planted in the western world."

Linguist Walt Wolfram, a professor at North Carolina State University says, "The Lumbee English dialect bears the imprint of the early colonization by the English, Highland Scots, and Scots-Irish. Moreover, Lumbee American Indians' speech is distinctly different from their Anglo-American and African American neighbors." Lumbee vernacular unites the tribe and is so distinctive that tribal members can distinguish one another.

Another consideration is John M Taylor's article, 'Lumbees – Descendants of the Lost Colony?' Excerpt: The Lumbee Indians were late being recognized as a Native America tribe, with the benefits that attend that recognition. It has been argued that this was primarily because in the early days of our nation they believed themselves so well assimilated with the European settlers along the Lumber River that they did not feel the need for separate recognition. An extract from the official Lumbee Tribe web site: "In 1885, the tribe was recognized as Indian by the State of North Carolina. The tribe has sought full federal recognition from the United States Government since 1888. In 1956, Congress passed the Lumbee Act, which recognized the tribe as Indian. However, the Act withheld the full benefits of federal recognition from the tribe. Efforts are currently underway to pass federal legislation that grants full recognition to the Lumbee Tribe of North Carolina."

And 'Origin of the Croatan Indians,' as told by James Lowry of Robeson Raleigh, Location: Thaddeus S. Ferree Southern Historical Collection. Manuscripts Department.

Wilson Library. University of North Carolina at Chapel Hill. James Lowry traces Lumbee origins back to Sir Humphrey Gilbert, who sailed to the American coast in 1583 with two ships, the Golden Hind and the smaller Squirrel. A hurricane hit, and most of Gilbert's and his crew weathered the storm, repaired the Squirrel as best they could, and sailed to Roanoke Island in North Carolina. At Roanoke Island they waited for rescue, but no one came. The crew intermarried with the Indians (which could have been a mix of Native and Portuguese); Sir Humphrey married Cherona, the daughter of Chief Cahwachaw. When Chief Cahwachaw died, he asked Sir Humphrey to be chief of the tribe. The Indians wanted more wealth, so they convinced Sir Humphrey to lead them west. When they reached Robeson County, Sir Humphrey, who was elderly, died. The Indians buried him there and settled near his grave.

Early reports of Lumbee circa 1900: Speaking of the language of this people, McMillan says: The Croatan/Lumbee have no Indian names and no Indian language-not even a single word-and know nothing of Indian customs and habits. The language spoken By Croatan is almost pure Anglo Saxon, Col. Fred A. Olds, a newspaper correspondent of Raleigh, says of their language: The language spoken by the Croatans is a very pure but quaint old Anglo-Saxon, and there are in daily use some 75 words which have come down from the great days of Raleigh and his mighty mistress, Queen Elizabeth. These old Saxon words arrest attention instantly. For man they say "mon," pronounce father "feyther," use "mension" for measurement, and many other words in daily use by them have for years been entirely obsolete in English-speaking countries.

My imagination is also of credit. I am positive that should you read the source material you will realize how easy it is for a writer to get carried away by a few facts, coincidental dates and well answered questions. Fairly though, I must mention that a great uncle of mine on my mother's side began the Smithsonian and that on my father's side my family is a 'family of interest' concerning the genealogy of The Lost Colony. At age eleven my comrades and I were exploring the woods and discovered Big Foot. We busted loose getting to the house and begged to call and report the sighting to the radio station, but were told it was time for dinner and to get cleaned up and warned to stay out of the woods. We never saw Big Foot in those woods again. Also, as a first grader I sold rocks to neighbors from a rickety red wagon because I wanted money for treats from the nearby store. I told them my daddy was out of work. I had to take the money back. But a lot of neighbors kept the rocks. That's how it is with fiction on fact.

Other sources include:

http://dna-explained.com/category/lost-colony/

http://www.lost-colony.com/Beechland.html

http://www.she-philosopher.com/gallery/powhatan-map.html
http://digitalcommons.unl.edu/cgi/viewcontent.cgi?article=1020&context=etas

http://www.elizabethan-era.org.uk/sir-walter-raleigh.htm

http://historical-melungeons.com/portuguese.html

http://sciway3.net/clark/freemoors/lumbee.html

http://en.wikipedia.org/wiki/Convento_de_Cristo

http://www.robertlomas.com/Orkney/scroll.html

http://www.econ.ohio-state.edu/jhm/arch/kens/kens.htm

http://www.blueridgeinstitute.org/moonshine/common_blue_ridge_moonshining_terms.html

http://en.wikipedia.org/wiki/Perceval,_the_Story_of_the_Grail

http://www.water.ncsu.edu/capefear.html

http://en.wikipedia.org/wiki/Rosy_Cross

http://en.wikipedia.org/wiki/Order_of_Christ_%28Portugal%29

http://mkharrison.com/Html/Lumbee_Indians.htm

http://www.grahamphillips.net/Ark/Ark_7.htm

http://www.washingtonwatch.com/bills/show/111_SN_1735.html

http://people.ds.cam.ac.uk/bv230/lang-var/wolfram%201999%20dialect%20identity%20in%20tri-ethnic%20context%20-%20lumbee.pdf

http://ashevilleoralhistoryproject.wordpress.com/2012/11/27/a-full-and-true-orphan/

http://www.lost-colony.com/surnames.html

www.huxford.com/genetics_lumbee_results.htm

www.huxford.com/genetics_lumbee_results.htm

http://www.ncga.state.nc.us/EnactedLegislation/Statutes/PDF/BySection/Chapter_71A/GS_71A-1.pdf

La Rochelle

Knights of Christ

Christopher Columbus

http://en.wikipedia.org/wiki/Cherokee_freedmen_controversy

The American Garden Vol. XI by L. H. Bailey. Also available from Amazon: American Horticultural Society A to Z Encyclopedia of Garden Plants.

In Reflection

This story explores a true life dilemma. North Carolina's state recognized Lumbee Indians seek full federal recognition as Native American Indians. NAI DNA within the Tribe is debated. And although sociolinguistics is a major origination factor Lumbees keep their old vernacular despite its lack of NAI influence and rich Spanish/Portuguese and Elizabethan English influence.

What if Lumbees submitted to other origination theories?

Why can't they be happy just to be?

And do you believe in psychohistory?

Considering psychohistory, is it odd that America's true pilgrims were cursed to repeat the cycle of forming a 'Second Society' to protect their Christian beliefs? Or to live as simple laborers, uneducated pidgin speaking moonshine runners? To live as infamous suffering souls who keep their most striking honor secret for fear of being kilt off? Considering that it is not odd for Christians to believe splinters of Jesus' crucifixion cross, now called the True Cross, behold healing powers, it is not odd to believe secrecy of protected groups with special knowledge continues.

A Catholic King's greed forced the public disbandment of the Knights Templar. However, the Grand Master of the Knights Templar did not confess to treason, as did others being burned alive at the stake, which was a cross. Instead he proclaimed a brazen curse against all who persecuted Christians. His direct persecutors died shortly thereafter. The Lumbee Indians refer to this type of negative conjuring as 'putting a root on' someone to this day.

The crucifixion cross was made of common fir, pine and cypress. In 1119 Knights built a temple on the ruins of the Temple of Solomon, a Holy site which to this day contains precious Christian relics. These Knights were called the Knights Templar. They banned together in a crusade against evil, against Islam and they protected Christians to the death. The Knights Templar also protected a piece of the True Cross, along with other Christian relics. The Holy Bible reads that when the Temple of Solomon is destroyed and rebuilt the third time Christ will return. Until then, crusaders protect Christian relics to place back into the Temple when it will be under the rightful watch of true Christians.

There are scores of manmade caves and tunnels built by the Knights dated to have been built during their four hundred year underground crusades in Europe and the Middle East. And there are scores of tunnels, newly discovered and some undiscovered in America, that were presumably made during the realm of The Underground Railroad, a movement to free Negro Slaves from Whites. This concludes that the war on freedom and righteousness is continual.

The Portuguese were master ship craftsmen and sailors. They both vigorously explored and sold their knowledge and skills to other countries. North Carolina's linguistic studies determine a strong relationship to the Portuguese language and the Lumbees.

And also of major consideration: Slip into Sir Walter Raleigh's shoes. He was an intelligent industrious man, a Christian man. In 1572 he witnessed the St Bartholomew's Day massacre where French Protestants were massacred by French Catholics in Paris. The slaughter of Protestants, Raleigh's fellow Christians, spread throughout Paris. It lasted several weeks. Modern estimates for the total dead vary from 5,000 to 30,000. So it was only logical for Raleigh to befriend the queen in order to find a 'New Found Land.' According to the The (Coptic) Church of Alexandria, the ancient Church of Egypt, one of the Oldest in Christianity, St Bartholomew's martyrdom, bloody as it is, is commemorated on the 1st day of the Coptic Calendar, which falls on September 11. The Knights Templar has always been crusaders against Islam. In America, September 11, 2001, will live on in epiphany for all American citizens.

So overall, will it make any difference which branch the Lumbees deem their ancestors? Is there an actual Second Society which holds pertinent knowledge and or Christian relics? Could a Second Society even be kept secret in the tightly-knit Lumbee community? As of 2013, fifty five thousand Lumbee Indians are recognized by the state of North Carolina as the determined Lumbee Council seeks full federal recognition as Native American Indians. This mostly Christian community resides in the Sandhills, on an area they claim as their swamp filled with fir, pine, cypress and shine.

One thing is certain. The psychohistory of religious freedom and the self existential quest bears over us like a mighty being's palm over an egg. And the only thing worth dying and sometimes even living for is a good friend like Jake Wilkes.

Stephanie M Sellers

About the Author

With a history in Language Arts, pottery, sculpture and military service, Stephanie has a diverse view. As a writer she interprets the world around her.

Her works include short stories, full length fiction and non fiction. She enjoys researching human behavior, sociolinguistics and psychohistory. Aside from writing for her children she has written stories for the non profit group, Wild Horse Rescue Center which is assisted by the environmental non profit, The Abraham Foundation.

Visit her website, Fiction on Fact with Stephanie M. Sellers.

Made in the USA
Charleston, SC
26 July 2013